PENGUIN BOOKS

THE ISSA VALLEY

Czesław Miłosz was born in 1911 in Szetejnie, then Tsarist Russia, to partly Polish, partly Lithuanian parents, and was brought up in the multi-national milieu of Wilno (Vilnius). He graduated in 1934 from the King Stefan Batory University with a degree in law. In 1935 he received the Diplôme Supérieur d'Études Françaises Modernes from the Alliance Française in Paris. During the years immediately preceding the Second World War he worked for the Polish State Broadcasting Company. With the coming of the Nazis in 1939 he became active in underground circles in Warsaw, where he spent most of the war. His experience of that time found expression in his novel *The Usurpers* (1955, published in an English translation in 1966). Between 1946 and 1951 Miłosz served as a member of the Polish Foreign Service, but despite his initial sympathies for radical change he eventually broke with the régime and in 1951 he left his post as Polish cultural attaché in Paris to remain in the West thereafter. *The Captive Mind* (1953) is his most influential and overtly political work. Among his other books are *The Issa Valley* (1955), *Native Realm* (1968) and *Emperor of the Earth: Modes of Eccentric Vision* (1977), a volume of literary criticism. His *Selected Poems* was published in 1973 and a revised edition in 1981. Other collections of his poetry include *Bells in Winter* (1978), *Separate Notebooks* (1984) and *The Unattainable Earth* (1986). In 1976 Czesław Miłosz received a Guggenheim Fellowship for poetry and poetry translation and in 1978 the Neustadt International Prize for Literature. In 1980 he was awarded the Nobel Prize for Literature. A self-exiled Polish poet, he has been acclaimed for voicing 'with uncom-promising clear-sightedness ... man's exposed condition in a world of severe conflicts.'

Czesław Miłosz is now Professor Emeritus at the University of California, Berkeley.

CZESŁAW MIŁOSZ

The Issa Valley

Translated from the Polish by Louis Iribarne

PENGUIN BOOKS

PENGUIN BOOKS

Published by the Penguin Group
Penguin Books Ltd, 27 Wrights Lane, London w8 5tz, England
Penguin Putnam Inc., 375 Hudson Street, New York, New York 10014, USA
Penguin Books Australia Ltd, Ringwood, Victoria, Australia
Penguin Books Canada Ltd, 10 Alcorn Avenue, Toronto, Ontario, Canada m4v 3b2
Penguin Books India (P) Ltd, 11, Community Centre, Panchsheel Park, New Delhi – 110 017, India
Penguin Books (NZ) Ltd, Private Bag 102902, NSMC, Auckland, New Zealand
Penguin Books (South Africa) (Pty) Ltd, 5 Watkins Street, Denver Ext 4, Johannesburg 2094, South Africa

Penguin Books Ltd, Registered Offices: Harmondsworth, Middlesex, England

First published in Polish as *Dolina Issy* by Institut Littéraire 1955
This translation first published in the USA by Farrar Straus and Giroux 1981
Published in Great Britain in Penguin Books 2001

1

Translation copyright © Farrar, Straus and Giroux, 1978, 1981
All rights reserved

Portions of this translation appeared, in slightly different form,
in *World Literature Today* and the *Kenyon Review*

Printed in England by Clays Ltd, St Ives plc

The Issa Valley

�খ৲ঌ৲ঌ৲ঌ৲ঌ৲ঌ৽

I SHOULD begin with the Land of Lakes, the place where Thomas lived. This part of Europe was long covered with glaciers, and the landscape has much of the severity of the north. The soil is sandy and rocky and suitable only for growing potatoes, rye, oats, and flax. This explains why such care was taken not to spoil the forests, which helped to soften the climate and offered protection against the Baltic winds. The forests are predominantly of pine and spruce, though birch, oak, and hornbeam are also in abundance, but not beech, the border of its domain running farther to the south. Here you can wander for long hours without tiring the eye, for, like human cities, the tree colonies have their own distinct character—forming islands, zones, and archipelagoes—and are set off by wagon ruts in the sand, by a forester's cottage, or by an old distillery with crumbling, weed-infested furnaces. From almost any hilltop you can glimpse a blue sheet of lake with a white, barely perceptible splotch of grebe, with a string of ducks winging over the reeds. The marshlands abound in every species of waterfowl, and in spring the pale sky reverberates with the whir of snipe—a *whew-whew-whew* —made by the air in their tail feathers as they perform their monotonous acrobatics, signifying love.

In the meadows the faint whir of snipe, the gabble of blackcock, so like a bubbling on the horizon, and the croaking of frogs (the number of which has something to do with the storks that nest on the rooftops of cottages and barns) are the voices of that season when a sudden thaw gives way to the blossoming of cowslips and daphne—tiny pink and lilac blossoms on bushes as yet without leaves. The two seasons most appropriate to this land are spring and autumn—a long and sunny autumn, thick with the smell of rain-soaked flax, the clatter of swingles, and distant echoes. This is the time when the geese show signs of restlessness, leaping clumsily to fly after their wild brethren summoning from on high; when someone would bring home a stork with a broken wing—a creature spared the sort of death by pecking such as is meted out by those guardians of the law on those not fit for the trip to the Nile; when word would get around that a wolf had made off with someone's suckling pig; and the woods would hear the music of the hounds—always a soprano, a bass, and a baritone—barking in pursuit of wild game, their pitch signaling whether they were on the track of a hare or a buck.

The fauna of this region is mixed, not entirely that of the north. Ptarmigan are not uncommon, but then neither are partridge. In winter the squirrels have a grayish coat, the shade of which may vary from red to clear gray. There are two species of hare: the first, the common variety, looks the same in summer and in winter; the second, the white hare, changes its color and is indistinguishable from the snow. The proximity of these two species has given the experts food for thought, though the matter is further complicated because, as any hunter will testify, the common hare has two subspecies—the wood hare and the field hare, the latter sometimes crossbreeding with the white.

Until recently, everything a man needed was manufactured at home. His clothes were made of coarse homespun, which women had spread on the grass and bleached in the sun. In late autumn, during that time of day given to tales and songs, fingers turned hanks of wool into yarn in rhythm to the measured beat of the spinning-wheel pedals. With this yarn the housewives wove dresses on homemade looms, jealously guarding the secret of their patterns: this one in a herringbone, that one in a twill; this color for the warp, that for the woof. Spoons, vats, and household utensils were hand-carved, as were clogs. In summer, bast moccasins from linden bark were worn. Not until the First World War, when dairy cooperatives and meat and grain markets were introduced, did the villagers' necessities of life begin to change.

Cottages are of wood, their roofs shingled rather than thatched. Cranes, consisting of a beam braced against a forked post and stone-weighted at one end, are used for drawing well water. The small flower garden at the entrance to the house is a woman's pride and joy. Here the women tend their dahlias and mallows—a plant that flourishes along the wall, not one that graces only the earth and can't be seen through the fence.

It's time to pass from the general landscape to the Valley itself, which in many ways is an anomaly in the Land of Lakes. The Issa is a deep, black river with a lazy current, thickly bordered with reeds; a river whose surface is barely visible in places under the lily pads, which winds through meadows and between gentle slopes noted for their fecundity. The Valley is blessed with an abundance of black earth—a rarity for us—with the lushness of its orchards, and possibly with its remoteness from the world, something that has never seemed to bother its inhabitants. The villages in these parts are more prosperous than elsewhere, being situated either along the only major road skirting the river, or high above it on terraces; and at night they eye one another with their window lights across an expanse that echoes like an echo chamber every hammer blow, dog bark, and voice—which may explain why the Valley is celebrated for its ancient songs, songs that are never performed in unison but divided into parts, with one village always trying to outdo a neighboring one with a more mellifluous and gradual ending of a phrase. Collectors of folklore have noted a variety of motifs along the Issa going back to pagan times, like the story of the Moon (which in our language is of masculine gender) rising up from his nuptial bed, where he sleeps with his wife, the Sun.

2

❧ᶘᶚᶘᶚᶘᶚ

THE ISSA VALLEY has the distinction of being inhabited by an unusually large number of devils. It may be that the hollow willows, mills, and thickets lining the riverbanks provide a convenient cover for those creatures who reveal themselves only when it suits them. Those who have seen them say that the devil is rather short, about the size of a nine-year-old; that he wears a green frock coat, a jabot, his hair in a pigtail, white stockings, and tries to conceal his hoofs, which are an embarrassment to him, with high-heeled slippers. Such tales should be treated with a certain caution. It is possible that, knowing the superstitious awe in which the Germans are held—they being people of commerce, inventions, and science—the devils seek to lend themselves an air of gravity by dressing up in the manner of Immanuel Kant of Königsberg. It's no coincidence that along the Issa another name for the Evil Spirit is the "Little German"—implying that the devil is on the side of progress. Still, it's hard to believe they were in the habit of wearing such a costume for everyday. If one of their favorite pastimes was dancing in the empty scutching sheds near the farm buildings, how could they possibly kick up clouds of grain dust without showing due regard for their appearance? And why, if they are endowed with a certain immortality, would they be apt to choose a costume from the eighteenth century?

There is no predicting whom they might impersonate. A girl lights two candles on St. Andrew's Eve, gazes into the mirror, and her future is revealed: the face of the man with whom her life will be joined, or the face of death. Is this the devil in disguise, or could it be the work of other magical forces? And how is one to tell them apart, those creatures coinciding with the advent of Christianity from those native inhabitants of bygone days, like the forest witch who switches children in their cradles, or the little people who stray at night from their palaces under the roots of the elderberry bushes? Are the devils and those other creatures joined in a pact, or do they simply exist side by side like the jay, the sparrow, and the crow? And where is that realm where both species would take refuge when the earth was plowed up by the tracks of tanks; when those who were about to be executed dug their own shallow graves by the river; and when, in blood and tears, Industrialization rose up, surrounded by the halo of History?

One can easily imagine a parliamentary session being convened in caverns deep inside the earth, so deep that it is warmed by the fires of the earth's molten center. The session is attended by hundreds of thousands of tiny devils in frock coats, who listen solemnly to speakers representing the Central Committee of Infernos. The speakers announce that, in the interest of the cause, all dancing in the forests and meadows will have to cease; that from now on, highly qualified specialists will have to operate in such a way that the minds of mortals will never suspect their presence. There is applause but it is strained, for those present realize that they were necessary only during the preparatory stage, that progress has consigned them to gloomy chasms, and that they will never again witness the setting of the sun, the flight of kingfishers, the glitter of stars, and all the other wonders of the uncircumscribable earth.

The peasant farmers along the Issa used to place, by the entrance to their cottages, a bowl of milk for the water snakes, which were not afraid of humans. In time, the inhabitants became fervent Catholics and the presence of the devils made them recall the struggle being waged for dominion over the human soul. What will they become tomorrow? In narrating such a story, one never knows whether to use the past or present tense, as if what has passed has not really passed as long as it survives in the memory of generations—or in the memory of one chronicler.

Or were the devils attracted to the Issa because of its water? It is said that it possesses properties affecting the personalities of those born along its shores, who are inclined to be eccentric, are far from being at peace with themselves, and whose blue eyes, blond hair, and somewhat sturdy build only give a semblance of Nordic health.

3

❧❦❧❦❧❦

THOMAS WAS born in the village of Gine at that time of year when a ripe apple thumps to the ground during the afternoon lull and when vats of freshly brewed ale stand in the hallway after the autumnal harvest. Gine was not much more than a hill, thickly wooded with oaks. That a wooden church was built there betrays a hostility toward the religious practices of the past, or may testify to a desire for peaceful transition, for it was here that rites were once performed in honor of the god of thunder and lightning. The church was buttressed by a stone wall at the back, and from the green in front, one could see river bends; a barge ferrying a cart, moving along a cable pulled by a ferryman's hand to a steady rhythm (there was no bridge at this point in the river); and through the trees, some cottage roofs. A little to one side stood the rectory, with its gray-shingled roof reminiscent of Noah's Ark. After mounting a few steps and pressing the door latch, the visitor crossed a parquet floor of worn tiles laid in a herringbone pattern, while the light fell from above through red, green, and yellow panes, filling the children with awe.

On a slope, in a clump of oak, was the cemetery where Thomas's maternal ancestors lay in a chained-off square, the chains joined by four stone posts. Bordering the cemetery on one side were several mounds, where, in summer, lizards flitted in and out of the wild thyme. These were called the Swedish Ramparts, and were built either by the Swedes, who had journeyed here from across the sea, or by their adversaries in battle. Occasionally, the remnants of armor would be unearthed among the ruins.

Past the Ramparts were the park trees, skirted by a steep road that was often turned into a riverbed by the thaw. By the roadside, the arms of a cross protruded from an eerie clump of hawthorn. To reach the cross, you had to climb through weeds and over the ruins of stairs before coming to the round hole of a spring, where a frog might stare up goggle-eyed from below the rim, and where, by kneeling and pushing aside the duckweed, you could feast your eyes on the eddy below. Craning your neck, you beheld a wooden, moss-covered Christ—one arm clasping his knee, the other supporting his chin in an attitude of sorrow —sitting in what looked to be a shrine.

A lane branching off from the road led homeward. Thick with lindens, it was more like a tunnel, descending all the way to the pond near the granary. It was called the Black Pond because the sun never shone on it. It was a spooky place at night; the black pig had been sighted there more than once, grunting and stamping its hoofs on the paths, vanishing only after someone made the sign of the cross over it. Across the pond, the lane climbed again, opening out onto a brilliant green lawn. The house was white and built so low to the ground that the roof, its shingles here and there tufted with grass and moss, seemed to be crushing it with its weight. Wild grapevine, whose berries made your tongue curl, wound about the windows and the two small porch columns. Another wing had been built onto the rear of the building; here they used to set up winter quarters, as the front of the house was rotting and sinking from the dampness seeping from underneath the foundation. The wing was divided into a number of rooms, housing the spinning wheels, looms, and ironing presses.

Thomas's cradle stood in the old part of the house, facing the garden, and birdsongs were most likely the first sounds to greet him. When he could walk, he spent most of his time exploring the house. In the dining room he was reluctant to approach the oilcloth sofa—less because of the portrait of a man clad in armor with purple trim, and so stern of gaze, than of the two horribly twisted ceramic faces standing on the mantel. He never ventured into the part of the house referred to as the "salon," and even as a grown boy he felt ill at ease there. Just off the hallway, the "salon" was always empty, the parquet floor and the furniture squeaked even in the silence, and somehow the room always bespoke a human presence. But the larder was the place he liked most to visit, which happened rarely. His grandmother's hand would turn the key in a door painted bright red and release a rush of odors: the smell of smoked sausage and hams hanging from the rafters, mingled with others emanating from the little drawers stacked along the walls. Sometimes his grandmother pulled out the drawers and let him sniff their contents. "This is cinnamon," she would say, "this is coffee and these are cloves." Higher up, in a place where only grownups could reach, shimmered little dark-gold pots that aroused one's desire, mortars, an almond-grinding machine, and a mouse trap—a tin box big enough for a mouse to climb onto by crossing a little bridge notched with stairs; when it reached the bacon, a trapdoor opened and sent it plummeting into the water. The pantry had a grated opening, and the room was always cool and shady. Thomas was also fond of the room off the corridor, next to the kitchen—the "cloakroom," as it was called—where the cheeses were aged and the butter churned. He loved to take part in the churning, to move the stick up and down, the buttermilk hissing at the opening, though he soon tired of it: it took so long before one could lift the lid and see the yellow chunks clinging to the little cross at the end of the stick.

The house, the fruit garden in back, and the little lawn in front were Thomas's earliest discoveries. On the lawn, three agaves, a large one in the middle, flanked by two smaller ones, were bursting out of their tubs, whose staves bore traces of rusty hoops above and below. The agaves seemed to merge with the tops of the spruce trees at the bottom of the park, and between them loomed the world. As a little boy, he was permitted to run down to the river and the village only when accompanied by Antonina as, a wooden trough braced against her hip, a paddle—or, as it can also be called, a *kijanka*—balanced on top, she went to do the laundry.

4

———————

❧ ❦ ❦ ❦ ❦ ❧

THOMAS's ANCESTORS belonged to the landowning gentry. How they had become squires was now lost from memory. They had worn helmets and swords, and the local villagers had been forced to work their fields. Their wealth was measured more by the number of "souls," or serfs, in their possession than by the size of their landholdings. In the past, the villages had rendered tribute in kind; later it was discovered that the grain which was loaded onto barges and shipped down the Niemen to the sea could bring handsome profits and that it paid to cultivate the land. It was around this time that those in servitude began staging revolts and massacring their masters;

they were led by the elders, who shared a common hatred for both the squires and Christianity, the coming of which coincided with the loss of freedom.

By the time Thomas was born, the manor was already in decline. All that was left was a modest tract of land that was plowed, sown, and harvested by a few families of farm laborers. Payment was mainly in the form of potatoes and grain, and the yearly allotment was entered in the books under the heading of *ordinaria*. Aside from the laborers, a few farmhands were kept "at the manorial table."

Thomas's grandfather, Casimir Surkont, bore not the slightest resemblance to those men of yore whose passion was the judging of horseflesh and wrangling over the merits of this or that weapon. Short, somewhat sluggish, he spent most of his time in his armchair, dozing with his chin propped on his chest, the gray wisps on his rosy-pink bald patch slipping down, his pince-nez dangling at the end of a silken cord. He had a child's complexion (only his nose would take on a plumlike color when the weather turned chilly) and blue, red-veined eyes. He was quite susceptible to colds and preferred his room to open spaces. He neither smoked nor drank, and, though he was expected to wear knee boots and even spurs to demonstrate his readiness to jump into the saddle, he preferred going around in long breeches bagged at the knees and in laced-up shoes. He kept no hunting dogs on the estate, and packs of all breeds, idled without the chase, moiled about the barn, scratching and plucking for fleas. Nor were any firearms kept. Grandfather Surkont valued above all his peace and his books on gardening. He behaved toward people much as he did toward plants, and was not easily swayed by the passions of others. He was understanding, but his reputation for being "too softhearted," along with his aversion for card playing and carousing, alienated him from his peers, who, unable to reproach him with anything in particular, would pronounce his name with a shrug. Visitors to the manor were always treated graciously, regardless of rank or calling. While it was customary for a gentleman to be treated differently from a Jew, a Jew differently from a peasant, Grandfather paid little heed to this custom—even when it came to the terrifying Chaim. Every few weeks, Chaim showed up in his britska and, whip in hand, dressed in his black caftan, his trousers hanging over the tops of his boots and his beard sticking out like a scorched plank, entered the house. He began by negotiating the price of rye or calves, but this was just a prologue, because then, wailing and gesticulating, he commenced chasing members of the household from one room to another, pulling his hair and predicting bankruptcy if he paid what they asked. It was as if he considered it a dereliction of duty on the part of a good merchant to go away without staging these little dramas of despair. And it always amazed Thomas how quickly these tantrums subsided, and how afterward, with something like a smile playing in the corners of his mouth, Chaim would settle down with Grandpa for a good, neighborly chat.

Surkont's benign way did not imply that he was apt to make concessions. The ancient feuds between the village of Gine and the manor were a thing of the past, and the lay of the land was such that it had not given rise to any quarrels. The same could not be said of Pogirai, a village to the other side, bordering on the forest, where the villagers bickered endlessly over the right to pasture. They would meet, wrangle, get riled up, and in the end appoint a delegation of elders. But the moment they sat down with Surkont to a table graced with vodka and cold meats, all their carefully rehearsed arguments faded. Stroking the back of his hand with his palm, Grandfather would state his case, slowly and sincerely; plainly, his self-assurance was aimed only at finding an equitable solution. They would yield ground, soften their position, compromise, and only on the way back would they recall all they had ne-

glected to say, rankling at how, once again, they had been
charmed and embarrassed in the eyes of the whole village.

As a young man, Surkont had studied in the city and
read the works of Auguste Comte and John Stuart Mill,
of whom hardly anyone on the Issa had ever heard. His
grandfather liked to reminisce, but the stories that stood
out in Thomas's memory were the ones about the formal
balls attended by men in frock coats. Grandfather and a
friend had shared the same coat; while one danced, the
other had waited at home, trading places a few hours later.

He had two daughters. Helen married a local land-
owner; the other, Tekla, a man from the city. Tekla, who
later became Thomas's mother, came to Gine for several
months out of the year, and then only rarely; most of the
time she had to accompany her husband on his travels, at
first in search of work, later because of the war. For
Thomas she was almost too beautiful to be real, and he
gulped with love at the sight of her. His father was practically a stranger to him, and he was constantly surrounded
by women; first by Pola, during infancy, and later by Antonina. Pola was white skin, flaxen hair, and the sensation
of softness, and his affection for her was later transferred
to a country bearing a similar name. Antonina had a protruding belly, wore striped aprons, and always carried a
bunch of keys on her belt. Her laugh was more like a
horse's whinny, and her heart bore malice toward none.
She spoke a mixture of both languages, Lithuanian being
her mother tongue and Polish an acquired one.

Thomas was very fond of his grandfather. He had a
nice smell about him and the gray bristles above his lip
tickled his cheek. He lived in a little room where a print
showing people tied to stakes, with half-naked men putting
torches to the stakes, hung above his bed. One of Thomas's
first reading exercises was to read aloud, syllable by syllable, the inscription: *The Torches of Nero*. In this way he
came to know the name of that vicious tyrant, the name he

later gave to one of the pups when the grownups, after examining the pup's mouth, had said it was bound to be fierce because it had a dark palate. Nero grew up showing not ferocity as much as cunning—he was shrewd enough to eat plums that had fallen from the tree; when none lay on the ground, he leaned against the trunk and shook it with his forepaws. On Grandfather's table were many books, illustrated with roots, leaves, and flowers. Sometimes his grandfather took him into the "salon" and lifted a piano lid the color of chestnuts. His fingers, somewhat swollen, tapered, skipped along the keyboard with a motion that astounded Thomas no less than did the sprinkling drops of sound.

Grandfather was frequently seen consulting with his steward, Shatybelko, who wore a parted goatee, which he had a habit of stroking and spreading apart while he spoke. A dwarfish man, he went around with knees bent and legs sticking out of his oversized boot tops. He smoked a pipe —huge in comparison with his size—with a curved stem and a perforated metal lid. His lodgings, situated at the far end of the same building housing the stable, coach house, and servants' quarters, were always shaded green by the geraniums planted in flowerpots and tin cans. The walls of the room were decorated with religious pictures, which his wife, Paulina, festooned with paper flowers. Mopsy, his little dog, trailed Shatybelko wherever he went. If his master was detained in Grandfather's room, the dog waited outside anxiously, for it was one of those dogs that, surrounded by a world of people and larger dogs, was forever in need of protection.

Except for Chaim or farmers on business, visitors were rare, seldom coming to the manor more than once or twice a year. The master of the house was neither on the lookout for them nor was he annoyed when they came, though the arrival of almost anyone was enough to throw Grandmother into a pout.

5

GRANDMOTHER MICHALINA, or Misia as she was called, never treated Thomas to anything and never doted over him, but what a character she was—slamming doors, cussing at everyone in sight, not in the least fazed by what others thought. During one of her tantrums, she was apt to retreat to her room for days on end. Catching her alone, Thomas rejoiced, much as if he had surprised a squirrel or marten in the brush, for, like them, she belonged to the species of forest animal. Her generous straight nose, nearly lost behind bulging cheeks, even bore a certain resemblance to theirs. Nut-brown eyes, smoothly combed dark hair—full of health and purity. In late May she launched the first of her expeditions to the river, in summer she took several baths daily, and in autumn she broke the ice with her foot. In winter, too, she devoted much of her time to ablutions of every sort. She was no less attentive to the house, or rather to that part of the house she regarded as her private domain. Otherwise, she was a woman of few needs.

Thomas seldom ate at the table with his grandparents, as his grandmother was not one to observe regular meals, something she regarded as a silly convention. If she had a yen to eat, she would duck into the kitchen for a crock of buttermilk, a snack of salted cucumbers or pickled cabbage (she had a positive weakness for anything sour or salty). Her distaste for the ritual of plates and dishes—how much nicer to sneak into a corner and munch something on the sly—sprang from a conviction that far too much time was squandered on ceremonies, and not least from stinginess.

Guests were a constant irritation, since they had to be fed and entertained, even when one felt no inclination to do so.

She wore no jerkins, woolen underwear, or corsets. In winter her favorite pastime was to stand by the tiled stove, skirt hiked, and warm her posterior—a pose that meant she was ready to engage in conversation. Thomas was greatly impressed by such gestures carried out in defiance of accepted customs.

Grandmother's tantrums were only on the surface; inwardly, protected by her aloofness, she must have enjoyed herself richly. Thomas was of the suspicion she was made of some durable substance, that inside her ticked some self-winding machine, completely oblivious to the world outside. And what pretexts she could invent to curl up inside herself.

Her ruling passion was magic, the world of spirits and the hereafter. The only books she ever read were the lives of the saints, though it was not the religious message as much as the language, the sound of those pious and god-fearing sentences that charmed her. (She never thought to instruct Thomas in morality.) In the morning, emerging from her warren, which always smelled of wax and soap, she and Antonina would sit and interpret one another's dreams. At news that someone had been visited by a devil, that a house was feared to be uninhabitable owing to reports of clanking chains and rolling barrels, she was all smiles. Any sign from the other world—a proof that man was never alone on this earth but always in company—was enough to brighten her spirits. She divined the clues and admonitions of various Powers in the most trivial events. For only through canniness, through vigilance, could the Powers be beneficial. Grandmother had such an abiding curiosity about those beings who swarm about us, and whom, unknowingly, we continuously brush against, that she gave special treatment to women said to be in possession of secrets and magical incantations, going so far as to loosen their tongues with a piece of cloth or kielbasa.

She showed little interest in the farm, and if she did, it was only to ensure that Grandfather, who preferred to steal rather than risk a scene, wasn't slipping things to his protégés on the sly. Not having to be of service to anyone —the needs of others rarely crossed her mind—freed of any guilt where family obligations were concerned, she was content simply to live.

Thomas, if he was lucky enough to visit her in bed— her bed stood in a corner behind a curtain, a prie-dieu with a carved rest and a red velvet cushion adjacent to it— would sit at her feet, bracing himself against her knees bent under the blanket (she couldn't stand quilted coverlets); and if wrinkles gathered around her eyes and her apple cheeks began to quiver more than was usual, that meant she was in the mood for telling funny stories. Occasionally, she might grump over some prank of his, call him a rascal or a clown, but he never took it to heart, knowing how fond she was of him.

On Sundays she dressed for church in dark blouses buttoned to the neck over a jabot. She wore a little golden chain with links the size of pinheads, and kept a locket in a little pocket on her belt, which she would open on request (it was quite empty).

6

VARIOUS POWERS would observe Thomas in the sun and greenery and pass judgment on him, each according to his province. Those able to step outside of time would shake their diaphanous heads in dismay, for they could foresee the effects of the ecstatic state in which he lived. Such Powers were familiar with the works of composers desirous of expressing felicity; but it was enough to crouch beside the bed of a child who wakes on a summer morning to the oriole's song outside his window, to a chorus of quacks, cackling, and gaggling from the barnyard, to a steady stream of voices bathed in never-ending light, to appreciate the futility of such musical exertions. Touch was also a kind of ecstasy—the feel of naked feet racing over smooth boards, onto the cool of a corridor's tiled floor, over a garden path's circular flagstones still wet with dew. And, let us also note, he was an only child in a kingdom that could be transformed at will. Devils, rapidly shrinking and taking cover under leaves at the sound of his footsteps, were forever imitating hens when, all in a flutter, they crane their necks and reveal a moronic look in their eye.

In spring, the lawn was covered with flowers known as the "keys of St. Peter," or cowslips. Thomas was wild about them, that sudden burst of bright yellow on a field of green, the way they clung to their naked stems so like a bunch of keys, and in each a little ring of red. The lower leaves were wrinkly, pleasant to the touch, chamoislike. As soon as the peonies were in bloom, Antonina would cut a bunch for church. Thomas loved to immerse his gaze in them, straining his whole body to enter their rose-colored palace, as the sun filtered through their petal walls and little bugs wallowed in the yellow pollen—once, when he sniffed too hard, a bug ran up his nose. When Antonina went to fetch meat from the storage cellar in the garden, he tagged along, hopping on one leg, crawling down the ladder, and savoring with his toes the slab of ice taken from the Issa and sprinkled with straw. A scorcher above, but so cool below—amazing! He found it hard to believe the cellar did not stretch beyond the stone foundation blotched with dampness. And the snails. After a rain shower, they shunted across the wet pathways, from one green patch to another, trailing a silver streak. Cupped in your hand, they retreated into their shells, reappearing the moment you said: "Snail, snail, give us a look-see and I'll buy you a cookie." Whatever pleasure the grownups took in such pastimes, it was always, as the Powers could easily attest, with a slight embarrassment, and they were not likely to be found contemplating the little white band on a snail's shell.

For Thomas, the river was gigantic and always full of echoes: the *thwack-thwack-thwack* of the wash paddles, immediately echoed by others, as if rehearsed. A whole orchestra, never a missed cue, the newcomer always sure to join in at the same tempo. Hidden in the bushes, Thomas would shinny up a willow and wile away the hours, listening and staring down at the water—at the water spiders, their legs ringed by little pools, engaging in their endless pursuit; at the beetles, those drops of metal so smooth the water never clung to them as they danced their continuous round, always a round. Sunbeams revealed whole forests at the bottom, traversed by schools of fish that darted helter-skelter, only to band together again with a flick of the tail, a scattering motion, then another flick . . . Now and then, a larger fish meandered from the deep into the light, and Thomas's heart throbbed with excitement. At the sound of a splash out in the deep, at the sight of a flash and a spreading of ripples, he was up on all fours on his tree perch. Dugouts were rarely seen on the river, appearing and disappearing so quickly they almost escaped notice. The fisherman, paddling with a double-bladed oar, a line trailing behind, sat so low he seemed to skim the water.

Thomas, who made his first pole at an early age, was a patient but unlucky fisherman. Until the Akulonis children, Józiuk and Onutè, taught him how to tie a hook. At first, he made only brief visits to their cottage on the outskirts of the village; later these visits became so routine that, if he was not at home, his whereabouts were never a secret. In the afternoon, he was handed a wooden spoon and told to sit down at the table; there he helped himself to *bonduki* and sour cream from the same bowl used by the rest of the family. Akulonis was an imposing man, with a back so flat it amazed Thomas: he had never known anyone who could hold himself so erect. The homespun pants legs around his calves were bound by strips of bast, wrapped all the way to the knees. Fishing was one of his passions; but most important of all—he owned a dugout. Behind the apple trees by the granary, the ground sloped down to a cove rank with sweet flag, through which the dugout had cleared a passage and where it lay beached. Forbidden to take it out into the water, the children pretended they were out canoeing by rocking back and forth at one end. Capsizable, the dugout, a hollowed-out trunk, was fitted with a pair of outriggers. Akulonis fished for pike in it, first letting out the line with the spinner, then looping it around one ear. At night he would set up the night poles, one of which he gave Thomas. This was a rod fastened with hazel forks; the forks were wound with line, one end threaded through a slit, a double hook going on the loose end. The ideal bait was a young perch, because once the hook was stuck in the small knife slit in its side, it could swim around the whole night; any other fish would have lacked the vitality, would have died too soon.

Credit for what followed must go to Akulonis, for it was he who picked out the spot and cast the line. Unable to sleep, Thomas sprang out of bed early the next day and bolted down to the river before the morning fog had lifted. Above the rosy, mist-covered, glasslike surface, he spotted the forks: empty. In disbelief, he began reeling in the line, yanked on it, felt it strain, then heard the splashing. Ecstatic, he darted back up the hill, eager to show everyone his fish the size of a man's arm. People huddled around. It turned out to be, not a pike, but another kind, one that

Akulonis said was a rare catch. Nothing even remotely similar had ever happened to Thomas, and years later he still spoke of it with pride.

He felt drawn to Akulonis's wife, whose fair skin reminded him of Pola, and went out of his way to be fondled by her. At home they spoke Lithuanian, slipping imperceptibly from one language into another. The children spoke a mixture, except when certain communal acts demanded certain time-honored exclamations, such as when the boys charged naked into the river, yelling: *"Ei virai!"* or "Forward, men!" *Vir*, as Thomas later discovered, meant the same in Latin, though Lithuanian was decidedly more archaic.

But all summers must come to an end. Then come the rains, noses pressed against windows, the boredom among the older children . . . And evenings in the kitchen, when the girls gathered around Antonina to spin or shuck beans, when everyone looked forward to new stories and would be disappointed if, as sometimes happened, something intruded to spoil their fun. Thomas, listening to their songs, was especially intrigued by one, all the more so when Antonina took on an air of secrecy, warning that such songs were not meant for him. In his presence she sang only the refrain:

Hey, little dress, spin all night,
Hey, little miss, have no fright!

The rest he caught only in snatches. The song was about a knight who had gone off to war, fallen in battle, and one night returned to his sweetheart as a ghost, mounting her on his horse and taking her away to his castle. There was no castle, of course, only a grave in the cemetery.

One song, sung by a girl from the Poniewież region, was about some carpenters, or at least that is what Thomas imagined it to be about:

> Boss, I'll thank you for my fee,
> 'Cause it's quittin' time for me.
> Just give me my pay,
> And I'll be on my way.

The last word was held for a long time, to show that the way was far indeed. The shorter songs were a little on the happier side.

> He grabbed his bottle and he grabbed his glass
> And made his way to High Ridge Pass
> And from High Ridge Pass to the county seat
> He rode in search of a wife so sweet
> With a thumpety-thump on his pony dear
> Till he and his horse at the church did appear—
> And I won't marry a soul, I swear,
> 'Less it's me Mike, oh dear, oh dear!

Or:

> Hop to the reel
> But don't bust your heel!
> My brother's name is Scratch,
> His shoes need a patch!
> Got me a hound named Black,
> Lose your shoes and he'll fetch 'em back!

During the fortune-telling, as the wax is poured, the most exciting moment comes when it sizzles in the cold water and starts to assume the various shapes of Fate. One by one, the figures are turned and their silhouettes studied, setting off a chorus of "ooh's" and "aah's" as the wreaths, animals, crosses, and mountains are gradually deciphered. For Thomas, one St. Andrew's Eve augured genuine horror. Only girls were permitted to look into the mirror, and at midnight, with a solemn air, to shut themselves up in their rooms. Once, as a joke, he tried to mimic them, but when the mirror reflected a pair of red horns, it ended in tears. Horns, or just the embroidery on a girl's blouse flashing in the background? No telling, but for a long time after that, he gave every mirror a wide berth.

One winter—there was always that first morning when you went tracking through the snow that had fallen the night before—Thomas spotted an ermine on the Issa. Frost and sunlight made the twigs of the bushes on the steep shore of the opposite bank stand out like bouquets of gold, lightly tinged with gray and bluish purple. It was then that a ballet dancer of remarkable grace and agility made her appearance, a white sickle, arching and straightening. With a gaping mouth, Thomas stared in awe and ached with desire. To have. If he'd had a rifle with him he would have shot it, because one could not simply stand idle when one's wonder demanded that the thing arousing it be preserved forever. But what good would that have done? Then there would have been neither ermine nor any sense of wonder, just dead matter lying on the ground; no, it was better to feast one's eyes and let it go at that.

In spring, when the lilacs were in bloom, they used to take off their shoes and let their feet squirm, every pebble stabbing like a nail. But it didn't take long for the skin to toughen, and from then until the first frost, Thomas would traipse barefoot on the trails, so that on Sundays his feet would roast and he couldn't wait to chuck his shoes after Mass.

7

NOT EVERYONE can be the hero of an adventure such as befell Pakenas. Thomas had always approached him with reverence. Perchlike, with a shiny, sharp nose, Pakenas worked as a weaver in the large workshop,

where he operated the ironing press used to press homespun cloth between sheets of cardboard, which long use
and the absorption of dyes had turned pitch-black. (People
from the surrounding villages brought their homespun to
the manor for beating and ironing.) Although the incident
took place long ago, it has not been forgotten, and there
was living proof that it was not merely rumored to have
happened, since Pakenas was always on hand to testify,
albeit reluctantly, to its veracity.

It all began in the Borek, a clump of pine along the
Issa and a favorite nesting place of the rooks that cawed
and circled above the treetops. The Borek had an evil
reputation. An old shepherd believed to have choked to
death on a piece of cheese was buried there.

"Choked to death?" asked Thomas. "How so?"

"Choked to death, that's how—while eating his supper in the pasture." The unusual circumstances of his
death may explain why he was never buried in the
cemetery. A chest left behind by Napoleon's army was
buried there as well; according to legend, they had stum-
bled on its iron lid while digging the shepherd's grave.

"And why wasn't it taken out of the ground?"

"Couldn't get a grip on it, ran out of time and
energy—" Here the explanations became rather vague.

Late one night, around midnight, Pakenas was making his way back from a village dance on the far side of the
river. Finding the dugout where he'd hidden it in the
bushes, he paddled across the river. But he wasn't a few
steps across the field when a column of vapor started in his
direction. He broke into a run, the column at his heels. His
hair on end, he ran faster, but the column kept pace.
Pakenas bounded uphill to the park and, howling in mortal
terror, banged on Shatybelko's door for help.

The slight embarrassment with which Pakenas later
recalled the incident had to do with some of the goings-on
at the dance. The appearance of the shepherd's ghost he

took as a punishment, a sign—he was, as they say, inclined to superstition. If he had emigrated to America like his brother and gone to work in a dry cleaners on some bleak Brooklyn street, all recollection of that night would have faded. The same might have happened if he'd been drafted into the army. But the treetops of the Borek—he could see them every day on his way from his room in the granary to the workshop—stood as a constant reminder. But, then, it is not for a chronicler to lavish details on every character who crosses his field of vision. A life such as Pakenas's can never be plumbed, and if we have alluded to it, it was only to state that once upon a time a certain Pakenas existed, at a much later date than many a learned man with his treatises disputing the existence of ghosts and gods. Suffice it to say that both his scruples and his timidity prevented Pakenas from ever marrying, and when Antonina and the girls chided him for clinging to his bachelor's ways, he would merely snuffle.

A waistcoat, a triangle of white shirt, clasped at the neck by a red-embroidered collar; a blank expression, a certain irritability accompanying his gestures—especially at the loosening of threads on his loom. Pakenas also had custody of the key to the granary. On his way out, he hid it in a crack under the doorsill. Once inside the granary—this, after Thomas mastered the trick of opening the iron-studded door—the feet crossed a floor sprinkled with grain and black rat droppings, and in the bins you could sit and shower your feet with the cool stuff. A tiny window in the loft—the outer wall was so thick the window was more like a tunnel—commanded a view of the entire valley. Pakenas's room was furnished with flour sacks and a bed; above the bed was a cross and a tin holy-water font, and draped over one arm of the cross, an aspergillum.

Every so often, while playing with Józiuk and Onutè in the geese pasture, Thomas ventured up to the edge of the Borek. The wind whistling overhead, the cawing, the dead silence below: it was an eerie, forbidding place. Once, plucking up their courage, they made it as far as the shepherd's grave, now overrun by a thick patch of nettles and wild raspberries. It was from this same patch that, summoned by the moonlight, a white pillar had risen up and slithered off among the trees. Had the leaves on the nettle bushes swayed, wondered Thomas.

8

THE WAY to the church cut across the Swedish Ramparts. Thomas, wearing a short jacket of prickly homespun, followed the movements of the altar boys in their surplices. The boys went right up to the altar, all shimmering in gold, swung the censers, answered the priest without the slightest unease, and handed him bottles with spouts resembling the beaklike tips of a crescent moon. Could these be the same loudmouthed boys who hunted knee-deep in the water for crayfish, grabbed each other by the hair, and got tanned at home? How he envied them that, once a week, they could be other than what they were.

Several church fairs were held annually in Gine. Peddlers set up their canvas stalls by the roadside, at the foot of the hill, hugging the path leading down from the cemetery oaks. They sold gingerbread hearts and clay-rooster whistles, but Thomas was most enthralled by the little violet, red, and black squares of the scapulars, by the clusters of rosaries, and by the color and multiplicity of tiny objects.

Of all the holidays, none could compete with Easter, not only because that was the time of year when poppy seeds were ground in earthenware bowls and Easter cakes raided for their nuts. All during Holy Week, when the pictures and statues inside the church were shrouded, and bells replaced by the hollow clatter of rattles, people made a pilgrimage to Jesus' tomb. The grotto was guarded by sentries, each armed with a lance and a halbred, each in a silver helmet festooned with comb and plume. Jesus' body lay on top of an elevated platform, the same body that normally hung on the crucifix, only now the arms were covered with myrtle leaves.

The most eagerly awaited event of the season was the performance on Holy Saturday. Fifteen- and sixteen-year-old boys, after weeks of rehearsing, came running into the church with a roar, bearing dead crows lashed to poles. Devout old women, exhausted by a strict observance of the fast and by endless prayer, their heads drooping lower and lower, were suddenly roused from their drowsy meditations by a dead crow dangled before their noses; those who had brought eggs in bundles to be blessed were similarly taunted. The skits were staged on the church lawn. Thomas's favorite was the persecution of Judas. First they ran him off his legs, corralled him, showered him with insults, hung him till his tongue bulged, and pulled down the corpse; then lest he got off too lightly, he was flipped over on his belly, pinched till he groaned, his drawers lowered, his rear end stuffed with straw, a soul blown into him, until, screaming that he was alive, Judas jumped to his feet.

When Thomas was a little older, Antonina and his grandmother took him to Sunrise Mass at Easter. After a few doleful songs and litanies, the choir burst into an "Alleluia" and the procession got under way: a filing toward the door, a lingering darkness outside, candles flickering in the breeze, branches overhead, a matinal chill, the women's kerchiefs shimmering in the light, the bare heads of the men—ending with a procession around the church and along the little stone wall. In time, all this became associated in Thomas's mind with the advent of spring.

Then came the sleepy holiday patter, the sweet taste of rolls—and the egg-rolling contests. The children's course was made of turf, slightly curved to the inside and lined with strips of tin to increase the momentum. No two eggs rolled alike, and you had to guess by its shape whether to position it on the right, left, or in the middle of the rut. And just when the coast was clear, just as your egg started catching up with the others, spread out like a herd of cows; when it was on the verge of hitting another egg and making its owner a winner, it would suddenly take to wobbling and, obeying its own private whim, either skirt it by a finger or stop just short of it.

On Corpus Christi, the church was decorated with oak and maple leaf garlands suspended from the rafters above the heads of the congregation. All during May, flowers were placed at the foot of the statue of the Virgin Mary, but now it was the altar's turn to be decked. The children were crowded into the sacristy and handed little baskets of rose or peony petals. Thomas's grandmother made him take part in the procession. They marched with their backs to the canopy, under which the priest carried the monstrance, and one had to step cautiously to avoid tripping over a rock. Corpus Christi almost always fell on a hot day; by the time it was over, everyone was drenched, wrought from carrying all the banners and the reliquaries. But it was still one of the most festive of feast days: bright skies, the twitter of swallows, the chiming of bells, and lots of white, red, and gold.

9

THE WORLD was at war, and barely had it begun than the Russian Tsar, with his army now in retreat, ceased to have dominion over the Land of Lakes. Thomas saw the Germans only once. There were three, all on beautiful mounts. They came riding into the courtyard where Thomas sat next to old Gregory, who, too old to work, passed the time weaving baskets. A young officer, narrow in the waist and ruddy-faced as a schoolgirl, jumped down from his horse, gave it a clap on the neck, and helped himself to a drink from the milk can. The servant girls crowded around him, but old Gregory sat still, not taking his whittling knife from the branch. The sight of a man dressed in such colorful clothes—his uniform was a grassy green—came as a shock to Thomas. Strapped to his belt was a leather holster, and in the holster an enormous gun with a protruding metal butt and a long barrel. Thomas all but fell in love with his agility, and with something else not quite definable. The officer returned the can, sprang back into the saddle, saluted, and rode off with his soldiers by way of the cow barn and the linden lane.

What remains to be told is the story of the man's fate, a fate that, though only imagined, is hardly beyond the realm of plausibility. On one visit to the church, he leaned against the little stone wall and drew furiously in his notebook. Possibly he was reminded of a similar wooden *Kirche* he had seen in Norway before the war. As he mounted his horse and dropped down into the stirrups, to a creaking of saddle straps, he inhaled the fragrance of the meadows along the Issa, possibly recalling the landscape of devastation on the Western Front, in France, where he had recently seen combat. He never noticed Thomas, not then or—why not?—twenty years later as he sat in a general's car, surrounded by comfort rugs and thermos bottles, his corpulent chin propped against the collar of his uniform, and was chauffered through the streets of an East European city freshly conquered by the Führer's army. Clenching his fists in his pockets (we can assume he did), Thomas refused to recognize in the conqueror the object of his short-lived affection.

The war had only one effect on Gine: it meant no more shopping trips to town, since there was now nothing to buy. The result was a number of new and exciting domestic enterprises. Like the making of soap. A bonfire in the orchard, a kettle on a tripod, a brownish mash mixed with a pole. Phew! It was a stench to beat all stenches, but what excitement, what a lot of wrangling over the outcome. Once the mash had hardened, it was carved up into pieces. Or the making of candles. For that you needed cut-off bottles, tallow, and a wick. A piece of string, soaked in kerosene, severed the tops; by wrapping the string around the neck and setting fire to it, you could get the glass to crack all the way around in exactly the desired place. They also bought two carbide lamps, whose shape and odor intrigued Thomas. To make up for the lack of tea, Grandmother began to use wild strawberry leaves. Honey was substituted for sugar, but it wasn't long before she discovered saccharin, and from then on, she never went back to using sugar, saccharin being just as sweet-tasting—and cheaper.

It was time for Thomas to begin his studies, but with no one at home to take charge of his education, he was sent to the village, to Joseph, nicknamed "the Black." And black he was: brows like thick brushstrokes, a drawn face, and graying at the temples. He lived with his brother and helped out with the farming, devoting all his spare time to various hobbies. He was always receiving books, drying plants between sheets of pressed newspaper, writing letters for people—and talking politics. He had once served a prison term for those politics, and had worked at a number of trades, though he did not behave at all in the manner of townspeople, and the embroidery on his shirts proclaimed that he was still a peasant. He belonged to that tribe on which our chroniclers of today have bestowed the name of "nationalists"; that is, he was dedicated to serving the glory of the Cause. And that was his downfall, the root of his undoing. For while his sympathies were clearly on the side of Lithuania, he was nonetheless obliged to teach Thomas how to read and write in Polish. That the Surkonts—the surname could not have been more Lithuanian—regarded themselves as Poles he took to be an act of treason. His hatred for the Polish landowners (because they were landowners, because they had switched languages to distinguish themselves from the people), coupled with his inability to hate the man who had entrusted his grandson to him, and all that combined with his hope of opening Thomas's eyes to the splendor of the Cause—such was the tangle of emotion implicit in the fit of coughing that overtook him every time the boy opened his reader in front of him.

Grandmother was not at all happy with these lessons, with this fraternizing with "country bumpkins" (she had never accepted the Lithuanians, although her photograph might have served to illustrate a book on the country's original inhabitants). But since hiring a tutor would have been too uppity, she finally consented to Joseph, grumbling they were bound to make a yokel of him. Thomas was ignorant of all these complexities and antagonisms, and when at last he did understand, he thought of it as something exceptional. Had he crossed paths with a young Englishman brought up in Ireland or with a young Swede raised in Finland, he might have found many analogies.

But those lands beyond the Issa Valley were enveloped by fog, and what little he knew came from his grandmother's stories—how the English ate compote for breakfast (which may have explained his attraction to them), how the Russians had exiled Grandfather Arthur to Siberia, how one should love the Polish kings whose tombs were located in Cracow. To Grandmother, Cracow—"When you're a big boy, you'll go there"—was the most beautiful city in the world. His grandmother's patriotism for something so distant; the tolerance practiced by his grandfather, so unconcerned with nationality; and Joseph's constant invoking of the words "we" and "our country" nurtured in Thomas his later distrust whenever heated reference was made in his presence to any flags or emblems.

The lessons with Joseph dragged on, due to the chaos of the intervening years, out of which chaos the tiny republic of Lithuania was born. Thanks to Joseph, construction on the first school in Gine was begun, and he eventually became one of its teachers.

The war was abating, its progress measured by what one saw down on the road—from one of the rotting benches, say, situated at the park's edge. From far away, from beyond the lakes, from the cities they came, all fleeing from hunger, their backs strapped with sacks and bundles, many of them pulling their children in little wooden carts. One such family, a mother and two boys, was taken into the manor on the insistence of Antonina, whom the practically grown-up Stasiek had charmed with his beautiful harmonica playing, his city songs, and above all with his pure Mazovian Polish. "What a fancy talker!" she squealed, squinting with delight. Stasiek, with his big ears and skinny neck, failed to gain Thomas's affections, even though the boy had made him a crossbow with a butt similar to one on a real carbine. Those evenings were full of girlish giggling coming from under the linden tree, and even when Stasiek sat alone with Antonina, Thomas would squirm and fidget in his seat, and eventually leave them—bored, and somehow irked, as when the afternoon sun suddenly ducks behind a cloud.

10

❧ℐ❧ℐ❧ℐ❧

IF ANYONE was hounded by devils, it was Balthazar, even though he had the look of a man born for joy. A gypsy's complexion, white teeth, over six feet tall, pie-faced, with a light down for a beard. Whenever he presented himself at the manor—dressed in a tightly cinched tunic, his navy-blue cap cocked back, revealing a bushy thatch—Thomas would come on the run to meet him, yelling all the way. With him he carried either a basket of mushrooms—boletuses and honey mushrooms, their tops the shade of a cut alder, their sides a dappled white—or some game: a snipe or a black grouse with a little red stripe over the eye. Balthazar was a forester, though not in the strict sense. He was neither paid nor was he obligated to pay, but made his home in the forest (built with a free allotment of timber), cultivated a few potato and rye fields, and plowed a little piece of farmland every year. His arrival at the manor was enough to give Grandmother a migraine. Sometimes Thomas caught her scolding his grandfather: "It's your favorite again! Don't you dare try to slip him anything!"

People were envious of Balthazar, and with good reason. Before he became a forester, he had nothing; now he had a farm, some livestock, and not just a cottage but a house with a plank floor, a porch, and four outbuildings. He later married the daughter of a prosperous farmer from Gine and had two children by her. Surkont was a pushover for any of Balthazar's requests, to the point of exposing himself to ridicule. The forester made few enemies, for he knew how to act with discretion: while he made sure no trees in the old oak forest were cut down, he would not object if someone from Pogirai felled a spruce or a hornbeam, as long as the stump was covered with moss.

For Balthazar, happiness was lounging on the front porch, a jug of homemade beer beside him on the floor—swigging from his mug, smacking his lips, yawning and scratching. A contented cat; but it was on just such occasions that he was given to fits. From time to time, Grandfather sat Thomas down beside him in the britska and rode out past the manorial fields to the forester's cottage. The britska was a buggy put to frequent use, as was the *linijka* —a kind of board on wheels, mounted horseback-style. Still other vehicles were kept stored in the coach house: a carriage, dust-covered and cobwebbed; another on runners, an open sledge; and one called the "spider," a long carriage painted a garish yellow, with enormous front wheels and smaller ones in back, an elevated seat for a driver or footman; and stretching the full length of the "spider" (which rather reminded one of a wasp), a bed of planks that, when jumped on, flipped high into the air.

Grandfather grabbed him by the waist every time the britska lurched. Past the fields came the grasslands and moors. Black pools in the grass-choked ruts concealed potholes deep enough for a wagon to sink up to its axle. Smoke, curling upward against a clump of hornbeam, signaled the barking of dogs, a rooftop and a well hoist. In the wilderness, alone, among animals that craned their necks from the brush and spied on the barnyard bustle—that was the life for Thomas. Balthazar's place smelled of resin, and the virgin wood made it gleam as though forged from copper.

Balthazar sat there, grinning, while his wife entertained them with food and drink, passing round the cold meats with a persistent "Please—help yourselves." Slight of build, with a jutting jaw, she uttered not another word the rest of the evening.

Thomas sometimes left the grownups and ran off to spy on the jays or wild pigeons—so many species of bird were to be found there. Once, among a pile of rocks in the brush, he discovered a nest of hoopoes; reaching inside, he caught one in his hand, a fledgling, which tried to frighten him by fanning its head feathers. When he brought it indoors, the hoopoe wouldn't eat, preferring to flit along the walls instead. In the end, he had to let it go.

Whatever was tormenting Balthazar, he would never have told Thomas. Not even he knew the nature of his affliction, only that it was getting worse. As long as he was putting up the house, everything was fine. But later, pausing behind his plow to roll a cigarette, he would lose all sense of where he was; when he came to, his fingers would be clenched, the tobacco spilled all over the ground. As a last resort, he doubled his work load, but his innate laziness made him finish any job in half the time it took normally; and the moment he stretched out on a bench with his jug of beer, his insides would go soft, do a slow somersault, and in a trance, as though half asleep, he would try to scream through clenched jaws. No luck. Sometimes he had an urge to jump up, bang his fist on the table, and take off for parts unknown. At times the whispering merged with the limpness, and Balthazar would fling his beer mug at his tormentor, who either crawled inside him or mocked him from a distance. When this happened, his wife took off his boots and helped him into bed. Balthazar submitted to her, as he did to everything else, with apathy and the feeling that something was wrong, that he had somehow been cheated. He was repulsed by her homeliness, which was hardly noticeable in the dark but inescapable during the day. Sleep brought relief, but not for long, and at night he would awaken with the sensation of lying at the bottom of a pit barricaded by high walls, from which there was no escape.

There were times when he did bang the table and break away. But then it was only to embark on a real binge, lasting no fewer than three or four days, during which time he would drink till the vodka burned his insides and the innkeeper's wife, a Jew, had to squat over him and piss in his face—a notorious, though incriminating, method of revival. Word would then get around that Balthazar was at it again, some claiming that it came from a life of fat and plenty, others that he was conniving with the devil—which was not idle gossip, because Balthazar was heard to blab many things during his drunken ravings.

Years later, after he had left Gine, Thomas had occasion to think of Balthazar, to summon all that he had heard about him, with its blending of fact and legend, and to recall the stone-hard biceps (Balthazar was a man of herculean strength) and roelike eyes. No amount of success or providence, he decided, could protect a man from such an affliction of the soul, and whenever the example of Balthazar came to mind, it always made him fearful of his own fate and of all that lay ahead of him.

I I

A GOATEE, a flickering glance, the meekly folded hands of a city dweller, elbows propped on the table: thus did Herr Doktor, the "Little German," manifest himself. "Scat," Balthazar muttered under his breath, trying to make the sign of the cross and scratching his chest instead, while the other went on, cajolingly, his words falling like the rustle of dry leaves.

"But, my dear Balthazar," he said, "I only want to

help you. You're forever worrying, and for no reason. You're worried about the farm, aren't you? You're worried sick because the land doesn't belong to you. Yours and not yours. Here today, gone tomorrow, right? You think someone else will take over the manor and turn you out."

Balthazar moaned.

"But does the land really mean that much to you? Well, admit it. No, deep down you're hiding something. Right now, this very minute, you'd like to make a clean break with everything. Oh, the world is such a big place, Balthazar. Big cities, nights of laughter, music . . . You fall asleep on some riverbank, alone, free, all your bridges burned behind you, one life finished and another just beginning. No more guilty conscience, a new world before you, one that's never to be . . . Because you're scared, Balthazar. You're trembling over your property, over your hogs. 'What,' you say to yourself, 'am I to be a nothing again?' All right, but of all the Balthazars, why choose the dumbest one? Wouldn't you like to know what the other Balthazar is like?"

"Oh, God."

"There's no relief in sight. Autumn comes, winter, spring, summer . . . then autumn again, and so it goes till the grave—that's it, Balthazar, drown your troubles in drink. And you know what the nights are like. But it wasn't I who advised you to get married against your better judgment, to pick out the ugliest girl because she had a rich father. Fear, Balthazar, that's what did it. You wanted security. And are you any happier now than you were at twenty? Remember the parties? The days when your hand took easily to the ax, your feet to dancing, your throat to singing? How you and your friends used to live it up in grand style? Now you're alone. A farmer. Though it's true, they might take away that house of yours."

Balthazar was paralyzed, a sack of sawdust inside. The other was on to him.

"You're out at the crack of dawn, dew on the grass, birds singing—but is that the life for you? No, you're counting. For you it's just another day, a day like any other. On and on, like a plow horse. And in the old days? You used to sing. But now? You look at the oaks, but they might as well be hemp. Or not even there. It's all there in the books, Balthazar. But you, you'll never know what's in the books. Better to hang yourself than to keep such a mess buried inside. Otherwise, how can you be sure life isn't just a dream? That's what it says in the books. Would you hang yourself? I doubt it."

"Why is everyone else so lucky and not me?"

"Because, my friend, to each is given a certain thread, and that thread is a man's fate. Either a person catches hold of it and is content with it, or he doesn't. You were unlucky. You weren't looking for your own thread, you were too busy trying to copy others. What makes others happy makes you unhappy."

"What am I to do? Tell me."

"Nothing. It's too late. Too late for Balthazar. You're losing more and more of your nerve. The nerve to hang yourself or run away. You'll rot."

The beer came out of the jug in a muddy stream. He was drinking and at the same time burning on the inside. The other grinned.

"And no sense worrying over that secret of yours. No one will ever be the wiser. It's strictly between us. Everybody has to die, right? A little sooner or a little later— what's the difference? True, he was young. But he'd been fighting so long he was almost forgotten in the village. His wife will cry for a while, but she'll get over it. So what if he had a plump baby boy to hug him; he was much too small to remember his father. Only you shouldn't go around crying in your beer about having some sort of crime on your conscience."

"But the priest . . ."

"Yes, I know, you went to confession. But you're not so dumb as to believe you can make a clean breast of it in the confessional. You lied. It's bad to be refused absolution. You were lying when you said you killed him because he jumped you with an ax. All right, he jumped you. But then what? Well, Balthazar? You shot him while he sat there eating in the bushes. You threw in the bloodstained biscuits after him, and that's how you buried him. Isn't that so?"

Balthazar howled and let fly with the mug. The intercession of the "Little German" also accounted for his later hell-raising in the taverns as he went about overturning tables and smashing lamps.

12

THE GROUND in the fir hollow being the quickest to heal, Balthazar had carved out a piece of turf, then packed it down again with the shovel. He would come just before nightfall, sit, and listen to the shrieking of the jays and scurrying of the thrushes. It was easier to endure the pain here than to brood over it from a distance. He was almost envious of the person lying there. Such a peaceful spot, clouds drifting above the trees . . . And how many years did he still have ahead of him?

After stashing the rifle in the trunk of an oak, he never touched it again. A converted army rifle with a sawed-off barrel, it had fit easily under his overcoat, leading the other man to believe he was unarmed. He had jumped him from the bushes lining the trail, his ax held high, and yelled: "Hands up!" A red beard, a Russian greatcoat much the worse for wear: a POW from a German prison camp, trying to escape through the woods. Why the ambush? To rob him of his civilian clothes, club him to death, or just some madman on the loose? The moment Balthazar swung the rifle to his hip, the intruder spun around and fled so fast the bushes swished. But he didn't know his way around the forest, wasn't familiar with its many tunnels and crossings. And once an animal starts circling, it'll always wind up where it should. Taking his time, Balthazar started stalking him. If the prisoner went that way, he figured, then he had to come out in the pine clearing and stop to catch his breath. What was pushing him? Revenge? Fear that the man wasn't alone, that he might attack at night? Or was it just his hunter's instinct, the urge to track down the animal, to get even with him? Sneaking up, crouching low, he glimpsed the gray coat more or less where he had expected to find it. Leaving him for a moment, he circled round by way of some saplings to get in closer range, then trained the barrel on the man's stooped shoulder—he was sitting sideways to Balthazar—his neck, and finally on his head with the visorless cap. Later, with all his might, he tried to remember why he had pulled the trigger, but just when he was sure of the reason, another took its place.

The Russian fell face down. Balthazar waited; it was quiet except for the hawks crying overhead. Not a sign of any movement. Satisfied the man was dead, he zigzagged up to the body and turned it over. Bright blue eyes stared up at the spring sky, a louse crawled out of the hem of the dead man's coat. Next to him, on the ground—a bag of biscuits, untied and spotted with blood. The heels of his boots were worn smooth, evidence of his long trek from Prussia. He went through the man's pockets but found only a pocketknife and two German postage stamps. He covered the body, along with the ax and other things, with some fir branches until he could come back with the shovel later that evening.

He made up his mind while brooding at the scene of the crime one day. He was almost willing to believe the idea was communicated to him by the Russian. Maybe the killing was meant to be. That night he slept well, and was out of the house at daybreak.

The wizard Masiulis bred sheep, many heads of them, and gate after gate had to be opened before entering the yard. Balthazar displayed his gifts: a tub of butter and several wreaths of sausage. The old man adjusted his wire-rimmed spectacles. His skin looked almost smoked, gray bristles showed in his ears and nostrils. They began by swapping the latest neighborhood gossip, but when it came time to reveal the purpose of his visit, Balthazar was tongue-tied. At last, he pointed to his heart, made a gesture as if to rip it out, then muttered, bearlike: "They're torturing me." The sorcerer said nothing, nodded, and led him into the orchard, out past the beehive, where an old forge, rank with weeds, stood among the apple trees. Taking down some sacks that hung on poles, he gathered a handful of dried twigs lying in a corner, made four little piles, and sat Balthazar down on a log in the center. Then he lighted the twigs, and, to a low patter, began sprinkling herbs from the little sacks onto the fire. The smoke grew fiercer and headier, as the bespectacled face, all the while intoning some prayer, loomed up on one side and then the other. When he stood him up and brought him back to the house, Balthazar lowered his eyes under the other man's gaze.

"No, Balthazar," the old man said at last. "I can't help you. What's fit for a king is a king, an emperor for an emperor. Every power has its equal, but this is one power I don't have. Maybe you'll find someone who has what it takes. Wait and see."

Thus did his hopes vanish. And to those who tried not to guess his secret, Balthazar smiled blithely, baring his teeth.

13

THE PRIEST seldom visited the manor, and Thomas first came to know the rectory the day he and Antonina, nervously fingering the fold of her kerchief, stood on the front steps, staring up at the magical window. The parish priest, a stooped, rumpled man, was nicknamed —after one of his pet phrases—Father "Well, well." The priest had him recite the Our Father, the Hail Mary, and the Creed, and rewarded him with a holy picture. The Virgin Mary in the picture reminded him of the swallows that nested above the hay ladders and in the barn rafters. A blue dress, a bronzed face, surrounded by a disk of real gold. He kept the picture in an almanac, approaching its colors with delight every time he leafed through its pages.

He had little trouble learning the catechism, though his sympathies were not evenly divided. First came God the Father, bearded and frowning and towering above the clouds. Then Jesus, with his gentle gaze, one finger pointing to a heart spoked with rays—but Jesus had gone back up to heaven and so He, too, was far away. But not so the Holy Ghost, that eternally living dove shooting shafts of light down on people's heads. As he prepared himself for confession, he prayed to the Holy Ghost to hover over him—it was so hard keeping track of one's sins. He added them up on his fingers, lost count, and had to start all over again. Brushing his lips against the much worn and polished grating of the confessional, listening to the priest's heavy breathing, he recited the list as fast as he could. But by the time he reached the Swedish Ramparts, he was suddenly doubt-stricken, slackened his pace, broke out cry-

ing in the lane, and, full of despair, ran to his grandmother: what to do about all the sins he had forgotten?
She told him to go back, and he cried the harder, now from
shame. At her wit's end, she took him by the hand and
brought him to the priest. Her presence had a calming
effect, and embarrassing as it was, it was better than having to face it alone.

From the start, therefore, Thomas had the makings of
what theologians call a "scrupulous conscience," the cause,
in their view, of many of the devil's triumphs. Try as he
would not to omit anything, he was always careful not to
include a certain secret among his offenses. Unable to see
it from the outside, he never imagined that it was both
his—his and Onutè Akulonis's—and that it existed, so to
speak, apart from them, in the sense that it had been invented before them. It went far beyond the usual—using
foul language, say, or spying on girls swimming naked in
the river, at the black crows beneath their navels, or spook-
ing them on Saturday nights when they squatted in the
orchard between dances and hiked their skirts.

Slipping away from their playmates, Onutè and he
would retreat to their secret hideout on the Issa, crawling
on all fours through a tunnel of blackthorn and then
branching off—one had to know exactly where. There,
on a sandy mound, safely huddled in seclusion, drawn together by the danger, they conversed in muffled voices and
listened to the fish splashing, to the whacking of the wash
paddles, and to the rumble of cart wheels on the road.
Naked, their heads turned toward each other and the shade
falling on their arms, they would find in this inaccessible
palace an even smaller sanctuary in which to dwell in mystery. Like her mother (and like Pola), Onutè had blond
hair, worn in a braid. And this is how It was performed:
Onutè would lie flat on her back, pull him toward her, and
squeeze him with her knees. And they stayed that way, as
the sun rolled across the sky, and he knew that all the time

she was waiting, waiting for him to touch her, and it made him feel *sweet* all over. Yet this was not just any girl, but Onutè, and nothing could have prevailed on him to confess their secret.

Taking Holy Communion early in the morning, on an empty stomach, made him woozy and gave him stomach cramps. He came back up the aisle from Communion with his hands crossed on his chest and his eyes glued to his shoe tips. It was hard to visualize the wafer stuck to his palate—and which his tongue would shyly peel off—as the body of Jesus. But he was noticeably changed by it: for one whole day he was actually quiet and well-behaved. What appealed most to his imagination were the priest's words comparing the soul to a room that had to be cleaned and made worthy of receiving its Guest. He imagined that, after the wafer had melted, it was later healed in the soul, returning to its place in the chalice that stood among the greenery on the altar. That he, Thomas, was privileged to carry around such a room filled him with pride, and he was careful not to sully or damage it.

The day was approaching when, as had been promised, he was to be made an altar boy. He had even begun memorizing those inscrutable Latin responses, when the old pastor was suddenly transferred to another parish. The new priest—young, imposing, with a prominent chin, and brows joined at the bridge of his nose—alarmed people by his impulsiveness. He kept those who were already altar boys and refused to take on any new ones, as he had more important duties to attend to.

His sermons were a far cry from that endless prating, larded with hemming, with that monotonous "Well, well . . ." to which the people of Gine were accustomed. Although not always able to follow them, Thomas like everyone else froze in expectation when the new priest stepped into the pulpit. He began informally, in a voice barely above a patter, but soon, at regular intervals, he rose to a loud and booming exclamation, and the effect was musical. Then came a raising of the arms and a vociferating to set the church walls to trembling. He fulminated against their sins, his finger pointed into the crowd, and everyone quaked, believing himself or herself to be the object of his wrath. And then—abrupt silence, as he stood, flushed and excited, and stared; leaning on the edge of the pulpit, he bent down and in a low, soothing, heart-to-heart voice presented them with visions of the happiness awaiting those who were saved. At that point, his listeners began to sniffle. Soon the fame of Father Peiksva began to spread beyond Gine and the neighboring villages, and people from out of the parish began coming to him for confession, and he was forever surrounded by kerchiefs, seen bowing low every time his female admirers went to kiss his stole or hands.

He was adored by Akulonis's wife, by the servant girls, and above all by Antonina ("When he cleanses your sins," she sighed, "it's like he was scrubbin' your insides with a steel brush"). Even Grandmother, though opposed in principle to Lithuanian sermons, became a convert of his after hearing one of his orations delivered in Polish. But the fervor didn't last long. Now the women's boast to outsiders that a great honor had been bestowed on Gine was accompanied by a scowl, and they would immediately change the subject. Nor did it take Thomas and the children from the village long to realize that it was better to steer clear of the rectory.

14

MAGDALENA'S COFFIN was delivered to the cemetery a few days before the Feast of the Assumption. The coffin, shrouded with an ornamented blanket, lay in a big wagon on a bed of straw. Pausing in the shade of the lindens, the horses buried their heads in their feed bags, lapped up the oats, and drowsily swished away the flies: they had come a long way. The news spread so fast that the driver had no sooner tied the reins to the fence than people began milling around in anticipation. Father Peiksva made his appearance on the smooth flagstone path farther up the hill—motionless, as if unable to decide whether to come down, as if bracing himself. At last, he began to make his way down, slowly, only to stop again, pull out his handkerchief, and stand there, twisting and crumpling it in his fingers.

The scandal involving Magdalena had lasted some six months, and she had no one but herself to blame. Peiksva had inherited her as the rectory housekeeper, and their relationship was strictly private—a priest was only human, after all—until she began acting improperly, strutting about with her chin up and swiveling her hips like a dancer. She took such obvious pleasure in flaunting herself before him, in dropping hints so as to put the other women on notice: you may kiss his hands and robes, but I have *all* of him. Words led to visions—of how the man who stood before the altar used to lie in bed naked with her, of conversations, of moments of intimacy . . . Granted, much can be forgiven in such matters, as long as one is not nagged by all sorts of images.

Looking back over Magdalena's behavior prior to that (for two years she had served as the old pastor's housekeeper), the inhabitants of Gine, after long discussion, soon discovered other improprieties. Had her marriage plans fallen through and her fiancé immediately married someone else because of her age—she was going on twenty-five at the time—or even because she was poor, the daughter of landless peasants? Her fiancé, against everyone's advice, against even his parents' wishes, was ready to marry her, owing obviously to Magdalena's special powers. But at the last moment, frightened by her passionate nature, he had a change of heart. Similarly, other things, one corroborating the other, began to appear in a new light. And for those who still had any doubts, there was now the coffin.

Because Antonina used to spit every time she uttered Magdalena's name, Thomas, even though she had done nothing to deserve it, was already prejudiced against her. Whenever he came to the rectory to visit Father "Well, well," he was lured into the kitchen and treated to a piece of cake. He was even enthralled by her, would get a lump in his throat at the sight of her. When she leaned over the stove to sample one of her dishes with a spoon, her skirts (they pinched her waist they were cinched so tightly) rustled, a lock of hair slipped down over one ear, and a breast shifted inside her blouse. Though she was unaware of it, they were joined together because he knew what she looked like. True, he had confessed the sin, but he had seen her—from his leafy perch in a low-hanging tree on the river, his heart racing, wondering whether she would ever come, the Issa slowly turning pink in the setting sun, the fish jumping . . . He was craning up at a flight of ducks when she appeared, testing the water with her foot. She entered the water not like a *baba* who plops down once or twice with a splash, but slowly, step by step, her breasts splayed, not too black under the belly, more like a smudge. Kicking up an occasional fountain as she went, she had dog-paddled over to the water-lily pads, then swam back and washed herself with soap.

Thomas was both shocked and confused by all the gossip. It was inconceivable to him that the same person who thundered against the fires of hell could himself be a sinner. If the person who granted absolution was no different from anyone else, then what was the good of absolution? (Such questions were never posed openly.) Thus did Magdalena acquire for him the magic of forbidden things.

But the grownups were resentful of her; they were able to make distinctions where Thomas was not: a woman was one thing, a priest in a surplice another. She had broken the covenant, disturbed their peace, and spoiled for them the pleasure of listening to the sermons.

Father Peiksva, accompanied by stares, came down the hill. What would he have them do with the coffin? As he approached the wagon, they looked the other way. Tears were streaming down his cheeks, his lips pressed together to stop them from twitching. Only once did he open his mouth, and that was to ask that the body be carried up to the church for the Christian burial he meant to give it. The blanket was removed, revealing a coffin of white pine. Four of the villagers hoisted it to their shoulders and began climbing uphill, so that Magdalena stood up perfectly straight.

15

IT TAKES a fairly desperate person to swallow rat poison, a surrendering to one's own thoughts so complete as to make one oblivious to everything but one's fate. Magdalena might have lived to know many cities, countries, people, inventions, books, and all the incarnations of a lifetime. She might have, but try explaining that to her, try proving by a wave of the wand that there have been millions of women in the same predicament as she. Nothing would have stopped her, not even the despair of all those who, at the very moment she was taking her own life, were fighting for another hour, another minute. Once the mind has surrendered, once the body finds itself face to face with the supreme horror, it's already too late.

Nor should one overlook her wrought state shortly before the old pastor's departure. Her fiancé had broken off the engagement, which had numbed her, convinced her that nothing would ever change, that things would remain irrevocably the same. She rebelled at such a future—day in and day out, month after month, year after year, until she woke to find herself an old spinster. At daybreak she lay in bed, horrified at the thought of getting up and going about her daily chores. Sitting on the edge of the bed, she cupped her breasts; spurned like herself, they would share her life of celibacy and wither idly away. And then what? Latch on to boys at village dances, go for a tumble in the hay, become a prey to their dirty jokes . . . ? By the time Father Peiksva took over the rectory, she had worked herself into a state of utter despair.

When you're on a swing, there comes a moment of suspended motion, followed by a breathtaking downward rush. For Magdalena, earth and sky suddenly changed places; the tree outside, even the clouds, lost their old familiarity, and every animate thing seemed suffused with pure gold. Never had she dreamed that life could be so transfigured. She was to be rewarded for her suffering; and even if it meant eternal pain, it was worth it. Not the least of her exultation sprang from satiated pride; poor and illiterate as she was, she had been singled out by such an educated man, a man head and shoulders above the rest.

And then—it should be borne in mind—she was driven out into the cold, this time for good. Peiksva, aware of the scandal and forced to choose, had found her a housekeeper's position with a pastor in a parish so distant everyone could see the break was final. In that house overlooking the lake, with only a carping old man for company, Magdalena did not wait long before surrendering to dark despair—a despair she had known before her brief interlude of happiness. She swallowed the rat poison while the wind was whistling in the reeds, traces of white foam were being washed up on the shingle, and waves lapped against the boats moored to the landing.

The pastor of the other parish refused to bury her, washing his hands of the affair by donating his wagon, a few horses, and a driver.

Magdalena's last journey—before she entered that realm where highbred ladies belonging to a bygone era were on hand to greet her—began early in the morning. Under fleecy clouds the horses trotted briskly along, the men stood sharpening their scythes for the second mowing, and whetstone chimed against metal. They traveled down a sandy road, through groves of juniper and pine, then climbed uphill before coming to a crossroad overlooking three stretches of water, joined by green clasps like a necklace of translucent stones. Again downhill and into the woods—into a village street, where Magdalena spent the afternoon hours staring up at the leaves of an old maple, till evening shadows began to fall and the heat let up and it was time to resume the journey. The wagon wheels bounced across the log-covered dam; before long, the thrushes began their evening concert, and a starry sky unfolded with a refulgence of moving spheres and universes. An immense calm, a deep blue space—and whoever was looking down from there, did he behold a tiny solitary creature who had discovered how to stop the beating of her heart, the circulation of her blood, and of her own volition turn herself into an inanimate object? A horse smell, a driver's idle patter—and so it went until late into the night. Came morning and it was over hills again, through oak forests, as the wagon drew near to its destination. Gradually they descended into the Issa Valley, while across the way, with a view of the river gleaming through the osiers, Father Peiksva recited his breviary and waited.

Decomposition sets in quickly in summer, and people wondered why he was delaying the ceremony, almost as if unwilling to surrender her to the earth. Yet no unpleasant odor was detected when it came time to lift her from the wagon—a fact duly noted later on. The priest had her buried on the outskirts of the cemetery, on the slope, where the loose ground was held in place by clusters of roots.

Father Peiksva's sermon on the Feast of the Assumption was brief, and was delivered in a calm and steady voice. He described how she who was without blemish had risen into heaven, not in spirit alone but with her whole body, just as she had been while on earth; how at first her feet had barely touched the grass, then how she had slowly ascended without moving them, higher and higher, the breeze playing with her long robe, such as was worn in Judea at the time, till she became a minute speck among the clouds; and how she was granted that with which we sinners—if we are worthy—shall be rewarded in the valley of Josephat; and how, with all her earthly senses and in possession of eternal youth, she now beholds the face of God the Almighty.

Shortly afterward Father Peiksva left Gine, never to be heard from again.

16

_____

❧✿❀✿❀✿❧

AMONG THE WOMEN it was a subject of back-yard gossip. The men, on the other hand, observed silence; their eyes fixed on a pinch of tobacco, they licked the paper and pretended to be focusing all their attention on the thing at hand. With the gossip came a mounting anxiety, though for a time the people were content to ponder it, were careful to avoid using certain dangerous expressions.

The person who contributed most to the spreading of rumors was the new priest, Father Monkiewicz, a rotund, baldheaded, high-strung man, who could hardly contain his unease when he could find no natural explanation for a continual knocking on the wall (always three knocks in a row). After all he had heard, he was never comfortable at home; his nerves couldn't take whatever was manifesting itself in all the knocking. At the sound of someone's hand on the door latch, he would jump up, open the door, only to find no one there. He had hoped that these weird intrusions would cease of themselves, but things only got worse. The sexton was invited to sleep in the rectory, and from that moment on, there could be no more room for speculation. Father Monkiewicz, beside himself, appealed to the local villagers, and at night, in two's and three's, they stood guard in the kitchen.

It seems that Magdalena's ghost was loath to leave the place where it had known happiness. Using an invisible cleaver, it split invisible logs and started a fire that crackled and blazed like the real thing. It moved pans, broke eggs, and scrambled them on an otherwise cold and empty stove. What did it use for tools and utensils? Or were these only echoes, a whole register of sounds imitating nature? Or does a ghost have access to another kind of kitchen, one equipped with a universal bucket, a universal frying pan, a universal woodpile, that are but the essence of all the buckets, frying pans, and logs that ever were? A mystery—nothing to do but be vigilant and try not to believe the evidence of one's senses. Not even holy water had any effect. The priest sprinkled the water, there was a letup, but not for long, because then it resumed, every night a little louder and more obtrusive, sometimes to the sound of splashing water and a clanging of pots and pans. Worse, the mysterious interventions soon shifted to the bedroom. To the continual knocking and tampering with door latches were added footfalls, the sound of papers and books being hurled to the floor, and something else— something bordering on muffled laughter. Father Monkiewicz made the sign of the cross, sprinkling first one corner, then another—not a sound; but as soon as he came to the fourth, he would hear giggling, followed by the sort of whistling made by blowing into a hollow nutshell.

News of the incidents traveled quickly to the neighboring villages, and if the people of Gine hadn't made it their own business, there would have been not three of them sitting around at night in the kitchen but three hundred. Barred from it, outsiders fell to gossiping so that the parish fairly teemed with the wildest rumors.

It was Balthazar who helped persuade people that Magdalena's ghost had outgrown the priest's house. His story might have been sloughed off as absurd, or treated with that sham gullibility with which one assents to the tales of drunkards so as not to risk offending them—were it not for one detail. Balthazar claimed, no less, to having seen Magdalena ride down from the cemetery to the river on a white horse. She was stark naked, he said, and both she and the horse had glowed in the dark. When a crowd later assembled at his father-in-law's place, he repeated the story, taking offense at the merest insinuation that he might have been seeing things. Someone suggested going to the pastor's stable to see whether the priest's bay was there. Sure enough, they found it—all lathered up as if just returned from a long gallop.

Naturally, the manor house was all astir at the news, a fresh installment of which was delivered daily by Antonina. "How awful," Grandmother Misia would say, and secretly delighted by these otherworldly pranks, she would invite the priest over to hear the litany of his woes. When, noisily gulping down his strawberry-leaf tea, he conceded with a worried look that his health was failing, that unless these manifestations stopped he would ask to be transferred to another parish, Grandmother's triumph would be complete; and implicit in her "Oh, do be serious, Father!" was a cheerful vindication, since, after all, she was on the side of the spirits, not men.

Then another incident, this one quite close to home, arose. One day, allowed into Shatybelko's bedroom when the steward had nearly recovered from a sudden illness, Thomas got the creeps. The sick man, his beard spread out fanlike on the quilt, his dog curled up on the bedside rug, could muster only a few words in a feeble voice. Although Mopsy had disgraced himself—he had run off, his stump of a tail tucked between his legs—the old man bore him no grudge. What had happened was this: during the threshing season, the boiler engine was parked in the shed by the barn, and after the day's work the precious transmission belt was stored in the shed, under lock and key. That evening Shatybelko had already settled down with his slippers and pipe when he was suddenly seized with doubt: had he or had he not turned the key in the lock? That he couldn't recall was enough to give him the jitters. At last, afraid someone might steal the belt, cursing under his breath, he pulled on his boots, slipped into his sheepskin coat, grabbed the lantern, and gave up a warm room for the cold and rain outside. It was so dark all he could see was the patch illuminated by the lantern. As he had suspected, the shed was unlocked. He went inside, squeezed through the narrow passage between wall and boiler, and checked: the belt was still there. But just as he was about to head back, he was visited by a monster. Shatybelko described it as a sort of bumpy log that moved sideways, level with the ground, and which was mounted with three heads—all with Tartar features, he said—baring their teeth in hideous grimaces. As the ogre slowly advanced, he made the sign of the cross and started backing into the shed, aware that by doing so, he was cutting off his only escape. So, waving the lantern, he tried to maneuver around it and in the process trod on the monster's body—a body "soft as a bag of chaff," he said later. Once outside, he wanted to run, but did not dare turn his back on the creature. Step by step, he backed across the yard separating the farm buildings from his door, the three infernal heads constantly twisting and writhing on that legless trunk—and gasping, keeled over onto his front doorstep. The entire episode could not have lasted more than a quarter of an hour, yet despite his previous good health, he suddenly came down with a fever.

Grandmother claimed it was the ghost of a Mohammedan, descended from the hill known as the Tartar Cemetery. (If not for that name, all recollection of those Tartar prisoners of war who had worked in Gine centuries ago would have vanished.) But why now—unless someone had put him up to it, ordered him to sow more turmoil? And who else could that someone have been if not Magdalena, in command of subterranean forces.

In time, all these episodes led to a straining of relations between Father Monkiewicz and the village. Now that all were agreed as to the cause, they argued logically that what remained was to remove the cause. At first they merely insinuated as much in his presence, discreetly, relying on parables and circumlocutions. When that didn't work, they came right out and declared it was time to put an end to all these spooky goings-on, and that there was only one way to do it. The priest waved his arms and screamed he would never condone it, never, and he denounced them as pagans. Once his mind was made up, he was adamant. There were those who were in favor of going ahead anyway, with or without his consent, though no one believed they would ever have the nerve. A stalemate. Meanwhile, another priest came to the rectory. During his brief stay, the rites of exorcism were performed.

17

THOMAS WAS AFRAID to stay out after dark —up until the time of his dream. It was a sweet and powerful dream, but also horrifying, and it was impossible to say which of these emotions prevailed. Words could not describe it, not the morning after, nor later on. Words cannot capture that mixture of smells, those indefinable qualities that attract us to certain people, much less the sensation of falling down a well, of sailing clear through to the other side of existence.

He saw Magdalena in the earth, in the solitude of the immense earth, where she had been dwelling for years and would go on dwelling forever. Her dress had rotted away, shreds of cloth had merged with dry bones, while the strand of hair that used to slip down over her cheek as she bent over the kitchen stove was now stuck fast to her skull. But at the same time she was close to him, looking exactly as she had that day he had seen her wade into the water, and this merging was like the recognition of another time. He had the same lump in his throat, the shape of her breasts and neck was unspoiled, while her touch became transmuted into a kind of dirge: "Oh, why must I fade, why must my arms and legs fade away? Why am I alive, yet not alive—I, who once lived, just once, from the beginning till the end of the world? Oh, the sky and the sun will still be there when I am long gone. Only these bones will be left . . . Oh, nothing, nothing is mine." And together they sank into the silent depths beneath the earth's many crusts, to which worms make their way and pebbles slide; only now it was he who was turning into a handful of rotten bones, lamenting through Magdalena's lips, and discovering such questions as "Why am I me? Why am I destined to die, to stop being myself, when I possess a body, warmth, a hand, fingers?" Or perhaps it was not a dream, for even as he lay at the bottom, under the surface of reality, he could still feel his bodily self—his doomed, disintegrating, and posthumous self; and even as he was taking part in the annihilation, he perceived that the person below was the same as the one above. He woke up screaming. But the objects outlined in the dark now became a part of the nightmare, defying definition. He was immediately plunged back into the same delirium, the same visions as before, but in ever new variations. Relief came at daybreak. Anxiously, he opened his eyes; he was returning from faraway places. Gradually, the light illuminated the crossbar joining the legs of the table—the bench, the chair. What a relief to rediscover the real world of objects, things made of wood, iron, and brick, so solid and full-bodied and rough to the touch. Things that only yesterday he had spurned were now a welcome sight, his private treasure. He feasted his eyes on all the knots, cracks, and crevices. Of that other world there remained only a delicious headiness, the remembrance of lands whose existence he had never dreamed possible.

From then on, he swore never to scream if Magdalena ever approached him in the dark, confident that she would do him no harm. He even wished at times she *would* appear, though the mere thought of it happening was enough to give him goose pimples—the good kind, the kind he used to get when he ran his hand over a velvet ribbon. But not a word about the dream did he breathe to anyone.

18

WHAT WAS DONE was done in secret, and it was some time before Thomas learned of the affair, which provoked in him feelings of great horror and sorrow.

Only the village elders, a dozen or so farm owners, were made a part of the conspiracy. They convened toward evening and drank their fill of vodka to quell their unease and to bolster their courage. Permission had been granted; that is to say, Father Monkiewicz had said, "Do as you please"—a tacit admission that all the means at his disposal had failed. Shortly after the other priest had left— that night, except for the sexton and the old housekeeper, the rectory was empty, the expectation being that the exorcisms had rid them of Magdalena—a loud cry was heard in the bedroom, and Monkiewicz appeared in the doorway, his long nightshirt in shreds. Magdalena had pulled off his blanket and started ripping the shirt off his back. When he later came down with erysipelas, everybody, including himself, attributed it to a bad case of fright, for which there was only one effective cure: magical incantations. A medicine woman was summoned to work her spells on him. These were people known to possess powers capable of exorcising any illness from the body; laced with threats, snatches of Christian prayers, and with chants of even greater antiquity, their incantations contained words that, once revealed, immediately lost their power, and whoever knew them was allowed to transmit them before death to only one person. The priest submitted to these remedies grudgingly, but who will say no, who will doubt them, if there's a chance of his being cured? A similar moment of weakness, coupled with the faint hope that the haunting would soon cease, made him acquiesce in that other matter as well.

Tradition dictated that it be undertaken at night. Although not necessarily a rule, it was something that had to be performed with a certain reverence—meaning, above all, in silence, without any spectators, attended by only a few solemn and trustworthy individuals. After testing the blades of their shovels, they lit their lanterns and slipped out by way of the orchards, singly and in two's.

There was a strong wind, a rattling of dry oak leaves. The lights in the village were already out, so that it was pitch-dark and quiet except for the leaves. As soon as all were gathered on the little square in front of the church, they set out for the appointed place and formed a circle as best they could on the steep slope. The flames inside their stovepipe lanterns pitched and tossed in the wind.

First came the cross, which had been stuck in the ground so that it would last as long as the wood held out, leaving only the buried part to rot and crumble, and eventually the whole to topple. They pulled it out of the ground and carefully laid it on its side. Then they leveled the mound of dirt on top of the untended grave—not a single flower was to be seen on it—and went to work in a hurry, so as not to prolong the eeriness. A body is laid to rest for an eternity; to open a grave after several months to see what has happened to it is a violation of nature, tantamount to planting an acorn or chestnut and then scraping the ground to see whether it has taken root. But perhaps they only meant to prove by their actions that a show of strength and willpower was necessary to counteract those doings so contrary to the natural order.

The sound of loose gravel signaled that the moment was at hand. A shovel clanged, but closer inspection with the lantern showed that it was only a rock. At last they struck wood, dug out the coffin, and cleared away the dirt so they could raise the lid. The vodka had done what it was supposed to do, supplying the sort of inner warmth that allowed them to feel superior to creatures less alive than themselves, not to speak of the trees, the rocks, the howling wind, and the phantoms of the night.

What they found bore out their suspicions. For one thing, the body showed absolutely no signs of decomposition. Later they reported that it was so well preserved it looked as if it had been buried only yesterday. This was proof enough, as only the bodies of saints and ghosts were endowed with such powers. Secondly, Magdalena was found lying not on her back but face down, which was also a sign. But even without such evidence, they were ready to do the prescribed thing. The presence of such signs only facilitated their task, relieved them of any doubts.

After the body was rolled over, one of them took the sharpest shovel and, bearing down with all his might, lopped off Magdalena's head. A spike carved from an alder was placed upright on her chest and hammered with the dull end of an ax till the point went clean through the bottom of the coffin and deep into the ground. Next they grabbed the head by the hair, stuck it between her feet, replaced the lid, and lowered the coffin again—now so relieved that they were laughing, as sometimes happens after moments of great tension.

Possibly Magdalena had been so terrified of decaying, so desperately unwilling to enter eternity that, ready to pay any price, she had consented to haunt the living, and in return was granted the privilege of preserving her inviolable body. The men swore up and down that her lips had been bright crimson. By cutting off her head and crushing her ribs, they had put an end to her bodily pride, to that pagan attachment to her own lips, arms, and belly. Skewered like a butterfly on a pin, her skull brushing the soles of the little shoes given to her by Father Peiksva as a present, she surely must have realized that she, like everyone else, was meant to dissolve into the saps of the earth.

After that, no more disturbances were reported by the rectory, and nothing was ever heard of Magdalena staging any more of her exhibitions. And why should she have, for it appears she had discovered that, even more effectively than by cooking on invisible stoves, by knocking on walls or by whistling, she could prolong her life simply by invading Thomas's dreams, as he never forgot her.

19

THAT AUTUMN—the autumn Magdalena was haunting the land—there was an exceptionally good fruit harvest, but for want of any market it ended up as pig feed, only the best of the crop going for canning and domestic use. Piles of apples and pears lay rotting in the grass, attracting wasps and swarms of hornets. Thomas paid for one such pear with a stung lip and a swollen face, because once a wasp tunneled its way into the pulp, its presence was hard to detect, and only by giving the pear a good shake could you get it to show its striped and pulsating belly. Thomas helped with the fruit-picking by climbing up the trees, secretly flattered that none of the grownups could match his skill in shinnying up, cat-fashion, even onto the skinniest branches. And every year there was a crop of new ones, each bearing a different name: sugar pears, butter pears, honey pears, bergamots . . .

During the summer–autumnal lull, Thomas got into the library. Until now, this corner room, with its painted walls and where even in hot weather it was shivering cold, had failed to arouse his curiosity. But by badgering he got hold of the keys to the bookcases, from whose shelves he was always pulling down new wonders. In one of them, a glass-paneled one, he found several red-bound illustrated books embossed with gold. Although unable to make out the captions under the drawings—they were written in French—he figured out that the girl in the long, lace-trimmed knickers was called Sophie. From another case, this one set back in the wall, under a cobweb and several scrolls of yellowed paper, he dug out a volume bearing the title *Shakespeare's Tragedies*, in whose company he spent long hours on the edge of the lawn, next to a green hedge-row redolent with moss and wild mint. This was also the favorite nesting place of ants—the large, red, biting kind—and it was not unusual to see him furiously rubbing one calf against the other. Between the spruce tops the air shimmered on the far side of the valley, and from where he lay he could see tiny horse-drawn coaches trailing long columns of dust.

The book was illustrated with men in armor holding crossed swords, or scantily dressed men (were their legs naked, or did they wear tight-fitting pants?) being stabbed to death, and the mildewed pages gave off a musty smell. He ran his finger along the rows of letters, but although the text was in Polish, in time he gave up, conceding that such things were only for big people.

He had more fun with the travel books. Negroes, armed with bows and arrows, were shown standing naked in reed boats, or towing a hippopotamus familiar to him from his natural-history book. He often wondered whether their bodies were really striped, or just painted, and dreamed of accompanying them on a long voyage to distant waters, and, among papyrus plants standing taller than a man, of building a village inaccessible to outsiders. Two of these books were written in Polish, and he read them both from cover to cover (it was from them that he learned how to read, that's how intrigued he was). Thus began a new era in his life.

He used hazel branches for making bows, but not those that were crooked from exposure to the sun. Instead, he crawled into the shady underbrush, among matted layers of dead leaves, where kinglets flitted with a tremulous *cheep-cheep-cheep*. The naked saplings that grew straight up to the light, not bending an inch, were the best. These dark grottoes also made excellent hideouts and arsenals for his weapons.

Armed with homemade arrows—for greater stability, he tacked on turkey feathers—he set out on hunting expeditions, freely inventing his game, a gooseberry patch often sufficing. His favorite stand was a footbridge—not on the Black Pond, but on another, situated between the wing facing the garden and the farm buildings—used for loading the water cans. Pretending he was in a dugout, he stood on the footbridge and took potshots at the ducks. This once led to an investigation when one of the ducks was found dead in the middle of the pond and he refused to take the blame. Since the Indians were known for hunting fish with a bow and arrow, he was constantly on the lookout for fish along the river shoals (so as not to lose any arrows), but they always got away in time.

On rainy days he sat at a little table bolted to the floor of the porch and practiced drawing swords, spears, and fishing poles. Here a certain quirk of his should be noted, for no sooner would he commence sketching a bow than he stopped and tore up the drawing. Bows were his great passion, and somehow he had formed the idea that one should avoid showing the things one loved, that they should be guarded in absolute privacy.

One day his grandmother took him along to the attic and showed him a box brimming with all sorts of odds and ends, mostly junk, except for one thing—books! Adventure books! One was about a stowaway on a sailing vessel who hid under the deck, kept himself alive on hardtack, and was constantly menaced by rats. The water which he later found in some barrels was called "sweet water." Did that mean it had been sweetened with sugar? So Thomas imagined, for how else could he explain the boy's ecstasy when he managed to bore a hole in the barrel?

The best place for daydreaming about these and other adventures was the outhouse, which stood at the end of a pathway sheltered by a canopy of currants. The outhouse door was latched from the inside, and the heart-shaped opening could be used as a peephole to spot anyone heading for the privy. A few cracks let in the sunlight, and there was always the music of flies, bees, and bumblebees. Now and then a hairy bumblebee, droning heavily, meandered from behind into the pit (whose stench Thomas inhaled with gusto). The corners were always full of spiders spinning their nets, the crossbeam dotted with patches of stearin left by the candles. There were also cracks in the side walls, through which, except for the leaves of a black elderberry, there was nothing to be seen.

Seeing Antonina flit past the heart in the door, he would snap out of his daydreaming and button his pants in a hurry. At the other end of the path was a garbage pit, the place where Antonina butchered the chickens. Her lips puckered and cheeks bulging, she cocked the arm holding the cleaver and maneuvered the chicken into position on the stump with the other; only mildly flustered, the chicken seemed pensive, whether from idle curiosity or indifference was hard to say. The cleaver flashed, Antonina's face wrinkled with pain, even a faint smirk, and a feathery clump was next seen flopping aimlessly on the ground. Thomas shuddered to see it, and just because he shuddered, he remained a spectator to it. One such beheading turned out to be extraordinary. A rooster, an enormous bird bristling with shimmering gold feathers, tried to take off without his head, with only his red stump of a neck sticking out. His speechless flight caused Antonina to drop her jaw in amazement—and in tribute, for the rooster fell only after colliding with the trunk of a linden.

Thomas seldom made any more fishing trips to the river, and seldom ran off to see the Akulonis children—partly because of Magdalena, partly because of his books. The more secluded places along the Issa now seemed forbidding. As for bow-and-arrow hunting, that was not to be shared with one of his companions and run the risk of ridicule: that wasn't dignified enough, not like fishing or carving reed pipes from willows. There were some games he preferred no one else to watch—games that might have been thought of as too childish for a boy his age. One was a game of war between two stick armies planted in the sand, with Thomas taking turns bombarding one and then the other side with rocks.

20

EARLY THAT WINTER, Grandmother Dilbin arrived from Dorpat, Estonia, and the room where she slept exerted a strong attraction on Thomas. Not much taller than he, ruddy-skinned, she was, unlike Grandmother Misia, a real busybody. She darned his socks and mended his pants, tutored him, and made him recite his catechism. She was, above all, different. She smoked cigarettes, the long-tipped Russian kind, a habit she had acquired from constant fretting—as she put it—which cigarettes had a way of relieving. From her trunk she removed a flat clothes box, revealing a wealth of tiny tins and wooden cases, minuscule packages bound with ribbons, and sundry trinkets meticulously wrapped in newspaper.

The rite of unpacking, just because it was such a rare occurrence, preserved its ceremonial character. For Thomas there was always some little present, some novelty, like a bar of genuine Chinese ink, the purpose of which was explained to him by his grandmother, though he was captivated more by its shape, its deep black color, and the clean angularity of its corners.

From her he learned, as never before, something of the ways of the world. Having spent her youth in Riga, his grandmother could tell him stories of the trips to Majorenhof, of swimming in the Baltic, and of the time she was nearly swept out to sea; about her father, Thomas's great-grandfather, Dr. Ritter, who treated children and waived his fee if their parents were poor; of his great popularity and his reputation as a practical joker, famous for his impersonations and disguises so convincing that even his mother, taking him for a beggar, had once tossed a coin into his hat. Thomas also heard talk of the theater and the opera, of swans that bobbed up and down as if truly waterborne. The name of a vocalist—Adelina Patti—was invariably pronounced with a sigh. She sighed, too, when reminiscing about the parties in Riga, about the crowds of young people, the games, the singing, the *tableaux vivants*. Not to mention the trips out into the countryside, to the Imbrody estate, near Düneburg, which had belonged to her mother's family, the Mohls. About the coach rides through brigand-infested woods, the secluded inns with conniving innkeepers. About "the guillotine"—a bed whose canopy fell at night, killing the unsuspecting traveler and then disappearing along with the corpse through a trapdoor in the floor. Of how, when a coach was ferried across the river, the horses would panic and drown its occupants. Then there was the servant girl at Imbrody whom the boys once spooked, installing long tobacco pipes behind the mirror—where she was fond of posing—and blowing big puffs of smoke her way. Once, as she slept, they made off with her bed and put it down in the lake; she later woke with a scream. And the boat trips on the lake, in the white sailboat . . . Of all the names and incidents mentioned, these were the ones that stuck in Thomas's mind.

He also had his grandmother to thank for tales of Bitowt and his comic exploits—Bitowt, a glutton and eccentric madcap celebrated all over Lithuania. In summer, Bitowt would get his cart into shape, load up the back with horse feed, put on his cape, take his place behind the driver, and shove off on a journey that usually lasted several months. He drifted from manor to manor, where he was always treated royally because of the fear aroused by his malicious tongue. He smoked cigars as he rode, tossing the butts behind him—once he barely made his escape after setting the rear of the wagon ablaze. Another time, at an open market in a little town, he went up to an orange peddler, a Jew. "How many oranges can a man tuck away at one go?" The Jew: "Five." Bitowt to that: "Sixty!" The Jew: "Free oranges to the man who can!" As Bitowt was starting on his fifth dozen, the Jew yelled: "Help! Many dozen oranges ze man has eaten! He vill die for sure!" At home he had a first-class cook, and they were always squabbling. In the evening, Bitowt would summon him to his bedroom and growl: "You rascal! You're through, finished! You've done it again! Your cooking is too good; I'm so stuffed I can't sleep!" But then he would call him back and ask him for the next day's menu.

Thomas, by chatting with his grandmother, managed to pick up a little history. A copper relief of the Virgin Mary, delivered up from her trunk, hung over her bed; above the nightstand was a portrait of a girl—beautiful, bare-necked, with an open collar. The girl's name was Emilia Plater, a distant relative of Thomas, on the Mohl side, which was supposed to be a source of great pride, as she was remembered as a heroine of the Polish Insurrection. In 1831 she had mounted a horse and taken command of a detachment of insurgents in the forest. She later died of wounds suffered in a battle against the Russians. As for the copper relief, it was once the property of his grandfather Arthur Dilbin, who in his youth had also chosen the forest. That was in the year 1863 ("Remember, Thomas—eighteen hundred and sixty-three . . ."). The battle cry of the insurgents, "For our freedom and yours!" had meant that they were fighting for the liberty of the Russians as well; but the Tsar was very powerful and their only weapons had been shotguns and swords. Grandfather's commanding officer, Sierakowski, was hung by the Tsar, but Grandfather was exiled to Siberia, from where he made his way back many years later and married. Presently Thomas's father and uncle were serving in the Polish army; they, too, were fighting against the Russians.

Around the house, Grandmother Dilbin dressed city-style, even with an amber brooch. Underneath—Thomas used to spy on her—she wore several woolen petticoats and cinched her waist with a sort of whalebone corset. Her pale blue eyes bulged, her mouth assumed a look of utter dismay whenever Misia hiked her skirt in front of the tiled stove. What exasperated her was the way she had of mocking the emotions of others. Gossiping about someone in love with one of the local girls, she would ask, in her usual Lithuanian drawl, as she rubbed her rump against the tiles, "Now what, pray tell, can he possibly see in her?" Over and over again: "What, pray tell?"—as if it was not enough that human beings longed, yearned, suffered. Grandmother would respond with an angry shrug, mumble something about how "pagan customs are slow to die"—which was true enough; yet privately Thomas seldom sided with her, sensing in her, kindhearted as she was, a certain weakness. At the mere sight of him she wrung her hands in despair, complaining that he was neglected, shabbily clothed, and wild as a savage. And did she ever spoil him. Until then, he had not thought twice about sewing on his own buttons with the help of Antonina's needle and thread; but now that he had someone to pamper him, he had to be waited on constantly.

There was something fragile in the curvature of Grandmother Dilbin's round shoulders, in the veins around her temples. Peeking into her room at five or six o'clock in the morning, he found her sitting up in bed, saying her prayers in a loud, keening voice, a vacant stare in her eyes, her cheeks bearing traces of two little wet streams. (Misia, on the other hand, slept till ten in winter, woke, and stretched with feline contentment.) Footfalls sounded in Dilbin's room till late in the evening, as, pacing the floor, she smoked cigarette after cigarette. The monotonous sound of her padding feet traveled through the house, lulling Thomas to sleep. Subject to chronic dizzy spells, in the daytime she never went for a walk in the garden unless accompanied by her grandson; often she would stop in the middle of a path, stretch out her hands, and beg him for his arm. Once they rode out in the carriage to visit neighbors; at the place where the road skirted a cliff, she shut her eyes, keeping them closed until she was sure the danger had passed.

Thomas was constantly tempted to tease and test her. Sometimes, when she pleaded for his arm on one of their garden strolls, he ducked behind a tree, deliberately provoking that round and pink little creature to tearful supplications.

21

THE DAUGHTER of Graf von Mohl was given in marriage to Dr. Ritter, and from that marriage six daughters were born, the youngest of which, Bronislawa, was destined to become Grandmother Dilbin. From that period of warmth, love, and happiness, lasting until her eighteenth birthday, a number of copybooks, inscribed with minuscule writing, had been preserved in her trunk—verses composed as a young girl. Several dried-out flowers had outlived those closest to her.

Constantine had played the piano beautifully, sung in a baritone, and was famous for his recitations of patriotic poetry at all the Riga soirées. But her parents were resolutely opposed: he was too young, too impractical, and, most damaging of all, penniless. Soon after they parted, there was another suitor, and Broncia, as she was called for short, experienced her first nights of solitary weeping, the terror that accompanied the sealing of one's fate. Arthur Dilbin, no longer in his prime, with a reputation for being rather staid in his ways, was surrounded by an aura of martyrdom: for his having taken part in the Uprising, his estate had been confiscated, though his management of the family property assured him of a steady income. He was found acceptable, and Broncia gave up the city of her youth for a remote country village, for a life of domestic chores and bookkeeping on quiet evenings, under the same lampshade where Arthur sat smoking his pipe.

A portrait of the man: broad forehead, narrow face, an expression of feral pride; hollow cheeks accentuated by a bushy blond mustache, big-shouldered, sober-minded, hand stuck in a buckled leather belt. At the manor he kept a pack of hounds, devoting all his leisure to hunting. He also had a passion for harness racing, that test of strength between a driver and his horses, when the pull of the reins can tear the skin from a man's hands. He was a gentle, discreet man, slipping payments to the mothers of his illegitimate children so that his wife was never the wiser. These children dated, for the most part, from his bachelor days. As a young blade he was credited with having saved a certain aristocratic family from extinction, thanks to visits to a local countess married to a senile husband. Such gossip did him no disservice; and whenever he passed the young count, he would size him up on the sly, stroking his mustache with approval.

Then the settling down, the burden of responsibility. And children. Bronislawa lavished all her affection on her children. When the older boy, Theodore, was seven, she brought him for the summer to Majorenhof, to the seaside, though she failed to recover the beauty she had once known there. Their younger son was born the same year that Arthur died of a cold caught while hunting. He was named Constantine.

However far back one searched in the history of the Dilbins, Ritters, and Mohls, Constantine bore no physical resemblance to any of his ancestors. Black eyes, pitch-black hair encroaching on a low forehead, an aquiline nose; the swarthy complexion of a southerner. Skinny and high-strung, he was a winning child with a heart of gold: ask him for something—anything—and he was ready to hand over what was his, down to his coat and jacket. He also showed signs of being exceptionally gifted. But when Bronislawa later moved to Vilno so that her sons could receive a proper education—which, left to her own resources, was no easy task—Constantine showed a reluctance to learn. The slightest effort enervated him. His mother pleaded with him, went down on her knees, promised him presents, cajoled him. But he knew her better than to believe in her bullying threats, and as for presents, he knew there was nothing his mother would deny him. He soon fell into bad company, cavorting with gamblers and people of loose morals, drinking, running up debts, and began taking up with girls from the clubs. His education came to an abrupt halt when he was expelled from the Gymnasium in his fourth year.

His older brother, Theodore, had studied veterinary medicine in Dorpat, and after graduating, he began supporting both his mother and his brother. Heir to his father's build and facial features, he was quieter and more given to romantic dreams. Burdened by his sense of responsibility and honesty, he felt the urge to travel, to seek adventure— all the Dilbins had been something of adventurers, one of them having served in Napoleon's army, taking part in both the Italian and the Spanish campaigns. Theodore married Tekla Surkont, whom he met while vacationing at the house of his cousin, in the vicinity of Gine. He later became Thomas's father. The outbreak of war he welcomed as a portent of change, as that "war of nations" prophesied nearly a century ago and promising to destroy the might of the Northern Tyrant.

Bronislawa's tears, although swallowed privately at first, streamed more and more openly down her cheeks, and she prayed to God to have mercy on Constantine and for the forgiveness of her sins if they were the cause of his suffering. Her pleas had risen in the early-morning hours —once, after she discovered that he had forged his brother's signature on some checks, and later, when after being drafted into the Russian army he was assigned to an NCO's school and from there transferred to the front. She trembled for his safety when he saw combat at the front, but not for Theodore's, who, as a professional man, was mostly stationed at the rear. Finally she received word that he had been wounded and taken prisoner. From then on, it was packages made of plywood, bound with canvas, and addressed to the Red Cross, reaching him at some unknown destination in Germany. She counted the days from one package to the next, sewing little sacks for sugar and cocoa, devising ways to squeeze the most into a package. She did this until the year 1918, until the day she received a letter from him telling her that his shrapnel wound had healed, leaving only a chest scar, and that he had been caught trying to tunnel his way out of a POW camp, but that he was free now and had enlisted in the Polish cavalry.

There was still a war on, this time between Poland and Russia, and the Tsar had been assassinated. Theodore, accompanied by his wife, had visited Bronislawa in Dorpat, stopping off on his way south, from up around Pskov, to fulfill his patriotic duty. Fingering her rosary beads, she tried to imagine the night marches, her son Constantine bent over his saddle in the sleet and rain, the charges with raised swords; his chest, already wounded once, ready to stop a bullet. She was haunted by visions of corpses—the Germans, in occupying Dorpat, had executed a number of Bolshevik commissars, dumping their bodies in the square and leaving them to lie there, glazed with frost, until orders were finally given for their burial.

She prayed that Constantine's life would be spared. But during the pre-dawn hours she would be seized by another fear, the terror of time, of both the past and the future. All the lies he had told, the sneaking into Theodore's bureau drawer, the banknotes lifted on the sly; her trembling as she confronted him with it. And the way he had blushed, pitied her, and then that dreaded moment when he had tossed back his head and assumed an expression of defiance, believing even in his own lies—that, for her, had been the most painful part. Resident in him was an inability to experience the world as it really was, the need to embellish it with fantastic schemes, always confident of discovering some new ticket to success serving to justify these occasional perfidies. She knew that it was too late for him to mend his ways. Her supplications for his return were not altogether pure. Her mind constantly swarmed with images of the consequences of his weakness, of his lack of perseverance and vocation. The sleazy, big-city haunts, the cardsharps with their fawning whores—and there, among them, her little Constantine. No, her incantations were not pure, and that made her feel guilty, that made her raise her voice and rock back and forth as she recited the words of the litany, by which gesture she hoped to exorcise her grief. Such was the intent of phrases like "O Tower of Ivory," "O Ark of the Covenant" that Thomas heard through the door.

Her sins? What sins she had committed, no one would ever know. Perhaps deep down, in the pulsations of her blood, in the very depths of her corporeal being, whose essence no tongue could ever convey, she had discovered the flaw, the guilty residue of her existence, of her having begotten children. Possibly. It was from her, in all probability, that Thomas had inherited his scrupulous conscience, a tendency to reproach himself for each and every thing, and his teasing of her was a revenge for the guilt aroused in him by her lamentations of "Oyey, oyey."

22

SPRING WAS in the air. The ice on the pond was melting, and the traces left by Thomas's blades were slowly being effaced where only a short time ago he had skated or amused himself by stamping his feet on the green slabs embedded with insects and algae. Showing signs of weariness, the snow dripped from the rooftops in the afternoons, the drops drilling little dotted lines along the sides of the house. In the evening, the bright pastel pink on the white hills would thicken into yellow and carmine, the tracks of animals and people darken with moisture.

Thomas, encouraged by Grandmother Dilbin's supply of illustrated German magazines, acquired a passion for sketching. He was especially inspired by pictures of artillery, tanks, and his very favorite plane—the Taube. Twice a Taube had flown over Gine, but at high altitude, causing people to congregate and point up at the sky, the source of the buzzing racket. Now, in magazines, Thomas could see what it looked like in action. His drawings showed soldiers charging (legs in motion were easily rendered by dashes bent at the knee) and hitting the dirt; rifles sent forth sheaves of straight lines, broken to mark the bullets. And sailing by overhead—the Taube.

Before moving on to the incident that is somehow related to these scenes, we must first describe the floor plan of the house. In winter, only the wing facing the orchard was occupied; that is, the part looking out across the angle formed by the old manor and the annex. First came the weaving room (where Pakenas worked), then nothing, then a storage room for wool and seed, then Grandmother Dilbin's room, then Thomas's, followed by Misia's little cubbyhole and, at the far end, by Grandfather's room. Awakened by a chill early one morning, Thomas curled into a ball, but there was no escaping the draft. He turned so his back faced the window, pulled the blanket up to his neck, and pondered the sunlight on the wall. Some flour, set out to dry on a canvas sheet, lay on the floor. Letting his eyes roam lazily over the surface, he became intrigued by the sight of something sparkling like ice or salt crystals. He jumped out of bed, crouched down, and lightly fingered it: glass. Mystified, he turned and glanced out the window. The pane was punctured by a hole the size of two fists, its jagged outline shaped like a star. He ran immediately to Misia's room, yelling that someone had thrown a rock from the garden.

It turned out he was mistaken. They searched high and low, until finally, under Thomas's bed, in the very corner, Grandfather flushed out a black object, which he warned everyone not to touch. They sent for one of the villagers, an army veteran. The black object, which Thomas later had a chance to examine at his leisure, had the shape of a large egg, only heavier, with a notched flange wrapped around the middle. In the orchard, below the window, they found boot tracks and a grenade pin. They recalled, too, how the dog-barking that night had been more fierce than usual.

The grenade had not exploded, but it might have, in which case Thomas would have been laid to rest under the oak trees, a stone's throw from Magdalena's grave. The world would have gone on as before; swallows, storks, and starlings would have winged their way back from their annual migrations beyond the seas; wasps and hornets would have gone on sucking pears for their sweet juice. Why it had failed to explode is not for us to judge. It had hit a wall, bounced to the floor, and rolled over to Thomas's bed, where the decision to explode or not to explode had ripened inside it.

Grandfather was sorely grieved. At news of another manor being attacked, inspired by what was happening farther to the east, he would quietly clear his throat and try to turn the latest scare into a joke. Not even when the woods had been infested with marauding bands of Russian POW's had he taken any special precautions. And which of his neighbors had cause to attack him? They had known him since childhood. Had he ever done anyone any harm? Even accidentally? And as for the traditional animosity between Pole and Lithuanian, wasn't it he who argued that the Lithuanians were entitled to their own state, and that those who spoke Polish were as much *gente Lithuani* as he? Still, there it was—the grenade. Someone had thrown it. Who? And for whom was it intended? They counted the windows: one in Grandfather's room, two in Misia's, and two in Thomas's room. Anyone well acquainted with the house would not have aimed for the boy's room, so it was either an outsider or someone who knew his way around but had simply miscalculated.

Grandmother Misia was not at all fazed that *she* could have been the object of such hostility. As usual, she let Grandfather have it, blaming it on his Lithuanian and peasant sympathies. Nor was she the least bit concerned for her own safety, though, in her case, protection would have been difficult: the wooden shutters to her room closed from the outside. Not so with Grandmother Dilbin, who was panic-stricken, so much so that her windows had to be padlocked. After Thomas's miraculous escape, she indulged him more than ever, taking from her trunk—which seemed to contain an inexhaustible store of treasure—a slender box full of watercolors and a paintbrush. His first painting was of a bullfinch, the reason being that bullfinches—they were forever husking seeds in the bushes by the house—were a big splotch of red, tinged with streaks of blue, gray, and black. Bullfinches and the speckled, red-hooded woodpecker, whose pecking brought down white patches of snow from high up in the trees, were among winter's greatest surprises.

The grenade affair failed to enter the realm of Thomas's military and travel fantasies. Even though tracks in the snow inspired visions of long boots, tightly cinched jackets, and hushed deliberations, his soldiers and pirates were not a surreptitious force, had nothing of the darkness of the night. He became suspicious, flinching whenever he met up with any of the local farmhands, whom the war had lent a somewhat menacing air. It had started the summer before, with Thomas sneaking down Indian-style to the Issa because of the way they sat in the bushes, whistling, making catcalls, and firing their army carbines so that the bullets skipped across the water like pebbles. They were not very popular in the village, and they kept to themselves. Akulonis used to threaten them with his fist and call them "jailbirds" because they scared the fish. Once, when they went so far as to fish with grenades, they provoked widespread indignation: that was too easy, a violation of the code.

To be on the safe side, a bed was put up in the weaving room, where Pakenas, now shifted from the granary, took up quarters. Not that he afforded any real protection; indeed, he had a reputation for being a terrific coward, probably dating back to his tumultuous escape from the shepherd's ghost. Imputations of this sort are generally promoted by a person's physiognomy, in Pakenas's case by a pair of bulging, lobsterlike eyes. Besides his knotted walking stick, Pakenas also had custody of an old revolver, the bullets to which, alas, were missing.

23

JOSEPH THE BLACK climbed the road leading up from the village and occasionally got mired in the snowy slush mixed with horse manure. Water trickled in the wagon ruts burnished by sleigh runners. He unbuttoned his gray homespun jacket, and as he passed by the roadside crucifix, he doffed his cap and squinted from the glare cast by the white slope, and higher up, at the park's edge, by the granary's white wall. Down below, in one of the Issa's inland coves, crows circled the Borek forest, their cawing a portent of spring.

Instead of turning into the lane, he passed the exit and, skirting the orchard, steered for the cottages. Once upon a time, these huts lining the road had been occupied by farmhands working the manorial estate. Only a few were inhabited now, the rest having been invaded by itinerant laborers. Joseph responded politely when greeted, but was in too great a hurry to stop. Past the cottages, near the cross under the tin-roofed lean-to, he swung to the right in the direction of Pogirai and the forest's dark border.

Pogirai was a long village, stretching well over a

kilometer, with one main street and one cross street. Fairly prosperous, it was distinguished by the absence of any thatched roofs or chimneyless hovels. Its orchards were as plentiful as those in Gine, and it was known for its apiaries, for the dark honey collected in fields of buckwheat, clover, and open forest meadows. When he came to the third cottage past the green farm belonging to Baloudis, the American, Joseph stopped and peered over a picket fence. An old man in a brown woolen caftan—brown and black sheep were a Pogirai specialty—was trimming a log. Joseph shoved open the gate, and as they stood shaking hands, he complimented the man on his choice of fir. The old man nodded and said it was for bracing the crib. The tree, no doubt, had made its way there thanks to Balthazar, but Joseph had other things on his mind than poaching.

Just then, the younger Wackonis, heavy with sleep, came crawling out of nowhere. He ran his fingers through his hair to comb out the straw and feathers, and somewhat shyly, eyeing him nervously, paid Joseph his respects. He had on a pair of navy-blue pants and a military tunic. His broad face turned sullen when Joseph said he had a little matter to discuss with him.

Putting down his tin cup and wiping his mustache with the back of his hand, Joseph stared at him in silence. At last he propped both elbows on the table and said: "Yeah, yeah—I know."

Sitting on the end of the bench, Wackonis fluttered his eyelids, then lowered them drowsily. A shrug of the shoulders. "Ain't nothin' to know."

"Maybe there is and maybe there isn't. I picked you because you're a simpleton. Remember who taught you how to read? Or have you forgotten?"

"You did."

"Well, now, is that any reason to start pitching grenades at folks?"

Wackonis lifted his eyelids. His face was now that of a grown man—serious, grim. "And what if it was me? Those ain't folks—they's gentlefolk."

Joseph laid a birchwood snuffbox on the table, rolled himself a cigarette, fitted it into a holder, lit up, and took a puff. "Ever see me siding with gentlefolk?"

"Nope, never did. But I do now."

"Your father, he won't tell you, but I will. You'd better listen to people with more brains than you."

Wackonis folded his arms on his chest; his cheek muscles twitched. "The gentlefolk sucked us dry, we don't need their kind round here. Kill one, two—they'll get on back to their Poland. Then the land'll be ours."

Joseph shook his head mockingly. "We don't need no gentlefolk in Lithuania, the land will be ours. Where did you pick that up? From me, that's who. And now you're going to teach *me*, huh? You want to go around butchering and burning like a Russian?"

"They don't have no more Tsar."

"Not now, but one day they will. You're a Lithuanian. We'll get it back one day."

"And who's gonna get it back?"

"Lithuania. The Slavs—Poles or Russians, what's the difference—they're all sons-of-bitches. I worked in Sweden —now that's the life for us!"

"The Poles are our enemies."

"The Surkonts have been Lithuanians for centuries."

Wackonis chuckled. "How can Surkont be a Lithuanian when he's a gentleman?"

Joseph reached for the beer pitcher, filled his mug, and asked, "Is that who you were aiming for?"

The young man's face emptied. "Naah—I didn't much care who it hit."

Joseph again wagged his head. "Oh boy, that's just fine. You can thank the Lord it didn't go off. And you know who it almost killed? Did they tell you?"

"Nope."

"The boy—Thomas. They found it under his bed."

"The Dilbin kid?"

"Yep."

Silence. The mug still at his mouth, Wackonis said, "Everybody knows where his old man is. Like father, like son."

"You jackass! How would you like to have been at the kid's funeral?"

"What for?"

Joseph curled his lip, bared his teeth, and blushed. "Listen here, Wackonis. I know who put you up to it, and I know who kept you company out there that night. Those pals of yours, those 'Iron Wolves,' they don't scare me, see? Oh, you know how to fight, all right—against women and kids."

Wackonis sprang to his feet. "None of your darned business whose idea it was!"

Joseph leaned back, fixed him with a stare, and sneered: "Spoken with all the arrogance of a born Pole."

24

❧❀❧❀❧

THE ICE on the Issa broke with a cannon's roar. Then came the floes, freighting loose straw, boards, branches, dead chickens—and crows, promenading on the ice with a delicate step. This was also the pupping season, and the bitch Dusty couldn't keep her litter a secret for very long; sooner or later the whimpering pups gave her away. Thomas loved to feel their fleshy warmth against his face, to immerse his gaze in their eyes enveloped by a blue film. Russet-colored, a cross between a wolf and a fox, her muzzle flecked with black, Dusty would quietly acquiesce, panting with a drooping tongue.

Pakenas packed the pups into a basket and Dusty was locked in the woodshed along with one of her pups, the brightest and the quickest. Thomas ran after Pakenas and caught up with him by the cliff overlooking the river. The steep bank, bright with yellow clay, was riddled with swallows' nests. The floes had moved downstream, leaving swirling little eddies in the swollen waters.

Pakenas cocked his arm and let go with one of the pups. It hit the water, a splash, then nothing, only a little pool, which was rapidly broken up and borne away by the current. A little while later, a head surfaced downstream; paddling its tiny paws, the pup again vanished from view, only to reappear as it rounded the bend. From then on, Pakenas took two at a time from the basket; throwing one, he would clutch the other against his chest. The last of them went under, but a second later came up, fighting bravely until, followed by Thomas's gaze, it too was swept out into midstream.

Going from the warmth, from a world of things they had not yet learned to distinguish, into the icy water, they were not even aware of the water's existence. Thomas walked back in a daze. Mingled with his curiosity was a shadow of his dream about Magdalena. He opened the shed door and began petting Dusty. The dog whined, sniffed him suspiciously, then bolted from his reach.

Then came the first warm spell: chickens grubbing by the woodpile, old Gregory sitting on his bench, whittling away . . . Gregory's knife, so worn down that the blade was more like a shoemaker's awl, could sever a branch at one swipe—in old Gregory's hand, that is, but not in Thomas's, who, even if he used the same knife, first had to notch one side and then the other before getting it to snap.

Mrs. Malinowski came to see Grandfather about leasing the orchard for the summer—called an *arenda*, an arrangement whereby a certain percentage of the harvest went to the landlord. An unusual request, but she said she wanted to give it a try; her son, Dominic, was now fourteen, and she was sure they could manage it together. He promised her the orchard, but the woman had come none too soon. A few days later Chaim came lumbering up to the manor in his buggy to propose some of his relatives as leaseholders. Chaim could cite professional guarantees, as well as custom, since traditionally the leaseholders were Jewish. But a promise was a promise. The scene ended with the usual pulling of hair, wailing lamentations, and clenched fists raised to heaven.

A widow, Mrs. Malinowski was the poorest in all of Gine; with no land of her own to sow or till, her only possession was a cottage down by the ferry landing. She was a squat, broadly built woman, and the crest of her kerchief towered above her freckled forehead like a peaked house roof. Her visit marked the beginning of a new friendship for Thomas.

Several months later, while he was busy exploring that part of the orchard out past the beehives (the path ran alongside the hives, within attacking range of the bees), he spotted a shed. A real cabin—not one of those trail shacks built by horse herders in the clearings—tall enough in the center for a man to stand upright, its straw roof held down by wooden poles. The peak, formed by the acute angle of an inverted V, was reinforced with nails. A small campfire was burning by the entrance, and next to it sat a boy roasting green apples on a stick. The boy showed Thomas in and around the shed.

Dominic Malinowski, freckle-faced like his mother but taller, with a shock of bushy red hair, was quick to get Thomas, for whom the privilege of addressing a nearly grown-up person as an equal was a source of discomfort, even embarrassment, under his control. Dominic let him smoke his homemade pipe—a rifle cartridge fitted with a stem. Thomas, who had never smoked tobacco before, tried, even though it irritated his throat, to keep the rolled tobacco leaf lit, determined, then as later, to win the approval of those cold gray eyes.

Whereas it used to be that when asked for Thomas's whereabouts, Antonina could answer, "At Akulonis's, where else?" now it was: "Up at the shed." The irresistible magic of smoke winding through the trees, the smell of straw and rotting apples, and hours spent by the campfire. Dominic could spit more than a dozen meters, blow smoke through his nose, fix traps for birds and marten (which used to chase squirrels around the linden trunks in the park, though the trapping had to wait for winter) and teach Thomas the art of cussing. Since he was illiterate and had an abiding fascination with everything, he made Thomas tell him what was written in books. At first Thomas was embarrassed—in the same way he was embarrassed by his kinship with Grandmother Dilbin—because knowledge acquired from letters of the alphabet seemed to him inferior; but Dominic was persistent, asking "Why is that?" "How so?" "If, then why?" But there were some things, things that had never occurred to him until now, that lay beyond his power to explain.

Attraction. Submission. Was it an attraction for the roughshod, the forbidden? Dominic emerged as a high priest of truth, because his sense of irony, his implied mockery, was a refutation of his, Thomas's, superficial knowledge, underneath which, he knew, there teemed something real. That something went beyond the long slugs they collected and roasted over coals to make them contract; beyond the horseflies whose bellies they packed with blades of straw to make them fly like airplanes; beyond even the rat Dominic once let loose in a tunnel of blazing coals. Far beyond that—farther and deeper. Every trip to the shed in the orchard held out the promise of some new discovery.

His instincts proved correct, for Dominic was always guarded in his presence, never revealing more than a fraction of his nature. He did not need any outward confirmation of his power over Thomas; he graciously, condescendingly accepted the homage rendered him. He spared him, in fact. Why? Perhaps he was disarmed by Thomas's naïve trust, or perhaps he found it more prudent not to jeopardize his relations with the manor house. His hemming, the way he had of wrapping his arms around his knees whenever Thomas insisted on entering forbidden territory—such gestures seemed full of implication about the very thing for which Thomas had such an urge. If, though, his reticence suddenly broke down, it was surely the fault of the devils along the Issa, or of Thomas's own stupidity—for having violated the rule that one should not always cling to those one venerates. If he was tactless, then it was because he lived with his fantasies and had never been snubbed.

Mrs. Malinowski seldom visited the shed. She would bring supper for her son in the afternoon, but not always, at which times Dominic would boil himself a batch of cabbage soup and use his jackknife to carve huge chunks from a loaf of black rye, wolfing it down with bacon bits. Not to mention apples and pears—charcoaled pears were like nothing in this world—or potatoes, roasted to a crisp, a jab with a sharp stick signaling whether they were done. Occasionally, Antonina would drop by unannounced and drag Thomas away by the scruff of the neck. Now and then, she came with baskets for the "inspection"—the term given that quota of the harvest owed the manor for the household—and their job was to help with the carrying.

Sometimes, in a lighthearted but mean sort of way, she would address Dominic with a pejorative word that meant "you relative of every conceivable kind of toad."

25

❧❧❧❧❧

DOMINIC, if the truth be known, was a king in disguise, ruling by means of an unspoken terror, the quietness of which he carefully guarded. He had been elevated to royal office by virtue of his toughness and by his talent for giving orders. Those who had tasted his hard fist obeyed him and whispered not a word of complaint to their parents. His court, which waited on him in the village pasture, consisted, as might have been expected, of his most trusted confidants, or ministers, and of ordinary acolytes, who were used for performing such menial tasks as keeping the cows in line. Only the closest confidants were admitted to experiments of a more serious sort.

A critical mind, which took nothing on faith and demanded for everything a scientific explanation, he scrupulously attended to anything that flew, jumped, or crawled. Severing their legs and wings, he was intent on plumbing the mystery of living machines. Nor were humans overlooked, such as the time he commanded his ministers to hold up one specimen by the legs—namely, the thirteen-year-old Vera. He was equally intrigued by technological inventions, capable of devoting hours to contemplating the construction of a mill, to the point of rigging an exact replica, together with his own modifications, and installing it on one of the brooks that emptied into the Issa.

By imposing his will on others his own age, Dominic

avenged himself for the humiliation he had endured since childhood. For as long as he could remember, he and his mother had worked the property of others, mostly wealthy farmers, these being by far the worst breed, whose holdings ranged from a hundred to two hundred acres. To have to look them in the eye and, cheerfully, fawningly, anticipate their every whim, their every command; to live in constant fear of being cheated out of a promised bushel of rye or a couple of pairs of old shoes—this was the stuff on which hatred thrived, the suspicion that the entire world was predicated on a lie.

Earlier that same summer, before he was moved into the shed in the orchard, something important happened in Dominic's life. For a long time he had been content to fawn, to do the bidding of others, until one day a war veteran began letting him handle his service rifle—this in reward for keeping silent about certain matters.

Now, the arrangement about the rifle coincided with an outbreak of rabies in the village, and people suspected one dog of having been bitten by a rabid animal. All agreed that it would have to be destroyed, yet no one was eager to do the job—until Dominic volunteered. The dog was surrendered, but with reluctance—who knew, maybe the dog *hadn't* been infected. The dog—big and black, tail erect, bristles sprouting from its muzzle—started fawning on him, happy to be unleashed, to exchange a life of yawning and flea-hunting for the freedom of open spaces. Dominic, after giving the dog something to eat, took it out to a place overlooking a small pond. Situated in the middle of a peninsula formed by a bend in the Issa, the pond was fed by a muddy ditch; in spring its warm shallow waters became a spawning ground for pike, before drying up again in summer, its bed of silt suitable as a permanent dwelling place only for stickleback. A thick wall of reeds ran all the way around, reaching as high as a man on horseback; on one bank, nestled among the reeds, stood a pear tree.

Dominic tied the dog to it on a thick cord and sat down with the rifle, a little distance away. Next, removing the bullet heads from the cartridges, he inserted wooden ones, specially carved for the occasion. The dog playfully wagged its tail and yelped with joy. To shoot or not to shoot. He braced the rifle butt against his shoulder and hesitated, more to savor the freedom of choice, the fact that the hound suspected nothing, that the decision rested entirely in his, Dominic's, hands. That and the knowledge that one jerk of his finger would change it into something other than what it had been. But how? Would it fall flat, spring into the air? Not only the dog but the entire landscape would be altered. Nothing like being killed by a bullet—a calm, a hush, as if devoid of human presence, and all done so effortlessly, so coolly, just a simple: "Fire!" The reeds sighed, a moist red tongue hung from the dog's yap. The mouth snapped shut: it had caught a fly. Dominic took aim at the gleaming hide.

Fire! For a split second, the dog was convulsed by something like shocked bewilderment. Suddenly it bolted forward, stretching its cord, snarling. Angered by this gesture of defiance, Dominic fired a second shot. The dog keeled over backward, rose again to its feet—and suddenly comprehended. With hide bristling, it backed away from some appalling vision. It went on taking bullets, which came at intervals—to prolong the moment—each one having a different effect, culminating in a dragging of the hind quarters, a whining, and a convulsive waving of the paws with flank to the ground.

Sitting with Thomas by the campfire in the orchard, Dominic began entertaining thoughts of a theological nature, inspired by memories of the act just committed. If he was superior to the dog, the arbiter of its fate, wasn't God in like measure the arbiter of human fate? He felt bitter toward God. He held against Him his insensitivity to the most sincere pleas. Once, just before Christmas, when there had not been enough bread in the house, when his mother had knelt before the holy picture, weeping and praying, he had wished for a miracle. Crawling into the attic, he had got down on his knees, made the sign of the cross, and, in his own words, said: "It can't be you don't see how worried my mother is. Perform a miracle, and I'll sacrifice myself to you. Kill me, so long as you make a miracle happen." Confident of success, he hopped down from the ladder, sat down on the bench, and calmly waited. But God responded with absolute indifference, and that night they went to bed hungry.

God, thunder-wielding God—thunder, after all, was a better weapon than a rifle—clearly favored hypocrites. Every Sunday, there they were, dressed in the latest fashions, the women in green velvet bodices, with gaudy kerchiefs tied under their chins. They sang in the choir, rolled their eyes to heaven, and piously folded their hands. But watch out when they got home! You could faint on their front doorstep before they condescended to share their cheese fritters smothered in cream and lard. And they knew just where to use a strap—out behind the granary, out of earshot. They hated each other and loved to backbite; stupid and vicious, once a week they assumed an air of virtue and piety. Divine retribution? How, when God had bestowed the greatest wealth on a man who slept with his own daughter—he had spied on them through a crack: the girl's naked knees, the panting old man, the girl's amorous groans . . .

The priest instructed them in the lessons of charity. But for men, no less than for animals, the only lesson was: kill or be killed. When he was younger, he was everybody's scapegoat. Not until he was bigger and tough enough to draw blood did they begin to respect him. God saw to it that the strong prospered and the weak suffered.

If only he could have flown to heaven and grabbed Him by the beard! They had invented flying machines, so why not a superplane? Dominic was floundering in a maze of complexities. Who went to hell, anyway? Maybe God was only faking that nothing fazed Him, maybe He was the sly type, like a cat that looks the other way and then pounces. If it weren't for the fear of hell—boy, what a picnic! And if anyone got in the way—whamo!—let him have it with the rifle. Clasping his knees and listening condescendingly to Thomas's rambling explanations, he looked for a way out of the labyrinth. Once he was struck by an ingenious idea. What if the priests were making it all up, what if God really didn't care about the world? Of course there had to be a hell, but that was something between people and devils—spirits who, like the invisible witch, Laume, changed their appearance at will and went after those stupid enough to court them. Maybe there *was* no God, maybe no one lived in heaven. But how to be sure?

Dominic, who, as has already been noted, had the sort of mind that appreciated the value of experiments, gradually formulated the following logical proposition: If man was to a dog what God was to a man, then whenever a dog bit a man and the latter reached for a stick, that was the same as when God was wounded by a man and punished him. The trick was to find something so offensive as to force God to use one of His thunderbolts. If nothing happened, that would be a proof.

26

A SHARP AWL, the kind shoemakers use. Dominic was continually testing the blade with his finger, carrying the instrument in his pocket wherever he went.

That Sunday, a hazy sunrise gave way to clear skies laced with luminous strands of Indian summer. By one of the Issa's steep banks there stood a moss-covered boulder, with a flat, altarlike surface. Dominic's ministers, now wearing shoes and clean shirts—they had just returned from Mass —sat on the grass facing the rock, puffing on little cigars, each trying to keep a poker face. Invisible creatures may also have been in attendance, their necks craned in anticipation of the performance.

Dominic, meanwhile, stood pensively on the riverbank, skipping pebbles across the water. He could still back down. And if what the priests had said was true? Then he would be struck by lightning. He gazed skyward. Not a cloud; a noontime sun high overhead. A bolt of lightning out of a clear blue sky—he'd give anything to see it. But by then it would be too late. The ripples pursued each other in ever-widening circles, rocking the flattened leaves on the surface, until one of them buckled and its green hide was overrun. Was he scared, or what? He tossed a pebble across the river, aiming for the strip of shade on the opposite shore, squeezed his fists inside his pockets, and felt the awl.

He headed straight for the boulder. Seeing him approach, his ministers began to withdraw, and he watched them with contempt as they kept moving farther and farther away. Then he took from his pocket a crumpled blue handkerchief, carefully unfolded it, and smoothed out its corners on the rock's rugged surface.

The Mass over, Thomas had tried to catch up with him but lost sight of him in the crowd. Someone had said he'd seen him heading for the pasture, and Thomas, picking up the trail, took off in the same direction. His tagging after him would have been enough to infuriate Dominic. But to show up at the climactic moment, at the instant the vertical fold between his brows expressed a firmness of will—that was unforgivable. Why did Dominic have to be distracted from his purpose? He yelled something at Thomas, who stood there, not comprehending, though somehow he grasped the impropriety, the painful ridiculousness of his presence, as reflected in the faces of the others. At a command from their leader, they pounced on him and flipped him to the ground, belly first. He fought back, but their hands, reeking of tobacco, kept him pinned down, immobile except for his upturned chin. They ordered him not to make a sound.

The stone table reached just above Dominic's waist. Something round and white shone in the middle of the handkerchief—the Holy Eucharist. He had brought it back from Communion, his hands folded on his chest, balancing it on his tongue and deftly spitting it into his handkerchief. Now he would find out. He grabbed the awl and aimed straight down at the body of Christ. He lowered it, then raised it.

He dug it in.

Keeping the blade in the wound, he searched the sky for some sign of retribution. Nothing happened. A flock of birds shimmered overhead, winging their way from the direction of the stubble fields. Not a cloud or a wisp in sight. He bent down to see whether the wafer, still transfixed by the knife blade, was bleeding. Nothing. Then he began to stab and stab, mutilating the little white disk to bits.

The moment he was free, Thomas took off on the run, his throat convulsed. He ran with the feeling that he was fleeing from the world's manifold evil, that he had been implicated in the sacrilege; it was not only the fear of possible mortal sin. Suddenly he realized how dispensable he was, the self-deception of all those times he had imagined himself to be Dominic's friend. He was, in truth, nobody's friend. He ran for an eternity. At home he clung fitfully to Grandmother Dilbin's arm, desperate for her help, and she kept asking him what was the matter, but all she could get out of him was spasmodic sobbing. That night, screaming he was afraid, he pleaded for the light to be left on in his room. He mumbled in his sleep, and several times his grandmother had to climb out of bed and anxiously lay her hand on his forehead.

Father Monkiewicz, to whom he immediately went to confession, not wanting to postpone it till the weekend—he could barely muster the words to describe it—was outraged by this sacrilegious act committed in his own parish. Coaxing and cajoling, the quicker to extirpate the evil, he twisted and squirmed inside the confessional. But Thomas refused to betray his former friend, despite the priest's insistence that it was his Christian duty to do so. Somehow the name refused to come to his lips. Only when absolution was granted did he feel somewhat relieved.

From now on, even though it meant missing the harvest, then at its peak, he avoided the shed in the orchard, resorting to various subterfuges when Antonina stuck a basket in his hands. This was around the time that he began disappearing, going into hiding at the mere glimpse of homespun pants through the trees. Crossing paths with Dominic, he lowered his gaze, pretending not to notice him.

In effect, that whole ritual conducted on the banks of the Issa had resolved nothing. As soon as it was over, the other boys, unable to seize the scientific relevance of the experiment, feeling somehow cheated—how different if there'd been a clap of thunder, or at least a little blood to show for it!—sat down and dealt a game of blackjack. Afterward, it should be noted, Dominic had gathered up the crumbs of wafer and eaten them: stabbing it was one thing, tossing it into the wind or trampling it underfoot was another.

Dangling his legs over the side of the cliff, he banged his heels against the clay and smoked his pipe fashioned from a cartridge shell. He was overcome by a feeling of emptiness. Better a bullying, fist-wielding, stick-wielding father than having no one to put on trial. He was oppressed by the sorrow of orphanhood, of his double orphanhood. Alone, completely alone.

The surface of the Issa quivered. A water snake was crossing to the other bank, bearing high its perpendicular head, with tentacle-like ripples forming diagonally in its wake. Dominic measured the distance with his eye and felt in his arm the certainty of a bull's-eye. But the water snake was a sacred being: whoever killed one did so at the risk of tempting fate.

27

EVERY AUTUMN, Thomas was on hand to witness the threshing. The boiler engine: the best part was the way it started up or blew off steam. On top of the boiler, a little off-center, close to a wood-fired furnace, the two large balls rotating on metal rods resembled a pair of outstretched arms, lowered at an angle. Did the arms ever stretch upright, he wondered. He never did find out, his attention being devoted exclusively to the action of the balls. At low speed—*prrr-whack, prrr-whack*—they were easily distinguishable; but at high speed they became a whirling, spinning, almost invisible blur: *pfft-pfft-pfft* . . . A couple of benches took up one corner of the yellow-painted shed, through whose roof the boiler's smokestack shot up chimneylike. Thomas, parking on one of the benches, was often joined by the men from the barn as they took time off from the threshing for a smoke. The other bench, the one opposite, was usually taken by young Sypniewski, stretched out on his sheepskin. The nephew of

Shatybelko, Sypniewski had charge of the boiler. Drawing up his knees, he lay there, head cradled in hand, meditating about only he knew what. From time to time, he would climb down from the bench, check the pressure gauge, flip open the little door, and toss a few oak logs into the belching pit, or lubricate the engine with an oilcan, even though the blacksmith was responsible for its maintenance.

With a flushed face and a nose full of grease smell, Thomas would come out for a breath of the fresh air that ruffled the leaves of the poplar. Outside, he was fascinated by something else: the transmission belt. Close to a meter in width, made of thickly padded hide, the belt connected the boiler's big wheel to a smaller wheel mounted on the thresher. What stopped the belt from slipping off the bigger wheel, wondered Thomas. There were times, in fact, when it did come loose, caused by a slack in the revolutions, producing cries of "Keep back!"—because when it came down, it was with a bone-crushing crash. All work was immediately halted while Sypniewski and the blacksmith tried to soften the impact by applying pressure on the belt with poles. By the time they jumped back, it slipped off without a sound. A surefire sign the machine was slowing down was if the patches on the belt could be seen on its rotations.

Inside the barn: dust clouds, reverberations, a frenzy of activity. The sacks, suspended on iron hooks, swelled in no time. Thomas liked to dip his hand into the streams of cool grain. One by one, the filled sacks were hauled away by the blacksmith, over to the poplar tree and onto the weighing machine. The threshing floor, aswarm with blinding, stinging dust, was a blur of white kerchiefs and sweaty faces. A sheaf described an arc on the end of a pitchfork; the thresher swallowed it with a *grrr*, the paws at the back, their bright-red finish now a faded pink, jerked fitfully back and forth, and sifted the straw between them.

Several teams of horses were needed to move the

boiler engine or the thresher. Sometimes, though seldom, it would be transported to one of the neighboring farms, accompanied by a lot of yelling and cracking of whips and laying of branches under the wheels. The only other boiler in the region belonged to Baloudis, the American, in Pogirai; elsewhere, the threshing was done by hand, with flails. The thresher might be lent to anyone, except to those living down below by the river: downhill was easy going, but uphill was too rough on the horses.

Previously at home among the threshers, Thomas first sensed, following the incident with Dominic, that his presence was somehow unwelcome—by the palaver of the men, by the way they ignored him or somnolently spat out their tobacco spittle. The brooding Sypniewski; the women, shooing him away from the threshing floor; the other children his own age, who were assigned special chores, such as fishing out from underneath the thresher the canvas tarpaulin used to catch the chaff—all made him feel like an outsider.

Other little unpleasantries took on a new meaning. The looks of amused condescension when he tried his hand at a scythe or plow, for example, or the *baraban*—a piece of metal strung on wires, which Shatybelko banged in the morning when it was time to go to work, and later in the evening at quitting time (during the threshing season, the signals came from the boiler's whistle, a blast so shrill it made people plug their ears). Shatybelko's clanging had a definite lilt to it, and people laughed because it sounded like "booby-boss, booby-boss." They laughed good-naturedly, but it hurt nonetheless.

In the servants' quarters, Antonina and the women gossiped about their masters, about them and about their forebears, those slave drivers of old. One ancient pastime held particular fascination for Thomas: a girl was forced to climb a tree and cuckoo while the men took potshots at her. Thomas loved it when the girls shinnied up the trees at apple- and cherry-picking time—it allowed him to peek up at the darkness under their dresses (panties were unheard-of in Gine). They giggled and called him names, but pleasure was written all over their faces. So what did they, those grandees of the past, do? Blast away from below? In Antonina's sighs he caught not only a brooding rancor but also a feeling of superiority—over him, who was, after all, one of them.

For these and other reasons he began to take refuge in Grandfather's company. Nodding, arms akimbo, he would listen to lectures on plants—how nitrogen was inhaled and oxygen exhaled, how every year forests were burned and grain sown, until the soil became barren, and how the three-field system was later introduced. In time, Grandfather became his chief companion; now, when Thomas turned the pages of his grandfather's books, he did so demanding explanations. He entered the verdant kingdom of plants at that time of year when leaves turn yellow and fall to the ground, a kingdom far removed from reality. Here was a sanctuary for him; plants were not mean or vicious, did not wound or exclude.

Nor was there anything menacing about Grandfather. Always patient, never so distracted by the affairs of grown-ups that he neglected Thomas's needs, he talked to him in earnest, always in his hemming manner—a sign denoting both amusement and affection. Even while he was washing, pomading his hair, or combing his bald patch, he was always ready to answer questions. Thomas once rubbed his hands with the pomade—a soaplike paste that came in a little paper tube—and sniffed it. Grandfather washed with warm water, with a towel wrapped around his waist, revealing a chest and stomach coated with a fine layer of grayish silver.

Grandmother Dilbin openly deplored Thomas's lack of proper schooling. Having no faith in Joseph, she began tutoring him herself, though much had changed since she

was a schoolgirl. She promised that when his mother returned she would take them both away with her, but that
day was continually being deferred. And what learning he
did acquire was not very evenly distributed. If he read
well, it was only because of his curiosity. He wrote in a
chicken's scrawl and spoke the local dialect, throwing in
Lithuanian expressions at random (which later was to
cause him considerable embarrassment in school). With
his sudden turning to Grandfather, he was initiated into
botany, becoming rather knowledgeable for his age, and
his grandfather was cheered that instead of growing up to
be a soldier or pirate he might one day become a farmer.

No photographs of Thomas remain from this period,
for the simple reason that none was ever taken. Of late he
had discovered the mirror, though he still did not know
how to view himself in comparison with others. He never
thought to use a comb or brush. A thick shock of untamed,
dark-blond hair swooped down over his forehead. Chubby-
cheeked, gray-eyed; the stubby, upturned nose of a little
boar—a nose identical to the one in the lilac-tinged photo
of Great-grandfather Mohl. Tall for his age.

"Tommy has a face like a Tartar's ass," he once overheard one Koreva boy whisper to the other. The remark
had added insult to injury. The two boys, sons of Koreva, a
neighbor from across the Issa, had stopped over in Gine
with their parents. They had bossed him, bored him silly
with their games, and hurt his feelings with their constant
elbowing in the ribs and teasing.

The suspicion arose that he had inherited an inability
to make friends. Was it from Grandmother Surkont and
her streak of self-willed independence? Grandmother Dilbin's timidity? Or was it simply due to inexperience? His
grandparents once took him along on a social visit. Not
only did he eye the host's daughter suspiciously, but he
shuddered when she took him by the hand and showed him
around the garden, stiffening his whole body and holding

his breath for fear of being brushed by her skinny bare elbows. Standing on a bridge over a stream, their backs against a birch railing, he had sensed an aura of expectation, but he was mute. He was reminded of Onutè, of their mutual excursions, and was mortified.

His social manners: he blushed and shuffled his feet in company. He had been to town several times, but that hardly meant a familiarity with the world at large. On market day he stayed put in the wagon, giving Antonina a hand with displaying the apples for sale. Some of the houses in the town sat so close to the river's edge they almost touched the waterline—the Issa broadened here, almost beyond recognition—the streets were paved with cobbles big enough to sprain an ankle, and Jewish shop-keepers stood on the wooden steps of their shops, beckoning to customers. The tallest and biggest building in town was a white mansion—overlooking ponds covered with duckweed—that had once belonged to a princely family but was now in the process of being converted into a school or a hospital. The railway station lay on the outskirts, which was why he preferred the longer but smoother route home that cut across the tracks, because then he got a chance to see a real train. He looked forward to the trip. Antonina handed him the reins and he would crack the whip. If they were traveling alone, she had them hitch the most sluggish horses—automobiles were a constant hazard. To keep them from bucking, Thomas would remove the blanket covering the hay seat, jump down, race around the front, and drape the horses' heads.

With his grandfather, freed from the proprieties and the coercing that came of being among people, he wandered through the wonderland of seeds that germinated under-ground—of shoots, crowns, petals, pistils, and stamens. He made up his mind to learn the different species of plants, enough to start a herbarium the following summer.

28

As A BABY, he was often placed on a bear-skin, at which time a sacred peace descended on him; half frightened and half enthralled, he would sit motionless, lifting his hands so as not to touch the shaggy beast. Worn and moth-eaten, the hide had come from the last bear in the region, tracked down ages ago during his grandfather's childhood. Though he knew them only from the rug and from pictures, bears nonetheless aroused in Thomas feelings of great affection. And he was not the only one, judging by the reminiscing of the older people. In former times, bears were kept on the manorial estates and were trained to perform certain chores, such as turning hand mills or hauling wood. Numerous anecdotes were told of them. One proud and self-respecting bear was still remembered in the village of Gine—a bear so partial to sweet pears that if the master of the house invited him to sit at table, he had to be careful to share everything fairly and equitably, for, if his pears were too soft or too green, the bear roared with indignation. Thomas sat up straight in his chair and was all ears when stories were told of one bear. The bear, who had a habit of strangling hens and had to be chained up, showed great cunning: sitting up on his haunches, he scattered sand around with his forepaws, and when the gullible chickens came within radius of the chain, he clubbed them unconscious, hiding his quarry beneath him and assuming a look of pious innocence. His favorite story, though, the hero of the most marvelous adventure of them all—this one was told by Grandmother Dilbin—was the bear who, seeing an empty carriage parked in front of some farm veranda, climbed aboard. The horses bolted, but the bear, which also panicked, froze in his seat. The runaway coach and its strange passenger reached the highroad. At a junction stood a cross; the wagon careened to one side, the bear grabbed hold of the cross and, still holding on to the driver's seat with the other paw, managed to uproot it from the ground, and so arrayed rode into the village street, terrifying the villagers, for it looked like the devil's work.

One aristocratic squire, the story went, used bears to show his disrespect for the Russians. The Governor General, a Russian, once paid him a visit, and this is what he saw as he pulled up at the manor: two bears standing in front of the porch, each holding a halberd, and down below on the steps, wearing a Russian peasant blouse, the squire in the act of bowing to the ground. The Governor General, taking this to mean: "We, the Emperor's wild subjects, half beasts and half men, welcome you under our roof," clenched his jaws and ordered an about-face.

In all these tales, the bears emerged as creatures endowed with a nearly human intelligence, making their treatment at the Smorgon Training Academy, as described by his grandfather, all the more cruel. The bears, wearing wooden clogs, were paraded on a sheet-metal floor heated by a fire from below; as the floor grew hotter, music was played, and soon the poor bears were sitting up on their hind paws—the forepaws were left intentionally bare. Later the music always made them recall the scorching metal and they commenced to dance.

That such huge and powerful animals were possessed of a benign, even timid nature only deepened one's sympathy. Their cowardice was borne out by a certain peasant, at a time when bears were still in abundance in the forests. The peasant had lost a cow—a maverick, given to straying from the herd; in a fit of anger, the peasant grabbed a pole and, finding the stray lying in a raspberry patch, began swinging. A roar told him he was mistaken. The man took off in one direction, the bear in another, so scared he dirtied the entire patch. Diarrhea in these parts is even referred to as "bear's sickness."

Grandfather could recall how the bear—the one that had bequeathed his skin—was smoked after the kill and how the hounds had recognized the meat by its smell and how their hides had bristled at the mere scent of it.

In winter, Misia used to spread an elkskin by her bed, the elk being prized for its cured hide, so thick and soft to the touch. When the soles of Thomas's moccasins wore down, his grandmother took a piece of leather from the cupboard, measured off a section, then cut out the part outlined in pencil with shears. This was also a vestige of the past, as elk were now scarce, with only a few being left at the mercy of poachers in a forest located some twenty kilometers from Gine.

The bearskin was associated with one of Thomas's earliest loves. One autumnal day Balthazar showed up at the manor and announced that he had a present for Thomas in the wagon. There, lying on a bed of straw, was a cage with wooden bars, and inside the cage—an eagle owl.

Grandmother Surkont acquiesced, though not without grumbling that the bird was bound to make a mess of the house. The owl stayed. Balthazar had caught it and raised it before it had learned to fly; quite tame, it allowed itself to be taken by the stomach, screeching in a shrill, chickenlike voice, for which reason Thomas named him Squeaky. It was as unlikely a sound as one would have thought possible. Though it was no bigger than a hen, its wings, when extended, were longer than Thomas's fully outstretched arms; it had a curved beak, a powerful grip, and the claws of a killer. Then a new era began: the plucking of rats from every conceivable kind of trap. Squeaky ate like this: he clasped the meat between his claws and tore at it with his beak. Quite capable of snapping at a hand if it came near the bars, he never went for a finger. At dusk Thomas let him out of his cage. A soundless flight, a rush of air—when suddenly, in midflight, he would drop a pile, splattering the floor (which indiscretion Thomas immediately cleaned up, to avoid angering the grownups), and then, from the top of the tiled stove, let out a real owl hoot. The flying exercise over, he was returned to his cage.

The softness of his feathers, the russet-gold eyes, the way he nodded, like a farsighted person struggling to decipher something in fine print . . . Thomas's attachment grew, to the point that he could predict certain of his habits. When the owl was placed on the elkskin, he behaved uproariously: his whole body jerked, his claws contracted, and then he started pawing the hide, shifting his weight from one leg to the other. One brush of the elk's short hide was enough to evoke memories of his ancestors that had once preyed on deer and hare. The bearskin, on the other hand, did not seem to bother him.

For Thomas, though he would have been too embarrassed to admit it, hair had many vague connotations and was close to being an obsession. Why the upraised hands when he was placed on the fluffy fur hide? And why were bears thought to be so nice and gentle? Was it because they were so hairy? And Magdalena that time in the river. And the owl. Weren't its spasms born of the same thing as what Thomas, in his dream, had felt as a shiver? By identifying with the owl, by embodying himself in him as he clawed the elk hide, he was on the verge of asking whether he had not felt an urge to claw Magdalena, or whether the sweet intoxication had come of the knowledge that she was already dead. But he didn't ask, and it was better so.

Hens screech, but then that is their nature. The owl, on the other hand, was by nature a dual personality: trustful, defenseless, his heart pulsating beneath your fingers, his legs limply dangling, graceless, veiling his eyes with his lower eyelids when he was scratched behind the ear, and a terror of the forest by night. But was he really the outlaw he was made out to be? If he was, it did not seem to affect his internal nature. Or did every Evil harbor some hidden vulnerability, a suspicion, the barest glimmer of doubt?

No sooner did Aunt Helen arrive and lay eyes on the owl than she and Grandmother Surkont began to conspire. The decision was made: they would sell him. Eagle owls commanded a good price among hunters, who, setting them out on posts as decoys, hid in blinds and shot down the owl's attackers. Thomas dutifully accepted their verdict, as if intuiting that no love should ever be extended beyond its limits. As for the money he was promised, he never saw a penny of it.

29

Whenever Thomas went into the library, he had to put on his little sheepskin against the cold; the room was never heated and his hands turned blue as he leafed through the sheets of parchment in the hope of finding something on plants or animals. Often, he grabbed a couple of volumes and took refuge in a warmer part of the house. One of the tomes abducted in this manner bore a title whose contorted, snakelike letters he had difficulty deciphering: "On the Office of Swordbearing . . ." Unable to cope with the rest, he went to his grandfather for an explanation of the contents. His grandfather—but not before putting on his pince-nez—read the title aloud: *The doctrines of the Church of Our Lord Jesus Christ/ being in Lithuania/ briefly summarized/ according to Holy Scripture. The defense of said office against all its adversaries having been written by Simon Budny. On the question of what is clearly prescribed by Holy Scripture/ that a Christian may own subjects, both freemen and slaves/ so long as they be treated in a God-fearing manner. This being the 1583d year A.D.*

Tapping the leather pince-nez case against the volume's musty cover, his grandfather began turning the pages. After a while he cleared his throat. "This is not a Catholic book. You see, Thomas, long, long ago there lived a man named Hieronymous Surkont. This book was his; he was a Calvinist."

Thomas knew that the word Calvinist connoted something bad, that it was even a derogatory term. But they, those infidels, who didn't go to a church but to a *Kirche*, belonged to the far-off world of cities, railroads, and machines. Protestants? Here in Gine? He regarded it as an honor to have been initiated into such a shameful secret.

"A heretic?"

Grandfather's fingers slipped the pince-nez back into its case. He looked out the window and stared at the snow. "Hm? Yes, yes, a heretic ..."

"And this Hieronymous Surkont used to live here?"

Grandfather suddenly perked up. "Did he live here? Probably, but we know very little about him. He spent most of his time in Kedainiai, at the court of Prince Radziwiłł. That's where the Calvinists had their parish and school."

Thomas sensed some reticence on his grandfather's part, some resistance, the sort of deliberate ambiguity the grownups used when they spoke of certain family members in hushed voices, falling silent the moment anyone entered the room. The faces of these outcasts, impossible to visualize, disappeared into the dark background as in some faded photograph, with not a trace of a brow or facial blemish left behind as a reminder. Whatever sins they had committed—grave enough to bring shame to their descendants—the age in which they lived, the degree of kinship dissolved into whispers or mild reproaches directed at the intruder. But this time it was different.

"There is a German side to the Surkont family. They are all descendants of Hieronymous. Nearly three hundred years ago, in 1655, the Swedes invaded our land. Hieronymous went over to the side of the Swedish king, Karl Gustav."

"Then he was a traitor?"

Grandfather liked to pinch the end of his purple-veined nose, puff his nostrils, then suddenly let go, producing a *pff-pff* sound.

"That he was"—*pff-pff*—"but if he'd fought against the Swedes, he would have betrayed the Prince he served. Either way, he would have been a traitor."

Thomas frowned as he contemplated the complexities of the dilemma. "So it was Prince Radziwiłł's fault," he declared at last.

"Now *there* was an ambitious man," said his grandfather. "He thought that once Karl Gustav made him a Grand Duke he would no longer be a vassal of the Polish king. As ruler of Lithuania, he could then force everyone to convert."

"And if he had," said Thomas, "we would all be Calvinists, right?"

"Probably." He scrutinized his grandson's face, grinning in a way that suggested he saw through the boy's questions, to the awareness gradually taking hold: Why are we what we are? Who or what decides? What would he have become if he were someone else? "But Hieronymous

Surkont wasn't exactly a Calvinist. He was a Socinian, another—uh—species of those who refused to recognize the Pope."

And he began telling him of the Socinians, or Arians, as they were also called, and of the new set of doctrines they had propagated—doctrines prohibiting, among other things, the holding of public office, whether that of voivode, judge, or soldier, a practice expressly condemned by Christ; and the ownership of serfs. This last point had been a cause of much dissension, many arguing that the Bible sanctioned it—this being the position of the book he had taken from the library. As for Hieronymous, following the expulsion of the Swedes he left the country, never to return, eventually settling in Prussia, somewhere around Königsberg.

Thus was the seed sown, and his grandfather had no way of knowing how long it would be nurtured in the vegetable sleep of seeds that patiently bide their time. The seed was sown: in it were contained the squeaking of wooden boards, the sound of footsteps slipping along bookshelves and numbered folios that glow among dark rows of leather bindings; elbows propped on the table in a ring of light cast by a green shade; a pencil bobbing up and down in mimicry of thought, which in the beginning is nothing but a haze, a blur without shape or outline ... No one lives alone; he is speaking with those who are no more, their lives are incarnated in him; he is retracing their footsteps, climbing the stairs to the edifice of history. Their hopes and defeats, the signs left behind, be it a single letter carved in stone—here is the way to peace, to mitigating the judgments he imposed on himself. Happiness is given to those who have the gift. Never and nowhere will they feel alone, as they are comforted by the memory of all who have struggled, like themselves, for something unattainable. Whether or not Thomas was rewarded, such moments as those spent in the company of his grandfather abided with him, anticipating an age when voices muted by time would become precious.

30

IT TOOK the Spaniard Michael Servetus more than two hours to die. It took so long because not enough wood had been piled, and through the flames he chastised the city of Geneva for its frugality. "Poor me, I can't even die a proper death! Surely the two hundred ducats and the gold chain they confiscated should have bought enough wood to burn me alive!"*

Meanwhile, Calvin had sat unbendingly in his chair, reading the Bible in the penumbra of his room, while his vicar, Guillaume Farel, his eyes smarting from the smoke, had shouted up at the burning heretic: "Believe in Jesus Christ, the everlasting Son of God!"

Such was the fate of Michael Servetus, after his having hidden among the papists in France for twenty years—a fate willed by the very man with whom he had secretly exchanged letters and in whom he had sought refuge. But Servetus had an indomitable spirit, the tongue in his charred mouth still stirred, and his weak voice could yet testify to the sacrilegious truth: "I believe that Christ was the true Son of God, but not that he was everlasting."

* A record of Servetus's last days, based on no longer extant sources, is given by Wiszowaty. See Stanislaw Kot's "L'influence de Michel Servet sur le mouvement antitrinitarien en Pologne et en Transylvanie," in the collection *Autour de Michel Servet et de Sébastien Castellion*, (Alphen aan den Rijn, The Netherlands: H. D. Tjeenk Willink, 1953).

He was survived by a rumor that spread from country to country, that caused goose quills to scratch in Basel, Tübingen, Wittenberg, Strasbourg, and Cracow as they went about copying theses secretly obtained from friends attacking the Trinity. When copies of Servetus's banned writings were discovered on some Polish students in Tübingen, the Prince sneered: *"Schwärmerei!"*; the university trembled and tried to hush up the whole affair. Servetus's name was never mentioned, and even Petrus Gonesius, now returned from Padua to propagate the new doctrine among the Protestant sects in Poland and Lithuania, was careful not to utter his master's name in public. But Melanchthon wasn't fooled. "I have been reading the work of a Lithuanian who means to summon Servetus from hell," he wrote. In Transylvania and Moravia, meanwhile, Jacob Paleologus was composing his great work *Contra Calvinum pro Serveto*—quite clearly written in defense of the Spaniard. But the chest containing his manuscripts was sealed by the hand of the Holy Inquisition, following his arrest and journey to Rome, where he died a martyr's death.

In the writing of any chronicle, people and events are re-created from certain minor details. Now, it would be dishonest to say that Hieronymous Surkont was a short or tall man, dark-haired or fair, when not the slightest physical description of him, not even the dates of his birth and death, has survived. This much was certain: that Rome was for him the seat of the Antichrist; that as he rode horseback in his elkskin jacket along the road skirting the Issa, he had contemplated with sadness this people incapable of embracing the true faith. For theirs was a fake Christianity aptly fitting popish superstitions: after singing hymns in church, the women ran and offered sacrifice to snakes, convinced that if they didn't their men would not be up to fulfilling their conjugal duties. Fables took the place of Holy Scripture, fables about a god of water and a god of wind who shook the world. And pagan rites, such as those observed when hunters assembled before the hunt. And furtive meetings under the oaks.

An inquisitive man, driven by what must have been a powerful thirst for knowledge, he had probably sought out those like himself, finding them in Kedainiai. He must have studied diligently to have felt an equal in those disputes held by candlelight, supporting his arguments with quotations from the Bible: "Your reasoning, my good sir, is fallacious, more properly deserving of the name of sophistry, because that passage in Hebrew can be interpreted otherwise." Or: "Fellow brother, is not the intent clearly evident in the Greek and Latin commentaries?" This was at a time when the Trinitarians, still loyal to Calvin, and the ditheists, and even those who, following the example of Simon Budny, refused to worship Christ, still tolerated one another, thanks to the moderating influence of Radziwill, who, even though he took as his model the Church of Geneva, refrained from banning theological disputes and was even inclined toward novelties. Not a few Arians from Poland had found a haven on his estate, though, to be sure, at the price of exercising a certain caution.

Was Hieronymous Surkont submerged; that is, was he baptized as an adult, in the manner prescribed by the Brethren, who were strictly opposed to the baptism of infants? No telling, though it is known that he ceased to be a Trinitarian, remaining loyal to the memory of Servetus, nearly a hundred years after that martyr's death. That the three-headed Cerberus substituted for the One God was a heinous insult to reason he took as self-evident. He embraced the revolutionary thesis that God was one, as was Holy Scripture, which was clear and unequivocal and did not require any official exegesis; one had only to read the Gospels, to return to the age of the Apostles, to traverse centuries during which Scholasticism had sought to obscure the simple words of the prophets and of Christ. Calvin had gone only halfway, killing Servetus in fear of the truth. Whoever failed to destroy Cerberus would never be entirely free of all the hocus-pocus, indulgences, Masses for the dead, pleas for the intercession of the saints, and all other things of a magical nature.

One can infer, from the scarcity of facts available, that in that religious controversy which for many decades divided the Brethren, Hieronymous Surkont leaned in favor of the legacy bequeathed by Petrus Gonesius. Placing all hope in Jesus Christ for the salvation of his soul ("I am a vile worm in the eyes of my Lord," Thomas deciphered in one of his books), he would have argued that Christ did not share in God's divinity; that the Logos, the invisible and immortal Word, became flesh in the Virgin's womb; in other words, that Christ was conceived of the Logos. He had embraced Christ's humanity with awe, gratitude, and joy, but not like the nonworshippers, who did not distinguish between Jeremiah, Isaiah, and Jesus, and who were more apt to invoke the Old Testament than the New.

But what of his thoughts on Gonesius's *De primatu Ecclesiae Christianae*, which he surely must have studied, and on the works of his disciples? Hieronymous Surkont could hardly have dismissed their arguments in the practical realm, arguments that had long reverberated in the synods of Lithuania. Their demands, after all, were given credence by the Gospels. For was it not written: "And unto him that smiteth thee on one cheek offer also the other; and him that taketh away thy cloak forbid not to take thy coat also." Was it not written: "Jesus said unto him, Follow me; and let the dead bury their dead." Was it not written: "And every one that heareth these sayings of mine, and doeth them not, shall be likened unto a foolish man, which built his house upon the sand: And the rain descended, and the floods came, and the winds blew, and beat upon that house; and it fell: and great was the fall of it." Jews, Greeks, slaves, and masters are equal; all are brothers. A Christian does not shed blood, but divests himself of the sword. He frees his serfs from bondage, sells his earthly goods, and distributes his wealth among the poor. Only thus does he become worthy of salvation; only thus does he distinguish himself from the hypocrites, whose actions give the lie to their words.

The period in question came after the synods of Lithuania had rejected these uncompromising demands, giving rise to bitter dissension among the Brethren. Surkont had set out to refute their arguments with the aid of the Old Testament, as well as with examples taken from his own experience. Granted, the serfs had endured great poverty and oppression—but free them from bondage? That would have been to invite paganism, barbarism, and banditry. Look what happened during the emancipation under Rekut, starosty of Samogitia: the serfs took cover in the forests, emerging only to murder and maraud. Then, too, there was the example of their own peasant rebellion with its revival of the old gods, serving notice on the landowners inhabiting the Issa Valley. Unbelt one's sword? The disciples of Gonesius had chosen a bad time to propose so drastic a measure: to the east, beyond the Dnieper, the wars with Ivan the Terrible were still going on unabated. Outvoted in the synods, they never recovered from their defeat.

Then came Karl Gustav of Sweden, brandishing the sword on behalf of an Imperium for Protestants. And Hieronymous Surkont? Did he suffer moments of vacillation? Of indecision? His Prince had painted a powerful vision of Lithuanians living under the protection of a Swedish king; stripping the papists of both land and serfs, they were to become bearers of light to the east and to the south, all the way to the Ukraine, wherever the black robes, their mouths full of holy Byzantium but not knowing a word of Greek themselves, had succeeded in keeping the people in ignorance. They had no choice: they were being threatened by a Jesuit invasion—the Jesuits, with their cunning methods of seduction, their theaters, schools, every year luring more and more of the faithful away; the desecration of temples, funeral processions being attacked by student mobs . . . Before long, nothing would be left of the Reformed Church in Lithuania. The Prince had played his last card, obedient to his vocation as protector of the faith. And to another ambition, off in the distance: the crown. And, who knows, even visions of Swedish, Lithuanian, and Polish armies standing at the gates of Moscow.

One suspects that he was driven not only by his loyalty to the Prince but also by his contempt for the blusterous nobility, roused by the priests to a holy war against the heretics. Never applying cold reason, never opening the Bible, guided only by blind, elemental instinct.

Faithful to the end. And the horror of it all: the initial reverses, the vacillation of even the most fervent believers, a fratricidal war, a country laid waste, the sinister indifference of allies . . . Death came to the Prince as the papists stormed the fortress, the last outpost. Then, for Hieronymous, the final hour of reckoning, the time when each man repeats after Christ: "Lord, why hast thou forsaken me," the final dissolution of pride and will.

We can assume that he found consolation in the Bible, or in the memory of their own Anti-Trinitarian martyr—his head crowned with straw drenched in sulphur; his body chained to the stake; his book, waiting for the first lick of the flames, bound to his foot. A detailed account of Servetus's death has survived, thanks to Hieronymous Surkont's co-religionists from the Protestant sects of Poland and Lithuania. It was they who copied the manuscript, otherwise not extant, bearing the title *Historia de Serveto et eius morte*, whose author was Petrus Hyperphragmus Gandavus. No, exile could not compare with bodily torture.

Surkont, nonetheless, had endured spiritual torture, the stigma of a traitor, the burden of self-doubt that came from not knowing whether he had made the right choice. Between his fealty to the King, the Res Publica, and to his Prince, who never begrudged him their theological differences. Between his contempt for the papists and his aversion for the invaders, whose successes—not defeats—he was obliged to wish for. A heretic in the eyes of the Catholics. A barely tolerated outcast among the Protestants. All he could do, in fact, was to repeat: "I am a vile worm in the sight of my Lord."

Quite by accident, it was discovered that Hieronymous's last descendant, a Lieutenant Johann von Surkont, student of theology, was killed in the year 1915, in the Vogesen. If his body lies on a slope facing the east, where thick rows of crosses descend into the valley of the Rhine, crosses that from a distance might be mistaken for vineyards, then the grass on his grave is brushed by the dry winds coming from his native Lithuania.

31

IN GINE, the *bitnik*, or beekeeper (from *bitè*, Lithuanian for "bee"), was Thomas's aunt, Helen Juchniewicz. As payment for tending the beehives, she was allotted a percentage of the honey and wax—though she was a member of the family, custom dictated it. Her arrival invariably signaled the removal of utensils from a special cupboard and the donning of special vestments. Pinning up her sleeves at the elbow, she slipped a mask over her head, a sort of basket of green muslin. Though she often dispensed with gloves, she was seldom stung. Thomas was assigned the task of loading the smoker (tin, with a wooden handle) with live coals from the kitchen, dry rot being needed to get the coals to smolder. In her mask, with a knife and pail in one hand, the billowing smoker in the other, she looked like—well, no metaphor could have possibly done her justice. With mouth agape, Thomas passionately devoured that figure trailing down the lane in the direction of the hives. Later, back at the house, she ladled out some curdled milk from a bowl, applying it to the stings. When it came time to extract the honey, Thomas got to operate the "centrifuge"—a metal pot that rotated manually on a stick, forcing the honey out of the combs.

Aunt Helen had the same large, pyramid-shaped nose and protruding apple-cheeks as Grandmother Misia, to whom, except for being somewhat larger-proportioned and blue-eyed, she bore a definite physical resemblance. She had a sugary smile and a look of piety, which obviously worked to her advantage, clothing her passions in innocence. Her ruling passion was miserliness, dictated not so much by frugality as by something so deeply engrained, so fundamental to her being, that it often sought justification in the most improbable of motives. If she had to go into town on some errand, she never took the wagon. "The weather's so lovely—I feel like a walk today," and so saying, she would hike the ten kilometers to town on foot, taking off her shoes the moment she reached the road, since, as she put it, "walking barefoot was healthier." The real reason, of course, was to avoid having to tip the driver and to save wear and tear on her shoes. When it came to dividing the honey and flour, she always made sure the choicest part went to others, except that the "choicest" part always contained some hidden flaw. Nor, if the rumors were to be believed, was she above feeding her domestic staff bad meat, worm-infested pork, for example, though no doubt she prided herself on not keeping them exclusively on a vegetarian diet.

From Misia she had inherited an iron constitution and endurance. She never took ill—but God forbid anyone calling a doctor if she had! Twenty kilometers were, for her, something of a country stroll, though at her brisk peasant pace she could easily have managed a hundred. Naturally, she didn't give up bathing in the river until well into November. Never had Thomas seen her with a book in her hands, not even a prayer book, as if she had vowed never to touch one, though the little French she knew said that she must have studied at one time or another.

The arrival of her husband, Lucas Juchniewicz, was always theatrical, contagiously so. Whooping and hollering from his carriage, he threw up his arms, jumped down, and with the flaps of his cape or cloak fluttering behind him, ready for a bear hug, came on the run, squealing in a high soprano, "Mama! Oh, oh, oh! How glad I am to see ya, what a sight for sore eyes . . . !" Smooch, smooch, mm-mm . . . But the chief attraction was the man's face: round, with a dark forelock drooping down over the forehead, a face all wrinkled with sincerity and emotion. "Good ol' Luke," Misia, by now smothered and wet, would reply, and behind his back mercifully sigh, "Good ol' loon." For Grandmother Dilbin, on the other hand, Luke was living proof that there was at least a grain of truth in the old saying: "Only fools and madmen are born along the Issa."

That summer, the summer Thomas built his herbarium (after managing to scrounge some cardboard from Pakenas), his naturalist's honor could no longer keep him from the beehives, heretofore off-limits; after considerable pestering, his aunt finally surrendered and agreed to take him with her to the apiary. He took no chances, wearing his grandfather's long pants tied at the ankles, an old mask with rusted netting, and a pair of rubber gloves. Although prized for their intelligence, although surrounded by a poetry of honey, bees assumed an altogether different aspect the moment their hives were opened—one not exactly compatible with the image of them buzzing in the branches of a linden tree. An acrid smell, a fury of motion, a mad ferment, the cruel severity of law: Gine most certainly was a poor preparation for life in society if Thomas was intimidated by something as cruel and mysterious as a beehive. Charging at him with their stinging intent, they descended on his glove, their curved bellies vibrating spasmodically, their diminutive feet clinging to the rubber —all in order to perform that fatal act and expire, helplessly and convulsively, in the grass. His aunt worked at a leisurely pace, nonchalantly flicking off her attackers, now and then cautioning him: "Easy does it, Thomas." But Thomas was less affected by the pain than by the hellish pandemonium of the beehive, with its own special, persistent rhythm. He couldn't take it; he began to run, the bees in hot pursuit, a hint of murder in their buzzing drone. He squealed, waved his arms—in short, the whole enterprise, his dream of accomplishing something worthwhile in the practical realm, ended in disgrace.

Plants were better, quieter. Some, after a thick *Economic and Technical Guide to a Herbarium* had been consulted, enticed one to prepare crucibles and mortars— a whole pharmacy—so alluring were the descriptions of their medicinal properties. Visions of different-colored decoctions that had to be blended and strained; extracts submerged in alcohol; jams and preserves made from roots popularly thought of as worthless. As in the family larder in Gine, the imagination was plunged into an aromatic penumbra. For now, though, Thomas was content to devote himself to less practical work: the collection of various species.

He had a weakness for orchids, which contained all the magic of creatures inhabiting warmer and more humid climates, being for northern regions emissaries of the tropical south. First there was the stem, the meatiness of their green bodies, contiguous with flowers concealing a multibranched candelabrum and smelling vaguely of something rotten, wild, so faintly that their fragrance had to be inhaled long enough to be named—alas, it was unnamable. In June they dotted the grasslands along the Issa, at that time of year when vapor rose from the floodwaters of the river deltas, still awash with silt and the decay of bulrushes, to mingle with the bright green efflorescence. The speckled orchid, a pale lilac-hued cone flecked with dark violet, was hard to catch in full bloom because it was immediately touched by the rust of decay. Thomas would kneel down and carve out the black earth with his pocketknife. (Pocketknives, though occasionally lost, belonged to the realm of objects marking various stages in his life; his last had been one with a wooden handle, his present one, flat-handled and of solid metal.) Carefully, he would lift the soil and slip out the bulb with its rough, fingerlike protrusions. Bursting from the bulb, the orchid rushed forth to meet the sun, then remained in darkness till the following year. Pressed between sheets of cardboard, the orchid gradually took on a rusty hue; the bulb began to flatten and assume the most bizarre configurations.

The white orchid had a purity of color that in a summer twilight was as luminescent as the white of the narcissus. A meadow full of orchids became, in the evening mist, a meadow inhabited by diminutive phantoms. But, when dried, the white orchid lost all its charm, retaining only its slender, roan design. The same was true of the arum. He soon discovered that plants growing in dry regions kept perfectly, undergoing hardly any discoloration, though he felt a greater attraction for the luxurious plants that thrived in wet, humid places. Even insects, armor-plated and quick of movement, bustling in hot sand and a riot of roots, lacked interest. The jungle—now that was the place for him! Why was it that a superabundance of light always resulted in a diminishment of being?

From among the many inhabitants of the sand dunes,

Thomas collected only mulleins, though they were too long for the herbarium and had to be bent zigzag fashion. Needless to say, he hunted most passionately for those flowers described by his guidebook as rare. And just because it was so rare, he especially treasured a globeflower (*Trollius*)—of the crowfoot family, similar to a yellow rose—plucked among some oaks by the cemetery.

He helped his grandfather tend the flower beds along the wall, to the right and left of the porch, weeding, transplanting the seedlings, and carrying water from the pond. Terraced steps, reinforced with stakes, led to the foot-bridge through a small wicket gate—why the gate was there was anyone's guess—in a fence invisible under heaps of hops and morning glory. As he dipped the watering can into the duckweed, large green frogs, startled by his intrusion, leapt in panic and took refuge among the debris afloat in the middle of the pond. Returning with the can, winded from the long walk, he would watch his grandfather water, trying to guess in advance when it was time for another trip to the pond. The evenings were redolent with the tiny bluish-gray night-scented stocks planted along the edges of the beds. Stocks, gillyflowers (with lustrous, velvetlike petals), and asters, which lasted until late autumn and the first frost, were the garden flowers Grandfather liked most to grow. Thomas's favorite was reseda because, although it was plain-looking, like orchids, it aroused an urge to inhale its insides, but also regret because it was so tiny. A reseda the size of a cabbage head—now that would have been something to smell!

Because Misia was of the belief that sickness was one of those things to which normal people were immune, the medicinal virtues of the vegetable world were never exploited. True, the larder was still called the "pharmacy," a relic of the past, but the medicines contained in its drawers had not been preserved, with the exception of arnica flowers, used for treating bruises, and dried raspberries, an extract of which was used by Grandfather as a sudorific against colds. Thomas knew that plantain leaves were the best remedy for wounds; first you applied the leaf, then wrapped it with a cloth bandage. If it still refused to heal, Antonina would moisten a piece of bread with spit and knead it with a spiderweb—a surefire home remedy. It was Grandmother Dilbin who introduced the use of iodine.

Thomas's botanical passions were fated to last no longer than a season. His herbarium, monumentally conceived, became more rarely enriched with a new specimen, the need for cardboard less urgent, as his interest in birds and animals began to revive, soon to the exclusion of everything else. This revival was less Aunt Helen's than Romuald's doing.

32

THAT AFTERNOON, Romuald Bukowski, dressed in his work shirt and work pants, finished mowing the clover, planted his scythe beside the ditch, and went for a dip in the river. He stripped leisurely and, standing knee-deep in the water, washed himself, the black string with the holy medal dangling every time he bent down. Contentedly, he lathered his flat stomach and his thighs; he was still a man in his prime. Wet, he slipped into his clothes and, the scythe safely back on his shoulder, was homeward bound by way of the path through the orchard. Barbarka dished him up a bowl of buttermilk from the underground cooler, elbowing him good and hard in the ribs in the process (something she never did in company). To his loud clap on her rump, she squealed, "Mind you don' spill the milk, Rom!"

The hounds whimpered and whined in their pen. In high spirits, he reached for the hunting horn on the wall, which hung under a shotgun and riding whips with deer-hoof handles. Horn in hand, he went back out onto the porch and began blowing, setting the dogs to wailing and baying for their freedom and the hunt. Later, in his bachelor's quarters, he opened a medicine chest and shaved in front of a tiny mirror—a hard growth, bluish in color—and brushed his sidewhiskers. A sunburned, brick-red face, leathery skin, a black mustache streaked with white—nothing to worry about.

He pulled on his shiny knee boots and buttoned the collar of his navy-blue jacket. "Where to?" pried Barbarka. "Bear-trappin'. Fix a man somethin' to eat and hold your tongue." From a pile of stirrups in the corner, he disentangled two saddles. "Go get Pietruk to saddle Blackie and Chestnut!" The freckle-faced Pietruk showed up a short while later, scratching his crotch through a hole in his pants. Romuald trailed after him to make sure the saddles were cinched properly. He mounted Blackie gently, his spurs jangling, and led the riderless horse by the bridle down into a little canyon, then uphill along a rocky road that cut through the woods. Whenever a hazel grouse fluttered, he bent over the horse's neck and followed it with his eyes.

On Romuald's finger was a signet ring—of some kind of metal, not gold. He wore a homespun jacket, dyed a dark blue. Starting in the sixteenth century, the Issa Valley had been colonized by settlers lured there by the Princes Radziwiłł, and the Bukowskis had come from the Kingdom of Poland in their covered wagons, through forests, across fords and uncharted wilderness, before reaching their destination in the virgin forests of Lithuania. Many fell on distant fields of battle—in the wars against the Swedes, the Turks, and the Russians. Some became impoverished, predestining their heirs for the life of a peasant or tradesman.

But Romuald had upheld the family tradition. His father had run the family farm just outside Vendigala; later, after the estate was parceled out, they migrated here. Not a fortune, but never mind: a man's worth was measured not by money.

Past a clump of woods, the road dipped down and leveled off into grazing pasture, threading a maze of fences —stakes lashed with dry branches. A well crane, steeply pitched roofs. As he rode past one of the houses, both men—the man on horseback and the one observing him— touched the visors of their caps. Masiulis, the wizard, sat with his back against the farmhouse wall, smoking his pipe. They were not on the best of terms. The magician laid claim to as much land as Romuald, but he was a peasant— a Lithuanian peasant. Masiulis followed the rider with squinting eyes, took a puff on his pipe, cleared his throat, and spat.

A mauve afterglow lingered behind the fir-notched horizon; a round wafer of a moon; the distant echo of a shepherd's song played on a wooden horn wrapped in birch bark. He let his horse break into a trot, admired the undulating earth, thought about nothing, rejoicing in the motion, his leg against the warmth, the animal's supple grace. Coming into view now were flat grasslands, fringing the park shrubbery; off in the distance, wrapped in a bluish mist, loomed the hilltops beyond the river valley.

At the park's edge, on a wooden bench overgrown with beards of gray moss, Helen Juchniewicz sat staring up at a moon gaining steadily in brightness. She had come out for a breath of summer air, and not, let it be emphasized, for a horseback ride with Romuald Bukowski; otherwise, she would have worn riding breeches. That she had jokingly, even flippantly, agreed to a rendezvous had completely slipped her mind: no sinful desires had guided *her* steps. When Romuald secured his horse to a tree down below by the roadside, climbed the hill, and made for the bench, she let out a startled "Oh!" He greeted her gallantly, bowing and kissing her fingertips. They talked about the weather, about farming; he told a few jokes and she laughed. When he invited her for a horseback ride, she demurred, saying that she was out of practice and not properly dressed for it. In the end, she consented, placing her foot in the stirrup with all the grace of a born trooper. "Which way?" she asked. "Let's try that way," he said, pointing straight ahead.

From Gine the dusty road ran along the Issa, climbing steadily to where the terraced land sloped down more steeply, twining inlets and meadowlands, taking refuge from the highland mass in the willows by the riverside, until finally, bypassing one and then another of the little villages where long bundles of cut reeds lay before the house to dry, the road made a fork: one way led across a ford to the far bank, the other straight up the side of Mount Vilainiai. The swift river current cut through willow-thick sandbanks. The ford was a comfortable one, with the waterline well below the axles, though dangerous in autumn, during the rainy season, when the horses snorted and balked in panic, leaving the rider to trust to the horse's instincts. Mount Vilainiai, dense with boulders and juniper bushes evoking sinister silhouettes, fell steeply down into the river gorge. The summit afforded a marvelous view of the winding blue ribbon below, of the holms around the ford, which had not prevented the mountain, by far the most rugged and desolate in the region, from acquiring an evil name. The smell of warm milk drifted from the cowsheds along their way, the evening silence was occasionally disturbed by the sound of milk squirting into a bucket, by a farm woman's whining complaint provoked by a swishing tail in the face. Through the twilight, through shafts of light issuing from open cottage doors, through a baying of hounds kept behind fences, they rode. Below them, a gleaming ford, a scaly surface. The clatter of hoofbeats on shale at the foot of the Vilainiai's steep talus caused Helen to pull up on the reins of her chestnut.

"What a spooky place," she said.

He smiled. "What's so spooky about it?"

"God help you, Romuald, if you so much as mention his name."

"Oh, *him!* I've got a way of dealing with him."

"What sort of way?"

"Well, you talk to him, see, real polite-like, then you invite him along."

"Honestly, how can you! I'm heading back!"

"Hold on, I was only teasin'."

They continued to climb, the darkness steadily thickening, a light breeze ruffling the mountainside grass. They reined in at a spot overlooking the gorge. The river shimmered faintly at their feet. Far below, the rueful cries of a bird in flight.

They sat motionless in their saddles, their bridles softly jangling. Helen sighed. Was it a sigh dictated by convention, one of those gestures well suited to the occasion? Or was it the sigh of someone wishing it could somehow have been otherwise?

The Milky Way, which in this part of the country goes by the name of the Bird's Way, was inscribing its luminous signs in the firmament.

33

WHEN ROMUALD, wearing his navy-blue visored cap, his hunting whip dangling from his saddle, rode up the lane to the veranda, Thomas had visions of a dark statue, a mobile perpendicularity on horseback. They soon became the best of friends. At the dining table, while Aunt Helen lavished their guest with sweetmeats, Romuald and Grandfather talked crops. Still, certain imperceptible signs visible in the behavior of the older women connoted a distance. Romuald, though a welcome guest, was of a different world. Such distinctions took nothing away from the powerful charm exerted by his presence, and for Thomas those visits, those conversations full of the lore of animals, held forth the promise of new marvels.

Although Borkuny lay no more than three and a half kilometers away, this was his first trip there—now, as he accompanied Aunt Helen, who, just by chance needing to call on the medicine man for some sheep medicine, had decided to pay Mr. Bukowski a social visit. A sharp right at the crucifix, down the road from the commune, took one to Pogirai; veering slightly to the right before gradually straightening was the way to Balthazar's; the left led to Borkuny. Before them loomed the timberline, and behind the first row of trees, another world: a knoll sloping down into a glen, a clump of woods, a patch of swamp, a maze of trails, and a set of wagon ruts through bouquets of green. Behind a clump of fir, at the very bottom of the hollow, the Bukowski farmstead sprang suddenly into view. The small manor house was fronted by wooden porch columns overgrown with purple lilacs, partially obscuring an orchard, scattered alder, and rows of pine in ascending height—from saplings to full-grown. The inside of the house was rank with leather, the corners cluttered with stirrups, saddles, and harnesses. Scattered among the piles and decorating the walls were objects of an unfamiliar nature: horns, whistles, bags, cartridge belts . . . Thomas went from object to object, wanting to know the purpose of each, in one instance grabbing hold of a gun—Romuald had cracked it to make doubly sure the chambers were empty—and pulling on the trigger with a clicking sound that brought Romuald over on the run. "You shouldn't do that, Thomas. Might damage the firing pin." It was a 16-gauge shotgun, medium caliber (a 12-gauge, broad-barreled, was for big game; a 20-gauge, for small fowl). Though antiquated—Romuald had inherited the gun from his father—it could still fire with accuracy. The entire barrel was embossed with silver ornamentation called damascene.

The table was laid with a tablecloth and they were served by a young woman with head modestly lowered. Thomas could not, as they say, tear his eyes from her, enthralled no doubt by the range of colors: a whiteness of skin that shaded, subtly, by degrees, into a ruddiness of cheeks; a braid of dark gold; a furtive glance full of a mysterious, dark blue lambency. There was something friendly in her look, or at least that's what Thomas had supposed, until, just as they were going out the door, he overheard her whisper, much to his distress, the word *"shutas"* in Romuald's ear, this vulgar Lithuanian epithet being obviously at his expense. The visit was spoiled. Even so, from that moment on, almost in defiance, out of a desire to repair something, he felt a strange attraction for Borkuny.

Romuald climbed into the britska with them. It was only a stone's throw, he said, and his mother would be tickled. Borkuny: three farms without a name, situated so that Masiulis's property was wedged between Romuald's mother's property and his own. Built on a rise, the porch overlooked a small lake at the bottom of a marshy basin. Catherine Bukowski was profusely polite and apologetic. But what a face! Bristly, tuftlike warts, shaggy brows of a faded ash-gray—it made Squeaky's look positively ravishing by comparison. Her voice was a deep masculine bass. Her physiognomy, he was quick to notice, was quite congenial to her reign. The farming was supervised by her son Denis, a bachelor, now well into his prime. Servile to his mother's every command, he had a habit of cringing every

time she barked at him. A nondescript man—at least in
Thomas's eyes—except in one detail: a pair of boots that
reached not to the knees but higher, with soft leather
shanks laced with buckskin and sheathing the thighs cup-
like. A third son, Victor, an adolescent going on young
manhood, had bulging eyes, rough-cut features, and stuttered so badly that even when he stammered out a sentence
he partially swallowed the words, managing only the vow-
els, along with a guttural signifying this or that letter; so,
for example, "The hay's been took in," might come out
sounding like "Ge gay's geen gook gin."

Again the same table-setting ritual, the exhortations
to eat, the hot homemade mead passed around. "You're
man enough to drink, laddie." And: "Your health!" The
raising of mugs, the clinking of glass. Thomas took a sip
and the burning liquor made his eyes water; but Mrs.
Bukowski emptied her mug in one gurgling gulp (she was
back and forth to the demijohn, Thomas later discovered,
rummaging in the cupboard on some pretext, when—
gurgle-gurgle—she'd slam it shut, with face aglow). Denis
poured round after round, with Aunt Helen keeping pace,
squinting and sipping her drink in her own quiet way. The
voices grew louder, the jokes more obscure; he was surrounded by adults and their adult silliness, and it bored
him. They began to sing songs; Mrs. Bukowski broke off,
ran over to the wall, and took down a guitar that hung on
a tapestry embroidered with a kitten. Standing in the middle of the room, keeping time with her foot, in her deep
masculine bass she began wailing:

> Oh, Annie, honey, sweet li'l Annie,
> Why did Mama spank your fanny?
> Was it for the coffee, was it for the food,
> Or was it for fear of your maidenhood?
>
> Not for the coffee, not for the food,

And not for fear of my maidenhood.
Mama gave me such a drubbin'
'Cause I can't help from lovin'.

Spurred on by the applause, she sat down and, strumming on the strings of her guitar and turning up the whites of her eyes in a surge of emotion, she sang of Wurcell. It was a song well known to Thomas—how often he had heard Antonina sing it—but one that strained credulity. How could someone loved for forty years still be "young as a berry"? Because the words went like this:

Oh, Wurcell, Wurcell, I loved you strong,
Forty long years, heartless and cruel,
My life, my life you had to rule.
Forty long years or more,
So many letters, buried in the drawer.

So marry, if you will.
May the knot be tied in hell,
And may a prince take my hand
Still young as the berry
That grows in the dell.

In Mrs. Bukowski's mouth such sentimentality sounded comical, reaching outright hilarity when she came to the song "Hitch up the team, I must find my love," with its refrain of "I must—I must—I must—I must." Bad as it was, Thomas preferred this sort of entertainment to the ritual of gorging and guzzling. If he resigned himself to it, it was because he understood the need for patience: adults never were able to concentrate on one thing for very long. Only once was his curiosity kindled—when Denis told of having sighted a wolf that evening, a full-grown one, at the edge of the swamp, a safe bet there was a den nearby; but the moment Thomas began probing him for more details, their conversation was lost in the clamor of voices, guffaws, and clanking dishes. Still, there was a lot to be learned at Borkuny. He felt less inhibited here than he did, say, at other manors. Table manners were not something that required constant vigilance. What reassured him, no doubt, was the sight of black-rimmed fingernails and calloused palms, not to mention the deference with which both he and his aunt were treated.

Of the two Borkuny farmsteads, Romuald's held by far the greater interest. While at Romuald's mother's the talk was mostly of crop yields, plantings, and the market price of flax, at Romuald's it was all horses, hounds, and guns. Thomas could hardly wait to get back, the more because of some gnawing recollection. For what was wrong with one admiring glance—or was one obliged to pretend the attraction wasn't there?

They started back after sundown, his aunt working the horses with the reins, her spirits high, yet giving no outward sign of being in her cups. The sunset out here was distinguished by the myriad sounds assailing him from both sides of the trail, communing in a multitude of voices from out of the scrub and from off the dank marsh. That quacking there, that croaking—were those frogs, wild ducks, or some other species of bird? Some goatsuckers cut diagonally across their field of vision. He was awed by it—filled with reverential awe for this tumult in the dark, for this proliferation of creatures whose habits and routine tasks, now secret, demanded to be studied and tracked. Breaking up the land was the work of stupid men. To travel between open fields was to miss the beauty of it. If he'd had his way, he would have made plowing a criminal offense. Let there be wooded lands where animals could run wild! Immersed in such thoughts—in such dreams—he vowed that when he grew up he would found a kingdom— a forest kingdom, of course—to which only a select few would be admitted. Like who? People like Romuald, for example.

34

AN ENTERPRISE to which Thomas became passionately addicted at Borkuny—this after he had won consent to spend a few days there—might have seemed strange to some. There are creatures protected by the sort of fear to which humans are susceptible in their presence, a fear or revulsion not necessarily springing from any explicit danger, being rather the vestigial traces of ancient tacit conventions and rites. To challenge openly that word-defying sphere was commendable, or perhaps not altogether so, but it was done only on condition that there was no risk of some unforeseen reprisal. Thomas, having once mastered his fear, saw himself as a knight sworn to annihilating evil.

We have in mind adders. Borkuny abounded in them, so bold they came crawling right up to the front porch, even inside the house—Romuald had once jumped one under his bed. They had two habitats. By the trail leading down to the stream was a small copse of birch, thickly wooded and carpeted with dry leaves. The leafy bed provided excellent cover; once inside, there was no finding them. The trail was their sunning terrace, and most likely the route they used when they went out hunting for field mice. Their second city was on a strip of swamp, where they sequestered themselves in the mossy islands under the pine scrub. To get at these, Thomas had to slip into Romuald's long boots and venture into enemy territory, his heart clutching as he passed the mossy clumps that stood nearly face-high.

The adder, taxonomically known as *Vipera berus*, secreted a poison inflicting serious illness and sometimes death. The most popular cures against snakebite were incantations, cauterizing the wound with a red-hot iron, and alcohol consumed to the point of delirium, preferably all three at once. The Borkuny adders were gray in color, with a black wavy stripe down the back, though the woodland was inhabited by others, smaller in length, distinguishable by their tawny color and their dark-brown, zigzag stripe. Romuald explained how, instead of depositing her eggs like other reptiles, the adder bore her young suspended from a branch, her head poised and ready to devour her offspring, but how with their born sinuosity they always escaped into the grass in time. Although not tree climbers by nature, they were known to attack people from trees—one girl was bitten in the face while picking nuts. They were a real scourge in Borkuny, so it was not surprising that Thomas aspired to the role of exterminator.

From Romuald he heard talk of other snakes. Some twenty kilometers away, deep in the forest, stretched huge quagmires inaccessible to man (the snakes infesting them were enough of a deterrent). Black-bodied, with a red head, they were the first to attack, without warning, always going for the face or hands. Death came instantly, before one could gasp "Holy Jesus!" Thomas felt drawn to the place—if only to know what animals could survive out there. They say it was the favorite refuge of the elk when stalked.

When the weather turned hot, Romuald used to sleep in the barn, not to escape the heat so much—the house was amply shaded by shrubbery—as for the love of it, for the abundance of fresh air. It took Thomas a while, several nights of itching and scratching, before he got used to all the gnats and little bugs. To make up for it, there was the fragrance of newly mown hay, which quickly made him sleepy. And the mornings! To wake to a bright babble of birds, first invading his sleep, then growing stronger, the sun blazing through shingles alive with the scratching of tiny claws, the flutter of feathers . . . And the guessing game: just swallows, he would wonder, or something bigger like . . . wild pigeons? Then up early in the morning and off to the well with Romuald. Ahead of him: the joy of a long summer day. After a breakfast of whole-meal bread washed down with fresh milk, after the pulling on of boots (for precaution's sake), he was ready, hazel stick in hand, for the hunt.

Snake hunting was an art, requiring a stealthy approach to keep the prey, once surprised, from slithering away into the birch wood. Usually he caught sight of a few from a distance—lying like stretched-out whips, sunning themselves—then it was attack, on the run, banging with the stick, aiming always for the head, their bodies leaping, twisting, squirming, straining for the salvation of the brush, and he trying to cut off their retreat. With another stick—forked at one end, a small branch wedged in the fork—he would bear down on the snake's head, then slip out the branch. Pronged thus, the snake was borne back to the house, writhing in contortions: snakes were known for their endurance. The snake was then hung out to dry on the same stick. The dried ones were greatly in demand as a remedy against various cow ailments, especially among the river dwellers, the adder not being indigenous to that region.

Hunting in the swamp, where every bilberry or rosemary bush might conceal a adder, required even greater stealth—and skill, because the soft mossy matting cushioned every blow of the stick. Later (not that summer, but the next), out alone with the shotgun, he jumped a snake coiled some eight feet away from where he stood. He fired a barrel and the strangest thing happened: the snake vanished into thin air, the more astonishing since, at close range, the buckshot barely scatters.

Thomas's war with the adders did not imply that he

was free from prejudice, from the hideous shuddering sensation provoked by that unpredictable display of energy. The ripple of energy convulsing their ropelike bodies, the slimy crenulation lining their underbellies, the vertical slant of pupil—what a strange aberration of the animal kingdom! If it was true that birds were paralyzed by something inherent in their advance, then it was easy to understand, for their power seemed to reside outside them, as if they were merely an appendage, an instrument of something else.

Next spring, in the woodland surrounding Borkuny, Thomas was privileged to witness a rare spectacle: the mating ritual of adders. He was stopped in his tracks not by the observation of anything in particular. No, it was more like a vibration, an electrical discharge, a dance of lightning streaks on the ground. By the time he realized what it was, they were gone.

That summer, the first summer of his friendship with Romuald, he became adept at more than just snake hunting. He was granted—under Romuald's supervision, of course—the privilege of firing the double-barreled shotgun. First at the side of the barn—to get accustomed to the gun's kick—then at a live target. A screeching jay, a silencing finger, a sneaking up on tiptoes. Young and reckless, the bird, instead of taking cover, had perched on an exposed branch. A shot. Thomas came on the run, yelling. But as he picked it up by the feet, as the wings unfurled and a drop of blood beaded the jay's beak, he experienced a letdown he was not eager to acknowledge. But one had to be manly, to stifle any squeamishness, if one was to earn the title of hunter and naturalist.

Soon he was initiated into the hunter's workshop. He weighed out the shot with a metal gauge whenever Romuald made cartridges, and cleaned the barrels with steel wool soaked in oil so that they took on a mirrorlike sheen when peered through—as through binoculars—

under the light. He mastered, too, the art of skinning birds.

The chickens were forever being menaced by goshawks, whose attacks were signaled by Barbarka's frantic cries of "A bird! A bird!" (her description for any flying predator). One hawk, after being chased away, retreated as far as the nearest alder, there to survey the yard: he was soon a dead hawk. On him, Thomas served his apprenticeship. First came the incision down the middle, over breast and belly; then the skin was separated from the sides, a penknife serving to part the tissue joining skin and flesh. So far, so good; the real challenge came first with the tail (the tail feathers had to be left intact), followed by the legs (the claws had to be peeled off together with the skin). Once these obstacles were overcome, the skin was slipped off like a stocking, the tiny skull emptied of eyes and brain —a painstaking operation because one slip of the knife, one jerky move, and the delicate eyelids were ruined. After it was rubbed with ash and stuffed with oakum, the skin was left to dry. Wire and glass eyes were needed to stuff the bird in a sitting position.

The first time Thomas was a spectator to the sort of cunning exercised by men in the stalking of wild game was when he came to Borkuny for a few days to help with the mushroom picking. Mild mornings, pale blue skies, patches of cold dew and early frost blanketing the grass. In the pine grove, the one adjacent to the house, there were enough saffron milk cups in the moss flooring to fill baskets. Romuald stood nearby, a basket draped over one arm, his other hand clutching his gun strap; and in the pocket of his dolman, a little bone birdcall on a string—"Never can tell," he said, "it might come in handy." Birdcalls were carved usually from an owl's wing, sometimes from rabbit bone, the latter being less pure in tone. The bone one was good at imitating the trill of a hazel grouse, otherwise indistinguishable from the bark of the pine, its favorite sanctuary in times of danger. At a given signal,

Thomas held perfectly still, his jackknife poised against a mushroom stem, while a tremulous whistle pierced the silence of falling pine needles. Slowly, noiselessly, they slipped into the shadowy undergrowth. Again Romuald put the birdcall to his lips; he blew softly, knowingly, his fingers playing on the pipe's holes. Silence. Thomas was afraid his pounding heart would give them away. Then a reply—a hazel grouse, and another, closer. A feathery flurry, and there, dead ahead of them in the auburn lighting, silhouetted on a spruce branch, Thomas discerned a shadow pivoting its head, searching for its companion. Then an upward shifting of the arm, but so quick the shot and the report seemed to coincide; and when the smoke had cleared (when it came to gunpowder, Romuald swore only by the smoking, rather than nonsmoking kind), the hazel grouse lay lifeless under a tree, scarcely distinguishable from the bedding of dry needles.

Romuald was worthy of being admitted to the Kingdom to which normal mortals were denied access. Was worthy because the presence of wild animals excited him, made his cheek muscles quiver, made him vigilance personified, wholly oblivious to everything else. His housekeeper, Barbarka, on the other hand, belonged to the world of grownups, the more regrettable because she was so pretty, so childlike in appearance. It pained him to think there were actually people who went about blind to the things that mattered most. How bored they must be. To be fair, Barbarka spent much of her time tending the flower garden—and what exquisite flowers they were: whole beds of fragrant reseda, giant mallows, and rue, which she knew how to keep green all winter long, pinning it in her hair, like the other girls, before going to church. But that lambent stare of hers, so full of curiosity and scrutiny and ulterior motive . . . No, that bespoke something foreign, grown-up. Oh, Thomas had long forgiven her the insult, shamming indifference ever since; yet it needled him, that condescending way of hers, the way she had of making everything he touched—like cleaning rifle barrels—seem frivolous. If, just once, he could have elicited from her some sign of admiration, of respect . . . But no; to his trophies borne back from his snake-hunting she reacted with a disgusted "Phooey!" screwing up the corners of her mouth in a kind of sneer, as if the whole enterprise bordered on the indecent.

35

ROMUALD HAD four dogs: three hounds and a pointer. Zagray, smoky-hued, with yellow brows, bayed in a deep bass. Full grown, he was prized for his tenacity and endurance, virtues compensating for a sense of smell barely above average. Losing the scent, he never moiled aimlessly about, but moved in circles, deliberately, according to a plan. Dunay, a tenor, a dead ringer for the other, only leaner, was a dreamer, hence lacking in any aura of respect. One day deserving of praise and the next day worthless, he let his devotion be dictated by his mood, often only faking fickleness, as if to say: "I can bay with the best of them, but let the others track today—I have a headache." The dog combining a great heart with an infallible sense of smell was the yellow bitch Lutnia, descended from a race of Kostroma bloodhounds. Her pure gold eyes flashed violet-blue, she braced her handsome paws affectionately on Romuald's chest when she licked his face. The threesome was kept chained up for summer, because once unleashed they were apt to stage their own hunt, running the game between them. Gossamer on the trails promised liberation, though for the pointer, Karo, autumn was a time for meditation by the stove, a time for sticking one's nose under one's tail and taking stock of one's smell.

All week long, Thomas counted the days until Sunday. On Saturday, he rode out with his aunt, who headed back the same evening, leaving Thomas to spend the night at Borkuny. Tense with excitement, he twisted and turned, kicked off his covers, and kept being prickled by the straw, but he soon fell into a deep sleep, warmed by the weight of his sheepskin coat, which someone had draped over him. He was awakened in the dark, around dawn, by a rapping on the window. Two faces, those of Denis and Victor, were flattened against the pane. They came inside, yawning. A groggy Barbarka, her uncombed hair spilling down over her shoulders, brought in a lantern with a smudged chimney, got a fire going in the kitchen, and rustled up some potato pancakes. Through the fog outside came the sound of thick drops dripping from the branches brushing the porch.

The brothers each drank one round at breakfast. "Bagaga, go gus go gnee," Victor insisted, which translated as "Barbarka, show us your knee"—a sign of hunter's good luck—to which the housekeeper responded with a thumbed nose. The dogs went wild on their leashes. Thomas was given charge of Dunay, and had to strain backward with all his might to keep him from breaking into a trot. They took the trail down to the stream, filed across the footbridge, and stepped onto the preserve. The forester was Romuald's friend and let him—with one eye closed—do a fair amount of poaching.

An immense silence. The morning fog had begun to lift, and with the lifting emerged a forest floor rank with wet grass and laced with russet-matted trails. Romuald's horn echoed far and wide, his cheeks swelling and his eyes reddening from exertion. With effort, if he worked at it, Thomas could get it to make sounds, but never anything like a tune.

Autumnal smells, the origin of which, the blendings of which lay beyond his or any other man's power to describe: the rot of leaves and needles; the dank effluvium of fungi and white filaments embedded in black, beneath the slime of decaying, peeling debris. They were surrounded by good hunting grounds. Glades broken up by brushlike rows of pine, a lane skirting the forest flank, with another, moss-covered, path-lined, diagonally across from it. Wild game was a slave to old habits. Flushed out of hiding, it tried to ward off its attackers by describing a circle, aiming for more familiar trails and crossings, its direction betrayed by the baying of the hounds. A hunter had only to guess the right crossing and be there in time. Distracted by the dogs at its back, unsuspecting of any danger ahead, it would then charge straight into his sights.

Thomas was not carrying a gun; he was there as a lowly apprentice. His instructions were to stay close to Romuald. The moment they were unleashed, the whining dogs bolted into the brush. Zagray reemerged once, nose to the ground, and moiled about with an inquisitive look. "Denis, you take the lane," said Romuald. "Vick, you get up to Red Meadow. Tommy and I'll stay here." The men receded into the distance, the gun barrels strapped to their shoulders slowly fading behind the trees. "Watch Lutnia flush 'im," Romuald predicted.

A woodpecker racket overhead, a scraping against bark. Suddenly, from far off, a dog's voice, thin and high-pitched. *"Aï, aï!"* "Didn't I tell you? Lutnia!" A lull. Then once again: *"Aï, aï!"* "She's picked it up, but it's a weak 'un, she's gonter have to work at it." It was then that Thomas, for the first time in his life, heard the music of the hounds. To the steady *"Arf, arf, arf, arf,"* was joined another voice. "Dunay!" Romuald shouted, shifting gun from shoulder. Zagray's powerful bass came at long intervals now. Thomas was amazed that such music could come from the throats of dogs, a choir muffled by distance, reverberating deep within the forest. "They jumped a hare. But he won't come out here. Come on, Tommy—run!" and Thomas chased after Romuald, at first keeping up with him, then falling back, panting his lungs out. They branched off from the lane, maneuvered through the hazel, dropped down into a ravine, and scrambled up a bank. "There—" Romuald pointed out Thomas's stand, a young spruce, as, taut of neck, shotgun in hand, he himself waited motionlessly out in the middle. The ridge, brown with needles, tapered down into a green gully, commanding a perfect view of it, along with a tawny strip framed by forest walls. The baying rose to the left of them, full of desire and courage and wildness—and then abated. *"Aï, aï,"* Lutnia wailed, still trying to pick up the scent.

Nothing coming their way . . . Wait—there it was! It looked mammoth, almost red against the green, as it slipped into the pocket opposite them. With mouth agape, glad in that instant to be without a gun, Thomas was gripped by hunter's fever as the animal, growing in stature, advanced; with eyes transfixed, his mouth still wide open, he was jolted by a shot. The hare went straight up, twisted in the air, and then it was over except for a convulsive twitching of the paws. Thomas was the first to get there. His gun back on his shoulder, Romuald strode up leisurely, grinning all the way. But the dogs had beaten him to it. Dunay looked up at the boy with a mouth full of fur. Romuald took out his knife, sliced off the hind paws, and tossed them to the hounds, giving Dunay a pat or two of approval; then he lit up. "That Dunay! He'd eat the wounded ones alive."

Thomas tried to get Romuald to explain how he knew where to get into position. Romuald laughed. "Got to play it smart. If they jumped him over there"—he pointed to the hazel ravine—"and he came back around this way"— he pointed to the left—"then he had to come out here. He'll always backtrack to where he lives."

He called in Denis and Victor with the horn, and he and the boy sat down on a couple of stumps. A pale November sun was burning a path through the mist. Thomas was curious to know what other game they were likely to meet.

"A buck. A fox maybe, but don't count on it. Got too much sense, a fox has."

As soon as the others came out of the brush, parting the damp pine branches, they held council, then moved out along the ridge, winding through the terraced, steplike trails braced by rocks. As they were making their way, leisurely, shooting the breeze, the dogs let out a powerful wail full of wounded pride. *"Aï, aï . . ."* They went for their guns. "They got it on the run," Denis yelled. Just then Thomas saw a hare's tail flit across the slope, the elongated shapes of the dogs right behind it. "Out of range!" Romuald said. "No sense chasin' now." And he told of some hunters who, seeing their dogs were so far out they were no longer within earshot, spread out under a tree for a game of cards, and of how the hare came bounding right down the middle, scattering their hands. The anecdote made Thomas indignant, as it bespoke an irreverent attitude toward the best, the most essential of tasks. He was gnawed by a suspicion, not without foundation, that for some people hunting meant not much more than vodka and cards, that it was just another idle pastime.

The ferocious whining subsided to a normal baying. The men spread out on the stands, taking their time about it, and the screeching of jays testified to the intrusion. Thomas had his gaze fixed to the line made by the trail in front of him, when a couple of shots rang out, echoing in the trees' whispering murmur. "Denis"—Thomas surmised. Two shots meant a double-barrel, and Victor was toting a single-barreled Berdan.

Around a bend in the trail, from behind some trunks, loomed a spectacle in miniature: Denis, a hare at his feet, surrounded by moiling dogs. It was evident, from Romuald's gentle needling, that Denis's first shot had gone wide, that he'd hit it only on the second. Romuald pulled out a felt-covered flask, jokingly offered Thomas a swig, who declined, secretly wondering whether the liquid stuff was befitting the honor of Romuald the Magnificent.

"Aw, Tommy, those shoes of yours are goners." As a matter of fact, the shoes he had on—they happened to be his Sunday shoes—were not the best for hiking in the wet grass. Now that he was almost initiated, he was entitled to wear boots, the long-shanked kind, preferably a pair that laced all the way up to the knees, if there was no chance of his owning a pair like Denis's hip boots. The one person likely to be moved by such a request was Grandpa, as neither his grandmother nor his aunt would be very sympathetic—for reasons of frugality alone.

36

GRANDFATHER, having never really explored the library before now—before his grandson began rifling the bookshelves—browsed through the tomes of Narbutt's *The History of Lithuania*. On the advice of his grandfather, Thomas brought the volumes over to Joseph the Black's place, whence they passed into the hands of Father Monkiewicz. No doubt both, each according to his interests, were rewarded for their efforts. The pastor gruffly cleared his throat and sat up in his chair as he read of the sheer abundance of gods and goddesses once worshipped in the land; of the familiar superstitions at whose extirpation he had so diligently worked. There was no telling how injurious such books could be to the soul. A person might close the book, take off his glasses, and turn to other tasks, when suddenly, out of nowhere, the image of Ragutis sprang to mind, as vividly as if freshly unearthed from forest sands—Ragutis, that corpulent idol of liquor and lusty living, hewn from oak, leering mischievously, his giant feet clad in clogs, standing there unsupported in all his assiduously carved indecency—*in naturalibus*. And once conceived, there was no getting rid of him.

Some chapters like those dealing with the goddess Liethua, guardian protector of freedom, compared by the author to Freya of the Scandinavians, seemed expressly written for Joseph. But not a trace, not a single grain of dust remained of Lejčis, impaled or hung by the lords, even though independence had, centuries later, been restored to his native land. Nor would any trace remain, if not for a name mentioned in a scrap of parchment, a royal charter dating from A.D. 1483. By said charter, the nobleman Rynwid had been granted land "in reward for suppressing an insurrection of serfs claiming more freedom than that accorded them by law, and for taking captive their leader, the one called Lejčis, who, in wanton disregard for the royal majesty and sovereignty, did brazenly flout the King in the name of Liethua's pagan freedom."

In 1805, the historian Narbutt, a nobleman like Rynwid and Surkont, gave his timepiece to a man who, at a country fair, aroused his curiosity by reciting for him the words of an ancient dirge addressed to the goddess Liethua. "Little Liethua," it ran, "precious freedom! Hidden in the sky, where are you? Is death our only refuge? Wherever a poor man turns—to the east or to the west— naught but misery, duress, and slavery. The great earth is flooded with sweat, with the blood of wounds. Little Liethua, precious freedom, step down from heaven, take pity on us." Clearly, this was music for Joseph's ears. And so, brooking no quarter, they went on debating the merits of that book in a room at the rectory, to the ticking of a clock and in full view of the dahlias spying through the window. The dahlias were from a lovely garden planted once upon a time by Magdalena, a garden now sorely in need of pruning.

One autumnal afternoon, Joseph, less given to nostalgia since becoming privy to certain libelous facts in the town, was reciting the litany of his grievances while the pastor, his arms folded on his paunch, his eyes half shut, sat and listened. There was nothing remarkable or unusual in this recitation, which belonged to the ritual of their regular confabulations, but this time Joseph was assailed by doubts, these having to do with the manner of reprisal.

Joseph finished calculating the acreage of Surkont's farmland and briefed him on what he had heard in the town. If the man considered to be a model of virtue was not above such trickery, well, that was worth at least a shrug. "What's he need it for? He can't take it with him to the grave, can he? And if they all find loopholes, who'll get the land? Don't they see their days are numbered? The Latvians were wise in leaving them only a hundred acres."

The priest muttered that it was not the number of acres as much as the corruption, the way officials kowtowed to the rich. Joseph: It's up to the villages to decide whose and how much land to confiscate. The priest: That would be to invite anarchy. Maybe so, but *something* had to be done.

Joseph could not condone the practice of informing, nor any other method that might have gone by a different name but which amounted to the same thing in the end— and if, then only as a last resort. So the choice was between sinning through indifference and doing one's duty, however bad the consequences. Nor could one ignore the effects on the next of kin. But, then, there was no talk of confiscating the whole estate, much less of killing or jailing him; he would just own a little less, that was all.

This being the general gist of his words, Joseph asked the priest for his opinion.

Father Monkiewicz reflected, stroked his bald patch, then hit on a solution. "Didn't Surkont promise to donate some lumber for the school?"

"He did, but not until the first frost."

"If he and the other farm owners live up to their promise, how much wood will you still be short?"

"Thirty cords, more or less."

"Hm..."

It was a "hm" rife with implications. Such a solution had never occurred to Joseph, and he was quick to seize on it. He had only to sit down with Surkont, insinuate that he was wise to him, make him see that he was cornered. That would put the old man in a bargaining mood, force him to make certain concessions, and the thirty cords would be as good as delivered.

He asked no more questions, and they moved on to politics; that is, to the age-old debate of whether, given the choice of siding with the Poles against the Knights, or with the Knights against the Poles, the Grand Duke could have saved the country. A controversy not without relevance when one stopped to ponder the consequences of the first alternative. Take only the case of Misia, who would have died rather than admit to being a Lithuanian. Or Grandfather Surkont and the thousands of others like him. Such were the ripples of history, still spreading outward centuries later.

"Any news of the boy's father?" asked the priest.

"What's there to report? He's not coming back. And if he does, he's sure to land in prison for serving in their army. No, he'll settle there and send for the boy."

The priest sighed. "They're ashamed of belonging to such a small country. They're too in love with culture, big cities. But Narbutt wasn't ashamed—except that in those days people didn't think of their nationality the way we do . . ."

"People are crazy, if you ask me."

The priest shook his head. "Things are so mixed up today. Old lady Dilbin, Thomas's grandmother, now she's a German by descent. But in Prussia you find both Polish and Lithuanian names, and yet they're Germans. As long as it doesn't spell disaster."

Several months passed before Joseph returned Narbutt's *History*, the discussions prompted by it leaving nary a trace, neither on the leather binding nor in any of the margins of its stiff pages. Restored to its bookcase, the work was again left at the mercy of creeping mildew, to the scurrying of insects that exult in inhabiting dank and dark places.

Joseph never did sit Surkont down and offer him silence in exchange for the lumber, though he long entertained such a notion. It had not been an easy decision: at one end of the scale was the school, a more immediate goal; at the other, the principle of the thing, that and the welfare of the cottagers, who stood to benefit most from the redistribution. Principle had prevailed. Not that this had prescribed the proper course of action. The first course: to tell Surkont right to his face and threaten exposing him to the authorities, because what was wrong was wrong. All-out war, in other words. The second: to stool on him. And the third: to wait and see what came of all the sleight-of-hand maneuvering. This last course was most to his liking, since haste was the enemy of reason and patience had a way of rectifying many wrongs.

37

Thomas had a kingdom all his own—a paper kingdom, admittedly, but one that could be assembled and reassembled at will. The inspiration for it came from the rolls of paper which Grandfather and Aunt Helen (now a frequent visitor at the manor) periodically unrolled on the table—sheets embellished with watercolor designs, rectangles of all sizes, and boundary lines making up the property map of Gine. The bright, smoothly executed color planes showed through the paper.

Thomas's kingdom, ringed by quagmires inhabited by the red-hooded snake, was absolutely impenetrable. Originally, it was to have been entirely forest, but on second thought he decided to relieve the landscape with meadows painted a bright green. No roads cut through the forest—how could a virgin forest be traversed by a road?—leaving the riverways, laced with blue strips of canals, and lakes as the only arteries. Those who were allowed access—by special invitation, of course—entered by way of secret passages marked through the swamps. All the kingdom's inhabitants—a handful at most, the land being primarily at the disposal of such animals as the bison, the elk, and the bear—lived exclusively off the land.

The arrival of the autumnal chill deprived him of his table, which was shifted to the wing from that part of the house closed off for the winter. But the various family conferences held around the table, where people huddled over maps and the word "reform" was a constant refrain, coupled with the anxiety aroused by Aunt Helen's nosy intrusions, soon forced him to transfer his mapmaking and other activities to a little table in Grandmother Dilbin's room. There he was not disturbed by anyone, least of all by his grandmother, who was mostly bedridden, though he had to pay the price of being made a captive of her incessant bellyaching: she was neglected, alone among strangers, wasting away in some godforsaken hole, never to see her sons again . . . Nor did she spare the Lithuanians for their black ingratitude. Just let Constantine and Theodore and the Polish army stop fighting the Bolsheviks—ha, then they'd see what was left of their Lithuania! And how had they been rewarded, Thomas's father and uncle? By being denied a few days' furlough in their native land, like a couple of common criminals! Their letters reached them by way of Latvia—late, naturally—all personal correspondence being banned between Poland and Lithuania. The song-and-dance routines that went into getting those letters! The cunning she had used in getting someone to ride to the post office if she had no way of going to town herself. Nor was she above shamming some fatal illness to have Dr. Kohn summoned to the house, no matter how miserable the weather. And later, her eyes blinking and her cheeks burning, he watched her fingers tremble as they tore open the letters.

Thomas was unable to take her seriously; he paid little attention to her whining, being somehow rankled by her constant brooding over Constantine—the "black sheep," as Grandmother Misia and his aunt used to call him. Fresh out of Officers' Training School, Constantine was now a career officer, a lieutenant in a Uhlan regiment, though no doubt he had enrolled under false pretenses, having completed only three years of the mandatory secondary education. Her exaltation of her son bordered on the comical, as did her imprecations at being stuck in Gine, at having to live off the charity of the Surkonts, the irregular meals, the lack of companionship, the way Antonina ruled the household . . . She even complained about the homegrown tobacco, which Thomas took great pleasure in rolling and cutting—the cigarettes achieved a pleasing shape the moment the loose ends sticking out of the cartridge were trimmed with scissors—and neatly arranging for her in a little box. If he was attentive, it was only when she spoke of his mother, of how when she returned, Grandmother would take them both away, and how wonderful that would be.

Two or three days out of the week, Thomas traipsed into the village for his lessons with Joseph. He exerted himself especially at handwriting, the praise of his teacher being of greater consequence than the deprecation heaped on him by his grandmother and aunt. Joseph, sitting with his elbows propped on the table, his shoulders hunched together, the Adam's apple in his sinewy throat bobbing up and down, had a fixity about him, an aura of dependability. Perhaps this was what Thomas needed most—someone to say this was right and that was wrong, and knowing it had to be so.

Whenever they were visited by Lithuanians on official business, Grandmother Misia and Aunt Helen ran for cover: to show them too much hospitality would have been a breach of decorum, would have been to risk social opprobrium by associating with those yokels—one of their favorite epithets—masquerading as officials. Thomas used to watch through the half-open door as his grandfather, seemingly for the sake of diplomacy, drank just to whet their appetite. Later, Grandfather and the officials would ride out to the granary, where Pakenas loaded their britska with one or two sacks of oats for the horses.

The more frequent the visits, the more intense became the "business talks," from which not even Misia, rocking sideways in front of the tiled stove, remained aloof. It was "business," too, which sent Grandfather on frequent trips to the city. Before leaving, he cached some money and documents in a little canvas pouch, strung it around his neck, and, just to be safe, pinned it to his warm under-shirt. Over this went a waistcoat and woolen jacket. A knotted cravat, looped with an elastic neckband, was then wedged between the corners of his stiff shirt collar. A watch chain spanned the pockets of his waistcoat.

Inspired by his trips to Borkuny, Thomas, after re-treating to his grandmother's room or, when he could bear her lamentations no more, to the dining-room lamp, began compiling a notebook, or rather a scrapbook, having the shape and feel of an actual book. Cutting sheets of paper to size, he glued the margins together and bound them with a cardboard cover inscribed with the word *Birds*. Anyone taking the liberty to pry (which no one ever did, not want-ing to risk Thomas's contempt, since confidentiality was the very heart and soul of the enterprise) would have found a series of headings, capitalized and underlined, fol-lowed by ornithological descriptions in small-case letters. Mastering his tendency to scribble—tongue out, pen la-boriously at work—was no small feat. But in the end his efforts were rewarded: the execution, as a whole, was flaw-less.

Take the section on woodpeckers. Naturally, the one that held him in the greatest thrall was the large, speckled woodpecker, frequently sighted in the park in winter. This large, redheaded woodpecker was a lone species, hence:

"The dappled woodpecker—*Picus leucotos L.*" And underneath: "Inhabits deciduous forests with lots of rot-ting trees and ancient coniferous forests. Winters near human habitations."

Or:

"The black woodpecker—*Picus martius L.* Largest of the woodpecker family. Black with a red patch on the head. Nests in pine or birch forests."

Thomas had spotted a black woodpecker at Borkuny —not close up, since it was impossible to view at close range, but as it streaked among the birch trunks, its shrill *kri-kri-kri* carrying.

He had no way of knowing, of course, that the *L.*, or Latinized "Linni," was in honor of the Swedish naturalist Linnaeus, the first bird taxonomist. Yet he scrupulously guarded against allowing any discrepancies between other taxonomies and his own, the Latin names appealing to him because of their sonority: *Emberiza citrinella* for yellowhammer, *Turdus pilaris* for fieldfare, *Garrulus glandarius* for jay, and so on. Some of the names were conspicuous for their proliferation of letters, forcing his eyes to jump continuously from his notebook to the antiquated ornithology at his elbow. Even the longer names, if repeated often enough, acquired a pleasant lilt, one of them, that of the common nutcracker, being absolutely magical: *Nucifraga caryocatactes*.

The notebook proved that Thomas had the gift of concentrating on things that excited him. To name a bird, to case it in letters, was tantamount to owning it forever. The endless multiplicity of colors, shadings, mating calls, trills, wing sounds . . . Turning the pages, he had them all before him, at his command, affecting and ordering the plenitude of things that were. In reality, everything about birds gave rise to unease. Was it enough, he wondered, to verify their existence? The way the light modulated their feathers in flight, the warm, yellow flesh lining the bills of the young feeding in deeply sequestered nests, suffused him with a feeling of communion. Yet, for many, they were little more than a mobile decoration, scarcely worthy of scrutiny, whereas, surrounded by such wonders on earth, people should have consecrated their whole lives to contemplating only one thing: felicity.

Such, roughly speaking, were Thomas's thoughts, and neither the "Reform" nor any "business matters" could compete, even though the passion aroused by their constant iteration gave him pause: "Pogirai," "Balthazar,"

"the meadowland" . . . He was big enough and bright
enough to grasp what was happening, but his heart just
wasn't in it. He surely wished his grandfather luck, but he
was decidedly not in favor of his holding council with
Aunt Helen.

38

❧❦❧❦❧❦

BALTHAZAR WAS gaining weight, the afflic-
tions of the soul giving rise to this condition being sometimes more acute than those that cause a man to lose
weight. When he first heard about the famous Rabbi of
Šilelai, he had sneered, but his laughter soon hardened into
fear: who was he to refuse help that might have been
heaven-sent? He waited until the roads were fit for traveling by sleigh. Then the first snowfall turned to ice. Numb
with cold, Balthazar stopped off at a pothouse, got stone
drunk, and slept it off on a bench. Came morning, a hang-
over, back on the road, and telegraph poles—so stark and
stiff they pained the eye—aswirl with billowing snow all
the way to Šilelai. The Rabbi's house was sprawling, had
a sagging wooden roof, and was situated a little below street
level and fronted by a sloping yard. In the hallway he was
immediately beset by three or four men—the whole place
swarmed with men, both young and old. Where from, what
brought him here? He dumped his whip in the corner,
undid his sheepskin, dug into his pockets for some money,
and counted out the amount he had been told was fitting.
That done, he was whisked into a room where a bearded
man in a skullcap sat facing him from behind a desk, inscribing something in a large book. He informed Balthazar
that he was not the Rabbi but that he, Balthazar, was to lay

bare the reasons for his visit, and that he, the Rabbi's assistant, would convey them to the Rabbi, because that was how it was done. Balthazar balked. Gestures of confusion, a scratching of a scruffy forelock, a look of helplessness. He still believed, in spite of everything, in that ray of light, transfixing and illuminating him. But *speak*? The moment he opened his mouth, the mere sound of his voice would ring false, and how to find the words, how to unburden his soul before some stranger, a Jew, who never let up with his pen, and who even took his sweet time offering him a seat? Then Balthazar began to babble, and this babbling only made manifest that he was without a place to call his own, alive yet not alive, doomed without the counsel of a saintly man. The Jew put aside his pen and fingered his beard.

"You have a farm?" he asked. "A wife, children?" And: "Your sins, they make life difficult, no? What kind of sins? Big sins?"

Balthazar, though he would have been hard put to state whence his unease came—from sins, or fear, or something else—assented.

"You pray to God?" the Jew went on with the interrogation.

This last question gave him pause. If someone ached, he wanted to get better, and it was up to God to heal. But what if He wasn't in the mood? If He was too far out of reach? Balthazar went to church, so he nodded: yes, he prayed.

He later waited in the hallway, his back against the wall, a bystander to all the comings and goings, to the continual shaking of snow from boots. Soon the pandemonium swelled, thickening with incomprehensible palaver and frantic gesticulations. Suddenly a shriek from the back, a stampede into the reception room—the same one —an opening of doors, a squeezing of bodies; and Balthazar, caught up in the crush, was flung into a long chamber converging toward a black table at the far end. Over the clamor and commotion and wild vociferations came a commanding "Shh!" which was taken up by one and all: "Shh! Shh!"

The Rabbi, trailed by his bearded secretary, entered through a side door. An elfin figure with girlish features—a double for St. Catherine's face in the picture that hung in the church in Gine. His cheeks were adorned with fleecy blond curls; his apparel, dark and somber. The collar stud of his undershirt glinted underneath and his head was covered by a silken skullcap. Demure of mien, eyes downcast. The moment his assistant motioned for Balthazar to come forward, the eyelids rose, the gaze turned piercing. He fixed him with a long stare, cocked his head, and stroked the lapel of his frock coat. In the Rabbi's presence, Balthazar felt the full weight of his impotent mass.

His eyes still fixed on Balthazar, the Rabbi uttered a few words in their language, unleashing a fury of whispers, a rocking and reeling at Balthazar's back, until they were silenced with a "Shh! Shh!"

"He says, 'No—man—is—good,' " the Rabbi's secretary translated into Lithuanian.

The Rabbi's voice again purled softly behind the table.

"He says, 'Whatever—wrong—you—have—committed—man—that—and—only—that—is—your—fate.' "

Balthazar felt a surging at his back as he attended, in a shushing silence fraught with expectation, to the bearded man's words.

"He says, 'Do—not—curse—your—fate—man—for—whoever—thinks—he—has—another—and—not—his—own—is—lost—and—will—be—damned—forever. Think—not—of—the—life—that—might—have—been—for—such—a—life—would—not—have—been—yours.' " He stopped speaking.

Balthazar knew that the audience was over; someone else stood before the Rabbi and his words were now addressed to him. Jostling his way through the crowd, Balthazar stormed out of the house in a rage. Was this what he had traveled twenty kilometers through the freezing cold for? Damn these Jews. And damn his own gullibility. But by the time his boot was slung over the lower crossbar and furrowing a groove through the white, anger had given way to disappointment. An hour-long sermon or a few words—what was the difference? It was the emptiness of it all, the absence that made a man want to howl: no angels' trumpets, no fiery tongues, no swords forked like fangs . . . All right, he was homeward bound, a livid blue forest in the distance, clouds overhead . . . What else was there to say? He had been born, he would die, and he would have to bear his burden. Priest or rabbi—it was the same old rigmarole, never getting to the heart of it . . . Now, if a giant head were to peer out from behind the horizon and huff and puff and suck up everything in one furious rush of air . . . But nothing doing. So why should he be sore at the Jew? He was just a man, no better and no worse . . . But show me the man who *could* do something. A man could have his guts torn apart, could ache like hell, and here they'd come, preaching their words of comfort, blah-blah-blah, the same with all their machines, inventions . . . But they didn't know anything except "he was born and he died."

Gradually he was willing to admit to having gained some wisdom at Šilelai. The Rabbi's first utterance had even filled him with hope. Maybe everybody was troubled and repentant but was afraid to admit it. Wouldn't it be easier if people confessed to one another? No man is good? What about those with small sins? Was it enough to be without sin? Ooo, that Jew wasn't so dumb . . .

He took off his gloves and rolled a cigarette. The horse moved briskly along, the harness bells tinkled in the emptiness of space. A hare sprang out from behind a bed of willows, bounded along a frozen brook. Dusk fell, over-taking him in the forest, but not so abruptly that his eyes couldn't make out the notches on the pine trunks. Trees marked for cutting. He had read about the big government sale to England. There was a pine with no notch. Too crooked. It had a good straight trunk before lurching to one side and shooting up like a ship's mast. Maybe that was the sort of fate the Rabbi had in mind. A pine couldn't start over; it had to start from what it was, what it had become, bent and all. Then it could grow tall and straight. No more than a man could start again from scratch.

He bore down with the whip, somehow unconsoled. A man was not a tree; a tree knew at least what it had to have—light. The trouble is, you think you're growing straight, but you're not. Life going one way, and you going back and forth, trying to change it. Straight as a bullet, you think; not until it's too late do you see it's not climbing straight but curving. So much for that Jewish wisdom of theirs.

Firmly resolved not to stop along the way, Balthazar began pulling on the reins as soon as he saw snowy clumps sparkling in the light of the tavern windows. The horses hitched to the corner of the building worked their feed bags up and down, their harness bells tinkling with every toss of the head. No one's fate but his own. So be it. He clutched the door handle. Did he go inside? He went inside.

39

If ONE accepted the thesis that the preference shown by devils for frock coats and knee stockings was an expression of their eighteenth-century sympathies, then the Land Reform, that taking of land from some and the giving of it to others, must have lain beyond the compass of their expertise. The devil having custody of Balthazar—a crow strutting around a wounded rabbit—must have felt duty-bound to take inventory. The demands of accuracy, therefore, compel us to give an exact rendering.

An inventory of Surkont's landholdings would have looked as follows:

Arable land	271.2 acres
Pasturage along the Issa, fallow land, etc.	19.7 "
Disputed pasturage adjoining Pogirai	75.0 "
Timberland, grassland, and land cleared by Balthazar	105.0 "
Total	470.9 "

The newly instituted Land Reform meant that all lands in excess of 200 acres were to be distributed among the landless peasants—at a rate of indemnity so low as to be almost negligible. Surkont—or rather his daughter, mindful of her own interests—had found a loophole: under the law, farm properties could be divided among family members, up to 200 acres per household head, provided the estates were independently managed and supported structures. Surkont decided to pacify the government with the seventy-five acres of disputed land, dividing the remaining 395.9 acres between Helen and himself. But what about the deadline? The statute expressly prohibited any land divisions after the stipulated deadline. One need only solicit the cooperation of certain civil servants, not immune to blandishments of one sort or another, to have an older title "mistakenly" recorded in the books. And soliciting it he was.

There was one hitch: the forest. Under the terms of the Reform, all timberland was to become state property. So what did Surkont do? He had the forest land recorded as grassland. It all depended on how the assessors looked at it, on whether they kept their eyes to the ground or glanced up at the unusual blades of grass. Not much was left of the oak forest, anyway—a few dark-shaded groves of young hornbeam, a sprinkling of fir saplings, and a lot of swamp clearings. Still, the land bordered on a state forest, stretching dozens of kilometers, and that made it all the riskier . . .

Two farms: his own and Helen's. But if another farm —where? It was Balthazar who, quite unexpectedly, came to their assistance. In indulging Balthazar his lifelong dream, Surkont was guided less by self-interest than by a weakness for the boy—Balthazar, whether at thirty or forty, was still boyish-looking. The forester's cottage would be the loophole.

This, in outline, was the situation and the principal strategy. The best beer, along with that aromatic homemade brew laced with nine varieties of forest herbs, now graced Balthazar's table every time Helen Juchniewicz came to call. But Balthazar knew her well enough to keep a vigilant eye on her, all the while grinning that goodnatured smile of his. Coyly, in her own sweet way, she was prying—into the barn, the crib. Women of her kind were the trickiest to handle.

There are those who believe the devil to be nothing more than a hallucination, a manifestation of inner turmoil. If that is so, then the world must appear to them an even more incomprehensible place, since hallucinations are the province of humans. Even if we were to grant, for the sake of argument, that the affectionate little creature promenading about the table, jauntily sidestepping the streaks of brew described by Balthazar's finger, owed its existence to an alcoholic stupor, what would that prove?

There were days when the old gaiety returned, when a whistling Balthazar came up behind the plow—when suddenly a wrenching of the gut announced some imminent terror. It was always like this: one, two steps out of bounds, and some external force was there to repel him, drive him back. Yes, external: the pain he felt was not, could not have been a part of himself; deep down, he was still the same happy-go-lucky Balthazar; whatever had him on the run was attacking from the outside. And the terror came from the certitude that it was not his own doing, that it was not he who was summoning a subtlety of reasoning in times of despair, but it was the work of an otherworldly clairvoyance. Even his foolishness was a part of the jinx, and his tormentor knew how to make the most of it.

"So there you have it, Balthazar," he said. "One life. Millions of people with millions of worries. And you? Surkont, Helen Juchniewicz, the property, that shooting accident . . . A drop in the bucket. Why you? You could have landed anywhere, like a falling star. But you had to land here. And you won't be born a second time."

"The Rabbi was speaking the truth."

"The truth? Look at you, you're chewing your knuckles over that Juchniewicz woman; you're worried sick she's going to chuck you out . . . and you're worried just because you're so worried. If only you could accept your fate—but you can't. The Rabbi, though, he had you pegged. A wise and experienced man, that Rabbi. But, then, were you really so hard to figure out? The dirty Balthazar feels sorry for the clean Balthazar. Only there's no such person."

His fingers dug into the table. Oh, he was just aching to swing away, to tear the place apart, to become fire or stone!

"Okay, so knock the table over. Then what? That's not what you really want; you've got questions. Go ahead —ask them, get it off your chest. You drink it away; it takes your mind off things—but only for so long, for as long as the stuff burns your throat. Do you want to know, or don't you?"

Balthazar slumped down onto the table, both elbows

spread out wide, at the mercy of some weak but predacious weasel.

"If you've done something, was it because you couldn't do otherwise? That's what's hounding you, isn't it? I am what I am because of what I did. At such and such a time, in such and such a way. But why did I act that way? Was it because I was always what I am now? Is that it?"

In the presence scrutinizing him from afar, assuming a multitude of faces yet itself remaining constant, he assented.

"What are you moping about? That you're bad seed? That a stalk of wheat didn't sprout from nettles?"

"That must be it."

"Take an oak. Any oak in the forest. You look at it standing there, and what do you think? That it's where it ought to be, that place and no other. Right?"

"Right."

"But supposing the acorn was dug up and eaten by a wild pig. Would you still look down at the ground and say an oak tree belonged there?"

Balthazar played with the loose strands of his unruly hair, winding them around his finger.

"No. Why not? Because once a thing is, it's like it had to be that way always, always and forever. Same as with a man. Later you'll swear you just couldn't have gone into town to squeal on him . . ."

"I won't turn informer."

"The good Balthazar loves Surkont. Not really, you're just scared it could backfire—you know he's been greasing their palms—he might find out, and leave you at the mercy of his daughter . . . And you're scared that if you win, they'll annex the forest. Okay, they might make you a forester, but they're bound to ask, 'Why so much land, Balthazar?' Don't try to lie. And don't think cursing your fate will get you off the hook."

"I never know why I do anything. Not even why I sent the matchmakers that time. Or that Russian. I didn't have to kill him; I could have given him a good scare. Can't remember why."

"Ahhh . . . !"

Balthazar's cry was the cry that wells up from inside and that nothing can ever suppress or overcome or contend with. And the crime of it is, we go on tearing leaves from the calendar, pulling on our boots, testing our arm muscles, living . . . And that gnawing recollection of past deeds, but without recollection of the reasons. Either these deeds are ours, issuing from our very being, immutable, signifying a sickening burden, a stench in the skin, or they are the work of some masked perpetrator, the more terrifying since that means they are beyond getting rid of, that they are part of a hideous malediction.

Balthazar foresaw that Surkont would succeed. Out of fatigue, distrusting his own nature and all those subterranean forces impersonating us, he chose apathy. Inertia gave fewer causes for regret later on. If his own life had gone foul, why shouldn't everything go foul. For a while he took to beating his wife, then stopped, withdrawing into a heavy, brooding silence. The most sensible thing would have been to leave home, apply for a homestead somewhere else—which the Land Reform now made possible— but was it really worth starting all over from scratch, roughing it in a log cabin, putting up buildings? Better to leave well enough alone. Dividing up the land didn't mean the Juchniewiczes were about to set up house in the woods. And if anything ever happened to Surkont, she was bound to take charge, anyway.

Then a third child, a daughter, was born to Balthazar. But when the village midwife from Pogirai brought the baby over for his inspection, he couldn't remember how it was done, which night, or whether he had even taken pleasure in it. She looked so like a little kitten, the spitting image of her father. Not until the day after the christening party, as he was getting out of bed, was he told—it had been sloughed off as a joke at the time—that he had gone after someone with a knife.

40

TINKLING BELLS, a snorting horse, the sleigh runners' noiseless glide, and a white landscape embroidered with tracks. The wobbly square denoted a hare; the elongated one, a hare on the run. A fox track—neatly aligned, one paw behind the other—ran straight up a knoll, up to where the snow scintillated in the sun, before disappearing in a birch wood bathed in violet. Bird tracks were the easiest to spot: three overlapping dashes, often accompanied by a tail smudge or a faint imprint of the pinions.

The cold brought out the veins on Aunt Helen's nose —dark red against her pink-flushed face—beetling above the collar of her sheepskin. Her sheepskin's original color had faded, but Thomas's was new, still preserving its tawny sheen reminiscent of a squirrel's summer coat, and just because it was so tawny and soft, he loved to rub his cheek against the sleeve, patiently pushing back his grandfather's cap with earflaps every time it threatened to flop down over his eyes. Helen wore a round cap of gray astrakhan.

The snow trails around the house at Borkuny were tarnished yellow from tramping, the grounds pocked with frozen water patches and little piles of horse manure a-swarm with sparrows. Inside, a hurrying Barbarka brushed past them in woolen stockings and wooden clogs. Refreshments were served, and the three of them sat down at table; but Thomas, tiring quickly of the table talk, got up and browsed among the hunting gear mounted on the wall. A sort of compact had arisen between Romuald and Helen, and it rankled him. This was a different Romuald he was seeing now, one unworthy of the real Romuald—an accomplice of adults, lacing his talk with cracks that incited his aunt to fits of tee-heeing. Another incentive for clearing out as soon as was politely possible was the sulking Barbarka, whose biting lips betrayed a curious rancor. When forced to remain at table, he became so ruefully introspective that his aunt's commanding "Eat!" had a jolting, almost waking effect on him. But she never divined his real thoughts—those thoughts of a somewhat indelicate nature.

The smiles, the constant cajoling to eat and drink, were for him a sign of affectation. Why all the posturing, the pretending to be something other than what one was? Not a sign, never a hint of their true selves. In private, one thing; in company, another. Romuald, the real Romuald, would say, "Time for a crap," crouch down beside a tree, and afterward wipe himself with a leaf, without inhibition, without concealment; but in the presence of Thomas's aunt, he was all gentility and courtly manners. Nor was Aunt Helen above squatting and dribbling through her legs, yet how ladylike, how primly proper was her bearing now, almost as if she was without any privy part, or had left it behind somewhere. Even Barbarka. Why "even"? Because how could someone so uncannily beautiful squat down and, with flushed cheeks, make a puddle with her hairy part? As he looked at her and tried to imagine her in this pose, he quivered: miles separated the smoothness of her brow, the blue lambency of her gaze from that other region below. If each knew the other's business, why pretend ignorance? He had always been contemptuous of the decorum of the visit, of those social occasions when he was forced to be a spectator to their tedious proprieties, but never so much as during those winter visits to Borkuny. Meanwhile, he entertained visions of them squatting naked, attending to their bodily needs, each in full view of the other. Would they, in that position, still have felt obliged to blab the same banalities, the same platitudes that, alone, they were too ashamed to utter? The perverse pleasure he took in conjuring up such visions was tinged with one desire: to triumph over their disguises, to strip them of pretense. He swore never to become like them. Yet it was Helen who bore the brunt of his silent protestations—for her having infected Romuald, for implicating him in all this ceremonial silliness.

At dusk, when the sky was suffused from below with a stark red, when the thin tree branches seemed to inflict an icy cold, blackcocks flocked to the birch by the brook. Thomas would observe their tail feathers in flight, the white lining of their wings. At sufficiently close range, the metal black of feathers took on a shimmering iridescence; at a distance, the birds became silhouetted among the crowns of trees. From the cupboard Romuald removed a wooden decoy, as faithful a replica of a real blackcock as ever was carved. Fastening it to the end of a long pole, with the decoy propped up to look like a roosting cock, he stood the pole against the trunk of a birch; taking it for one of their companions, the blackcocks would swoop down out of the sky to within shooting range. Romuald promised to take him along on one of his trips, but the promise, for one reason or another, was never kept. A bad cold spell kept them indoors that winter, the result being they made only one leisurely stroll into the forest—in the company, alas, of Helen. Romuald pointed out a track in the snow—a wolf's, he said, after giving it careful scrutiny. How could he tell it was a wolf's and not a dog's? Hm, would have had to be a pretty big dog, said Romuald, adding that the pads on a wolf's paw, because they were more spread out, made for a deeper, cleaner print.

Romuald was not much of a churchgoer, though he aways stopped off at the manor when he went. But Barbarka was at church every Sunday, and with her head bowed over a thick missal, her kerchief's triangular fold falling between her bent shoulders, her presence was not nearly so intimidating. Church had a way of mitigating what was otherwise fearful; even Dominic, whose unkempt hair made him stand out among the men, seemed tamer, less belligerent. For Thomas, although he was reconciled to it, church attendance was a cause of some frustration. During Mass, a person's inner feelings had to ascend straight up to God; otherwise, he thought, he was guilty of cheating. Not wanting to cheat, he would clamp his eyes shut and try—without success—to let his mind soar up through the roof and into heaven. But it never worked; God was like air, dissolving into nothing, no matter how the mind conceived of Him. Then back it came, that irresistible earthly curiosity about who was seated next to him, who wore what, the facial expressions . . . And even when he was able to break loose and hurl himself into space, it was always to take the place of God, to gaze down on the church and on all those assembled. Through roofs and clothes made miraculously transparent, he would contemplate them. Their shameful parts, while hidden from others, were now fully exposed; their minds laid bare. With his giant fingers he would reach down and pluck one at random, cradle him in his palm, and study his movements. However much he fought against such fantasies, they reasserted themselves with every flight to heavenly spheres.

One book affected him deeply: a book about the first Christians and the Emperor Nero (the one shown making living torches of people in the print that hung in Grandfather's room). To it must be attributed his dream about purity. The dream: a group of Christians, with Thomas among them, stood singing in the arena of a Roman amphitheater. Tears streamed down his face, but they were tears of joy, the joy of a martyrdom willingly endured, bringing with it a cleansing of spirit that transformed him live into a flowing river. Once—and it happened only once —on his grandfather's orders, he'd had his hide tanned for some more serious transgression. Antonina had held him, while one of the farm boys whipped his bare behind with a switch. Painful as the punishment had been, the recollection of it somehow remained precious: a lightness of spirit, an exhilaration, a joyful expiation—the same tears of exultation and plenitude that had attended his dream about death.

The lions advanced, their serrated jaws coming closer and closer; the sinking of fangs into raw flesh, the gushing of blood, and the sensation of luminous exoneration, of eternal reconciliation with the Good.

But this was just a dream. In reality, that same week —the week of his dream—he created an awful scene when the black-bound book from whose pages he diligently transcribed the Latin names of his birds was missing. He searched high and low, exasperated the grownups with his pestering, but the book was nowhere to be found. What had happened to it? He discovered it by chance—in the same room where, among drying seeds strewn on canvas sheets and stacks of wool yarn, Aunt Helen slept. One of her turned bedposts had a foot missing; the bird book was there in place of it. He screeched, yelled, clenched his fists vengefully while his aunt, in a state of shock, demanded to know the reason for this tantrum. Damn fool woman! A book or a brick, what did she care! What were birds and animals to her—she who couldn't tell the difference between a sparrow and a yellowhammer! The owl, yes, the owl had mattered, but only because of the money it fetched. She was no more interested than she was in what Romuald had to say about hunting; it was all an act, a hoax, part of her flirtatious designs. Such malevolence was unworthy of a Christian. But Thomas wasn't bothered by such qualms. His contempt sought revenge; it inspired visions of punishment, both for this latest crime and for the crass stupidity she embodied. Visions, for example, of lacing her soup with belladonna berries. But the berries now lay under the deep winter snows, and a few days later his hatred abated. Anyone that blind to things deserving of love wasn't even worthy of being poisoned.

Thomas built his snowman on the front lawn, rolling the balls of snow in the winding sheet of down stirred up by his momentum. Three clumps, one on top of the other, the smallest—the head—fixed with coal eyes and a twig pipe. But by the time it stood erect, the hands were frozen and the fun already over: there was only so much one could do with a snowman. On winter mornings he gave Antonina a hand with lighting the fires. From the hallway her footfalls resounded crisply in the house—so hushed it seemed bedded in cotton—as she entered, trailing the cold and dumping the glazed firewood on the floor with a clatter. It was then up to him to lay the birch bark and erect a little tent of kindling—debris dried in the gap between tiled stove and wall. The bark, licked by the flame, would curl into trumpets. A moment of suspense: would it catch or wouldn't it? Next Antonina, her arms full of wood, with Thomas tagging behind, would march into Grandmother Dilbin's room, where everything was still a blur, and straightaway open the shutters, causing both Thomas and his grandmother, hunched in front of a pillow braced upright against the headboard, to blink from the sudden burst of light. On her bedstand, next to a thick prayer book, medicine bottles filled the room with their sickly odors. Having no inclination to linger, as he sometimes did in autumn, he resorted to any excuse to escape her weepy jeremiads. Poised on the edge of his chair by her bed, he felt conscience-bound to stay, but, unable to endure it for very long, he would invariably sneak out, his guilt made none the worse by his escape: his grandmother, because she was sick and weepy, belonged to those things that lent themselves to dispassionate observation, even annoyance, and from this detachment came both satisfaction and shame.

An important event: that winter Thomas got his boots, the ones he'd had his heart set on. Hand-sewn by a cobbler from Pogirai, they were a size too big (to allow for growth), but still a snug fit. To keep the foot from sliding, the soft shank could be tightened by a strap in the instep. Another strap, looped through eyelets, kept the shank tight around the knee.

41

THAT SPRING was unlike any Thomas had ever known. Not only because of the sudden thaw and the ferocity of sun. That year, instead of waiting passively for the leaves to appear, for the yellow keys of St. Peter to blossom, and for nightingales to trill in the bushes, he went out to meet it. The naked earth barely steamed in the cloudless light as, whistling and singing and flourishing his stick, he made his way to Borkuny. From the moment he slipped into the forest behind the farm that afternoon, he felt like joining himself to it, so painful was the swelling from within, so great the urge to proclaim his rapture. But he checked the urge, treading softly enough not to snap a twig, freezing in his tracks at the slightest rustle. This was the only way of gaining entrance to the kingdom, birds being panicked less by the sight of a man than by his movement. Dappled thrushes promenaded nearby, and he knew how to distinguish them from the fieldfare by their gray-brown, rather than bluish, head plummage. Circling a small spruce, he discovered a new hawfinch nest; and if not for their anxious screeching, he would have missed a jay's nest, so well camouflaged that it was hardly to be detected from below. The young spruce, its branches hugging the ground, was easy climbing at first; but the higher he climbed, the thicker became the needles, and it was a scratched and sweaty Thomas who finally surfaced at the top, his head adjacent to the nest. He swayed, held on with both arms to the thin trunk, while the frantic jays threatened attack from higher up, clearly intent on spearing him with their beaks, only to recoil in panic, resume their places, and renew the attack. He refrained from touching the eggs—there were four, all light blue and russet-flecked. Why were mottled eggs so common among forest birds? No one had been able to give him a satisfactory answer. Nature's way, he guessed. But why? He slid back down, extremely content with his accomplishment.

He returned, flushed with his impressions of the forest spring, whose beauty derived not from any one thing in particular but from a myriad of voices comprising a chorus of promise. From the treetops, now black against the western sky, came the long-drawn melodies of thrushes—the *Turdus musicus*, which only an ignoramus could have mistaken for the *Turdus pilaris* or *Turdus viscivorus*; from overhead, the winnowing of snipe in flight, like a bleating of lambs in the distance, somewhere beyond the rose-green swath of silk. Antonina pretended these sounds were the work of the witch Ragana, spurring her mount, the devil, transformed by her into a flying goat; but Thomas knew that it was only the wind whistling in their feathers.

To Barbarka he made a present of a bouquet of rose-petaled daphne, hyacinthlike in their fragrance, and they were graciously accepted. Romuald sat in the twilight, holding the barrel of his shotgun up to the lamplight for inspection. He asked a question that left Thomas momentarily speechless, even made him pale a little. Whether from pity or respect for Thomas's ability to incarnate the forest spirits, he inquired: "Want to come?"

His happiness was marred only by the burden imposed on him. The stalking of wood grouse, guided only by their song, was a recognized feat. One careless step, and the hunt was over; yet Romuald had trusted enough in his abilities to invite him along. His honor compelled him not to betray that confidence.

Thomas, no stranger to the ways of the wood grouse, had never seen a live one before, as it kept to the interior, away from human habitations—bird symbol of the wilderness. It was stalked two or three steps at a time, at the end of each song, when the bird was deaf to any movement in the dim light—it called only at daybreak, in the interlude between winter's thaw and the first greening.

Thomas's exultation over the lore of the wilderness, over anything having to do with nature, was deceiving. Was it the image of the bird itself—turkey-sized, long-necked, fan-tailed—that fired his imagination, or visions of himself stalking in the penumbra? The thrill of adventure, the prospect of participation as a genuine hunter, moving stealthily in the forest, mute and vigilant, his ears on the baying of the hounds? For he was capable of picturing not only the details, not only the trappings, but himself in the act of registering them; he exulted, in other words, in the role as much as in the thing itself. The arching of foot while stalking, for example, was a sign of his own proficiency, all too consciously perceived. And grownups were deluded if they supposed they didn't indulge in similar games. If they were honest, they would admit to a greater fascination with the role of lover than with the object of that love; to their wanting to savor the situation, the source of their pride. No wonder their words and gestures were artificial; they were performed, under censorship, on behalf of some ideal. Their affections had to be commensurate with their own ideal; when lacking, they had to be invented and their sincerity constantly reaffirmed. Acting was their stock and trade: one half impersonated someone the other half knew to be false. Thus, much can be said in Thomas's defense.

The fanaticism with which he divided people into worthy and unworthy, depending on whether he sensed in them the presence or absence of some passion, testified to his heart's exorbitant demands. Once he acknowledged birds as the supreme beauty, he vowed to remain faithful both to them and to his chosen vocation. His tenacity could be read in his exemplary conduct, in the steady grinding of teeth: "I will be what I choose to be."

The following afternoon, they set off in Romuald's one-horse britska. The sandy, deep-rutted road cut straight through the forest before weaving through the moorland, the spare landscape being relieved by a few scattered pine left for seed and by clumps of seedlings so young they were nearly transparent, many of them already crumpled and broken, grasslike, by the snows and winter winds. The moor, its barren aspect in stark contrast to the lush verdure along the Issa or around Borkuny, evoked little sympathy in Thomas. In the mixed forest past the range, Romuald looked for the logging trail used as a shortcut. Here the ground was already dry enough not to risk a sunken axle; the shadows now and then reverberated with the thumping of hoofs on hardened snow. They came out on a highroad lined with ditches, and a half hour later a clearing, the sky above it wreathed with chimney smoke, rolled into view.

"Jaugele," said Romuald. "In that village, everyone's a poacher."

In the vesperal light, the brushwood, mantled with mist, looked gunmetal blue against the black timberline. After crossing a little bridge choked with alder, they headed up a levee that led to the forester's. A stork nest on the rooftop, its occupants freshly returned, seethed with beaks and feathers. A dog bayed and stretched his limbs in front of the door, where a big-boned woman, wearing a dark green skirt, informed them that her husband was camped out in the woods. She invited them inside, but anxious to reach him before nightfall, they stayed only for some milk, served them in an earthenware jug. Following her directions—a right, then a left past the pine tree with the beehive, then another right by the peat bog—they picked up the trail, a horse track matted with wood chips and a bedding of pine branches. It was dark now; barkless logs shone by the trailside. Before long, they spotted a fire burning in the distance.

The lean-to of freshly cut pine took on a dark coppery glaze in the light of the campfire, around which a couple of peasants sat on their spread sheepskins. Thomas was quick to spot a pair of shotgun barrels leaning against the sloped pine shelter. The calling was nearing its peak— they were told by the gamekeeper and his partner—and the sunrise promised good weather, with little chance of rain. "The boy"—the gamekeeper nodded at Thomas. "Out here for the grouse hunt?" He stroked his bushy mustache, a facetious grin playing underneath, shook his head, and eyed him up and down. Thomas felt uncomfortable under his scrutiny.

Sparks showered and shot up and scattered in the soft black. Thomas stretched out his legs toward the fire and felt the generous warmth through his boot soles. Lying flat on his bed of fir, he covered himself with his sheepskin and listened to the sighing in the fir crowns, to an owl screeching somewhere far off; to the drawling voices of the men, who sat up trading gossip: a wedding, a lawsuit, the case of a man who accidentally plowed someone else's property . . . Occasionally, one of them got up and disappeared, to reemerge from the dark, hauling a dry log, which he tossed onto the fire. Lulled by the campfire patter, Thomas turned over on his side and fell into a drowse, the voices and the crackling reaching him through that half sleep between dream and wakefulness.

He was awakened by a tugging on the arm. The camp-fire, now out, was ringed by ash. The firmament, slightly paler in one half of the sky, glittered overhead. He shivered, as much from anticipation as from the chill.

42

IT WAS pitch-dark—silent except for a boot colliding with a root, a barrel scraping a branch. A hunting party of three; the fourth, the friend of the game-keeper, had gone to try his luck on other stands. The path narrowed and the smell of pine needles slowly gave way to the smells of the swamp. Pools of water glimmered in the gray pre-dawn light. They waded into the water, circled around it, got stuck in the bushes, and later balanced their way across slimy logs laid out bridge-fashion among the phantoms of dry reeds, forming something between an embankment and a levee. To the left, beyond a ditch resonant with a bullfrog's croaking, loomed a wall of pine scrub; to the right, a dark density of swamp forest, in whose interior Thomas made out here and there a light-barked trunk, the tangled underside of an uprooted tree, clumps of rushes, brake, and sedge. The sky ahead of them was saturated with rose; the longer the eye lingered on it, the blacker became the circumscribing darkness.

They stopped occasionally, ears perked. At one point, Romuald squeezed Thomas's arm. "There he is," he said in a whisper. But it took Thomas awhile to register the sound —a sort of muffled sigh, unlike any other creature sound he knew. At times it sounded vaguely like a hammering, an uncorking, but no—it eluded definition. They shook hands with the gamekeeper, who immediately dropped out of sight.

"We'll keep on at the same pace for a while," murmured Romuald. "He's too far out of range now. But later on—watch your step."

Clutching his gun with one hand, keeping his balance with the other, Romuald waded into the brush. Thomas trailed behind, straining to maintain the silence. But how to avoid making any telltale sounds when the foot, even before it had touched the ground, met with a matting of dry stalks? He found a way: before setting his foot down, he first dug his boot into the matting, or else sought out the moss. The grouse did indeed have need of the wilderness as a protection. Barricades of fallen tree trunks occasionally blocked their way, and Romuald debated whether to crawl under or over. The calling carried more distinctly now—a strenuous, quickening *tek-ap, tek-ap* . . .

Such scenes remain fixed forever in one's memory: giant aspen, made even more towering by the pearl-gray lighting between night and day, their boughs brushed with a radiance announcing the sunrise; roots like gigantic appendages fingering the dank dusk; the rush of naked stems, surging up to the light; and Romuald, no more than an ant beside them, cutting a path through the underbrush, his gun held high. And the song of the grouse. Thomas understood now why the grouse hunt was so celebrated. Nature could have invented no better song with which to convey the wildness of the spring. Neither a melody nor a graceful trill—more of a drumming, cadenced, causing a throbbing in the temples, a merging of grouse song and heartbeat.

Thomas imitated Romuald's every move and gesture. The moment Romuald turned and signaled, he halted in his tracks. The time had come. From now on, they had to take leaping steps. The bird broke off. Silence. Tiny birds, warbling shrilly, flocked overhead. Then it started up again. *Tek-ap* . . . faster and faster, until the calling was joined by another sound, rather like knife-grinding; that's when Romuald took his first hop, followed by a second, turning stock-still on the third. Thomas was afraid to budge before he was sure of his timing. But the instant the grouse began a new series, he was ready; taking his cue from the whetting, he jumped together with Romuald. One, two, three. He knew why the interval: the bird was momentarily deaf. They could risk a clamor now, so long as the body was prepared to become a statue on a moment's notice.

One, two, three. He concentrated entirely on the exercise, and prayed: "Please, God, make it work. Make it work." Once executed, there was no improving one's position—you stayed where you landed. But as his leg was probing for a mossy island, he lost his footing on the third hop and slid into the muck with a loud gurgle. He could have hoisted himself out by grabbing hold of a sapling at his back, but he was afraid the rustle might give him away. In despair he sank into the mud, while Romuald shook his fist at him.

He lost one sequence during the time it took to extricate his foot from the swamp. Soon he was jumping in tandem with Romuald, his anxiety steadily mounting at the prospect of flushing the bird, so close was the calling now. He found safe footing for the next series, poised, but nothing happened. Minutes passed. It was over. It had escaped. Terrified, Thomas implored Romuald with his eyes to bring it back.

Then the grouse started up again, exactly as before, only a little higher up. Had he merely shifted his perch? From Romuald's repeated crouching and scouting, Thomas surmised that he was plotting the most surreptitious approach. The sky above the forest roof had brightened; ahead of them, a clump of aspen was tinted red by the sun's rays. Romuald, taking huge strides, steered in that direction, motioning for Thomas to follow.

The grouse sat high up in a gap among the spruce. Kneeling and craning his head, Thomas observed it from behind a tree trunk. It seemed small enough to be a blackbird. Wings lowered, tail feathers beetling at an angle, buff-gray against its black spruce perch. Romuald, bent low, ducked under a needle curtain: he was trying to outflank it.

A shot. Thomas watched as the grouse, wings arrested, was pulled from the branch; saw the long path of descent, heard the thump, the shot's rippling echo. He licked his lips—joyous and grateful to God.

When he grabbed the bird by the head—a metallic sheen, a crimson brow, an ivorylike beak—and hoisted it shoulder-high, it hung down to his feet. It did not know the world of humans; once or twice, it may have heard men's voices from afar. It was oblivious to Aunt Helen, books, boots, the shape of a gun; oblivious to Romuald's and Thomas's existence, too. Nor would it ever know. Struck by a thunderbolt, it had died instantly. But he, Thomas, still resided on this side of the thunderbolt; they had met in the only way possible, and he felt a twinge of remorse that it could never be otherwise. The truth was that Thomas hungered for a sort of impossible communion with living creatures. Why this barrier, and why become a hunter if one loved nature? It had been the same with the owl: he had secretly dreamed of the day when the owl, by some word or deed, would cease to be an owl, if only for an instant. But the dream never came true; hence what was to be gained by keeping it locked in a cage? Since it was not within his power to assume another form—that of a grouse, say—all that was left was to bring the dead bird back, inhaling its smell, the smell of the forest's savage interior.

The sun was up. The tree craters and swamp patches congested with rushes now took on a more mundane aspect. Soon they were back alongside the ditch, which, to his astonishment, seemed closer in the daylight. He had a liking for this walk by the ditch: a ruthless dawn caught in a chaos of leaning, overlapping pine; this man with his black strip of a gun; a blue wreath of cigarette smoke, and himself, bearer of the trophy.

43

THOSE WHO have never stepped out of the house at the break of day and heard the babble of black-cock must lead sorry lives indeed, because such have never known spring. Nor will they be able, in times of despair, to conjure those weddings celebrated in places far from what afflicts them. But did it really matter if they could not experience such ecstasy, if someone else could? That time when lilac-hued flowers, powdery yellow on the inside, their stems coated with velvety down, were born among the needles; when cocks danced in the glades, trailing their wings along the ground and brandishing their tail feathers, ink-colored on the outside, white on the inside, their throats so surfeited with song they could only swell from the excess.

Romuald never hunted blackcock at Borkuny, taking care to preserve the wildlife there. The same birch wood that provided sanctuary for the adders bordered on a young pine forest; it was here that the blackcocks had chosen as the place for their mating rituals. Though sparsely wooded, the trees there were luxurious, their boughs bent to the ground, the floor beneath them like a mosaic: islands of close-cropped moss, patches of gray lichen, and clusters of red whortleberry. Blinds, fashioned to look like bushes, were favored for hunting; the hunter hid in them just before daybreak and waited, commanding a view of the blackcocks' ballroom. Thomas regarded it as a matter of honor to rely only on his naturalist's cunning; that is, he hunted without a gun, the challenge being to get close enough so that, if he had been armed, he would not have missed.

A milk-white mist, a child's pastel-pink sky. Such mists were not uncommon at any season, but none so breathtakingly serene as this. In the mist, against the white dew or frost, the luminous blackcocks resembled metal-plated scarabs. The mating grounds, the site they had selected for their love games, was for Thomas an enchanted garden. Crawling up on all fours, he would spy on them, though only once at close range. Another time he was startled by the mating call of a blackcock perched in a young pine. *Choo-shee!* Translucent drops glistened and sparkled on the needle tips, yet the bird was the focal point of space, equal in size to a planet. The bird flew away on its own, unprompted by any careless move on his part. How he longed for the cap of invisibility from the fairy tale, though there were times when he knew indeed how to make himself invisible.

The spring was gaining in strength: bird cherries along the Issa, overpowering the senses with their bitter perfume; young girls tiptoeing to pluck sprays of flowers so fragile they scattered at the slightest jostle; and those evenings on the village green, where a little drum and horn played accompaniment to the monotonous village reel known as the *suktinis*. And the house in Gine, now suddenly buried in clouds of lilac.

That year, Thomas's hand never once touched the four-pronged spear that he used to take pike-fishing, either with Pakenas or Akulonis, and the line on his pole was corroded by their rusty hooks. This neglect of a boyhood passion left him with a guilty conscience; but he now had other, more urgent things to occupy him, both at Romuald's and at old lady Bukowski's at Borkuny. What drew him there was neither the old woman nor Denis nor Victor, but a lake.

It was a small lake, secluded from both fields and roads, which made it all the more appealing. It was surrounded by marshland, and though a trail gave access, one had to slosh ankle-deep in water before reaching the shoreline. The lake was thickly ringed by tall rushes, but Thomas had discovered a small cove with a panoramic view, and an alder stump, where he would sit for hours in rigid contemplation. A perfect placidity, a sheet of another sky, traversed by water birds trailing long creases. The lake had its permanent residents, and Thomas was perennially on the lookout for them. The ducks came whirring down out of the sky, skimmed long and low over the surface, their triangular wing tips at first brushing the water, then ruffling it and sending ripples back to the shoreline. The ducks were preyed on by wailing hawks from above, and he once witnessed an attack in midair; the drake escaped by taking cover in the reeds. But the habits of the grebe engaged him most of all. Sometimes they surfaced close by: red-billed, crested, rufous side-whiskers on a white neck. He was mystified by their bizarre ceremonies, always performed out in the middle of the lake. Their snakelike necks suddenly elongated, they streaked across the water's surface with prodigious speed, the snake-necks now arched and their heads lowered. Their forward thrust was all the more astounding in that they barely touched the water and didn't fly. Like the motorboats in Grandmother Dilbin's illustrated magazines. How did they do it, he once asked Victor. "Gey gage geag goger guz ger gugid"—that is, "They chase each other because they're stupid," an explanation not likely to satisfy a naturalist.

Victor, because of his lumbering, stuttering ways, was not really the best company. He plowed, harrowed, tended the feed troughs, and even milked the cows with the servant girl. Always busy with menial chores, something of a hired hand. His stuttering, no doubt, had its origin in maternal terror. The old woman had a habit of sitting with her legs apart, huge of belly, fists clenched on her knees, and this brooding pose was of a decidedly different order from the crooning and the upturned eyes that went with the guitar playing. Thomas was always shocked to hear her sing, much as if a bull were imitating a nightingale.

Mrs. Bukowski bred many ducks, and one aspect of their behavior gave Thomas pause. The ducks waddled about the house, nibbling on the grass, or dabbled in a hollow, which, except after a rainfall when water collected at the bottom, was either a mudhole or, during drought season, a cracked basin. "Why don't they go down to the lake?" he asked. Victor sneered, and his response, or at least what could be salvaged from it was: "Ha! If they only knew!" They were unaware that close by was a diver's paradise, offering warm water, algae, sprawling pads adrift on somnolent depths, and sanctuaries among the reeds. As he contemplated their flattened, lapping bills and billowy cheeks, Thomas took pity on this strange debility of theirs. What could have been easier than to migrate over to the lake? A ten minute's journey, at most. Not until some years later was Thomas to pursue this philosophical insight, now only vaguely formulated, to its logical conclusion. Mankind was a pitiable lot. Not unlike those ducks.

The beauty of that spring—his twelfth—did not spare Thomas certain anxieties, and may have even contributed to them. For the first time he perceived that he had two selves, and that they were not altogether commensurate: the one he felt inside, and the outside one, his bodily self, the one he was born with, and nothing of which was really his. Barbarka, had she known of his admiration for her, would never have wounded him by calling him a "*shutas.*" She had judged him by his exterior, and this allegiance to his own face ("Tommy has a face like a Tartar's ass"), to his own gestures, for which he was held responsible, weighed heavily on him. And what if he was fashioned differently from others, not as well proportioned? Romuald, for example, was sinewy, lean in the hips, and had tapered knees. Thomas, measuring with his hands, found his thighs too big around; standing sideways before the mirror, he would examine his prominent backside, pretending, the moment he heard footsteps approaching, to be merely passing by. Others were able to part their hair down the middle, but no matter how often he combed or brushed, it was like trying to groom a dog's hide against the grain.

We live inside ourselves as in a prison. If people make fun of us, it's because they can't see through to our true selves. We carry inside images of our physical selves closely bound to our souls, though all it takes is another person's glance to dissolve that bond, to show us that we are not at all what we flatter ourselves to be. Chastened, we go around, existing inside ourselves, all too painfully aware of ourselves from the outside. This discrepancy made him yearn all the more for his Kingdom of the Forest, the map to which lay locked in a drawer. After due thought, he decided that women should be barred from the Kingdom, whether they were like Helen, Mrs. Bukowski, or Barbarka. Men, too, were adept at posing, but women were somehow to blame for their cold, squinting glances. Men whose minds were fixed on more noble aims did not have to bother with their appearance.

The linden leaves around the manor house in Gine had unfurled to become green hands concealing a little bell that hung in a worm-eaten shelter in a tree fork. Thomas could not recall anyone ever having used this bell; no cord was attached, and it was situated too high up for anyone to reach. During the month-of-May devotions to the Blessed Virgin, a yellow afternoon light fell through the windows into the church, heavy with the scent of flowers clustered at the foot of the blue Virgin.

Warm rains. The rains left the trails awash with

shoals of silt, laced with rivulets tunneling through the loam. If you stepped barefoot in the mud, your toes secreted a squishy paste. Then came the water, seeping back into the impression and filling the print left by the naked sole.

44

THE WINDOW of Grandmother Dilbin's room was open and, though it was still light outside, a nightingale trilled in the brake by the pond. Waking from a sleep heavy with premonition, she felt someone standing by her bedside. "Arthur!" she cried out. But there was no one, and then she remembered where she was, and she remembered that years had passed, and that the gold lettering on the gravestone had probably been washed away by the rains.

Bronislawa Ritter, a little girl with two blond braids who had just caught and freed a butterfly stranded on the windowpane, stared up at the evening shadows inscribed on the ceiling, two strands of gray hair now stuck fast to her down-filled pillow. The walls of her family home in Riga had been a protection from evil and the encroachment of time. A too happy childhood, followed by life's rapid descent, had left her unwilling to admit to the reality of it, to admit that laughter would never again resound—a bright and sunny laughter to dispel the irreversible. What was the meaning of it all? The little spoon used for serving jam; the iridescent silk gown belonging to her mother; the sister who used to tie her ribbon; the ringing at the front door; and Father, back from his patients, placing his checkered medical bag on the pier table . . . ? Of all the possible roads, why this one? Hard to accept that it had happened, hard but irrefutable, even without the reasoning of it, like a tearful novel that could be put down at will, no, that could *not* be put down ... Why me?

The descent. It began the day she and Arthur rode back from the church, with the snow melting on her eyelashes. The flickering candlelight of the candelabra, the creaking floor, the house that was to become hers from that day forward. "No, no!" It was like the discovery of death. The paper chains used to decorate the Christmas tree, and the caroling, and the flowers, and the hoop-spinning in the garden—all scattered, dispersed, leaving cruelty as the only reality. "No, no!" *Consummatio* forever. Arthur had been a good man. And she had ceded to it, to that monstrous order of the world with which he was at home. The smell of tobacco and leather stirrups had introduced her to a land where a person counted for nothing more than an object, a land where the cultivation of gracious customs was revealed as an affectation, a feeble mask covering the severity of law. And always the same bewildering question: "Was this it?" A land where nobody rebelled, where everything was sanctified and acknowledged, where no word could reconcile, where nothing could be changed.

She had hardly known the man, not even when his mustache had stood out in relief against his waxlike face, when, tending to the wicks by the coffin, she had yielded to the thought: "A thing." A man who could suppress his impetuous nature merely by sucking on a pipestem. A discreet man, reticent about the past. A man whose back bore the scars of Russian knouts—"for leading a revolt in the camp," he once muttered, grudgingly. A man who had traveled by reindeer in the land of eternal night and eternal day—in the Siberian tundra; taken cover in the forests during the Uprising, tall and lanky in his Polish overcoat and buckled belt. And the pride he took in his marksmanship . . . Like the time he knocked a Russian officer out of the saddle with a boar gun. And all the notes and IOU's left behind: "Fifty rubles to Matyda Zidonis." "To T.K.—twenty rubles." Although she suspected him of having betrayed her, he never gave any outward indication of it. Only later, in his will, there were those mysterious legacies to boys in the neighboring villages: his sons.

A whirl of dates, winters, springtimes, minor incidents, illnesses, guests . . . Theodore was born in the year 1884—yes, she was barely nineteen at the time. Had she wept the day she got the news that Constantine had drowned in a swimming accident—Constantine, a man she could have been happy with? She couldn't remember. Staring fixedly, she probed deep into the past, transfixed the way one's gaze can be arrested by an eddy or a flame. The sketchbook containing his drawings still lay in her trunk, preserved there to this day.

The nightingale cried out, was answered. Dampness seeped through the window. Whatever has been cannot endure; it fades, flickers, scatters; a man, doubting that he has been, can only pray. If a star ablaze in the bluish-green firmament was millions of miles away, and beyond it other stars, other suns; if all that was born passed without leaving a trace, then only God could rescue the past from insignificance. Even a past full of pain. Oh, if only one could say with certainty that it was not a dream.

"Shut the window, Tommy; it's cold."

Her voice now grated like a rusty-hinged door. He registered the change. He had been studying her for a good long while: the fingers intertwined, the once-full cheeks sagging, the deep furrows dividing them from the chin, the thin neck doubly creased. She turned her face toward him, her eyes, as usual, partially distracted by something.

Her grandson. Good or bad blood? Had he inherited Arthur's manliness, passion—or her own fear of everything that assailed us on this earth? Or did he have the blood of those—savages? It was her fault that Theodore was not like his father, that he was soft and even weak. She was also to blame for Constantine. If the boy took after her, he might well turn out like Constantine.

"Shatybelko brought back a letter. Look, Thomas, there it is."

Lying on one corner of the medicine table were several sheets of stationery, partially concealing an envelope. The slanted, jerky, practically illegible handwriting belonged to his father. The other, in which some letters had been doubly inscribed, as if to ensure their legibility, was his mother's.

"Mommy writes that she'll be home soon, in a few months at the most."

"Which way is she coming?"

"Everything's planned. You know the border's closed, there's no way to cross legally. But she writes that she knows of a little town where it's easy to cross."

"Will we go back the same way, or by way of Riga?"

His grandmother looked around for her rosary beads. He bent down and picked them up from the floor.

"You two will go. That's all I care about."

"Why do you say such things, Grandmother?" Secretly he registered no emotion, and he reproached himself for it.

She said nothing in reply. Groaning, she tried to raise herself up in bed. He leaned over and helped her, her sloping shoulders wrapped in a fustian morning jacket, a band of wrinkles running from the back of her neck to under her earlobe.

"These pillows. Look how they sink. Maybe you can straighten them a little."

Thomas's pity was somehow deficient; he wished it could have been more sincere, but that would have meant forcing himself, and he winced at this inability to feel genuine emotion. At the moment his grandmother seemed less

irritating than usual, for what reason he didn't know—
more open, perhaps, free of her usual craftiness.

"Lots of nightingales this year—eh, Thomas?"

"Lots, Grandmother."

As she began fingering her rosary beads, he couldn't
decide whether to leave or to stay.

"With all the cats around," she said at last, "it's a
wonder the birds aren't afraid to sing."

45

WHO SAID there were no witnesses? The
lush grass, crushed underfoot, had not yet recovered as the
booted feet went on trampling more weeds, rough stalks
rustled against leather shanks, and a frightened thrush resumed its caterpillar hunting. A couple were sitting at the
bottom of a small, leafy-walled hollow, under a sky of drifting clouds. A dark arm was wrapped around shoulders
sheathed in a white blouse. An ant, suddenly encumbered,
was trying to free itself from its unwanted burden.

This was the time when the cuckoo's song trailed more
and more into laughter, before lapsing into silence until
the next spring. But no one was counting the trills now—
the number of which was a portent of how many years a
person had left on earth. Whispering was heard on the
green floor below, along with the soft jangling of spurs.

Treading lightly, the wizard Masiulis strayed closer, a
small gunnysack, used for collecting herbs, slung over his
shoulder. Stooping, he put down his walking stick and dug
out a plant root with his knife. The sound of a human
voice. He took a few steps, parted the leafy curtain, and,
unobserved by anyone, squinted wryly. The woman's ges-

ture—he had just caught her in the act of straightening her dress—said that what had happened never happened. The deed irrevocably severed, she had begun talking of mundane matters, somehow relieved, as if just returned from adventures encountered in the kingdom of the night. The wizard let go of the branches, made his way back to the edge of the forest, sat down, and lit his pipe.

Masiulis was not without his passions. His wisdom, so far as one could tell, was the sort nurtured by mockery and contempt. Contempt for human nature in general, and for his own in particular. Wasn't it he who told someone (for what reason, it was difficult to say): "Man is like a sheep. But on top of this sheep God built another sheep, this one of air, and the live sheep wants never to be itself but the other"? Contained in this fable was the whole secret of Masiulis's magic. Given such a vision of human nature, nothing was more natural than wanting to help those sheep which could not sustain themselves in air.

There was no reason for Masiulis to think kindly of the couple in the woods. The sight of any couple somehow offended him—how they distanced themselves from others, the privileged air they assumed . . . Not so much offended as amused, to the point of provoking his sarcasm, for the same reason people threw sticks at dogs for making a public spectacle of their lust: their drooping tongues and lovesick glances communicated a recklessness, a disregard for their own silly exhibition, for everything but the savoring of their pleasure, seemingly given only to them. "Eh, you old jade," Masiulis grumped, his anger having been aroused by Helen's modest gesture.

Several days later, by coincidence, Barbarka came to call on Masiulis for advice, there being no one else to whom she could appeal for advice and medicine. At least Masiulis didn't ask, as the priest did in the confessional, "How many times, my child?" To be fair, Father Monkiewicz, after hearing the confessions of his parishioners, required of them only sincere repentance. Repentance means pleading to God to take note of our ardent desire to be rid of all sinful desire—so that He will be lenient with us the next time around. Since He is All-seeing, surely He must see that we are angels, that we surrender to temptations of the flesh against our wills, without our consent, even with grief for having been made thus and not otherwise. No sooner was she out of the confessional, no sooner relieved of one burden, than Barbarka knew, as did all who went to confession, that she was ready to assume another.

There were time-honored remedies for dealing with Barbarka's dilemma. It was enough, for example, to add a portion of menses to a man's food to make him feel bound by invisible threads. But either this remedy had failed her or she was simply seized with a desire to confide in someone. The wizard, receiving her cordially, spoke at length, until her tears fell one by one onto her fingers. They were tears of remorse, but also tears of shame. Because if Romuald had learned of her coming, he would have beaten her, and rightfully so. For Masiulis was inciting her against him—his festering grudge against the Pole had been aggravated by the couple in the woods. And instead of giving her a portion of lovage—the prescribed remedy, a liquid extract which was added to a man's food in small doses—he advised her to stop wasting her charms on an old lecher, on that traitor of a nobleman who had eyes only for ladies.

Puffy-eyed, Barbarka made her way home. She lingered for a while on the forest path, pensively blurring the horse tracks with her bare foot. "Eh, what does he know?" Did he know Romuald? Not the way she did. Old? But what man his age . . . ? Crooking her big toe, she scooped up the sand and needles. No, it would have to be done her way.

Barbarka was twenty-two years old. Her skirt fluttered and grazed her thighs and her steps gradually gained in surety. She strutted now with her head held high, her lips pursed in a smile of confidence. At the spot where the farm buildings came into view, she stopped and surveyed the rooftops, the well crane, and the orchard, as if noticing them all for the first time.

Her way. But how? Give it time, it would come. For now, it was enough that she had in her head the vague outline of a decision. Nothing like a good cry to change one's outlook on things, to make one see the fallacy of humbly submitting to one's fate. Leave Borkuny? Never.

Her visit with the wizard had not been in vain, though its effects were not exactly those anticipated by Masiulis. He had yielded to his passions, which were of benefit only when they fostered wisdom, not when they took command. No, he had acted contrary to his vocation.

Romuald stood in front of the barn, mending the plow with a hammer. In the kitchen, Barbarka scooped some water from a pail, wiped her face, and looked into the mirror. Mustn't let it show. A woman's cunning—yes, but unawares. And she licked her lips to make them look less chapped.

46

LUKE JUCHNIEWICZ, a man as easily given to sulking as to effusiveness, sat whimpering on one end of the couch. "But, Lukey"—Grandmother Misia tried to console him—"maybe the land won't be parceled. Nothing's happened yet, has it?"

"Not yet, but it will," he whined. "It's for sure now. The crooks, they'll make beggars of us all." He wiped his eyes with the back of his hand. "What's to become of us, anyway?"

It was hard to contradict him; the Juchniewicz estate was one of those scheduled for redistribution under the Land Reform Act. Aunt Helen sat beside him, her gaze fogged with mild resignation. Grandfather, seated opposite them, cleared his throat. "You'll move in with us, of course. It'll be better all the way around. You can help us run the farm, and Helen can take up residence here."

"Imagine Joseph turning informer," sighed Helen.

"The skunk. I warned you, didn't I? So much for your Lithuanians!" Grandmother turned to her husband and said, mimicking him: "They're so nice and loyal and innocent. Leave it to me, I'd teach them a lesson—with the whip, the whip!"

Grandfather fidgeted with his cuff-links, something he did when he felt uncomfortable. "The official gave me his word. Joseph won't give us any trouble, so long as we keep greasing their palms."

"If you ask me," said Helen, "we should move out to the cottage. That way they'd see Daddy on his property and me on mine," she said, placing undue emphasis on the word "mine." "Home is home, after all."

Thomas looked up from his book and listened until the voices suddenly merged into a meaningless patter. He was seated on the couch, having warmed a little hollow in the cold leather upholstery. The dining-room window was atwitter with sparrows clinging to the wild vine that wound its tendrils about the window frame. The leaves of the agave on the lawn stood upright, bronzed by the late-afternoon sun.

"The poor thing," said Grandmother mockingly, "he'll never survive. Ugh, what a seedy, good-for-nothing lummox, a moonshiner, a bootlegger, a damn fool drunkard. Besides, he's so fat it's disgusting. Good riddance, I say!"

"Well, well . . . hm . . . he did build himself a house," said Grandfather in Balthazar's defense. "And he does look after the forest. No, no, that's not the way to treat a man."

"A man! But he's no ordinary man—that's our darling Balthazar, the apple of our eye, dearer than our own daughter!"

"God forbid," said Helen, raising her hands in horror. "I would never dream of bringing harm to anyone. Why, he could be put up at the manor; Shatybelko's getting old, and he could help out around the farm. Or what about one of the cottages in the commune?"

Thomas perked up his ears, curious to see how Grandfather would respond.

"Yes, that's a possibility," he conceded. "It even makes sense. Only you see, Helen . . . hm . . . the way things are, if you offend them, get them riled up . . . You'll have to admit that right now . . . I mean, it's just a matter of getting the divisions approved . . . No, now is not the time for making enemies. And he does know the forest . . . As it is, we have enough trouble on our hands with Joseph."

The vision of danger evoked by Grandfather had a silencing effect on the women. Luke clutched his head. "What awful times we're living in! Don't rile them, treat them with kid gloves . . . Oh, deep down I feel so sick."

"Poor Lukey. He could use some drops." Grandmother's suggestion went unheeded by Helen.

For Thomas, Luke was an enigma, a man who acted like none of the other grownups and the very sight of whom was enough to provoke a snicker. But no one ever laughed, and that made Thomas distrustful of his own instincts. On the other hand, Luke was someone who wore long pants, was married to Helen, and who knew when and where to sow and harvest. Thomas suspected that behind the rubberlike face—a face that could alternately stretch

from an excess of sympathy and shrink in times of despair
—there was hidden the real Luke, a man not half as stupid
as he looked. Yet he never found any evidence of that
other, more intelligent Luke. Still, there had to be more to
him than that. Thomas was forced to conclude that he was
an exceedingly cunning man, that he was only shamming.
Even his manner of dress was different, was supportive of
the comic role he had adopted: he wore a pair of tight-
fitting checkered knickers, straps under the soles of his
shoes, and a hat identical to those pre-war hats that,
sprinkled with naphthaline, lay stored in a huge trunk in
the attic.

Aunt Helen was always amiable but, as Thomas
could not help noticing, also patronizing toward her husband. Luke had a knack of never volunteering his opinion
about anything.

"Well now, one room would do it. Just one little
room. Enough for the officials to see—" It was Helen
speaking now.

Grandmother groused in disgust. "Helen, how could
you? All alone in the forest, at the mercy of that . . . that
bumpkin? Ugh!"

"Well, it wouldn't have to be forever, just once every
few days, enough to let the news get around that the
Juchniewiczes were running their own farm. That wouldn't
be too much to ask, would it, Papa?"

"Hm, I suppose I could have a chat with him. No
harm in talking to him, I guess," Grandfather answered
evasively.

Thomas went back to his book, but was soon distracted when the grownups turned their invective on Joseph. He was a chauvinist, a fanatic; he would have killed
if he could; he was the sly type; he had been showered with
wood for teaching the boy a little arithmetic, and with so
many other blessings. Grandfather held his peace, and not

until after a long pause did he shyly mumble: "If you look at it his way, he might be—well—justified."

Grandmother Misia clasped her hands and raised her eyes to the ceiling, calling on heaven as her witness. "Oh, good Lord!"

47

THE DAY was at hand. Back at Borkuny, they had decided to stay clear of the flood waters around Joniškiai: the place was so thick with sweet flag as to be almost unnavigable by boat, and so crowded with the local peasants during opening season as to be a shooting gallery. Their choice had fallen on Lake Alunta, a little out of the way, but worth traveling the extra distance. "Wait'll you see all the ducks, Tommy!" The guns: Thomas was to use Victor's Berdan; Victor, the muzzle-loader. With the muzzle-loader went a bag full of accessories: powder in one pouch, shot in another, firing caps in still a third, along with a good supply of hemp. To load it, a powder gauge measured the right amount into the barrel, a long wooden ramrod being used to drive home the hemp; then came the shot and another wad of hemp. Uncocking a Berdan was tricky, but Thomas soon got the hang of it, squeezing the trigger with his index finger, gently lowering the hammer with his thumb. But the muzzle-loader was trickier; the sight of the little round cap exposed was enough to evoke visions of the hammer slipping and firing.

The choice of dogs was carefully weighed. Karo was left behind; duck hunting was bad for pointers, ruining their stance. Dunay was not to be trusted because of his flightiness; any moment, he could bolt into the brush.

Lutnia was out, too—no challenge in it; besides, she was in pup. That left Zagray—serious, systematic Zagray—for flushing the ducks.

A rack wagon, littered with straw, with Romuald, Thomas, Denis, Victor, and Zagray aboard. A cracking whip, dust swirling up from behind the wheels, and Thomas, lying on his back, watching the recession of rock, trees, and settlement fences. Romuald whistled, and Thomas chimed in; they were traveling, spirits were high. A half hour later the food sack was raided, the kielbasa passed around, and there was a lot of gnawing and chewing and lurching with the bumps.

The plan was to get there before nightfall, spend the night, and head for the water at daybreak. Would they manage to get their hands on a boat, Thomas wondered. What're you worried about; a village on a lake was bound to have its share of boats and dugouts.

Water loomed in the distance, bluish-red from the western glow. They took the high bank, the lake clearly outlined below. Oval-shaped, one end sharply tapered; the near shore bordered by hillside meadows; the far shore, starting from about midway around the oval, by a blackish mass in which here and there, silhouetted against the sky, stood the perpendicular feather of a pine. Over there were the big swamps in which they would be hunting. By the roadside, on a mound so round it could have been man-made, they passed the ruins of a castle, then dipped down into the fenced lane that was the entrance to the village of Alunta.

At the cottage, they ate curdled milk from huge earthenware bowls. Later, at twilight, Thomas scaled the castle slope. A full moon was on the rise; crickets chirruped in the hushed grass, still warm from the afternoon sun. Tiny waves shimmered at his feet, scalelike. His hand touched slabs of rock—remnants of the castle wall. Was it from here that she had plunged to her death, he wondered.

For Romuald had initiated him into the lore of the castle —how following its conquest by the Teutonic Knights, the pagan priestess had chosen death rather than surrender. He had visions of a woman's figure, arms outstretched, wailing, a white cloak fluttering. Then the same scene, only in a slightly different version: a slow descent, a waist girded with cloth, a head crowned with a green wreath, a woman's voice intoning chants to her god, and a body, gradually arching over the shoreline. Her soul—where was it now? Had it been damned for refusing baptism? The Knights had been enemies; they had burned and killed and pillaged in the name of Christ and bestowed baptism as a protection against hell. Maybe her soul inhabited neither heaven nor hell but these ruins . . . Something rustled behind him; he flinched. A field mouse, probably. And even though he had come up in search of some thrill, he bolted back down the slope, taking refuge among cottage roofs, human voices, cows, and chickens.

Zagray, curled beside them in the hay, sighed in his sleep; Thomas, being the lightest, kept sliding down into the hole Victor had burrowed in the hay. Someone came crawling up the ladder and began stepping over them. "Who's that?" asked Romuald. "A friend," came the answer. Then silence, and Thomas fell asleep with his eyes fixed on a star peeking through a slit in the barn roof.

When you wake up in the hay, you always find yourself shifted around. Thomas woke to find himself dangerously close to the edge of the hayloft, a snoring, wheezing Victor no longer beside him but huddled at his feet. His unoccupied horse blanket lay creased and crumpled in the gray dawn; Romuald and Denis buried in the hay, with Zagray sprawled on top. Thomas yawned restlessly, was about to wake the others, when the barn door creaked open, there was a burst of light, of cold air, and a voice sounded from below: "Mr. Bukowski! Time to get up!"

They assembled their gear on a bench in front of the

cottage. Romuald and Denis buckled on their cartridge belts while Thomas stuffed his pockets with shotgun shells, breakfasting on a little milk so as not to have to awaken the women from their Sunday sleep. Their host and his son, who were to accompany them, their pants legs rolled up nearly to their calves, lowered the poles and oars from hooks under the eaves.

The lake was mantled with winding strands of mist. From high up on the steep path, they spotted the boats, one end beached on the shingle, the other in a mist revealing here and there a flawless smoothness, with their ribbed interiors seemingly immobilized forever. By the time they reached the boats, patches of water were already agleam with sky.

48

DUTIES AND pleasures are never evenly divided. Handsomely feathered, the drake prefers solitude to the tedium of sitting on eggs and the guardianship of the young. A duck is either nesting during the best months of the year—May, June, and July—or trailing a string of quacking creatures, her freedom of movement always checked by the last, graceless link in the chain. The first and most urgent exercise the young are taught is the art of taking cover under the leaves of water lilies, totally submerged except for their bill tips. Next comes flying, the hardest part being not the flapping as much as the breaking away. They are a long time in mastering it—beating the air, kicking up a spray, straining for flight but never quite achieving it . . . The opening of the hunting season invariably finds them in this latter stage.

The boats smelled of tar. In one of them sat Thomas, crouched in the bow, with Romuald and the dog at his back, then their guide, rhythmically transferring the paddle from one hand to the other. They glided, pushing deeper into virgin territory, as rippling waves slapped against the sides. The other boat, along with the heads of the men, loomed up out of the shimmery mist as if suspended. They were steering straight for the opposite shore. As soon as they made out the gaunt shapes of bulrushes, their guide, laying down his paddle, switched to the pole, each thrust against the bottom pitching his body forward.

A flock of ducks: a floating city, a concentration of blotches wrapped in mist. The skiff picked up speed, cutting off their escape route into the rushes; the ducklings, lined up behind their mother, broke in panic, their shrill cries denoting helplessness and desperation. Laughing, Romuald yelled: "Steady, or you'll be taking a bath." Thomas braced himself in the bow, ready to fire. They were nearly alongside when the ducks took wing; there was a frenzy of flapping, water spray. Thomas fired first—bang —then Romuald—bang, bang—the surface was pelted with shot, leaving little circular pools, along with three oblong shapes, immobile, and a fourth, spinning in one spot.

It's hard to explain to someone who's never done it what it's like to retrieve a duck killed by one's own hand. Either you strip and swim out from the shore, in which case the bird will rise to eye level on the swell of your approach; or you maneuver your boat alongside it and stick out your arm. In both cases, it's the interval between seeing it up close and touching it that counts. In the beginning it's no more than a floating object to which you're drawn by curiosity. When touched, it becomes a dead bird. But at the very moment it lies within reach, barely an arm's length away, when its speckled belly lies bobbing up and down in the water, there is always the promise of a surprise. For we never know whom we may have killed—a duck-philosopher perhaps, or a duck-explorer—and we half expect, without seriously believing it, that we will find a diary on it. And with waterfowl there is always the hope, seldom but occasionally rewarded, of finding an identification tag, inscribed with numbers and the markings of some research station located in a faraway land.

They picked up the four mallards and, skirting the reeds along the shore, searched the coves. Thomas spotted a duck under a tangle of stalks and fired: there was a flapping of wings, a toppled bird. "Good spotting!" Romuald commended him. Just then there was a clamor of wings on water; a column of birds, all well advanced in flying, surged upward, and Romuald brought down two with one shot. Denis and Victor responded with a barrage nearby.

The shoreline separating land from water was blurred by a hide of matted grass. They turned Zagray loose. Going under with every step, half treading and half paddling, he splashed resolutely forward, barking all the way. The younger ducks scurried ratlike in all directions, but with such speed there was barely time to take aim. Bulrushes scraped against the hull as their guide pushed them through to a clearing rank with plant roots. It was in one of these little lagoons that it happened. As he was searching for a new target, Thomas discovered—a tribute to his keen eye—that what had looked to be a slight bulge in a pad was a bird's head. Its presence was betrayed by an inability to keep still. With gun already to shoulder, he decided to grant it a reprieve: how could he shoot something so scared to death, so confident of its camouflage? By not killing it, he assumed greater power over it than if he had killed it. Later, as they were working their way out of the marshes, pulling on the stalks to help the rower, he consoled himself with the thought that the bird was still there, alive; that it would never know its life had been spared by a man, would never know that he had contemplated it; that he had reckoned what he could do but had willed otherwise. From that day on, they were forever joined in a pact.

Thomas gave up shooting at ducks in flight, having tried once and failed miserably. Nonetheless, he marveled at Romuald, whose aim was so sure that not even the rocking of the boat could disturb him. Especially with garganeys. So swift they made the air whistle, they were much smaller than mallards; but Romuald never missed—three already lay stretched out beneath the rower's bank.

"How'd you make out, fellas?" Romuald asked of the two Bukowski brothers. Victor started stuttering, while Denis kidded at his brother's expense. "Aw hell, by the time he loaded up, they coulda been nestin' on his head!"

Thomas felt a twinge of discomfort for having deprived Victor of his Berdan.

A light breeze creased the lake, which now matched perfectly the color of the sky. A bell in the village was announcing Sunday Mass. Terns cried as they circled the channel poles sticking out of the water at an angle. A buzzard, aiming for the forest, lazily flapped its wings under a cloud.

Their guides suggested making a detour by way of the river. The river ran off the lake behind the castle; the village of Alunta, hugging the tip of the promontory, was wedged between the old fortress on the hill and the river. At the mouth of a tunnel cutting through the reeds, they flushed some birds, which fluttered upward, eddylike. Romuald brought down one of them—a teal, the smallest of the species.

Lagoonlike, sheltered from winds and storms, the region recalled that African interior where Thomas had once built settlements inaccessible to humans. Protruding black poles, bearded with algae rocked by the current, marked the place where a bridge had once stood. Peasant cottages bordered on the sweet flag; the imprints and depressions left by their beached boats were visible up and down the shoreline. There were apple trees in every garden, the backdrop for fishing nets and laundry strung out to dry. White ducks and geese splashed by the footbridges where the laundry was washed. Viewed from such a tranquil river, a village assumed the dimensions of a country or a kingdom, the details of which escaped notice or were shrugged off as commonplace when observed from the street.

Victor and Denis, their boat now in the lead, had just flushed some mallards, but they held their fire—tame or wild ducks, they couldn't be sure; their ungainly flight triggered three barrels at once, killing one of the birds. The hunting over, they turned back and added up their kill. Romuald and Thomas had twenty-three between them, seven of them Thomas's. The other two boasted fifteen, including one white-eyed duck, and one merganser, gray, with a ruddy head and a hooked bill.

Now facing in the direction of the fortress on the hill, they squinted from the glare. The castle ruins shimmered in the luminescent haze. The pagan priestess who had once lived within those walls, and who was still very present at night, had disappeared forever, taking her place among ghosts and fairy tales. Zagray, suddenly restless, put his paws up onto the side of the skiff. Thomas turned around and held him back by his collar. With the butt of his gun resting on the bank and the barrel against his chest, he had the look of a hunter. But his duck, the one he had left behind, was still hugging the shore. What was it doing? Preening its feathers? Flapping its wings and quacking joyously, now that the danger had passed? Was it God who had decreed that its life should be spared? If it was God's decision, then He must have whispered to Thomas not to shoot. But if that was so, why this feeling that he alone was the arbiter of the bird's fate?

49

※♪♫♪♫※

SAULÈ, THE SUN, wanders in bright raiment through the sky above the earth where all that lives must perish. Those who would endow her with masculine powers can only cause consternation. Her face is the face of earth's mother. Her time is not our time, and of her doings we know only what a mind prey to the terror of its own solitude can fathom. Immutable in her rhythms, she nonetheless has a history of her own, as narrated in the song of antiquity. Long, long ago, during the first spring, before which there was only chaos, she was wedded to the Moon, Ménuo. When she awoke in the morning, her spouse was gone. During his solitary wanderings, he had fallen in love with Aurora, Aušra. Seeing this, Perkunas, god of thunder and lightning, cleaved the Moon with his sword. A just punishment, perhaps, since Aurora was the Sun's daughter by birth. The memory of Aurora's acquiescence to her stepfather's advances may explain Perkunas's later vengeance. The songs, composed by those in whose memories these events were preserved, are mute as to the reasons, testifying only that on Aurora's wedding day Perkunas drove through the gate and struck a green oak, shattering it. Blood gushed from the oak, spattering Aurora's dress and her maiden's wreath. Sun's daughter wept and asked her mother: "Where, Mama dear, shall I wash out the blood?" "Go, daughter dear, to the lake fed by nine rivers." "Where shall I lay my dress out to dry?" asked Aurora. "In the garden, O daughter, where nine roses are in bloom." And the last, most fearful question of all: "When shall I wear my white dress at the wedding?"

"Not until nine suns shine, O daughter, will you wear it."

Of the customs and cares of those who stir in realms above us, we know very little. To this day the nuptials have never been celebrated, but, then, the passage of a thousand years need last no longer than a second. We owe what information we have to a girl who once lost a sheep—this at a time when mortals were still in communion with deities of the sky. "I went to Aurora," the girl sang, "and Aurora said: 'Every morning I must build a fire for Saulè'" (hence the belief that Aurora is unmarried and lives in the house of her mother). "I went to the Evening Star," she continued, recounting her futile efforts, "who said: 'At night I must make up Saulè's bed.'" And the Moon also refused to help her: "Look at my pitiable face cut in half by a sword." (Thanks at last to a sign from Saulè, she discovered her sheep bleating in the distance, somewhere in the polar regions of northern Finland.)

Was Father Monkiewicz a planet? For a butterfly fluttering over the nasturtium and reseda beds, he surely was. Refracted in the butterfly's many eyes, who knows what charm was exerted by the summit of that shiny bald pate? An insect's lifespan of only a few days, but who's to say whether its ephemeral existence didn't find compensation in the ecstasy of shape and color denied us humans?

Father Monkiewicz. And beneath the surface: the toiling of planetary machines, the circulation of blood, the vibrations of a billion nerves. There were those who regarded him as little more than an ant, who would have been provoked to laughter by the sight of his drawers and of something once suggestive of a bathrobe (his cassock was never worn at home, to save on wear and tear). Breviary in hand, he rocked as he paced the yard, this man who, if his mother had not decided to spare at least one of her sons the life of a peasant, might now have been swinging a scythe. Circumstances more compelling than his wanting or not wanting had destined him to become a faithful servant of the Church. Yet it was this man who went about the daily exercise of his duties aimed at reassuring people they were worth more than a mountain, a planet, or the universe itself. Conceived in lust, infants slobbered and wailed as he administered the pinch of salt signifying a life of bitterness; as with the baptismal water he imparted the seal of the Word, elevating these products of Nature to dwelling places of the Holy Spirit. From that moment on, wrenched from the order of the immutable, they were justified in seeing themselves in opposition to Nature. And later, when the body's house began to crumble and the heart to slacken, Father Monkiewicz—or someone else invested with the very same power—would describe crosses in oil on limbs about to be turned to dust: thus was the contract between matter and breath dissolved.

Not all of Father Monkiewicz's time was devoted to pondering his duties. Just now, for example, he was flushing a butterfly from the grass to observe its flight; attending to a bee hovering above the chalice of a white lily; and, with one finger stuck in his breviary, was thinking: "The cheapskates!" The insult sprang from a recollection of the last christening. Hard-strapped, eh? A likely story. And he kicked himself for having settled for less than what was customary.

Thomas took off his cap as he squeezed the gate latch. He stood before the priest, fully conscious of the gravity of his mission. The tone of his words was suitably solemn, tragic. "It's Grandmother Dilbin, Father—she's in a bad way. The doctor said she won't pull through."

"Ah . . . !" uttered the priest at the news. "Right—I'll be there in a jiffy."

He was already tripping toward the stairs.

"I have a britska hitched down below."

"Fine, fine. You wait right here."

Though the rectory was practically next door, sending the britska was obligatory. Grandmother Misia's expression, her hushed consultations with Grandfather and Helen, their changed behavior in the proximity of the Unspoken—swelled Thomas with pride, the pride that came of participating in the most solemn, most grown-up event of all. With all hands out in the fields—it was the start of the harvest season—the task of fetching the priest had fallen to Thomas. Though he knew how to hitch a horse, the straps were always getting tangled, so as usual Grandfather had to lend him a helping hand. There was no road through the Swedish Ramparts, which meant going down the hill and past the shrine—reins tight, feet braced against the front, making a gradual descent toward the bend at the bottom. Once past the crucifix, you could let up on the reins—first, because there was no holding back the horses; and second, because custom allowed it.

The presence of Grandmother Dilbin, who lay motionless in the dark, somehow smaller, was enough to make Thomas, utterly consumed by his role of grandson and man of the house, tiptoe. He pictured the return trip home: the ringing of the bell, the faces peering out from behind fences, the piously bowed heads, himself in the driver's seat.

It was as he had imagined. The priest yelled over to the nearest hut, a small boy climbed aboard, sat down next to Thomas on the front seat, and shook the bell. Thomas drove cautiously (such a responsibility!), glancing furtively to the left and right. Unfortunately, most of the houses stood empty—their occupants were out in the fields —and their progress was observed only by an occasional old man or woman emerging from the yard, where, making the sign of the cross, elbows propped on fence, they followed with their eyes the most important traveler of all.

The warm afternoon sun drew beads of perspiration on the priest's bald pate. Neither the Sun nor the Moon nor the Dawn was any match for Father Monkiewicz. He was a Man, and if that did not suffice, there was always the object he held in his hands to tip the scale, for the planets and stars weighed no more than the sand on the road. His homespun shirt was stained under the armpits and gave off an animal smell, yet it was through such as he that the promise would be fulfilled: "It is sown in corruption; it is raised in incorruption: It is sown in dishonor; it is raised in glory: It is sown in weakness; it is raised in power: It is sown a natural body; it is raised a spiritual body."

50

"A LETTER!"

A barely audible squeak from out of the dark relieved only by a luminous crack in the shutter.

"No, Grandmother, there's no letter."

He was lying; a letter lay on Grandmother Surkont's nightstand. The censoring had begun some time ago—and not without cause, as it turned out. Thomas had eavesdropped on the conversations provoked by this last letter bearing a German stamp and reaching them by way of Königsberg instead of Latvia. God forbid she should ever lay eyes on it! The letter, in the gentlest way possible, had confirmed what Thomas's mother had written privately to her parents. Charged with embezzling army funds, Constantine had been sentenced, given a dishonorable discharge, and was presently applying for a job as a policeman. Theodore must not have taken the news of his mother's illness too seriously if he could be so indiscreet about his brother's misconduct.

The news was never to be divulged. It happened and

at the same time did not happen, reaching only those who were apt to slough it off as just another misdeed. A bullet lethal enough to pierce the human heart, forever buried in wood.

"I'm dying. Call the priest."

How often during her illness had she said she was dying, exaggerating every pain like the fairy-tale princess who complained of being pricked by a pea through seven layers of eiderdown. And perhaps just because they were so natural, so routinely familiar, these sighs—the sighs of hypochondria—actually did bring her some relief. The more we can show by our words that we are in control of our demise, the surer we are it will never come to pass.

"My dear, you will outlive us all," Grandmother Misia hastened to reassure her. "But a priest can't do any harm, can he? Why, if we'd sent for him right away, by now you'd be up and around the garden."

Reassurances. Sick people, refusing to accept what the mind knows to be true, are grateful for the sound of human speech, for that inflection of voice that precludes passage into the realm where there are no voices. Thomas was somehow irritated by Grandmother Misia's saccharine bedside manner. Why exaggerate so much?

That same day the priest climbed the steps framed by vine-covered porch columns. The changes wrought by the forty or fifty years since infancy had not been enough to efface the rustic cattle boy. His feet, now shod, had once borne the red and blue traces of autumnal frosts. Bracing himself with his crop, he contemplated, with the sort of curiosity evoked by rare animals, the procession of gentry arriving either on horseback or in glittering carriages driven by liveried coachmen. And now, as he entered the low-ceilinged rooms, it was not as a vicar of Christ: trailing him by the hand was the person he was once, the one almost too shy to cross the manorial threshold. The respect paid him did not exempt him from the fear of humiliation. He took refuge, therefore, in his surplice and stole: they gave him support, lent a dignified air to his gestures—if a rolypoly figure on short legs is capable of any dignity.

Then the door closed, and Grandmother Dilbin found herself alone with the priest. Despite Misia's false assurances, she could have few illusions now, not when a rustling descended, when the blurs of faces parted to reveal a flickering of white, a violet luster. That premonition of the end, an end so evident to those persisting in the external world, was gradually taking hold, as it must all of us, although it is difficult, if not impossible, to admit to the deprivation of our own private sphere, and that all must submit to the inescapable: the cipher that defies our imagination.

"Are you up to confessing, my daughter?"

"My daughter": thus did this squat Lithuanian shepherd address Bronislawa Ritter from the Hanseatic city of Riga.

"In the name of the Father, and of the Son, and of the Holy Spirit. Amen. Don't worry, my child, just repent your sins and God'll be satisfied."

But Broncia Ritter was wandering through a fog, frantically parting it with her hands, struggling toward some unattainable realm of clarity. "I sinned," she whispered.

"Sinned? How?" He brought his ear up close to her lips.

"I doubted in God . . . that He is, that He hears me."

Her fingers clutched his sleeve. "I sinned."

"Go on, I'm listening."

"I never loved my husband . . . I beg his forgiveness."

Groping through the fog was hard, very hard. Then a soft rustling of leaves: "My son . . . I must tell—"

The priest raised his hand and said out loud: *"Ego te absolvo."* The white disk of the Host descended in the pale light filtering through the partially open shutter.

A ball bounces off the gravel path into a waiting hand, grass glistens with dew, birds sing, generations of birds come and go ... Grandmother Mohl, the one now buried in the family grave at Imbrody, sits unraveling some wool: "Broncia, spread out your hands like this," and slowly winds a soft strand around her wrists. The coral crucifix given her by her grandmother, the one with the tiny window in the center, through which the peeking eye can see the Last Supper being celebrated. Jesus breaks the bread, His brow swarming with rays translucent against the room's cracked wall. All becomes equal, great and small: a peek inside brightly veined coral, a woman's voice in the worn-out dawn of childbirth ("A son!"), the scraping of sleigh runners, the fear of spaces, the gestures made by Christ that were not but are now, time foreshortened, where nothing can be measured by a clock or by the sand in an hourglass ... Mouth too weak to open ... help is coming from outside, from out there ... The Host clings to the tongue ... the coral opens ... she enters, diminished in size, goes up to the table, and receives a piece of the bread broken by Christ ... the legs already far away, in another land, far from the touch of Father Monkiewicz's spatula-like hand, the swollen finger of a plowman's son and grandson, descendant of reapers, now smearing her skin with oil.

Whenever he stood by the bedside of the dying, the priest felt the presence of the Invisible Ones—squatting in a row on the floor, fanning the air, always to a noisy ferment, to a clanging of swords. Those enticed by mental anguish reveled in the effluvia of despair haunting that place where the future had been abolished. Their whispered exhortations were aimed at abetting the self-obsessions of the dying, at trapping them in their own snares;

even as they were conjuring images of past happiness, they showed a Necessity impossible to breach. No wonder they sat in vigil of the blasphemy, the cursing of life's cheat, of the promise betrayed.

By making the sign of the cross, Father Monkiewicz drove them away, those who call for the demanding of proof, always proof, and in that way ensure victory for themselves when the hidden God is put to the test. Just reveal a fraction of your power and I will believe I am not dissolving into nothingness, into the rot of the earth: they crawl alongside, trying to sustain the idea amid the dissolution of all ideas.

But lying on Michalina Surkont's nightstand was a letter, a letter bearing news that prayers are rarely answered. If her having begotten bad fruit was interpreted by her as an affirmation of her baseness, then the letter could only worsen her grief. Was there any wisdom in keeping it from her? Perhaps she was being put to the supreme test: the necessity of trusting when all reason for trusting had been refused. By taking pity on her, by sparing her the blow, people were helping her the only way they knew how: through the sharing of illusions. For those verdicts delivered from on high were judged to be excessively severe.

"Asleep yet?"

"Barely."

Dr. Kohn left behind some morphine and told them how to use a syringe. At first, when he was asked about her illness, it was "probable cancer," then simply "cancer," meaning there was little he could do. Not so Father Monkiewicz, for no sooner did he leave than her chest began to heave and her breathing became more regular.

Gathering the folds of his cassock, the priest, always more sure of himself when seated at table, sat down in the dining room. After uttering a few appropriate remarks, he commented on this season's exceptionally good crop.

"The mercury is falling." Grandfather sighed. "I hope they can get in the harvest before it rains." He offered him some sweetmeats.

The priest was itching for the latest political and domestic gossip.

"Poor Mrs. Dilbin. All alone without her sons. They're so far away."

More he didn't learn.

"Far, far away," Grandfather repeated. "Ah well, a man's home is where he finds work."

"Not everywhere are things the way they are here." Grandmother could not let go an opportunity to vent her sarcasm.

"Duty first."

The priest attributed the flour sacks in his britska (a welcome gift, coming as it did just before the harvest) to the man of the house, as Surkont's wife, that miserly skin-flint of a woman, would have taken advantage of his timidity in laying claim to any worldly compensation. Thomas slipped the harness over the horse's head and forced the bit between lips stained a yellow-green. The lindens gave off a honey smell; the bees, clinging to their humming flowers, went about their work as Bronislawa Ritter slowly meandered on the outskirts of time.

51

STACKING A rack wagon is like putting up a house: both require skill. Once the structure is up, a rope, one end looped around a log laid lengthwise on top, is fastened to the platform; the beam, round and smooth from years of hauling, is used to brace the load, to keep it from spilling every time the wagon lurches. Another rope is strung at the back and two men are needed to cinch it, the risk being that the beam, if it ever slipped out, could fracture the horses' necks. When the driver climbs up on top, he looks down on horses not much bigger than squirrels and has to lie flat to clear the barn door. All day long, these rectangular yellow ricks wobble down the lane, blades of straw among the branches marking where a wagon has brushed a hazel bush. A sultry air, swelling clouds, and by evening it begins to rain—a light drizzle that gradually becomes a downpour lasting until daybreak.

Thomas sensed an air of impatience around the house. Misia and Antonina took turns at Grandmother's bedside, but privately they bore her a grudge. Pity combined with sleepiness often makes one impatient for the end. But then the weather turned sunny, the air shimmered from the heat, and the patient was given a shot of morphine. Thomas thought of Borkuny; no telling how long before he could make another trip out there. To air the room, they opened the shutters and window, letting in a swallow, which described a circle around the room.

On the afternoon of the third day following the priest's visit, Antonina barked out Thomas's name from the porch. He jumped up from the lawn, annoyed at having been discovered there: it gave the impression of keeping a deathwatch. Semidarkness. He found Misia struggling with the trunk lid—the same trunk from which Grandmother Broncia had produced so many trinkets. Packed inside the lid was a funeral candle. "When it's time for me to die, remember where it is."

There was a wavering and remitting in the sick woman's eyes that somehow complemented the grating voice of recent days. Antonina knelt down and, reading from a book, began reciting a litany in Lithuanian, while

Grandmother Surkont, her nose—the nose of a big mouse —beetling over the head of the bed, fussed about, turning the wax candle in her hand.

Thomas, more acutely aware than ever of his physical self, stood by the window, rubbing one bare foot against the other in the warm patch of sunshine on the wood-stained flooring. His heart was ticking, his gaze taking in every detail; he was aching to stretch, lift his arms, take a deep breath. His grandmother's fading swelled him with a triumph odious even to himself. It was cut short by a sob. He looked at her, her chest fighting for one more breath, so small and defenseless against the monstrosity bearing blindly down on her; and full of remorse for all his past injustices toward her, he collapsed at the foot of the bed, crying "Grandmother, Grandmother . . . !"

Though apparently still conscious, she was oblivious of their presence. He rose to his feet and, swallowing his tears, endeavored to fix her every gesture, her every twitch; her fingers opening and closing on the bedcover, the rasping sound escaping from her mouth. She was resisting the flight of language.

"Con-stan-tine . . ."

A match was struck, the wick took, burning low; the deathwatch had begun.

"Jesus!" she said in a distinct voice.

And then, in a low whisper, one which trailed into silence but which was still overheard by Thomas: "Save me."

Father Monkiewicz, had he been present, would have said that the Invisible Ones had been defeated. For the law which says that whatever dies must scatter into ashes and fade into oblivion had been defied by a single hope: by Him who has the power to break the law. Without demanding any proof, despite all arguments to the contrary, she believed.

The whites of her eyes were motionless; a hush except

for the sputtering candle. But no: her breast heaved. A deep breath, an interval lasting several seconds, and the body which had appeared dead exhaled—a startling, fitful, unrecognizable rattle. Thomas shuddered at this surrendering of one's humanity. The woman lying there was no longer Grandmother Dilbin, but death itself; neither the shape of her head nor the complexion of her skin denoted anything anymore; even the terror conveyed by her "Oyey, oyey" was gone. In the space of a half hour (it might have consumed a lifetime), her mouth became fixed, parted in the act of inhaling.

"May eternal light shine upon her, amen," whispered Misia, and she gently lowered the dead woman's eyelids with one finger. Slowly, solemnly, Grandfather crossed himself. They debated where to move her. The bed sagged so much they were afraid the body would stiffen in its half-crouched position. They decided to bring in the long table, and Thomas helped them to get it through the door. The table was covered with a dark blanket.

He helped move Grandmother Dilbin onto the table. As he wrapped his arm around her torso, her nightie shifted and he quickly averted his gaze. Glancing down at the bed sheet when they had her in the air, he in front and Antonina in back, he saw a blotch of feces excreted during the death spasm.

He came back after the washing and dressing. Hands folded on breast, heels touching, soles spread apart, jaw bound with a handkerchief. The open window let in the sounds of evening: the quacking of ducks, the slow rumbling of a cart, a horse's whinny. The world outside was so different, so serene, that it made what he had just witnessed seem unreal.

They sent him to get the cartwright, easing the pain. The cartwright, serving both the manor and the village, lived in the commune. Thomas brought him to the manor and helped him with the measurements. But that evening he had trouble getting to sleep. How could he sleep if next door her body lay in repose, if she could read his shabby thoughts from the other world. Yes, he had derived pleasure from watching her die. A bitter pleasure, like the taste of berries, which, however much they may burn the tongue, keep tantalizing us to eat more. Candles were burning in two tall candle holders beside the table-catafalque, prayers were being recited, but she was all alone in the dark night.

Early the next morning—the wax in the candleholders was embedded with a moth's wings; his grandmother's eyelids had parted, revealing a thin strip of white —he went to see the cartwright go about the art of coffin-making. The yard in front of the shop was littered with rimless wooden wheels stacked one against the other and with piles of cut lumber. Thomas was already familiar with the workbench, with its surface rough and scored with cuts and indentations, with its hand vises at the sides, whose threaded bolts screwed in and out with such ease, and with the constant smell of shavings underfoot. He could, as now, sit rapt on a stump, spellbound by the back-and-forth motion of the wood plane.

"Pine's no good; let's use oak," said the master carpenter. (Because of his beetling nose and bulging cheeks, Kelpšis bore a slight resemblance to Misia.) The backs of his hands were a tangle of veins, a landscape of mountains and valleys. A ribbon of shavings curled up from the chink in the plane, and Thomas rejoiced at this mastery over wooden matter; if a board could be planed, then anything could be planed, made smooth. Thus were Grandmother's cheeks to be graced forever by oak-grained filigree. The coffin made him relive his dream of Magdalena. He wondered about the worms, whether they could squeeze through the slits. A white skull, deep sockets for eyes, the durability of wood. His grandmother most certainly was dead, not in a stupor or coma. The gruesome stories she had told of coffins that had been known to bang after being sealed and even after being lowered into the grave, and of how, after clearing away the dirt and raising the lid, they had found people suffocated inside, their bodies convulsed by the struggle to escape. Grandmother had been so afraid of waking to discover she had been buried alive that she insisted it was better to verify death as someone in her family had done: by shattering the skull with a hammer.

Oak was also chosen for the cross. The cartwright took a fat pencil from his pocket, wet it with spit, and drew the outline of a cross on a wood chip. He handed it to Thomas, seeking his opinion, and he again savored a grandson's prerogative. The sketch showed a sort of lean-to spanning the arms of the cross.

"What's that for?" he asked, pointing to the little shelter.

"Got to. Two boards nailed together—uh-uh, not very pretty. Anyway, it'll keep the rain off, keep it from rotting."

According to Antonina, the soul circles the shell it has just abandoned. It hovers about, examining its former self, amazed that it could have seen itself until now only in relation to a body. As the hours go by, the face, once the soul's mirror, begins more and more to resemble rock moss. That evening Thomas witnessed a change in his grandmother's appearance, but suddenly withdrew in panic: she had looked at him! He bolted for the door, all set to yell that she was waking from a coma. But she made not the slightest movement. It was an illusion, caused by a further parting of the eyelids and the play of candlelight in the whites of her eyes. A soul no longer lived inside. If Antonina was right, it was floating about the room, brushing familiar objects, biding its time until the funeral, when with a clear conscience it could finally abandon what, after all, had once been its own.

52

CLOUDS GATHER into big-bellied shapes; a dragon with a twisted tail, fins, and streaming jaws journeys across the sky; the jaws become more attenuated, frazzled, until a tiny cluster of white detaches itself and, propelled by the dragon's breath, is borne swiftly away. A slender cross traverses the dragon's flank; the cross is held by the sacristan, who is followed by the priest, then the coffin carried by Balthazar, Pakenas, Kelpšis, and the young Sypniewski. The procession files across the Swedish Ramparts, from the top of which the eye can make out diminutive figures moving between the peaked sheaves that line the steeply sloped fields on the opposite shore.

Luke Juchniewicz, who arrived yesterday with Helen, runs up to the coffin to relieve Pakenas, his coattails parting to reveal a pair of dark checkered pants. He shifts his head under the load, the coffin sags, wobbles as his mincing steps throw the others off stride. Thomas's hopes are again betrayed: Luke has lived up to his comic role. But Luke is stubborn and with face tearfully contorted he bears up. Shatybelko has on a dark blue capote; his wife, a silk scarf embroidered with black flowers.

They seat themselves in the church pews. Thomas tries to pray but can't help thinking of the freshly dug grave. The family plot has room for only two more graves —one for Misia, the other for Grandfather—so Grandmother Dilbin has to be interred nearby. In digging her grave, they struck an oak root that had to be cut with an ax, leaving white wounds in the clay. The roots will enfold, possibly invade the coffin, and Grandmother will be trapped as in a bird's claws.

The others are still trailing toward the exit by the time he is threading his way through the tombstones. Here it is, on the outskirts of the cemetery, chosen for its proximity to the Surkonts, and where, only a few steps away, now partially eroded and tufted with weeds, stands another mound, that of Thomas's friend, Magdalena. Somehow they must meet, and he tries to imagine it, knowing that in reality there was no imagining it. They reach out to one another —Magdalena's head is now restored—and burst into tears.

"Why, oh, why did we punish ourselves so? Why were we strangers until now? Why did we have to suffer in solitude? You could have stayed with me. I could have found you a husband, and you, with your courage, could have helped me through life. Too bad people can't love each other until after they die. What's it like to poison yourself? I'm curious."

"Hard," Magdalena sighs. "I prayed for God's forgiveness, on my knees I swallowed the poison, but right away I got scared, cried out for help . . ."

They look young—Grandmother exactly as in the old photographs showing her cinched snugly at the waist. They call each other by first name.

"Why did you spook people?" asks Grandmother.

Magdalena smiles. "Why ask when you already know?"

"Yes, now I know . . ."

Thomas could not admit to their inhabiting separate worlds, no more than he could assent to Magdalena's soul being among the damned. Damned were those who failed to evoke pity or love. There, around the freshly dug grave, the others are already clustered as he begins a Hail Mary, digging his nails into his palm to add fervor to the recitation. He commends Magdalena to the Mother of God.

The coffin is lowered in a sling, seesawing, getting

snagged on a severed root before finally settling on the bottom. Thomas looks down while Father Monkiewicz delivers the graveside sermon. He thinks: For hundreds, thousands of years they have been burying the dead like this; if all were to rise at the same time, one beside the other, their millions would make a solid wall. Every living person knows he must die—Grandfather says they are waiting for him between the chains of the Surkont plot. They know, yet don't seem to care. Death—the passing from one life to another—is so terrifying, why aren't they screaming, tearing their hair out . . . ? But, no—nothing. Their calm, their shrugging it off with a "That's the way it is . . ."—baffled him. He believed there was a secret that God revealed to those who wanted Him to very much: that death was not inevitable, not what it was made out to be. Or did they know more than they were letting on, and was that why they took it so calmly? Thomas, in other words, gave them credit, just as he did Luke, who, if he did not possess another, more intelligent self, would have demolished an entire order; just so, grownups would have been nothing more than pathetic children in disguise. What looked to be simple could not be so simple.

One day he too would be lowered in a sling. Even if he became Pope? Even. But if the grenade had gone off that time, he would have died without knowing he was dying. The grouse brought down by Romuald had not had time to feel the terror. Oh, God, don't let me die a slow death like Grandmother.

"You throw first," Misia said, half aloud. Yes, as her grandson, he was the closest, indeed the only blood relative present. He picked up a yellowish clod of dirt and threw it, watching it shatter as it landed; others fell, drumming on the wooden coffin lid, and then came the shoveling, creating a narrow ridge of earth along the top plank. They worked quickly, filling the cracks between the coffin walls and then the surrounding gaps until the brown-stained boards assumed the tawny color of earth. If the coffin had aroused curiosity from the moment it was sealed, from the moment it contained a body, the urge was all the greater now: an empty space, a tiny pocket of air, a segment of tunnel.

Oaks overhead, some so old they must have sheltered Hieronymous Surkont on his horseback rides. At the foot of the close-cropped slope, a stream ran under a footbridge before emptying into the Issa. Orchards and huts on the other side of the canyon. Such was the view marking the end of the journey.

"We mustn't forget to order a plate," Thomas's grandfather said.

"It should read: *The widow of an 1863 insurgent*," Thomas intruded, knowing how proud she was of the past.

"Thomas and I will plant some flowers," promised Antonina.

Kelpšis held steady his cross with the shelter and planted it in the ground, shoring it up with dirt and leveling the rectangular-shaped grave with his shovel. Here our chronicler rests his pen as he tries to visualize those who will come to this place many years hence. Who are they? What sort of trade? Parking their shiny car down by the bridge, they will hike the rest of the way on foot. "What a funny old cross. Look at those oaks—what a waste of good lumber!" It's obvious they do not like death; the mere thought of it diminishes their dignity; their feet squarely on the ground, they proclaim, "We are alive!" Yet each is endowed with a heart, a heart that is sometimes gripped by terror, and their feeling of superiority over those who have passed is scarcely a protection. Bluish-gray lichen will hang from Kelpšis's shelter, the name on the plate will have faded. And clouds will gather into big-bellied shapes, just as on that day, long ago.

53

IT WAS a sound unlike any the human throat could make, but Thomas soon got the hang of it. It was hard going at first, but he practiced it to perfection, to a point where he almost believed he could speak their language. In the forest near Borkuny there was a hollow, thick with alder, and in spring the hollow became a lake. It was just after sundown, the treetops stood black against the orange sky: the time was right. He stood facing a solid wall of young trees, immersed in slime and the effluvium of rotting leaves, and with calculated fury, avoiding any abrupt movements, he picked off the mosquitoes attacking his face and neck. The mosquitoes were so bloated with blood that his palms were streaked from swatting. Softly, he released the safety on his Berdan. The Berdan, borrowed from Victor for the summer, had somehow become a part of him.

"What you need it for, anyway?" Romuald had told his brother. "You're too busy to take it out. It just hangs there, don't it? So why not let Thomas do a little huntin'."

Victor had consented.

Goshawks nested deep in the forest, deep enough for the swampy ground to make access tricky. Once they had got their wings, the young spent the day circling the forest, high up in the air, in imitation of their parents; by evening, the family was homeward bound for the night. The day before yesterday, Thomas had tested his baiting call and was answered on several sides. The secret was to pick a time when not all were back yet, because that was the time of their mutual summoning. The shrieking was getting closer; soon he spotted a pair of gray wings contoured among the leaves, heard the flutter as the hawk, oblivious of Thomas hidden in the shadows below, lighted on the slender treetop. He called and waited for an answer. Then ever so slowly he brought the barrel to eye level and squeezed the trigger. It fell! He spent a long time searching for it, afraid he might have to wait until dawn, when he practically tripped over it, its buff coloring almost bright against the dark-weeded swamp. And those flight feathers, stretching to full length as he picked the bird up by the wing . . . He nicked his finger while prying apart its tightly clenched claw. But one bird was hardly enough, not when he had gained the advantage. He waited a whole day before trying his luck a second time.

"Eee-eee!" The shrillness came from a constriction of the throat muscles, which, if done often enough, produced a painful cramping sensation. He could hear them deep in the forest. Would they fly back today, or not? Silence except for the buzzing of mosquitoes, a vertical column dancing up and down in the sunlight. He tried again: *"Eee-eee . . ."* What exactly this sound meant in their language he didn't know, though there was no mistaking the tone of longing, of urgency in it. They were coming, he could tell! He sent out another call; it carried in the silence that had already found other birds perched for the night or preening their feathers. Then it happened —that unremitting keening reaching him from several directions at once. They were out there, all right.

He savored his moment of triumph, trying not to make too much of it. The younger hawks were not yet trained to distinguish the real thing from an imitation, nor were there any jays to warn of a human presence. He called a third and final time, knowing that at close range he might give himself away.

Above the tree line—one bird shape, then another. In flight, but that still didn't mean anything. Heads up—a shadow just flitted through the brush, in among those young alders. It was perched. Where? The mosquitoes lining Thomas's arms and forehead could now feel secure; he was paralyzed. He could hear it crying from another treetop, but the foliage blocked his view. If he moved closer, by as much as a few steps even, the bird would spot him and resort to that peculiar flight when flushed by a man: the flight of mystery.

He would have to risk another call. Intent on getting it right, losing all sense of himself, he incarnated the soul of a goshawk. *"Eee-eee . . ."* Suddenly alerted, the bird responded. A flutter of wings gave Thomas his target. He took aim, guessing more by instinct the location of the mouse-gray blotch against the black. A report: the bird lurched forward, bunched up into a ball, and fell, arresting its descent as it brushed the boughs. Thomas came on the run, the branches whipping his face. A second kill! a voice piped inside him. He found the bird lying on its back, still alive, its claws exposed in self-defense. Instead of a companion or its mother—whose keening had beckoned so unerringly—there now stood, leaning over its inert body, a giant. The goshawk was a predator—Thomas thought by way of justifying the act—one that fed on the meat and blood of pigeons and chickens. Holding the gun upright, he clubbed the bird's head with the stock and watched as it veiled its golden eyes with its lower eyelids. After the skinning, the meat would go to Lutnia and the stuffed skin would preserve indefinitely the appearance of a discrete being—until the moths set in.

If Thomas was troubled by a guilty conscience (as he frequently was), he told himself that a creature killed by one's hand would have had to die anyway, that it didn't really matter when or how. That these same animals might have had an urge to live could not distract him from a higher ambition: the need for a trophy. The sky was already a deep shade of blue as he emerged from the forest and crossed the little footbridge over the stream. Through the bushes he saw the house lights burning. Barbarka was fixing supper. What would she say to this second kill?

But on the third try his luck ran out: the gunfire had scared them away. His bird-calling ability continued to bring him glory, until one morning (not that summer but another), as he went to test it, his voice broke. It had changed, become huskier, and he never recovered the purity of that signal that was something between a cat's meow and the whistle of a bullet.

54

BARBARKA slapped Romuald's face so hard it echoed in the orchard. "What's got into you?" he kept saying as he backed away. Taking the enemy by surprise was always the best tactic, and Romuald's surprise could not have been more genuine. A peaceful Sunday morning, unmarred by any squabbles or spats, when suddenly: "You cheater! You skirt chaser! Take that! That's what you get for cheating on me!" Romuald, no less stunned than if he'd sighted a comet, could have easily chased her off his property; but thinking she might have gone berserk, he quietly acquiesced. A moment later, a sobbing Barbarka was running down the forest path.

Though the tears were sincere, the slapping had come of a mixture of anger and premeditation. Her woman's instinct had told her that, win or lose, this was the only way, that moping and sulking would get her nowhere. The jump was best measured by the eye, not by any arithmetic. Romuald was the enemy, but not only. He was pleased with her service, and she knew it. Besides, he would have been hard put to replace her, to find another housekeeper with her love of cleanliness and tidiness and her willingness to try her hand at any kind of work, even plowing (once, when Romuald had taken ill, she had plowed practically on her own after the hired farmhand lost his temper and walked off the job). She was also a better cook than most. Romuald was getting on in years, was rather set in his ways; breaking in someone else would not be easy. But there were other reasons for her self-assurance.

They led a secluded life, but were not in need of company. Spring and summer, a time of endless chores, passed quickly. Barbarka spent the autumn canning apples and pears; the rainy season, at her spinning wheel (she knew how to weave a tight weave). They raised their own flax and bought their wool from Masiulis. She made linen from homespun; on her loom, cloth. In winter the thump of the shifting foot pedal lasted until sunset; in the evening she could spin almost blindfolded—weaving required greater light and concentration. A wooden loom and a handful of skirts stored in a chest were her only dowry.

The busy work week ended with Saturday's bathing ceremony and a trip to Sunday Mass, either in the britska or on foot. Romuald, not a fervid churchgoer, often skipped several Sundays in a row for the sake of his hunting.

The bathhouse was built with Romuald's own hands, on the river, and it was built according to plan. There were two rooms. In one he installed clothes-pegs, even a hand-carved bench for dressing and undressing. It also housed a log fireplace, the flat stone on the other side reaching such temperatures that a pail of water tossed on it was immediately converted to steam. In the other room, three shelves, built steplike one on top of the other, stretched from wall to wall. To keep out the wind, the scourge of any bathhouse, the gaps between the logs were stuffed annually with moss.

The ceremony began with the washing of Romuald's back and shoulders, with Barbarka doing the scrubbing. Romuald then got up a good amount of steam—the thicker, the better—and took to the highest shelf, a bucket of cold water within easy reach (it was her job to see that it got there), a splash of cold water being one way of prolonging the thing. Standing below, besom in hand, Barbarka would then run the birch branches over his chest and belly, which took some know-how: exposure to the steam left the skin so sensitive that the slightest brush of the twigs, even more than a lash, burned like a red-hot poker, the trick being therefore to alternate the flicking and the whipping. Romuald would sigh and holler "Ahhh! More! More!" roll over on his belly, scoop water from the pail, yell "Come on! Harder! Harder!" then, red as a lobster, bolt outside and welter in the snow for as long as it took to numb the body against the cold. Then it was back to the shelf, because now it was Barbarka's turn, and he kept her up there, and how he did, and she groaning "Oyey, I cain't take it no more," and he saying "Sure you can; just turn over," working her with the switch, and she laughing and screeching "Cut it out, hear? That's enough!"

If he dismissed her, who would go to the bathhouse with him? Who would scrub his back and shoulders? He liked to look at her; she could tell. She was all health and youth, her breasts just the right size, sturdy in the haunches and shoulders. Skin a light pink, almost white alongside his. Yes, she satisfied his male pride in more ways than one.

In more ways than one. In submitting to the love ritual, Barbarka would invoke the most sacred Biblical names (which may not have been appropriate, but at such times who cares what is appropriate and what is not?), screaming in a whisper at the height of her panting: "Romuaaald!" Motionless, he would contemplate the wave breaking on him, the wave he himself had set in motion. (In love, as in everything else, Romuald was a perfectionist.) He liked it when she caught her breath, and he again heard that incoherent litany of hers. Nor did she grumble if he went at it again and again and again . . . No, parting was out of the question. And if, despite time-honored methods, a kid was born? Well, so? And the next morning it was a new world, dew on the window, a trembling in the knees. And songs at the loom, joyous songs.

But at the moment she was crying as she pictured him in the orchard. His coming down the path, the sound of his footsteps, the creaking boards, and that voice—"Out!" *Let* him throw her out—he would be the one to suffer most. He didn't need this fling with Helen Juchniewicz. An aristocratic whim, so like a man, one of those male stupidities women had to put up with. Underneath all the masquerading, he was a man like any other. High time he saw how he was messing things up, chasing after highbred ladies just to prove he was no worse than other folk.

If not for old lady Bukowski . . . Now, there was the real enemy. While she did not oppose Barbarka's staying with Romuald—he needed company, same as any man— she kept a vigilant eye on them. The old lady would give him hell if he as much as sat her down next to him in the britska on the way to church: What would people say? A servant girl should know her place.

Yes, the old lady was an obstacle. An obstacle to her dream of becoming mistress of Borkuny, secure in the knowledge that she could never be evicted. But no Bukowski had ever married a peasant, not even a richly dowered one, much less one like herself. Sitting and staring into her lap, her knees spread wide apart, her skirt taut, Barbarka gave way to despair. Oh, if those were her only worries! When he came in, she would go down on her knees and beg forgiveness. Just let things be as they were.

The back of Romuald's neck—a robust neck, scored with tiny oblique rectangles—was red as a turkey's crest. Standing in rigid concentration, he suddenly made for the house, quickening his stride. He paused in front of the porch, then slowly mounted the wooden steps, went into his room, and took down the shotgun.

The forest, provided one attends to its whispering, can counsel a man what to do. Whether owing to the forest's counsel or the premise that men are tough only on the outside, that afternoon Romuald said nothing. But that evening, after the milking, his matter-of-fact voice rang out: "Barbarka!"

Quivering all over, she entered the room.

"On your belly!"

In his hand was the lash with the deer-hoof handle. He pulled back her skirt and, with measured but painful strokes, began whipping her bare buttocks. She winced and writhed and dug her teeth into the pillow; but she was happy. His punishing her could mean only one thing: She was *his*! And the punishment was deserved.

What came later was, in a way, a reward, the greater in that love mixed with tears and pain takes on a sweetness all its own. For it is one of man's stranger habits that even as he nears the moment of ecstasy, even as the body is surrendering, the mind continues to wander, more conscious than ever of the cleavage. The holy names that fell from Barbarka's lips proved that she was a faithful daughter of the Church, that the power of her emotions could be contained in no other language, all the while the mind was contemplating its triumph. For the same woman who a moment before would have been perfectly content with things as they were, that same woman was now plotting against old lady Bukowski. While the visible Barbarka hungered for the violation and the engorgement, the invisible Barbarka was insinuating that there were far worse things than having a baby. Thus was a certain alliance struck between them.

55

WITH THE blackcock hunt only a week away, the incident with Aunt Helen thrust Thomas into perplexity. However great his dislike for her, he was bound by a sense of family loyalty. The incident: They were on their way to Borkuny (he couldn't resist tagging along when she decided to go), Thomas working the whip and reins, the two of them seated side by side, and the horse had just started climbing the wooded knoll when—it was hard to say which came first, the seeing or the hearing of it—out from behind a young spruce came a burst of white and a woman's shrieking, and both the screaming and the whiteness belonged to Barbarka, but now so strangely altered that Thomas was awestruck.

Flushed, eyebrows knitted, brandishing a hazel switch in one hand, she screeched: "Bitch! I'll teach you to do yer romancin' round here!" Then a stream of cuss words in two languages. "If I ever catch you around Borkuny again, you'll git such a whippin'—"

There was a *swish* and Helen cupped her cheek with both hands; then another, only this time she stuck out her arm for protection. Thomas, thoroughly overwhelmed, gave the horses the whip and there was a clatter of wheels.

"Back, Tommy! Back! Good Lord, what did I do, what did I do! Back, Tommy! I'll never set foot out here again, so help me!"

Turning around on a narrow trail was easier said

than done, but he managed it, wheel scraping against the side, crushing young scrub, and almost tipping over in the process. Big tears ran down his aunt's face; now it was she who was flushed, and her muted voice expressed shock. Prayerfully clasping both hands together, she turned up her blue eyes and implored heaven to exact revenge for the outrage she had so innocently endured.

"What a beastly thing to do. I don't understand. Why? How could she do such a thing? She must be deranged."

Thomas concealed his discomfort by gazing straight ahead, affecting concentration. Romancing was the word for it, all right. All those sugary looks and dewy-eyed, plum-eyed glances . . . But how did Barbarka fit in? That he couldn't quite understand. Maybe Romuald had tired of all the sweet-talk; maybe the ambush in the woods was his doing. But why plot against his aunt with the help of a servant girl?

Thomas had a hunting date with Romuald. Theirs was a friendship between men, far above the petty bickering of grownups. But what if his aunt was to stop visiting Borkuny, if she forbade him or anyone else to go for reason of decorum? Or would she? Although for Thomas such matters bordered on the inscrutable, he sensed in his aunt's behavior the residue of some shame. She said nothing, not a word, but her silence was the beginning of a pact between them. She sat beside him in the wagon, her mouth hemmed by deep creases, seesawing like an owl.

"What? Back already?" asked Grandmother Misia.

"Nobody home," Helen said, lying effortlessly.

Thomas thus emerged not only as a victor but as an accomplice. For his recollection of the avenging Barbarka was tainted with memories of a more private nature. Not long before, while out brush-breaking with the Berdan, he had walked out onto the forest apron skirting the hay fields of Pogirai. He was spotted by an old peasant, who stood high up on a rack wagon, stacking the sheaves which another man, this one younger, pitched up to him from below. Thomas greeted him with the traditional *Padek Dèvu*—Lithuanian for "God's help"—when the old man broke off, stood up straight on the haystack, and began reviling him with his shaking fist raised sunward. Thomas, who hardly knew the man, and then only by sight, was mortified by this show of contempt, especially since he had done nothing to deserve it. Anger provoked by anger was understandable; but he had been polite, and his civility had met with the old man's fury and for one reason only: he was a Polish *pan*. Stranded out in the open, Thomas shuffled off at a deliberately slow pace—so as not to give the impression of running—his cheeks on fire, his horse-shoe-shaped mouth (though he would have been the last to admit it) quivering.

Something about Barbarka's ambush reminded him of that day. Only here it was he and Helen in the britska, and Barbarka . . . But if Romuald was behind the conspiracy— And inexplicably, inexorably, the image of Dominic came to mind—idolized, sacrilegious Dominic, who more than once had appeared in his dreams in the guise of Barbarka. "Nice company, this Mr. Bukowski"— Misia used to say, laying undue emphasis on the "Mister." "Honestly, the riffraff we let into this house!"

Romuald smelled of tobacco and masculine strength and Thomas had no desire to lose him. When he suddenly realized what was at stake—the hunt, the gun, everything —he was aghast at having had such thoughts.

He managed to pry out of his grandmother some cloth scraps for leggings and fixed himself a pair of moccasins from bast: for where he was going, the marshland, nothing else would do.

56

BALTHAZAR's distillery was located in the forest, far from the beaten track, and if the police came at all, it was to sample Balthazar's homemade brew up at the cottage, a couple of bottles sufficing to ensure the right kind of report. The liquor served not only Balthazar's own private use (he couldn't get drunk on beer), and not only as bootleg. Ever since the Commission's inspection of the forest—under his supervision—the village of Pogirai had borne him a grudge. Surkont's hospitality toward the three officials, their high spirits and flushed faces as they climbed aboard the britska, how they had sung most of the way, how one almost fell out—none of it had gone unnoticed. (Spirits later got so high they really couldn't tell the grass from the trees.) There were reasons, all carefully elaborated, why Pogirai was anxious for the forest to become state property, even at the expense of giving up certain privileges, such as poaching. Although no one except Joseph knew the real story behind the filing date of the Surkont land division, people's instincts told them that the timberland would be crucial to negotiations with the manor over the disputed pasturage. They were sore at Balthazar for conniving with Surkont, and the moonshine was used to quiet the most vociferous throats. One refusal and they were liable to take revenge by leading the police straight to the distillery in the woods.

Now when the men huddled after Sunday Mass by the church wall in Gine, the talk was mostly of the forest.

"That Surkont's a weasel." It was the young Wackonis, no longer wearing his military tunic but dressed like

Joseph the Black in a high-necked homespun jacket. The episode with the grenade had never been broached again; it was a thing of the past, buried and forgotten.

"You can bet," he said, running the tip of his tongue along the seam of his hand-rolled cigarette, "you can bet *he* ain't gonter give up what's his."

A poker face, without so much as a stare or facial twitch to give away the man's intent. But the mockery—a mockery aimed at the gullible—was not lost on Joseph.

"Maybe not now he won't," he conceded. "But give him a year or two."

"Balthazar's coverin' for him."

"He's tying his own noose."

"And it's gettin' tighter all the time. They say that Juchniewicz woman is gonter give him the boot."

"Who said?"

"Today, in the commune. Came lookin' for a house for him. He moves out, she moves in."

Joseph spat as a sign of his disgust. "A hired hand, eh? Uh-uh, he ain't that dumb."

"Think he won't?"

"Ain't nobody goin' to make him quit the forest. He'll fight it all the way. Take him to court and you can wait another ten years . . ."

"No more. He's runnin' scared. Down comes a pine cone and he thinks it's the sky fallin'.'"

"What drink won't do to a man."

Wackonis's attitude, thus expressed, proof that one's judgment of others should always be based on strict observation, spoke for the majority of the villagers: plenty of bad blood and plenty of revulsion. Where another man would take a hundred steps in stride, Balthazar was the sort who ran in circles, panting his lungs out, banging his fists against imaginary walls. But Balthazar was ignorant of their feelings, of that mixture of disgust and pity. The prison in which he was wrestling was real, and if anyone had told him he was imagining things he would have sloughed it off as the speech of blind and stupid men. And the liquoring was just to see their faces momentarily brighten, to hear a word of praise, to prove to himself that he was "a good man." So far, the liquor had done the trick; a little envy maybe, but that's as far as it went. Now there was this damned Commission, all these shady dealings of the manor . . . Wasn't it bad enough they'd made him an outcast, why had Surkont to go and mention his daughter —true, only one sentence, roundaboutlike, but enough to stand as a warning.

A batch of brew seething in a kettle, a big-cheeked face coppered by a blazing wood fire. Balthazar sat on the edge of the ditch staring down at the distillery below him, the darkness unrelieved except for the hazel leaves shimmering at his back. A hand blotting out the stars, aiming for the forests, guided by moonbeams over the waves of the Baltic . . . Oh, why didn't someone's hand reach down and seize this tiny speck on the rotating earth, pick it up, and whisk old Balthazar away? Anywhere, didn't matter where, into the orchestra pit in the middle of a big-city concert, music stands flying, audience in an uproar, and he, Balthazar, sprawled on all fours, a fury of motion in long-legged boots, would rise to his feet, rocking, wild: "Yell!"

And obedient to the command of his tormentor, he would proclaim his secret affliction, that illness affecting so many of us born along the shores of the Issa: "It's not enough!"

"Not enough!"

"It was not enough just to live!"

"Yell!"

And then a savage howl: "It's wrong! All wrong!"

A cry protesting the fact that the earth was the earth; the sky, the sky. Against Nature's boundaries. Against the law which says every "I" must be itself and nothing more.

But instead of being borne away by a hand, Balthazar got the hiccups. He scratched his chest through his open shirt and wrapped himself in his sheepskin against the chilly, transparent night.

The villagers of Pogirai were revulsed by the sight of a man who didn't know what he wanted, who made life hard for himself, embroiling himself in order not to be alone with his fear, that nameless, faceless terror. But who knew whether another fate did not await him, one which had been there all along, since the beginning of the world, that only he could fulfill but which had not been fulfilled, so that in the place where an oak should have stood there was now only empty space containing the barest outline of a branch.

Balthazar slid down from the edge of the pit, squatted, and stuck a tin cup under the spout. A long swig. From deep within the forest came the keening of a bird being torn apart. Dead silence except for the crackling fire. The sky was getting paler; a falling star traced a perfect line across the darker half.

"Kill somebody."

"Who?"

"I don't know."

57

A SNIPE is a gray bolt of lightning, taking wing, then zigzagging low above the ground before straightening its course. Why this particular pattern is hard to say, almost as if the invention of the gun was foreseen in the primeval scheme. A quivering Karo stood with forepaw raised, and Romuald brought down a bird even before Thomas had time to shoulder his Berdan.

The above took place in a marshy meadow agleam with rust-stained patches. He was wearing his snug-fitting moccasins and leggings—a protection against stalks and adders—and the water felt pleasantly cool. They marched single-file behind the dog through sun-dappled dew. It was to have been a party of four, but Denis had backed out at the last minute, leaving only Romuald, Thomas, and Victor.

Once a lake, its former basin was now a sprawling meadowland covered with sharp sedge and, up ahead, with moss, thick with pine scrub and clumps of tangled withes. As they crossed the scrub line, Thomas inhaled its familiar fragrance. The moorland was a kingdom of fragrance. The moss sprouted bushes of marsh tea (*Ledum palustre*) with narrow leathery leaves, and blue bog bilberries the size of pigeon eggs thrived on the warm, vaporous air. The berries were invigorating to the taste, but too many could put a man in a trance (whether from eating or smelling was unclear). The moor made a good feeding ground for the young blackcocks, still under their mother's guardianship —the older cocks, spending the summer in solitude, took refuge in the brush in the molting season and during that time became too lethargic to fly.

"Flush 'im, Karo, flush 'im!"

Karo kept circling around, flashing his white and yellow-spotted hide, wagging his tail, now and then throwing an inquisitive backward glance. Romuald pointed out the direction. He wore his high-necked dolman, a cartridge belt around his waist, and the strap of his game bag spanned his shoulder blades. Victor hoisted the leather pouch with the muzzle-loader accessories.

Thomas had kept his hunting date, arriving at Borkuny as if nothing had happened, greeting Barbarka as if he had never been aboard the britska that afternoon.

Later, as they were hiking along and had a moment to themselves, Romuald asked nonchalantly: "Will your aunt be dropping by one of these days?"

Thomas gulped. Why pretend ignorance? But if I meddle—he thought—I'm sure to make a mess of it. "I— she has lots of errands, I think."

That was all that was said of her. His barrel leveled straight ahead, Thomas fixed on the moiling Karo in anxious concentration. It rankled him that he had yet to bring down a bird on the wing—he didn't count the slew of wild ducks he and Romuald had bagged on Alunta. It was time he got one; the blackcock would be as good a test as any. The first kill of the day—Romuald's snipe—had only quickened his anxiety. The ability to track a bird in flight, to know how many meters to anticipate, and all that in the space of a split second, seemed to him a feat beyond mastery. If only he'd had time to get a bead on that snipe, but the spasm in his throat had barely subsided when Karo was already retrieving.

"They're lyin' low," said Romuald. "Dog's gonter nose 'em out into the open. Eyes to the ground, Tommy."

They waded knee-deep through the moss.

"They're over there, I betcha!"

But Romuald had guessed wrong, and so they kept plowing through the moss and Karo pulled in his tongue and went back to work.

The worst was not knowing when to expect it. You went along, concentrating for a while, bearing down on every bush, then bit by bit you let up, lulled by the rhythm of your own footsteps, until pretty soon a bed of reeds, like those up ahead, became just another obstacle, something that had to be circumvented. And that's when it happened, out of meanness.

For a moment they lost sight of Karo. Suddenly Thomas was pelted by a loud fragmentation, an explosion in midair, a violent sundering of the world: panic—gun bursts—blood rushing to the face—a blurring of vision—trembling hands. There they were! But so close he could see their elongated necks, their chickenlike bills beetling through a frenzy of flapping wings. He took aim—no, he merely pulled the trigger, hurriedly, pulling blindly and praying for a miracle. And there was Victor right beside him, all hunched up, shouldering his gun any old way, not a hint of any grace or style; and Thomas heard him fire, heard the report; and he saw his own bird in the distance, and the other one—Victor's—falling, and the dog jumping back and forth, not knowing if he was to sink his teeth into Victor's or Romuald's . . .

Ejecting the empty shell, Thomas, even though the sunny sky had become a funeral pall and his heart was racing something awful the way it does after some terrific scare, tried to bear his defeat courageously. He had counted—assuming he had had time to think at all—on a miracle. It was his own fault; next time he would be smarter.

Victor was reloading his blunderbuss of a gun, packing the charge with the ramrod.

"Gel gack em"—meaning, "We'll catch 'em," a tactful way of telling the boy not to take it too much to heart.

Thomas's gloom, the more painful for having to be concealed, soon began to lift: there was always the future. Just keep calm—above all, calm. The gray blight of stunted pine, their desiccated undersides hung with beard lichen, loomed everywhere. Romuald raised his finger, his eye constantly on the pointer's movements. "He's got it, he's got it."

The dog froze in its tracks, its tail perfectly rigid. The men closed in, lengthening their strides, guns at the ready. Thomas's insides implored the heavens.

"Get 'em, Karo!"

Karo inched forward, then froze again, fixated on some point.

"Get 'em!"

Others might have withstood it, but not Thomas. No sooner had he vowed to maintain his composure than there was an ear-splitting *wh-r-r-r*. It was unlike anything he had expected: a vibrating, a clapping of white wings low above the ground, then a shot—Romuald's.

"Ptarmigan! At 'em, Karo, at 'em!"

The ptarmigan was a beige-brown bird in spats, its snow-white wings in stark contrast to the rest of its body. Glancing furtively at Romuald's game bag, Thomas, instead of rejoicing at the discovery, at the prospect of recording a new species under its Latin name, felt only envy.

But he had contained himself, and that gave him heart; he had exercised restraint, thus absolving his hunter's conscience. He felt a surge of hope, one that somehow made up for the extricating of feet from slime, for the squishing of water from his bast shoes every time he took a step forward. Along the way they killed an adder—Karo had barked at it furiously, curling its upper lip and grimacing the way a human does at the taste of something sour. The dog slowed, as if to give them time to cultivate a proper vigilance, carefully moving one paw ahead of the other, glancing back to check their progress, to see if they were attending.

An explosion. Lord, how easy, how easy . . . Here it comes, take your time, get a good bead on him . . . Oh God, make it work! A shot, and Thomas, stunned, not conceding the worst, stood and watched as the cock kept on its leisurely course. This discrepancy between what was willed, between the incantation and the fact, utterly demoralized him. For at heart there had been the certitude, then as now, of some magical bond between himself and the animal, one that made of the leveling and the aiming something superfluous, the result of some special dispensation.

Two young cocks, winged by a blast from Romuald's

double-barreled shotgun, fell practically at his feet. It was one of those hits that paralyzes, grounding the bird but leaving life intact. Thomas picked them up, their necks twisting. It was a task he felt obliged to perform, now that the other had eluded him. Grabbing them by the feet, he banged their tiny skulls against the butt of his Berdan; it didn't work; shrilly, they cackled in protest. He took a bitter pleasure in unburdening his anger, an anger tinged with shame that he nonetheless suppressed by invoking necessity. Putting aside the gun, he swung and whacked them with all his might against a pine. Not hard enough, eh? Take that! The bludgeoning continued until the blood oozed from their bills.

"Snack time, fellas, the old stomach's growling. Must be pushin' noon."

They sat down on a clump of moss and Romuald broke out some dark bread and cheese from his game bag. Thomas, who had sat among these men so often in the past, never felt so apart, so far removed as he did now: a whole world divided them. Not even Victor—stuttering old Victor—had come back empty-handed. They were made of a different substance. What was it? He could stalk with the best of them. Hadn't they said so themselves? What was the secret that even Victor in his own clumsy way seemed to grasp but that he never would? A bright afternoon glare overhead, the soporific heat of the swamp, lizards scurrying to their arid islands among the lichen. He sat with eyes closed, seemingly bathing his face in the sun, but there was sadness inside, and it weighed him down like cold lead shot.

"Why don't you ever fire your gun, Tommy?"

How could he? If he had, it would have only magnified the dimensions of his failure. What a day! Soon it would be over, then back to Borkuny, by way of the roundabout trail skirting the hill with no trees, the same trail they were now steering for.

But just as they were hitting dry ground they flushed a flock, and Thomas—thinking he deserved some reward, some consolation at the very end, that he did not deserve the banishment—really let loose.

Romuald gazed wistfully down at Thomas's smoking barrel, then up at the escaping blackcock. "Not your day, Tommy. That happens."

His words did nothing to redeem the situation, and Thomas hated himself for having betrayed his confidence.

58

THE BLACKCOCK hunt was the more painful to recall in that it confirmed certain debilities, long suspected but never acknowledged. A hunter's hunter when it came to baiting, stalking, imitating a tree or rock, and even a fair shot from a blind, Thomas nonetheless panicked at the slightest stirring. If the blackcock hunt was to be the final test, then Thomas was up against something truly formidable; and unless he overcame it, he would never be a real man, and his self-image, so carefully nurtured, would be shattered. How he had hungered to become a citizen of the forest, had so accustomed himself to the idea, and now, by a supreme irony that would deny him the one thing he craved most, he was hearing: "No." So what was he really? Who? Was this the end—the map to his kingdom of the elect, his partnership with Romuald? Unable to part with his Berdan, he took to the forest, deeply aggrieved, and there found relief.

The flickering in the crowns, the sighing in the tree-tops calmed him, were a distraction. Here there were no tests to be passed, no expectations to be fulfilled, nothing to be tracked, hunted down, only the joy taken in the halting and advancing, the aimless silent treading, the ability to avoid detection by various creatures. At such times he would admit to being happiest without a gun, that he could do without the killing. On the other hand, breaking brush empty-handed looked funny; people were nosy, wanted to know why, and there was no explaining to them; but just say you're "out hunting," and no more questions asked. Besides, a gun barrel slung over the shoulder lent an element of adventure; no telling what sort of bird or animal you might jump along the way.

No gun was needed the time he surprised some roe. He was on one of those smooth, needle-strewn trails that dropped down to the swamp and whose ice-packed surface in winter made it ideal for sledding, when his legs buckled. An undefined presence, but a presence nonetheless: red tree trunks engaged in a dance, columns of light prancing among fern quills. No, not trees—live creatures sheathed in reddish-brown bark, existing on the very periphery of the plant kingdom. Feeding on the grass in front of him, they glided on tiny hoofs, their necks rippling; one turned its head in his direction but failed to distinguish him from his stationary surroundings. He had only one urge now: to prolong it, to dissolve into air and, thus made invisible, become a part of it. But whether it was a twitch of his eyelids or his scent that alerted them, they bounded nimbly into the hazel scrub, while he was left behind, on the verge of not believing his senses.

On another occasion, he had a similar encounter with a young fox foraging under a stump. Not content to contemplate its snout and tail, he had felt duty-bound to kill it and bring it back to Romuald as a trophy, thus redeeming himself for past sins; but the moment he touched his gun strap, the fox vanished without a trace, without so much as a quivering leaf to remind of its presence.

One day he yielded to temptation, and forever regretted it. In the crown of a hazel he observed a shimmering, coil-like movement, half in green and half in light. It was a squirrel, the horizontal advance making it appear more elongated, more magically iridescent. From the lower branches came the wailing of small birds: the squirrel was raiding a nest. Unable to restrain himself, driven by sheer love for the animal, he fired.

It was a young one, so slender that what he had taken for a squirrel was not a squirrel but the shimmer of color deposited in its wake. Its body bending and unbending on the moss, it clutched its chest with its tiny paws, at the bloody patch on its little white vest. It didn't know what death was; it was trying to remove it, as if it were a spike on which it had been impaled and around which it could only pivot.

Thomas, his face twisted with anguish, knelt beside it and wept. How to stop it, how to stop it. He would have given half a lifetime to save it, but he could only participate passively in the agony, the mere sight of which was a punishment. He bent down, and the paws, with their minuscule fingers, became joined as if imploring his help. He took it in his hands, and while he might otherwise have felt an urge to kiss and pet it, his lips were now clamped shut, because it was no longer the urge of possession that welled up in him but of self-sacrifice—for it, the squirrel— and that was clearly beyond his power.

The hardest thing to endure was the littleness of it, and the writhing, like quicksilver trying to defer the moment of congealment. And for a brief moment, so brief he immediately lost access to it, a mystery unfolded. Then the writhing turned to convulsive jerks; the fluffy down on its cheeks was permeated by a dark trickle. The spasms slackened. Dead.

He sat on the stump, the drone of the forest in his ears. A second ago it had been alive, playing, gathering nuts. Grandmother Dilbin's death, for reasons he could not altogether fathom, affected him less than did this creature's. A being, unique, never to be repeated, never to be resurrected. Because it was itself and no other. But where had they gone—the warmth, the suppleness, and above all the feeling of being itself? Animals were without souls. When they were killed, it was for keeps. They could not be saved, not even by Christ. But Grandmother could; she could cry "Save me" and Christ was there to receive her, to show her the way. Why not a squirrel, then, if He was almighty? Maybe a squirrel couldn't pray, but this one had prayed, because wasn't praying the same as wanting to live? And it was all his, Thomas's, fault. How low.

Bury it? It would just rot away to nothing. Take it with him? He didn't have the nerve to look people in the eye. It was best just to turn around and head home. As he was backtracking, an anthill caught his eye. A tall one, well camouflaged with pine needles. Abandoned? Wait, what about those mobile trails converging on it. When Thomas peeled away the top and probed it with a stick, the whole began to heave. He dug deeper until the collapsing tunnels gave up a stampeding, panic-stricken horde. Retrieving the squirrel, he laid it inside the hive and covered it. It would be stripped clean, leaving nothing but a white skeleton. It would be waiting for him when he came back. What then? No telling. Put it in a box and ditch it somewhere; that way, it would last longer.

Yes, low. To miss those able to protect themselves through skill and grace and hit only the vulnerable, the unsuspecting . . . That squirrel hadn't even seen him, it had not had any warning. He could feel the necks of those young blackcocks twisting inside him, could hear their tiny skulls thumping against the tree. A vision so palpable he could feel the brittle pine bark, could see the flakes flying with every clubbing blow. And other things that weighed on his conscience. Grandmother Misia told of how as a child he used to fill his basket with snails and toss them into the Issa out of pity (he was moved, perhaps, by the sight of them taking to the paths after a rainstorm), believing that he was doing them a favor, swelling with magnanimity even as they were drowning at the bottom. Then he remembered the duck whose life he had spared. But it was not a consolation.

If only he could have leaned on someone, cried his heart out, protested. He passed an oak on the edge of a clearing, and suddenly yearned for it to be alive, his stomach caving in, collapsing with the sort of suction and terror one feels on the swing's downward plunge. A roller—or, as it was recorded in his album, *Coracias garrulus*, one of those birds he was continually stalking but which always eluded, there being only one other bird, the kingfisher, arrayed in the same resplendent blue that was such pure color in motion—crowed from its perch on a dead branch, but Thomas passed below without raising his head.

And all the time they kept saying: Mommy is coming, Mommy will be taking you to the big city, to school . . . Always the same: next month, won't be long now, and—nothing, no sign of her. "Mommy, Mommy—please come!" he kept intoning as he strode along, hunter-fashion, his Berdan at the ready, his legs sheathed in knee-high boots, and the tears streaming down his face leaving a salty taste in his mouth. The incantation evoked no particular memories, only an aura of softness and light.

He had need of another luminosity now, not the mirrorlike glare of an August afternoon shimmering above the stubble. Recently he had been given to strange moods. Everything—people, dogs, the woods, Gine—was as before, only somehow different. To hollow out an egg, you puncture one end and suck out the insides with a straw, leaving only the shell, the outward appearance. The same with Thomas's world. Outwardly the same, but inwardly gutted.

And boring. When we bolt from bed in response to the joyful summons of work or play, the day hardly seems long enough to contain our expectations; but when the summons is absent, then all the purpose and planning are lost.

"What, Thomas still asleep?"

"What's the matter, Tommy, not feeling well?"

"Naah, I'm okay."

He would stand on the banks of the Issa, not comprehending his former infatuation. Leaves covered with a thick coat of roadside dust, a midsummer heat, a lazy current adrift with the oily film of floating debris ... He even dug out his poles, got the rust off his hooks, held the squirming earthworm between his fingers, and started to bury a hook's tip in the little pink opening when—the heck with it, he'd bait up with bread crumbs instead. He would watch the float, not really caring whether it jiggled and went under, the fishing being merely the repetition of a ritual that had once connoted something else. As much as he tried to rekindle the passion, he soon gave up.

He pulled out his arithmetic notebooks, neglected ever since his lessons were interrupted by Joseph's denunciation. His plan to devote one hour daily to his exercises lasted only as long as he began to founder, and then was abandoned. He took to rummaging in the library again, finding among other things a translation of the Koran, which he knew to be the sacred book of the Mohammedans—someone, evidently Thomas's great- or great-great-grandfather, had taken an interest in Islam. Despite the inscrutability of certain passages, Thomas took pleasure in reading it, delighting as much in the moral strictures as in the sonority of its phrases.

The Berdan hung idly on the wall and made him ashamed of his neglect. He planned a trip out to Borkuny but kept putting it off. Romuald, meanwhile, had stopped calling at the manor. Thomas's aunt, who must have known from Misia that Thomas had joined Romuald on the blackcock hunt, affected indifference.

"Thomas, go help bring in the apples."

He helped. Lugging the baskets for Antonina, though exhausting, afforded some satisfaction. The apples were freighted on a carrying pole, the baskets being attached to hazel hooks. The orchard now had a new tenant, a relative of Chaim. The cavernous barn cellars were lined with shelves for the choicest apples and smelled of stone and packed earth. He bit into a rennet, delighting as always in the firmness of its pulp: so he *hadn't* changed, after all.

Almost a month had passed before he remembered the skeleton, and even then he had to force himself to make the trip back. He found the anthill in the forest, all right, but the squirrel was gone. He never did find out what happened to it.

59

THE SELF-IMPOSED fast observed by Thomas was a strict one: two days on water only. He was driven to it less by the hope of having the stigma removed than by a need for self-mortification. Such self-punishment, he sensed, was only right, proper, justified.

He had his reasons. As if to prove that he was different, not the same as ordinary people, he came down with a strange affliction. In the morning he sneaked a mugful of water and tried to rinse out the spots on his bed sheet. There were nightmares; Barbarka, naked, would wrap him in her arms and whip him with a birch switch. Melancholy thoughts. How to breach the curtain. For the things around him seemed hollowed out, or veiled, their shapes no longer full but flat. And behind the curtain was the secret he kept pursuing, dreamlike—gaining steadily on it, the legs weighing like lead, only to lose it . . . God: why had He created a world where there was only death and death and death. If He was good, why was there no sticking out one's hand without killing, why no moving down a trail without crushing caterpillars or beetles no matter how one tried to avoid them? God might have created a different world, but He hadn't; He chose this one.

In this way his failure as a hunter, along with his shameful abnormality, by barring him from human company, thrust him into lonely, solitary contemplation. The fast was meant to cleanse, to bring a restoration of normality, and to permit of understanding. He who punishes himself shows disgust for his baseness and invokes God with his punishing part.

It was, he ascertained, an effective remedy. An empty stomach early in the morning, like fasting for Holy Communion. A few hours later came the hunger, a sudden and terrific urge to eat, then the resisting of temptation: aw, come on, just a bite of apple . . . But the longer it went, the easier it got. Most of the time he lay on his back and drowsed, inwardly ennobling himself. Of greater importance was what it did to the objects in his proximity, to the sky and trees, when he went outside and stood by the porch. He made the discovery that the weaker the body, the more he got outside it, elevating himself—condensed, specklike—to a point just above his head. The look of this other self was intense, embracing the part left behind, as the latter shrank, withdrew below, taking the earth along with it, whole and unaltered in all its surface details, down to the very bottom. The melancholy lifted, a new vista unfurled. Antonina used to tell of the goddess Varpeia, who sat in heaven, spinning the threads of fate, and of how a star dangled at the end of each. When a star fell, it meant she had cut the thread, that someone somewhere had died. But Thomas, instead of sinking, drifted skyward, like those tiny spiders that, hoisting themselves by means of an invisible thread, ascend nimbly to a higher branch.

What he set his mind to, he did, though by the afternoon of the second day he felt woozy and dizzy every time he got up. At supper he ate a plate of curdled milk and potatoes. Their fragrance—they were drenched in butter —never seemed so lovely.

By way of consolation, God rewarded him with hitherto unknown thoughts. One of his favorite pastimes had been to stand on the front lawn, bend over, and, through the arch of outstretched legs, survey the park on the other side: seen upside down, it came as a revelation. So, too, the fast transfigured not only him but everything the eye met. Not that the world ceased to be what it had been previously. No, both the old and the new converged. So maybe it was wrong to impugn God for the way He ran things; who knew, maybe one day we would wake to a new surprise. Maybe God looked down at the earth through straddled legs, or did so after a fast infinitely longer than Thomas's.

But the squirrel had suffered pain. Was there another angle from which to view it, from which to say the squirrel had suffered only in our imagination? That, no one, not even God, could say.

Thomas's fast had opened a chink admitting illumination. Touching the trunk of a maple, he wondered at its density. For inside was a realm where, made smaller, he would have roamed indefinitely, pushing to the very core, to those wood-locked villages and towns beyond the border of bark. Only figuratively, of course. For there were no towns inside, only in the imagination, though a maple was a colossus that, no less than the one looking on, contained the possibility of endless permutation.

Thomas was burdened by his loneliness, yet more

than anything he aspired to self-dissolution and a communion without words. He was quite demanding. Grandmother Misia—yes, but there was no confiding in her, not in Grandmother Misia. Nor was he much for confession; the examining of one's conscience according to a prayer book, according to questions requiring simple affirmation or denial, always omitting the most essential thing, repelled him. His guilt was inside him, a guilt too pervasive to be divided into sins.

God, let me be like the others—Thomas prayed, and the demons, plotting their next move, strained to listen. Make me a good shot with a gun, don't let me forget my hunter's, naturalist's vow. Cure me of that illness (a loud guffawing among the baser demons along the Issa, of which there were a great many). Let me understand your world when it pleases you to enlighten. The way it really is, not what I imagine it to be (here the demons fell to sulking, for the topic had turned grave).

If Thomas was subject to conflicting desires, they were not so for him. He brooded over pain and suffering, not for their own sake, but as attributes of the order of which he was a part. And since this order lay beyond the exercise of his will, he had to attend to his status, a status bestowed through the art of killing. Even though he wanted to keep up his friendship with Romuald and have access to the forest without the blood-spilling, he abdicated responsibility, without completely shirking it.

60

"Mama! Mama!"
Denis's whining supplications had little effect.
"Satan!" she ranted, banging her fist on the table.

"The Satan! Curse the day he was ever born! The scum!"

Her color—she was very flushed—worried him. She sat hunched over in her chair, breathing heavily, clutching her belly. "Oyey, what cramps!"

The lamentations went on: "He's disgraced us, dragged us through the mud. And him, he don't care if it kills his own mama. Oy, Denis, I feel so sick!"

Denis went to the cupboard, poured half a glass of vodka, and set it down in front of her. Emptying the glass in one gulp, she wiped her mouth, then gestured with the glass. Denis, pleased to see her not refuse this medicine, poured.

"Victor, keep me company awhile."

Denis stepped out onto the porch, where Romuald was sitting on a bench, smoking and brooding.

"Well?"

"Still rantin' and ailin'. Best not to show your face for a while."

"Got no mind to."

"What you have to do it that way for? Couldn't you have broke it to her more gentlelike?"

Romuald shrugged. "You know her better than that. Gentle or not gentle, she'd have taken it hard, either way."

They broke off. Hens clawed the ground under the apple trees; the earth was powdery and hollowed out and track-embroidered from the constant scratching. The cock, pursuing one of the hens, pounced on it, flapped its wings, then clumsily dismounting, let it go. The hen fluffed its feathers, dazed as usual by the whole procedure, oblivious even before it had time to be aware. A horse, its forelegs hobbled, bolted, heaving its mane. Denis took off on the run: the horse was trampling the poppies. He picked up a stick, flung it, and waved his arms. Ducks trailed through the grass, quacking plangently; it was a scorching, dry September day.

"What now?"

"Aw, she'll simmer down."

"She won't give her blessing—she said."

Romuald's face was drawn, stubbled, darkened by the ordeal. "If she don't, she don't. My tough luck. You—you're different, you obey. Don't marry, she says, and you don't. Can't do this, can't do that—there's no pleasin' her."

"Still and all, Rom, a farm girl . . ."

"Yours was highbred and Mama was again' her."

Not against her, really. She had opposed it more for her son's sake, almost out of jealousy, out of a determination to keep him single. But this latest—as imperceptible in its unfolding as the stages by which a fly gets trapped in a spiderweb—was too horrifying to contemplate.

The family coat of arms. Buried in a large chest were the family records, lying there undisturbed since the death of old man Bukowski, the only one still capable of deciphering them. To mingle the blood of the Bukowskis with the blood of slaves, whose backs bore the scars of centuries, was to sully the family blazon. Never mind that the Bukowskis had worked the soil, that outwardly they were indistinguishable from peasants; their ancestors had once elected kings, and that made them the equal of kings. Not one of their forebears—not the father, his father, or even their great-great-grandfather—had ever bowed and scraped, and the Bukowski had yet to be born who would surrender to the dark impulses of servility, docility, or cunning, impulses more proper to those of baser stock. Marry a peasant and the recollection of who one was and all that was owing the family name would cease to be a protection, would be to debase the line and efface it in the slime of the crowd which neither knew nor cared to know anything of its lineage.

Old lady Bukowski, that guardian of the purity of the blood, had reason to despair. She also had herself to blame. She had never objected to Romuald's keeping Barbarka at Borkuny; she had counted on his good sense, though certain signs—the woman's strutting self-confidence, the little liberties she took—should have been a warning.

Romuald had the banns published. Father Monkiewicz showed no surprise, though his heart ran with honey: what had been unchristian was now made Christian, and here at last was a nobleman with heart. One might question whether, for his own sake, it was wise of Romuald to have the banns announced. If it was to keep Barbarka on at his place, to have someone to scrub his back in the bathhouse, then he had acted wisely. Still, it would be hard to go on living the life to which he was accustomed; that was to be expected. It was a decision made not without certain qualms, a decision facilitated by the grudge he bore Helen Juchniewicz, who had dallied with him until by shunning him she had finally betrayed her genteel, aristocratic airs: hers was a threshold too tall for him.

Breaking the news to his mother had taken a feat of courage, and Romuald had sweated through the ordeal. He had gone on about the farm, about needing someone to help run it, about how it was high time he got married—Married? Who to? Well—uh—and then the name, followed by a belly laugh, and Romuald saying his mind was made up, and then a ranting, a throwing of chairs, a flailing with the cane . . .

Denis, after going back inside, found his mother staring fixedly into space, her fists clenched on the table, the vodka bottle down. Victor looked on from the bed with mouth agape.

"A disgrace." She wagged her head.

Then again—softer, to herself: "What a disgrace."

Denis loved his mother greatly and felt sorry for her. But he had run out of things to say. From his stool he gawked up at St. Aloysius, whose hand, the one bearing the palm branch, was speckled with flies. The glass fly trap on the sill was also blackened with specks that still stirred in the buttermilk. The stronger ones were crawling over their mired comrades, gracelessly dragging their wet wings.

61

GRANDMOTHER MISIA was the picture of serenity. Rocked by the waves of a mighty river, she lived in a perpetual hush of timeless waters. If birth was a passage from the protection of the maternal womb into a world of sharp, wounding objects, then Grandmother Misia had never been born, having always existed, wrapped in the silk cocoon of that which Is.

A foot, delighting in itself, in the very gift of touch, feels the soft quilt and lifts it. A hand draws the fluffy material up to the sleeper's chin. A white mist outside, the babble of geese, an autumnal dawn streaking the windowpane with dewdrops. Still time to sleep, or rather to linger on the border, beyond the reach of that which can be formulated in words and thoughts, in a world as yet undifferentiated into blankets, earth, people, stars, leaving only this spaceless realm—and awe.

The experience of those mornings had taught Misia the relativity of names given to objects, the relativity of all things human. Not even the teachings of the Church, we may presume to tell, were a match for that truth of hers—instinctive, profound; and the only prayer she ever required was one that could be reduced to a single, incantatory: "Oh." Grandmother Dilbin always spoke of her as "that pagan," and she was right. For Misia was unencumbered by the sort of flaw that reveals itself in our human striving. Incapable of exerting her will on behalf of some goal, disdainful of all goals, she relinquished. No wonder she was mystified by the cares and needs of others. Desires, needs? What for?

Fully awake, lying in bed with her eyes wide open, she dwells on details of a mundane nature, never exaggerating their importance, never racing out of bed to perform some errand she neglected the day before or which urgently demands her attention. Mindful of her place in the infinite, caressed by a giant hand, she is content to purr. The worries of others belonged to the sphere of things that happened, nothing more. Luke's, for example (what a couple they made!), or Helen's (thank goodness that's the end of her dalliance with Romuald!), or the Reform . . . Or Tekla, who had postponed her homecoming so often that people had ceased to give it any credence.

If Grandmother wasn't bothered by such things, the Invisible Ones, those spirits promenading about the parlor's squeaky flooring and furniture, *were* bothered by her indifference. Besides, they had long given up on her. There was no attacking the innocent, those never burdened by the awareness of sin. Even so, their experience came in handy in subjecting Thomas to a new brand of temptation.

Picking his nose, a habit favoring autumnal meditation, Thomas began, for the first time in his life, to pass judgment on Misia as a person. She was a horrible egoist, in love with no one but herself. But no sooner was the verdict pronounced than doubts were born. Granted, one had only to look at her to detect the pleasure she took in her own knees, her pillow's indentation, the way she sank into the eiderdown of her own interior (Thomas could feel—or imagined he could feel—Misia on the inside). But what made him think he was any different? He, too, loved to savor his own smell, to curl up and exult in his being *him*. Wasn't that cause for gratitude to God, for prayer? Or was it deceiving? His grandmother was pious, churchgoing. True, but wasn't she the celebrant of her own private Mass to herself? We say: God. But couldn't the saying of it be our self-love in disguise, a way of ennobling what we really adore: our own warmth, our own heartbeat, the wrapping of ourselves in the snugness of a blanket.

There is no denying the cunning of demons. How ingenious of them to undermine Thomas's confidence in his own internal voice, to rob him of his peace of mind by appealing to his scrupulosity. No longer could he implore God for illumination; genuflecting, he would always have the feeling he was kneeling before himself. Thomas wanted to confide in the Real, not in a cloud that, nourished by what is inside us, hangs overhead. Hardly had he finished fasting, therefore, hardly had he freed himself somewhat from his self-torture and tasted a few mornings of felicity, than he again lost his footing. He wiped the fog from the window, his face trailing tears of solitude.

Meanwhile, every morning at dawn, Grandmother reveled in her delectations, never dreaming how corrupting she could be.

62

"Soon it'll be over."

The voice—a signal—vibrated above dry grass resonant with the chirruping of crickets. Swaying on his feet, Balthazar stood on the trail, struck by the derangement of everything. What was he doing out here? Objects, blurred and flat-surfaced, zigzagged before him, taunting him with their unfamiliarity. He was hovering at the center of a vast emptiness, made even worse by the absence of any center, of any earthly support, the ground eluding, slipping away, senseless. He kept going, passing through a spray of sparks: insects, always the same, jumping without purpose.

"Soon it'll be over."

Creaking porch steps, an empty room—the wife and children were in Gine, visiting with the grandmother—a jug of beer on the table, a loaf of bread beside it. He tilted the jug, took a few swigs, then brought it down full-force on the floor. Streams of brownish-gold liquid fanned out starlike over the rough planks. He grabbed hold of the table, sickened by the smell of lye-coated wood, by the household rankness. His searching glance landed on the ax braced against the tiled stove. He walked over, picked it up, and, dragging it along the floor with his free hand, went back to the table with a rocking motion. Taking deliberate aim, he swung and hit the table from above, not crosswise but lengthwise, collapsing it. The loaf of bread rolled along the floor until it came to a rest, upside down, exposing its smooth, mealy underbelly.

Balthazar then brought in a wicker-bound bottle from the other room, stood it on the floor, and kicked it. He leaned against the wall, and watched as the bubbling liquid spread out and encircled both the wreckage and the overturned loaf. He was captivated by it, by the spillage that, detached from its surroundings, now stood out in greater relief. The swollen peripheries lazily seeped under the bench, leaving little islands that momentarily were inundated. There was something inexorable about its movement, some element of necessity, and it was the only thing on Balthazar's mind as he took the matches from his pocket.

Then it came: the recognition of that moment at the border of what a second ago was not and what a second later was, once for all time, till the world's consummation. As one hand squeezed the box, the fingers of the other approached the little stick with a darkened tip. Perhaps all along he had wanted to be only this: pure action, the sheer tension of doing, with no consequences to oppress him when, inaccessible to the past, he would be concentrated on a new action. He rubbed the match against the box and became fixated on the flame, as if it were a discovery, until the flame began to singe, and then the fingers parted and the match dropped to the floor, extinguished. He took out another, struck it hard, and tossed it in front of him. It went out. He lit a third, bent down, and slowly brought it up close to the spilled kerosene.

On his way out, he toppled the bench into the path of the creeping flame. His tunic, unbelted, was open; his pocket bulged with tobacco and a bottle of vodka.

"Soon it'll be over."

The future. What future? A voice calling in the distance; a pale, clear sky; crickets chirruping; day, night, day . . . Never to be again, superfluous. And the certitude, which came from somewhere, fortified itself. He walked with no destination in mind. Aimless wandering. Turned around once, and then came the horror of the aftereffect, of the irreversible provoked by the sight of the smoke seeping through the windows; and in protest—Balthazar's eternal protest—against the law which leaves nothing alone but chains us to its consequences, he clutched the bottle with trembling hand, weltered in the grass, got up on all fours, and let out a sound that we know to be a scream but which issues from the throat as a gurgling, rattling whisper.

Balthazar was sentient enough to run back and put out the fire. But such a course never occurred to him, the stifled scream coming not from the deed itself, not from what had been done, but from the necessity of its doing; and he sensed, possibly even as he had held the match, both that he was free and that he would do what had to be done. Just as surely as he must have known, kneeling on all fours like an animal, that there was no going back to quell the flames.

A figure, describing straw-colored swirls in the air with a wooden sword, was bellying toward him like an adder. Balthazar could make out a pair of vertically set eyes, a body crouched furtively low. He leapt to his feet, tore out a large fence post, and took a deep breath: the grass was empty. Only some gossamer threads, signs of Indian summer, waved in the air: slightly arched lines of incandescence. A gilded forest, a midsummer hush. Neither friend nor foe; no one except for some ungraspable—and therefore menacing—presence. He spun around to fend off an attack from the rear. A magpie screeched up from a nearby gully. By now the smoke from the windows was intertwining, gathering into strands that trailed along the roof shingles and mantled the crowns of the hornbeam with a cloudy haze.

"Soon it will be over."

63

"THE FOREST."

"State preserve."

"No."

"Whose?"

"Balthazar's."

"It's Balthazar's place on fire."

The people of Pogirai began spilling out of the orchards, out onto the aprons and stubble, for a better view. They sounded the alarm, grabbed buckets, hook-tipped poles, axes, and started stampeding. Dogs and children ran behind the men, a party of women, driven by curiosity, bringing up the rear.

In the next sequence of events, let us distinguish between appearances and reality. In the reconstruction of any past incident, no matter how logically consistent the facts, there are always some hidden gaps which, when filled, cast everything in a different light. If the effort is seldom made, it is because people are more content to rely on what is immediately taken for granted.

Balthazar, after setting fire to his house, lay in ambush out where the fence line ended on either side of the gangway. He was on the lookout because he knew that the fire would be spotted from Pogirai and that they would come to put it out and that he couldn't allow it. Those were the appearances. In reality, he was innocent of any such motives, but sat in the grass, teeth chattering, menaced by reptilian shapes and supernatural magpies. A lot was due to the discordancy between body and soul. The soul was given to chaos and terror, even as the body remained alert, its reflexes intact—heavy-limbed but still powerful. To others, this looked like the obeying of some will, bent on a definite goal.

They could see the flames now, could hear the dog, whose pitiful yelping said that the fire had already spread to the kennel. Diverted by the spectacle, they were all the more amazed when he sprang up, all mussed and disheveled and fierce, his hand still clutching the fence post. He cocked his arm in self-defense. He hadn't expected them, these people advancing like a mobile stone wall radiant with a multitude of faces.

At the head stood old Wackonis. When he saw Balthazar bring up the arm with the post, he shielded himself with his ax. Balthazar's body, registering the danger, did what it had to do. With all the strength bestowed by his arm and shoulder, he lowered the post on Wackonis's skull, felling him.

"He killed 'im!"

"*Killed* 'im!"

And then another cry, one to summon the communal spirit: "*Ei virai!* Forward, men!"

It was in a clearing of cut stumps interspersed with young oak, the green cover being here and there pocked by the dark craters of former grubbings. A dozen or so people in clamorous pursuit, leaping over the craters with shirt-tails flapping. Balthazar was seeking the safety of the tall forest. Knowing, without thinking, that it was a matter of life and death, he was entirely at the command of his self-protecting body and the destination dictated by it: the sawed-off carbine stashed in the oak.

They tried to cut him off, knowing they stood to lose him as soon as he hit the forest; he swung to the left; again they cut him off, forcing him to backtrack around and take to the alder grove. On one side of the grove was pasture-land; on the other, farmland—crop fields separating the grove from the timberline.

As Balthazar's feet sank in the mud, his boots chewed up clods of black peat. He was too winded to keep running; tried to keep on the move, but not having the breath for it, he dropped down on all fours and crawled, his heart banging, his voice wailing. The others took time off from the chase to hold council. Only one way to catch him: surround the grove and track him down hunter-style. They took up their assigned stations. Balthazar, hearing them, searched the ground for a club—he had discarded the fence post while fleeing—grabbed a branch of debris so moldy it fell apart in his hand, and finally had to settle for a rock.

The people of Pogirai had many scores to settle with Balthazar, with this criminal who had jumped them with his murderous intent, and all because they had tried to lend him a neighborly hand. Naturally, they had in mind a killing. But they knew his strength, knew they would have to gang up on him, and they spurred one another on with their foul imprecations.

Clock hands twitching spasmodically forward; gestures, glances, and motions performed simultaneously the world over; a comb touching long sleek hair; scintillating mirrors; reverberating tunnels; ship screws lashing seawater . . . Balthazar's heart was ticking off time; saliva drooled from his mouth. No, not yet! Let me live, no matter where, anywhere, just let me live! Seeking cover, he hugged the marshy floor, pawed at it as if to burrow a hole, to hollow out a hiding place. Because the present—his being there, trapped—was like the confirmation of some voice or dream, of that which must be, inexorably. But there was nowhere for him to hide. The alder grove, thick-shrubbed at the rim, was starker where he was, too dark for any bushes to grow, and the ground bulged with rugged roots laced with cow tracks and the flattened mushrooms of manure. An easy target. The carbine. To have the carbine now. But there was no carbine.

Balthazar probably should have gone to meet them with hands held high. But that presumed an ability to distinguish between the fire and the phantoms, and the people of Pogirai, but for Balthazar the people were a part of it, were in a way its executioners. His eyes bulging, loosening from their sockets, he squeezed the rock in his fist.

The men paddled the tree trunks like regular brush-breakers. Balthazar's strategy must be attributed to what little remained of his sentience. Rather than wait to be taken, he went on the attack, charging at those closing in from the side of the crop field. Surprise, he had figured, was his best chance of escape. But he was too heavy, kept getting mired in the mud, couldn't get up the momentum.

A young man, acclaimed by the girls as the best dancer at all the village reels, was the first to be met. They came within two feet of colliding. Balthazar aimed for the face. Now, to be a good dancer is to be endowed with a certain grace; the lad ducked—not a quarter of a second too soon—and the rock creased the side of his head. Only a tree behind which he had jumped saved Balthazar from an ax blade. A yell went up.

"Over here! Over here! Over here!"

Again on the run, Balthazar wrapped both hands around a sapling and pulled it up by the roots. How he uprooted the tree, a feat surpassing human strength, was unclear. Brandishing the sapling like a giant cudgel, muddied, he stood his ground against his attackers.

"Over here! Over here! Over here!"

Some sheep were raising a cloud of crop dust in the sun. A hedgehog rustled among the leaves of an apple tree. A ferry barge was moving away from the shore; on it was a man who held his horses by the bridle, steadying them as they inhaled through snorting nostrils. From high above the forest's moss-like expanses came the calls of cranes in passage: *kruuu-kruuu*.

They came together in a clearing. The air swished as Balthazar swung, at the same time a pole landed on his shoulder, loosening his grip and forcing him to drop the sapling. A long, iron-hooked staff, the kind used for putting out roof fires, its thick ashwood shaft held by Wackonis's son with both hands, rose up into the air.

If only a moment of everything's happening could be arrested, fixed, examined in a glass jar; if only it could be peeled away from the moment before and the moment after, and the tissue of time stretched into an ocean of space! But no.

The gaff came down on Balthazar's skull. He reeled, fell with his whole length. Silence except for the breathing of tired men, reverberations of the phrase "Over here!" and the tramping footsteps of the others, coming on the run.

Balthazar's house, stable, cow barn, and pigsty were

turned to ash. Of his farm in the forest, all that survived was the hayrick.

"He had it coming."

"The son of a devil."

64

OLD WACKONIS died, but Balthazar lived. He was carted to his father-in-law's place in Gine. Surkont sent for the doctor at once. Thomas had never seen his grandfather so irritable. Always an even-tempered man, he now snarled when he spoke, turning abruptly on his heels, his gray, close-cropped mustache bristling, his lips holding back some unutterable phrase. Balthazar still lay in a coma, so Grandfather went down to the village to keep a bedside vigil.

A large kerosene lamp burned brightly on the bench. Balthazar lay in bed, his head propped up by a single pillow. He had already been washed clean, leaving no trace of the caked mud and blood, and his livid face stood out against the white bandage of thick homespun. He was given Extreme Unction, but later, contrary to all expectations, he opened his eyes. His gaze bespoke puzzlement, peace. He seemed unsure of where he was, confused by all the fuss.

The priest, bound by the seal of confession, divulged nothing of what he was told, declaring only that Balthazar was in full possession of his faculties. (It may have been the shock that delivered him from the web of his entanglement.) He was alone with the priest for a long time. Of their conversation nothing is known, although later, with the passage of time, Father Monkiewicz began alluding to it, at first discreetly but then more boldly, justifying these indiscretions by the use he made of them. For it was his habit, when taking up the evils that lay in wait for man's soul, to illustrate his sermons with examples; thus did many facts in the Balthazar case become public knowledge.

Despite all his experiences as a confessor, despite all he had heard in the confessional, Father Monkiewicz was shaken. Not by the gravity of Balthazar's sins—sins never before confessed until now, as if the realization of their sinfulness had just been borne in on him—as by the man's stubborn, even resigned insistence on his own damnation. The priest said he had no right to speak that way, that God's mercy was infinite, that repentance was all that was needed to obtain forgiveness. And Balthazar did repent his sins, so fervently, so sincerely, that he repented all he had ever been, sparing nothing. He listened closely to the priest but at a given moment butted in: "Nothing can save me. *He's* around."

The clarity with which the past was revealed figured in Balthazar's imagination as a bright circle rimmed by shadow, from which he had come and into which he would return. He had learned to anticipate those subterfuges, perpetually new, by which he had laid on him the same suffering burden. And his words "He's around" rang with such surety that Father Monkiewicz had tossed a nervous glance about the room.

A hopeless dilemma. How to grant absolution and the last rites to someone guilty of so grievous a sin. The priest, obedient to his conscience, tried to wring from Balthazar at least a semblance of hope. What he got was a dying man's acquiescence, as the man was visibly too weak to protest. The hours spent in Balthazar's company left the priest feeling edgy, as if the affliction he had been called upon to cure was contagious; as if, being powerless against Evil, he had been called upon to act merely as a witness.

When the others entered the room, Balthazar, whether deliberately or from delirium, gave no sign of acknowledging their presence. Transfixed by some point in space, he muttered: "The oak."

This may have been a reference to the carbine in the oak tree, a normal deathbed reflex, that of retrospection, or it may have been an allusion to something else. He fell into a coma again.

Dr. Kohn arrived late that same night. He said that maybe, if he could be operated on . . . but that it would mean a long haul by wagon and then a train ride to a big hospital—which, in effect, meant keeping vigil and letting nature take its course. Balthazar did not live to see the sunrise. The darkly pitted shields of the sunflowers were just emerging from the mist; chickens, clucking somnolently, were shaking the dew from their feathers when Balthazar, wearing the same puzzled expression, took one last look at the roof beams overhead and the faces of the people.

"All together now, fellas."

Those were his last, inscrutable words, and a few minutes later he was dead.

By morning there was nothing more to see. The image of the live Balthazar thus remained for Thomas what it had always been, unaltered by the mask of deathly repose: the slightly upturned, somehow virginal upper lip; the rounded, boyish-looking face with its fugitive shadows and traces of a smile. So be it always.

"Didn't I tell you? Drank himself to death, the skunk!" Grandmother Misia made the sign of the cross, then added: "Lord, shed light upon his soul."

Antonina breathed a deep sigh and lamented man's fate: "Alive today, rot tomorrow." Helen had lost all recollection of her plan to resettle Balthazar and to move into the forester's cottage herself. She only regretted that so much property had gone up in smoke, her regret springing less from selfishness than from solicitude for the fruits of human labor.

The whole manor turned out for the funeral. Rain fell during the burial, and Thomas clung to his grandmother's side, holding the umbrella over her. As the priest shook the aspergillum, drops of holy water merged with the downpour rioting in the oak leaves.

The more he brooded over the Balthazar affair, the more confounded the priest became. Whatever conclusions he drew acquired for him the force of personal conviction only after he was used to proclaiming them out loud, to fortifying his belief through constant iteration. He talked of those who denied entry to the Holy Spirit; of man's free will, so fashioned as to accept or reject the gift. He likened the will to a spring on a mountain peak—rushing forth, spilling aimlessly, looking for a way until, guided by the force of its own momentum, it ran down this side or that.

After Balthazar's passing, Father Monkiewicz, though not a particularly skilled preacher or theologian, suddenly became adept at moving his audience, his success owing not least to a tacit understanding: they could always see the man behind the example. From then on, Balthazar occupied a prominent place in the memory of the parish. Women would invoke him to reform their husbands of their intemperate ways.

Thomas's grandfather had several Masses said for the repose of the forester's soul. The priest humbly accepted the money, at the same time rankling over this unnecessary —but incurable—display of humility before his masters. Privately, he had his own thoughts. At times he was even a little tempted to see Balthazar as a victim of the manor— only a little, but tempted he was.

Balthazar was now departed, the word "departed" being hard to imagine when pronounced by lips that some minutes or years hence would also find themselves among the departed. But the vats belonging to Balthazar's distillery were imaginable, all too tangibly. The people of Pogirai moved them closer to the village and made profitable use of them, and in time they became the cause of much bickering and even accusations of theft, these coming from the family of the deceased. The wild pigs, meanwhile, made good use of Balthazar's garden.

65

BIRCH GROVES in May are pale green; framed by dark spruce forests, they give off a light more befitting the planet Venus. In autumn their bright-yellow leaves become shimmering flakes of sun, and the aspen blazes red in the crowns of its chandeliers. Swollen rowanberries, buff plant hides, and matted leaves on the trails add further color to October in the forests.

They were hunting the place where the hills ran down to the marshland and saw before them slopes heaped up in a multitiered beauty. The morning air was cool, limpid. Romuald curled his hand into a trumpet and called in the dogs: *"Ha lee, toh lee! Ha lee, toh lee!"*

"Ohhhleee"—came the echo.

Thomas stood at his side, relieved of all his doubts and self-torment. They had lost their reality the moment Barbarka had come up to him after Mass and told him that Romuald would be waiting for him a week from that Sunday because that was the day he was planning to take out the hounds. Barbarka. The news of their wedding had been received at home with a shrug of the shoulders and some unflattering remarks, and Thomas, now more than ever, felt uncomfortable around her. Still, Romuald had sent word—nothing else mattered. So there were no bad feel-

ings, it was all his imagination. Romuald's welcome—
"Long time no see! What you been up to?"—was the
clincher.

Thomas was happy. He took in the sharp smells and
his lungs swelled him with a sense of his own power. He
flung back his shoulders, certain that if he jumped, his
resilience would carry him a hundred or two hundred
meters.

He cupped his mouth in imitation of Romuald. *"Ha
lee, toh lee!"*

"Ger gacktracking," Victor stuttered. His finger was
pointing to a glade down below.

The dogs were running in a pack. Lutnia in the lead,
followed by Dunay and Zagray. With no scent to follow,
they were running wild; time to call them off and move on
to other stands.

The world rose up luminous, simple; the chain binding him to the Thomas obsessed with his own thoughts
severed. Forward, march. He could feel the gunlock on his
Berdan grazing his back, and he reveled in its coolness.
Whatever was meant to happen today was bound to be
good.

To Thomas the future was always a storehouse of
things already prepared, waiting to be fulfilled. It was
gained through premonition, was somehow present in the
body. It even had its own emissaries in certain animals—
the cat, for one, if it happened to cross your path. Above
all, one had to have an ear for that inner voice, to be able
to tell the bright sounds from the dull sounds. But if the
future was already given, if it didn't shape itself as it went
along, free to become whatever it willed, then what was
left to our own willing and endeavoring? That was something for which Thomas had no answer, knowing only that
he would have to submit to the decrees being ordained
through him and that every step he took was both his and
not his.

Today he was submitting. The voice was full of brightness; it had the ring of crystal. The feet sank into a carpet of moldering leaf, his gun clanked against a ring on his belt; a hush among the pine; a nutcracker, dapple-necked, on the wing; anthills without motion, the movement now shifted to the interior, to kingdoms already giving way to their hibernal sleep. Thomas could have wandered like this for hours—if Romuald hadn't pulled up and, rubbing his jaw, pondered the best route for them to take. Three trails came together; they settled on the one skirting a cliff with a steep drop. In places they had a bird's-eye view of the spruce tops tapering to a point just below their feet; elsewhere the forest, ribbed with ravines trimmed by half-naked hazel shrubs and bright green at the bottom, arched gently down. Romuald stationed Thomas near the edge of one of these ravines and told him to keep a close lookout for any movement on the trail and in the narrow crossing below. As he watched the backs of Romuald and Victor grow smaller, he felt somehow cheated: those who get to keep going always seem to have the best of it.

He stood leaning against a pine trunk. Then he sat down on the ground, balancing his Berdan across his thighs. A crinkling noise—opposite him. He turned in the direction of the rustling and saw a mouse, its tiny nose poking out from its hole under a bedding of roots. With snout comically tilted, it sniffed the air, decided the coast was clear, and took off on the run, blending so well with the buff-colored matting that Thomas soon lost track of it. Another rustle, this one more like a brittle flaking, coming from a neighboring branch, snapped his head back. He rose to his feet and craned his neck: it was a giant spruce, from which a sprinkling of scales fell. Small birds were fluttering in the crown, but except for the fluttering and the flash of a sun-pierced wing he could make out nothing. He circled the tree but without improving his view. It gnawed at him not to know their names; the small ones, just because they were so hard to identify from a distance, always gave him the most trouble. Romuald, when asked to name their species, would brush it aside with a "Aw, who the heck cares."

He was jolted by the pack, by a sudden surge of yelping from the interior that rose up like the blast of a pipe organ in church. Not the voices themselves but a chorale that launches from the opening bars into its soaring, swooping pattern made even mightier by the echo. Thomas gripped his gunstock and kept shifting his gaze from the russet path to the bottom of the ravine, then back again to the path. There was no reading any direction in it, in the baying, in that constant rising and falling, the blending of which, the accreting of which into a steady, deep-throated rumble was so impressive that he gave up trying to locate it. With Romuald beside him he would have had the meaning of that music, would have had the thrill of it, but on his own he distinguished nothing, an incomprehensible language.

Then it seemed to fade. And with the dwindling of prospect came the sort of apathy one gets when the figures all tally and the thought of a recount palls, when things are such as to rule out the accidental. The green at the bottom, the footpath, by their sheer presence, were a denial of some unexpected intrusion. And Thomas was not mistaken: unsure of the boy's aim, Romuald had posted him in a spot where there was little likelihood of a killing (he knew it to be a crossing seldom used by the hare).

Relieved of having to answer to the call of the forest, Thomas fell to daydreaming. Idle, freed from his hunter's duty, even gladdened by his leisure, he cleared a hole among the needles and began carving little furrows in the ground with the edge of his boot. It was one of those games of make-believe not altogether compatible with his years: let this one be a canal, let that one be the river, now another canal over here . . . Meanwhile, the pack continued its discourse with space, and high above the howling, the wind whistled through the crowns of the tall-timbered forest.

How could he have detected the unfamiliar in their baying, the warning contained in their voices: Beware, beware! No; lost in his daydreams, distracted by his frivolous pastimes, he could not suspect that the verdict had been passed and that a tragedy was in store.

Everything was calculated to make sure the blow struck with maximum cruelty. A hero's confidence. The fear he had long nurtured, the overcoming of that fear, then the acceding to the weakness, to the loving and desiring, without which man would not be vulnerable to fate's wrath; the illusory rejoicing, and the promise that what was suffered once would never be repeated. Without ignorance, there can be no tragedy. But there it was, heading his way—the beaming light of illumination, in whose folds he was now playing idly under the vigilant scrutiny of speechless spectators: a fool, a madman, suspecting nothing, seduced by the magic of sound, furrowing the little trenches of his undoing.

The dogs had jumped a buck. Following the scent, they had described a huge arc, so that the baying now reached Thomas from the valley. He raised his head and fixed absently on the source, too distant as yet to be a warning. Then a bolt of lightning; not that he was jolted by the seeing of it; rather, with his whole body he felt the composition of the ravine suddenly rearrange itself into something new and unknown. Everything came at once: the wonder, the shouldering of the gun, the shot, and the realization: "A buck!"—but in a frenzy, in despair of the outcome, when even as the finger is bearing down on the trigger the mind has thrust upon it the certainty of a miss.

Thomas stood open-mouthed. He had yet to fathom it, the sense of what had happened. A groan wrenched itself from his mouth, the gun angrily hit the ground, everything emptied, and heaving, run through by the cruelty of fate, he dropped down on his haunches.

A breeze rocked the pine's fluffy paws. No more sound came from the dogs. So the idle daydreaming had been a trap. Why, why, when his inner voice had made him so confident? How would he ever bear the humiliation? Only now, under the fingers pressing his eyelids, did the buck—its forelegs tucked, its neck bent back—become a reality. Just one second sooner, just one single second. But it had been denied him.

There was a rustling nearby; out of the scrub came Lutnia, whimpering, her eyes searching his, followed by the other two, bewildered. Their disillusionment—a man had shot and brought discredit to the man—only made it worse. He sat still on the stump, cradling his burning cheeks. A twig snapped under a boot: his judges were coming.

Romuald pulled up in front of him. "Where's the buck, Tommy?"

Not a gesture, not even to look up. "I missed."

"But he was heading straight into your sights. I coulda dropped him myself, but I said, 'Let Tommy have 'im.'"

To Victor, who was coming up the trail, he said: "Tommy let 'im get away."

Every word—a cold blade—stabbed. No escape. He did not dare to look them in the eye. Forced to retreat, to go back into his prison, into the body that had betrayed him and which he could not renounce, he clenched his teeth.

Not a word on the return trip. The trail, its twists and forks so magical a while back, was now a dismal skeleton. What had he done to deserve this? Even worse than the shame was the rancor he bore himself—or God—for having believed in the promise.

When they reached the fork in the meadow, Thomas

said they were expecting him at home, and went his own way.

"Thomas! The gun!" they shouted after him.

The Berdan had been left leaning against an alder. Without turning his head, he stuck his hands into his pockets and tried to whistle.

66

THOMAS WAS going on fourteen when he made a discovery: after every great disappointment comes usually a great joy, one to make us forget what the world was like when there was not that joy.

Asters white with frost. A titmouse takes wing, and the slender branch, knobbed with minuscule white globes, rocks. He stands under a pear tree, facing the window of the room once occupied by Grandmother Dilbin, and inhales the tawny, shriveled-up pears on the ground, the effluvium of the garden's fading. His attention is on the closed shutters. Too early yet. Or could she be awake? He slips up to the shutters, carefully undoes the hook, but at the last moment withdraws his hand.

His latest worry was that, deep down, he was really unworthy of her. Whenever they sat with the fruit basket between them, he would deliberately choose the most bruised apple. In setting the table, he took pains to see that she got the best plates—there was hardly a dish in the house that wasn't chipped or cracked; laying out the cutlery, he would hesitate, decide his own fork was nicer, and promptly switch.

Did he feel like waking her? Of course he did, but he also knew that it would have been selfish of him.

The thresher's fitful grinding echoed from across the pond. He circled around the manor house, bounded up onto the porch, sidestepping the nasturtium seeds laid out to dry, and bumped into Antonina on his way through the kitchen. Years of traipsing back and forth had left shallow depressions in the hallway's plank flooring. He peeked inside the "cloakroom." What about weighing a bundle of cotton to kill time? He took the steelyard down from the wall, knotted the four corners of the sheet on the hook, and slid the brass weight back and forth. The machine managed to distract him, but not for long; he abruptly chucked it and put his ear to the door. Unable to restrain the urge, he pressed down gently on the latch, straining, without allowing any creaking, to open the door a crack for a peek inside. But it creaked, and then came a voice—hers: "Thomas!"

After the last hunt Thomas had taken sick, starting with shivers on the way back. His teeth chattering, he hurriedly undressed and slipped between the cold sheets. To make him sweat, Misia gave him a sudorific of dried raspberries. There was no telling how long he had been nurturing it—perhaps the other morning's false delirium had signaled a fever coming on—or whether it didn't answer to some need. Doubled up, with his chin grazing his knees, he was stricken with one desire: to burrow under the covers, to feel the weight of the quilt and sheepskin on top of him. That was several weeks ago, though it seemed a lot longer.

His mother sat before the mirror, her head tilted to one side, braiding the chestnut hair that had lain on the pillow as Thomas approached in the dark. Earlier he had touched her cheek with his lips and sat down on the edge of the bed, on its side frame. A brooch—or something else that defied closer definition—gleamed mysteriously on her nightstand. Later the shutters were opened, and Thomas stared at her from behind: at the eyes visible in the mirror, slightly slanted, gray, their shading made deceptive by the light reflected in them; the thick eyebrows that collapsed whenever she laughed and caused the eyes to disappear in the slits between brow and cheekbone.

From his early childhood, he knew of only two incidents involving his mother, and then only secondhand. He had gone over them so often in his mind that certain details had taken on the force of memory, though actual recollection was impossible, since he was much too young at the time.

The "bath" was an open stretch of shaded shoreline along the Issa, access to which was by a footpath dropping down from the fields. His mother had set him down next to the path, was already in the water when she saw a dog, its tongue out and its tail between its legs (rabies was quite common in the district), running straight in their direction. She jumped out of the water and, stark naked, dashed uphill to the park. The hand towel she had snatched up on the run and that had fluttered behind her, the way her panic was transmitted to him, the mouth gasping for air, the wildly pounding heart . . . Did he only imagine these things? He could even see the dog—reddish-brown, with hollow flanks—and hear it panting at their heels. Or were they from a dream?—he was haunted by such fleeing nightmares. Paralyzed, entirely at the mercy of her running, he had been scared stiff that her legs would give out, that she would collapse from exhaustion. This "she" was no more than a sign, bearing no resemblance to the woman in the photograph or to the real person he could now touch any time he liked.

In his talks with her, he kept returning to this childhood incident, and after she had repeated it from the beginning, he would ask: "But the towel. What about the towel?"

"What towel, Tommy?"

The other incident was one he never broached in her presence. He was one and a half at the time and deathly

ill with diphtheria. So close was he to dying that, according
to Antonina, his mother had butted the wall and crawled
about the room on her knees, wailing and imploring God's
mercy. With hands prayerfully raised, she had vowed that
if her son recovered she would make a pilgrimage on foot
to Vilno, to the shrine of Our Lady of Ostrabrama. Recov-
ery came quickly. But when he later pestered the grownups
about her vow, they became evasive. "Well, you see,
Tommy, times were rough then, there was a war on . . ."
Thus was born the recognition: no pilgrimage. He was
reminded of it during her talks, held usually in her room,
with Helen and Misia. And what thrilling stories she could
tell about her wartime adventures near the front: of how
she made it across the border—out in the wilderness, at
night, alone with the smuggler who had showed her the
route, of how it was so dark she lost the trail, and how,
terrified of running into a border patrol, she had hid in
the bushes until daybreak— "Really? Honestly, Tekla?"
Helen would cut in. But left alone with Misia, she would
begin with some condescending remark like "Well, well,
that's Tekla for you . . ." implying that she was flighty,
whimsical, had wonderful adventures but never any
money, and so on. Misia, from her perch by the oven,
loved to incite her to more of these prissy complaints, but
the woman was too dull-witted to see that Misia was simply
having fun at her expense. Thomas, who had never forgotten his mother's broken vow, was deeply wounded by his
aunt's insinuations. Maybe she really was the flighty type
. . . And then it surfaced, the resentment, born deep down,
at having been left behind, alone. The one time he caught
himself thinking such thoughts, he immediately confessed
to his guilt. To punish himself, he chose the most severe
penance—for three straight days he neglected to go into
her room to say good morning—most severe because it
was bound to create the wrong impression. The next time

he was tempted to sit in judgment of her, he shut his eyes and forced himself to think of how beautiful and courageous she was.

Leaves turned a dark red, the Issa steaming amid patches of rusted sweet flag. From time to time they would harness a horse and drive out to the villages to visit some of his mother's girlhood friends. Pitchers of beer on the table, the puffing of long-stemmed pipes, and the toasting, the children, the hounds, and the flowery green chests, the cheese smells in the vestibule, the buttermilk, the apples, the chickens fluttering in their roosts; the leisure of the village hut at that time of year when the fields have been worked and the farm retreats to the four-cornered sanctuary of the yard; when the mud on the roads spills over the rims and whistles in the spokes; when the tiled stove is fired and to sit at dusk staring at the fire and thinking of nothing is a fine thing; and then the pink turns to rose and you wish it could last and the fire slowly dies and it's not what it was and with the darkness comes a slackening of the will.

The wick of a globe lamp, green on the outside and white on the inside, has to be specially trimmed to keep it from leaving black whiskers on the chimney. Thomas sits doing his lessons; his mother puts aside the sweater on her needles and licks the pencil's lead tip. Her chair next to his, shoulder leaning against shoulder, a ring of lamplight, together, here, while from outside comes the hooting of owls in the orchard.

Still, what has already been cannot be so easily dismissed. One day she asked him what he would like to be. He blushed and lowered his head. "I . . . might become a priest."

She gave him a quizzical look. "Why a priest, of all things?"

"Be-because . . ."

He was swallowing his tears; he couldn't help it. He

was unable to come right out and say, "Because I missed a buck and it makes me sad that you forgot your vow." Besides, that would have been only partly true.

"Because . . . I'm bad."

A priest's surplice gave the one who wore it the right to be different; things expected of others were not expected of him. That was what he had meant to say.

His mother made a face.

"I am."

"What a perfectly silly thing to say."

He turned away and, clenching his teeth, said: "I don't ever want to be alone."

The door opens only once like this: the face above the high-necked gray sweater, the face of a stranger, radiant, beckons, waits, summons; and he, stock-still, confused, suddenly lets out a cry, jumps, and arms enfold—it's *her*. Never again.

Sleep brings peace. She tucks him in and her kiss softly accompanies him into the brushwood of night. Her footsteps fade as, burying his nose in his pillow, he thinks of what he might give her as a present. The bird book? No, that was something of a different order.

"But I do love her, don't I?"

67

It was St. Andrew's Eve, and when the wax was poured, his mother's augury was a garland—flowers or thorns, no telling—and his a leaf that, magnified by the shadow, loomed like the African continent with a cross on top. And then the snows, when people came in blowing clouds of vapor, stamping their feet to shed the glassy stuff, all the while the Issa's noisy mobile ferment was turning to ice. Christmas that year was celebrated in the traditional way, except that the empty plate which custom dictated be set out for the wayfarer on Christmas Eve was now really intended for a stranger, and not, as in years past, in the secret hope that his mother would show up. Now it was she and not Antonina who, assisted by Thomas, took care of the holiday festivities. It was she who cooked the borscht with mushroom pasties; she who made *slizyki*—sheets of dough rolled up cylinder-fashion and baked until stone-hard. The *slizyki* were served with syrup—a crock of which stood on the table—whose ingredients were water, honey, and ground poppyseed. The dishes served between the borscht and dessert were nothing compared to Thomas's favorite, cranberry pudding, which he ate by the heaping bowlful; and when the feasting finally caught up with him, the hay stuffed under the linen tablecloth in memory of the Christ child's manger made a comfortable little mattress for his elbow. Later, under the Christmas tree, he and his mother joined the others in caroling—she even taught him a few he had never heard. The stable lantern lit, they would set out for Midnight Mass, wading the whole distance through the powdery snow.

Thomas's mother, being a practical-minded woman, decided to sit out the winter in Gine. Crossing the border in the dead of winter was strenuous enough, but there were other reasons for postponing it. Thomas's father, who had been having his ups and downs, mostly downs—the fault of his peregrine, itinerant life—was now living hand to mouth as a municipal clerk. Since Helen had already been given her share in land, Tekla was entitled to something, too. But to raise a cash crop meant waiting for the threshing season and for the market price to rise. Then his mother hit on an idea, one that drew a loud "You're crazy!" from his Aunt Helen: why not smuggle a couple of ponies across the border—the short, stocky Lithuanian breed was much prized abroad—and make a present of them to her husband. But how, if she barely had made it across by herself, would she ever manage it with *horses*? Rubbish, it would *have* to work.

The border—open only to smugglers, wolves, and foxes for the reason that the Poles thought of the city of Vilno as theirs, while the Lithuanians claimed it as their historic capital illegally seized by the Poles—was a nuisance for many. His mother picked out a pair of horses, four-year-olds, both sorrels with a dark stripe down the back. She was relying on them for the journey home, on luck, and, if they were caught, on the leniency of the border guards (as long as no officers were around).

Window recesses powdered white, a hush except for the steady twitter of bullfinches husking lilac seeds. The prospect of a journey abroad awakened in Thomas an interest in geography. A German atlas, published in 1852, served as his textbook. Because it was so old, his mother had to pencil in the boundaries of certain states, many of which now bore different names. Although the atlas showed neither Gine nor any of the surrounding localities, something it could easily be forgiven, Thomas became fascinated by maps—by the way the finger went down, and under it were born forests, land tracts, roads, villages, and vast multitudes of people in motion, each distinct, each somehow distinguishable from the other; but how, the moment it was lifted—*poof!* And just as he had hungered for flight, for a higher perspective on those kneeling in church, so now he ached for a magical magnifying glass powerful enough to bring out all that was hidden beneath the paper's surface. The more we devote ourselves to that realm of contours, zones, and lines, the greater our enthrallment. The thrall is as great as when the mind tries to imagine what lies between two numbers. Now, if a map could be drawn to include every house and human, stationary or in motion, that would still leave all the horses, cows, cats, plant species, fish in the Issa—not to mention fleas on dogs, shimmering beetles in the grass, and ants and many other things. That meant a map was always approximate. Another discovery gained through his map explorations: Seated up here in the chair is one me, but down there under the finger being held on the blank spot that ought to have been Gine is another. I am pointing at myself, at the shrunken me. The second me is not the same as the one up here; down there, it is merely one among many.

The days were getting longer. Grandfather came back from one of his "business trips," flushed with success: he was told that the property division would be approved. In the end, money had spoken louder than Joseph's accusations. The Juchniewiczes were to move in after St. George's Day; as feared, their property was to be parceled.

It was a cold and snowy Palm Sunday—spring was late that year—without a catkin in sight. Blue crowfoots were already pushing up through the rot of last year's debris when it dawned on Thomas that this was to be his last spring in Gine. He took his time scouting the park, finally found the right spot—a rectangular clearing on a slope—dug up a young chestnut, bore it back, and planted it. If he ever came back to Gine, he would run down first thing, locate the clearing, and gauge the tree's growth.

The Issa was still iced, its surface a mirror reflecting cloud banks, but the shoreline was already giving up the first cornet-shaped leaves of a pale green. One day, on the brush-lined trail overlooking the river, he ran into Onutè, companion of his childhood games. He had laid eyes on her several times in the past, but never at such close range and never like this. Stopping in her tracks, she stared at him quizzically, even bewilderedly. She was grown-up. Ducking his head down, with a burning in his cheeks and behind his collar, he passed her with a stern, hard look.

The sternness was a mask, but Onutè could easily have mistaken it for the arrogance of a *pan*, which he nearly was. All this occurred to Thomas much later, long after the danger had passed, and it touched him with sadness.

68

━━━━━━

❧❀❀❀❀❧

Six months after the wedding, a baby son was born to Romuald and Barbarka. The thawing fields already bulged with naked black hummocks when an early April freeze forced them to take the sleigh to church. The baby was christened Witold.

The sky was cloudy, crows cawed in the sallows, and Romuald's red-tasseled parade whip lazily flicked the horse's spine. Barbarka folded back the corners of the plaid shawl: the baby was asleep. They were traveling, naturally, in complete obliviousness of that time designated not only by the return of spring and winter, the waving of ripening grain fields, and the migrations of birds. The earth under their green-lacquered sleigh was not volcanic, did not belch fire, nor was there any cause to think of those floods and conflagrations by which the history of mankind was made.

They had not reached the porch when Witold started wailing. Barbarka laid him in the cradle and, with one hand on the rocker, fixed her gaze on the table already laid out for the reception. Happiness was being the mistress of one's house. Now, when she opened the cupboard doors, she was filled with a sweetness equal to that of the pungent, freshly baked rolls inside. My rolls. My husband. My son. And, let us also note, my floor—whose planks squeaked in concert with the squeaking of laced-up shoes. Hence the woman's beaming face as the guests began to arrive, as Romuald, wringing his hands, said: "Well, Barbarka, time to serve up, bring on the feast!"

Old lady Bukowski took one look at her grandson and declared a resemblance to her son. This was her way of consoling herself—another was by emptying glass after glass. Night thickened; a thaw wind whistled in the branches. Someone drawn there by the light would have looked in on people laughing, reclining on chairs, and, out in the middle, on dogs—allowed into the house because of the winter cold—scratching their hides. The one scratching his neck with his hind paw, he's thumping the floor—but the sound is muffled by the window.

A wolf on the outskirts of the forest lifts its head in the direction of the well-lighted window and attends to the inscrutable habitat of humans, those creatures forever segregated from what the wolf is trained to understand. Others more cunning than it may also be enticed by the lighted square. But woe if there are any frock-coated devils among them; their interest in what goes on inside human dwellings will not go unpunished. By attaching too much importance to such trivialities, they will never survive an age demanding a sense of proportion. Soon no one along the Issa will testify to having seen one swinging its legs from a mill rafter, to having heard them dancing their jigs. And even if someone were to spread such tales, no one need assent to them.

The thaw wind came from the west, from the sea. Out there were ships, pitching and sounding their horns as they plied the waters between the shores of Sweden and Finland, between the Hanseatic city of Riga and Hanseatic Danzig. But Barbarka was here, changing her son's diapers, holding him by the ankles and lightly tilting the little fanny that always roused her to such tenderness. Such sentiments, like those she had when she offered her son her blue-veined breast, were not to be transposed beyond the realm of experience proper to them. We are given to live on the border of the human and the bestial, and it is good so.

69

❧❧❧❧❧

IT WAS around this time that Romuald hired a new farmhand: Dominic Malinowski. Whatever had caused him to leave his native Gine, the reason must have been serious.

They were in the barn, flailing—Dominic and the farmer in whose service he was that winter. The fight might have been avoided, even though it had been building since morning. Dominic was a master of self-control. His mouth was always clamped shut, drawn tight by the holding back of things he would have liked but never was able to say. The more he approached young manhood, the more he resembled a scrawny predatory bird. Many times he had been on the verge of taking this bully of a man by the throat, knowing at the same time the danger of surrendering to his impulses. "Wham!" echoed the old man's flail. "Whack!" answered Dominic's, and so it went, duet-fashion, with the threshing that afternoon. They broke only once, when the old man took out his bad temper on someone in the house. That's how it started.

That someone was a servant girl, the same age as Dominic, whom Dominic thought stupid for letting herself be bullied so easily. That he had taken a liking to her is beside the point; the fact is, he spoke up in her defense. The old man's stubborn, sclerotic pride then got a taste of Dominic's muscle. He held him up by the throat, felt his Adam's apple under his fingers, and hurled him to the ground, where he lay, groaning. Dominic was already beyond the gate when he heard the outcry.

A moment of triumph. "You won't boss *me* around." He was not yet back at his hut by the ferry when he began to consider all the possible consequences. And consequences there were. His former boss managed to incite the other farmers, including the wealthiest, against him; they made common cause and for a long time Dominic went unhired. Until Borkuny, that is.

Meanwhile, he stayed at home, carving spoons, kneading troughs, clogs—enough to bring in a few pennies every day. His mother would often sit on the bench opposite and follow the agile movements of his hands. "Land," she would say, and her son would raise his eyes to that face scored with wrinkles, to that mouth caught in the cramp iron of deeply engraved folds. It was the same every day: her petition for land under the Reform. "But Joseph said . . ." And: "They're parceling it out everywhere . . ." Dominic hung his head in silence and dug his knife into the limewood with greater intensity than usual. Lost in thought, he brought the knife back toward him slowly, plowing a long groove with the blade.

70

THEY PUT off leaving until June. Thomas's mother had the wagon rigged with a canopy—a hazel bow-frame, spread with a tarpaulin—similar to the one on a gypsy's. With a hundred kilometers to go before reaching the border, and another forty on the other side, it would be a shelter from both rain and night. She also got up a good supply of provisions: dried cheeses with caraway, cured sausage, and black-smoked hams, a favorite of Thomas's father.

The day before, Grandfather showed him into his room, shut the door behind him, sat down, and took to hemming and hawing. He talked of how city people were corrupt, of how one should avoid falling into bad company . . . but when asked how one could tell good from bad company, he broke off with a nasal *pff! pff!*—as if too ashamed to answer: "Well, you know, vodka, cards . . ." —and pulled him to him, and Thomas felt a powerful wrenching as he kissed his bristly cheeks, and then, just as abruptly, his grandfather freed himself and began fumbling in his pockets for a handkerchief.

At breakfast the next morning he blistered his lips while gulping down his tea and left the table without finishing it. He saw the wagon's white tarpaulin framed in the window, overheard the last-minute conversations, and raced outside, across the porch and down the sloping lawn, past the row of blooming peonies. Through a gap in the park trees, the valley rim lay in mist, a sunny day was coming up pink and clear above the dew, birds were singing. He wanted to hold it in his memory. "You'll forget us, oy, you'll forget us," said Antonina when all were huddled on the porch steps and she held his face in her hands, sadly. Misia's cheek smelled of wet rennets. Luke was his usual squeezing, slobbery, bear-hugging self. Then came the blessings, signs of the cross traced in the air. "All right, Thomas," said his mother gravely. Thomas gripped the hardened leather of the reins. Now, at all such partings there comes a moment when someone must do the breaking—and the more abrupt it is, the better. Thomas cracked the whip, wheels clacked, cries went up; looking back over the canopy's canvas cover, they saw, in the shrinking aperture of the lane's green tunnel, a flurry of handkerchiefs and hands in the air.

With reins taut, they eased their way down the rutty,

rain-washed road, and soon a brooding Christ flashed among the dense foliage. Back up the way loomed the granary's outer white wall. Thomas let the horses break into a trot, and without changing stride, they passed the cemetery oaks, under which lay Magdalena, Grandmother, and Balthazar, forever left behind. Gine vanished around the next bend; before them, the unknown.

Later, as the horses began pulling for the uphill climb, the Issa, twining in and out of meadows, shone for the last time. The water of one's native river is sweet in recollection. Muscles rippled under horsehide, and they took the incline, but down on the flats it started up again, the whipping and the cajoling: "Hey, Birnik, you're gonna get it!"

The horses, destined for a new home abroad, far from their native grounds, were named Smilga and Birnik in commemoration of their former owners. Smilga had a reputation for being honest, hardworking—a horse that pulled for all it was worth and never got fat. Birnik was just the opposite: immune to the whip, round as a cucumber, a faker and a shirker. But when it came to climbing, Birnik went at it with a fury: a hill was an obstacle, an offense to his lazy nature, and had to be quickly overcome.

His mother had on a flowery kerchief, the straw seat shaped itself to the sitting, and no sooner were they out on the road than the horses' drinking pail, though well secured, began to clank and something went wrong with the whiffletree. They crossed forest meadows, tails flailing against flies, and steered for the big-lake country, traveling the same route as the one taken by Magdalena in the coffin. An afternoon meal in the shade of an oak, a clean tablecloth spread on the grass. Just before nightfall, they looked down from a high elevation on a new terrain, where as far as one could see there was more water than earth, where lake adjoined lake, peninsulas blurred with isthmuses, and the eye beheld a green archipelago. Then it was downhill, through foothills and between boulders, some so tall and erect they resembled petrified animals. The haymakers were already at work in the meadows—row upon row of tiny human figures, rocking in unison to a common rhythm. Night lodgings in a fishing village; silence, boats reeking of pitch, and the crunching of oats in feedbags.

The time has come, Thomas, to wish you luck. Your future can only be guessed, for no one can predict how you will be shaped by the world that awaits you. The devils along the Issa have fashioned you as best they could; the rest does not belong to them. But keep an eye on Birnik. He's falling asleep again, slacking off, not knowing that thanks to you his name will one day be worthy of mention. You raise your whip—and here our tale is ended.

READ MORE IN PENGUIN

In every corner of the world, on every subject under the sun, Penguin represents quality and variety – the very best in publishing today.

For complete information about books available from Penguin – including Puffins, Penguin Classics and Arkana – and how to order them, write to us at the appropriate address below. Please note that for copyright reasons the selection of books varies from country to country.

In the United Kingdom: Please write to *Dept. EP, Penguin Books Ltd, Bath Road, Harmondsworth, West Drayton, Middlesex UB7 ODA*

In the United States: Please write to *Consumer Sales, Penguin Putnam Inc., P.O. Box 12289 Dept. B, Newark, New Jersey 07101-5289*. VISA and MasterCard holders call 1-800-788-6262 to order Penguin titles

In Canada: Please write to *Penguin Books Canada Ltd, 10 Alcorn Avenue, Suite 300, Toronto, Ontario M4V 3B2*

In Australia: Please write to *Penguin Books Australia Ltd, P.O. Box 257, Ringwood, Victoria 3134*

In New Zealand: Please write to *Penguin Books (NZ) Ltd, Private Bag 102902, North Shore Mail Centre, Auckland 10*

In India: Please write to *Penguin Books India Pvt Ltd, 11 Community Centre, Panchsheel Park, New Delhi 110017*

In the Netherlands: Please write to *Penguin Books Netherlands bv, Postbus 3507, NL-1001 AH Amsterdam*

In Germany: Please write to *Penguin Books Deutschland GmbH, Metzlerstrasse 26, 60594 Frankfurt am Main*

In Spain: Please write to *Penguin Books S. A., Bravo Murillo 19, 1° B, 28015 Madrid* ·

In Italy: Please write to *Penguin Italia s.r.l., Via Benedetto Croce 2, 20094 Corsico, Milano*

In France: Please write to *Penguin France, Le Carré Wilson, 62 rue Benjamin Baillaud, 31500 Toulouse*

In Japan: Please write to *Penguin Books Japan Ltd, Kaneko Building, 2-3-25 Koraku, Bunkyo-Ku, Tokyo 112*

In South Africa: Please write to *Penguin Books South Africa (Pty) Ltd, Private Bag X14, Parkview, 2122 Johannesburg*

READ MORE IN PENGUIN

Published or forthcoming:

Ulysses   James Joyce

Written over a seven-year period, from 1914 to 1921, *Ulysses* has survived bowdlerization, legal action and bitter controversy. An undisputed modernist classic, its ceaseless verbal inventiveness and astonishingly wide-ranging allusions confirm its standing as an imperishable monument to the human condition. 'Everybody knows now that *Ulysses* is the greatest novel of the century' Anthony Burgess, *Observer*

Nineteen Eighty-Four   George Orwell

Hidden away in the Record Department of the Ministry of Truth, Winston Smith skilfully rewrites the past to suit the needs of the Party. Yet he inwardly rebels against the totalitarian world he lives in, which controls him through the all-seeing eye of Big Brother. 'His final masterpiece . . . *Nineteen Eighty-Four* is enthralling' Timothy Garton Ash, *New York Review of Books*

The Day of the Locust *and* **The Dream Life of Balso Snell**
Nathanael West

These two novellas demonstrate the fragility of the American dream. In *The Day of the Locust*, talented young artist Todd Hackett has been brought to Hollywood to work in a major studio. He discovers a surreal world of tarnished dreams, where violence and hysteria lurk behind the glittering façade. 'The best of the Hollywood novels, a nightmare vision of humanity destroyed by its obsession with film' J. G. Ballard, *Sunday Times*

The Myth of Sisyphus   Albert Camus

The Myth of Sisyphus is one of the most profound philosophical statements written this century. It is a discussion of the central idea of absurdity that Camus was to develop in his novel *The Outsider*. Here Camus poses the fundamental question – Is life worth living? – and movingly argues for an acceptance of reality that encompasses revolt, passion and, above all, liberty.

READ MORE IN PENGUIN

Published or forthcoming:

The Diary of a Young Girl Anne Frank

This definitive edition of Anne Frank's diary restores substantial material omitted from the original edition, giving us a deeper insight into her world. 'One of the greatest books of the twentieth century ... If you have never read Anne Frank's diary, or haven't read it for years, this is the edition to buy' *Guardian*

Brideshead Revisited Evelyn Waugh

The most nostalgic of Evelyn Waugh's novels, *Brideshead Revisited* looks back to the golden age before the Second World War. It tells the story of Charles Ryder's infatuation with the Marchmains and the rapidly disappearing world of privilege they inhabit. 'Lush and evocative ... expresses at once the profundity of change and the indomitable endurance of the human spirit' *The Times*

Oranges John McPhee

From Thailand, where the sweetest oranges are as green as emeralds, to Florida oranges so juicy it is said they should be peeled in the bath, the orange exists in bounteous varieties. John McPhee has woven together history, anecdote and science to create a definitive guide to the world of oranges. 'A classic of American reportage. McPhee is quirky, original and intensely curious' Julian Barnes

Wide Sargasso Sea Jean Rhys

Inspired by Charlotte Brontë's *Jane Eyre*, *Wide Sargasso Sea* is set in the lush landscape of Jamaica in the 1830s. Born into an oppressive colonialist society, Creole heiress Antoinette Cosway meets and marries a young Englishman. But as Antoinette becomes caught between his demands and her own precarious sense of belonging, she is eventually driven towards madness.

READ MORE IN PENGUIN

Published or forthcoming:

A Confederacy of Dunces John Kennedy Toole

A monument to sloth, rant and contempt, a behemoth of fat, flatulence and furious suspicion of anything modern – this is Ignatius J. Reilly of New Orleans. In magnificent revolt against the twentieth century, he propels his monstrous bulk among the flesh-pots of a fallen city, a noble crusader against a world of dunces. 'A masterwork of comedy' *The New York Times*

Giovanni's Room James Baldwin

Set in the bohemian world of 1950s Paris, *Giovanni's Room* is a landmark in gay writing. David is casually introduced to a barman named Giovanni and stays overnight with him. One night lengthens to more than three months of covert passion in his room. As he waits for his fiancée to arrive from Spain, David idealizes his planned marriage while tragically failing to see Giovanni's real love.

Breakfast at Tiffany's Truman Capote

It's New York in the 1940s, where the Martinis flow from cocktail-hour to breakfast at Tiffany's. And nice girls don't, except, of course, Holly Golightly. Pursued by Mafia gangsters and playboy millionaires, Holly is a fragile eyeful of tawny hair and turned-up nose. She is irrepressibly 'top banana in the shock department', and one of the shining flowers of American fiction.

Delta of Venus Anaïs Nin

In *Delta of Venus* Anaïs Nin conjures up a glittering cascade of sexual encounters. Creating her own 'language of the senses', she explores an area that was previously the domain of male writers and brings to it her own unique perceptions. Her vibrant and impassioned prose evokes the essence of female sexuality in a world where only love has meaning.

READ MORE IN PENGUIN

Published or forthcoming:

The Chrysalids John Wyndham

Genetic mutation has devastated the world. In the primitive society that has emerged from its ruins, any sign of deviation is ruthlessly hunted out and destroyed. David lives in fear of discovery, for he is part of a secret group who are able to communicate with each other through their thoughts. As they grow older they feel increasingly isolated. Then one of them marries a 'norm' with terrifying consequences.

The Waves Virginia Woolf

The Waves traces the lives of a group of friends from childhood to youth and middle age. While social events, individual achievements and disappointments form its narrative, the novel is most remarkable for the poetic language that conveys the inner life of its characters: their aspirations, their triumphs and regrets, their awareness of unity and isolation.

Heart of Darkness Joseph Conrad

In Conrad's haunting tale Marlow, a seaman and wanderer, recounts his journey to the heart of Africa in search of the enigmatic Kurtz. He discovers how Kurtz has gained his position of power over the local people, and radically questions not only his own nature and values, but those of his society. '*Heart of Darkness* seemed to reach into the heart of Conrad himself' Peter Ackroyd, *The Times*

The Garden Party and Other Stories Katherine Mansfield

Innovative, startlingly perceptive and aglow with colour, these fifteen stories were written towards the end of Katherine Mansfield's short life. Many are set in the author's native New Zealand, others in England and the French Riviera. All are revelations of the unspoken, half-understood emotions that make up everyday experience.

READ MORE IN PENGUIN

Published or forthcoming:

Seven Pillars of Wisdom   T. E. Lawrence

Although 'continually and bitterly ashamed' that the Arabs had risen in revolt against the Turks as a result of fraudulent British promises, Lawrence led them in a triumphant campaign. *Seven Pillars of Wisdom* recreates epic events with extraordinary vividness. However flawed, Lawrence is one of the twentieth century's most fascinating figures. This is the greatest monument to his character.

A Month in the Country   J. L. Carr

A damaged survivor of the First World War, Tom Birkin finds refuge in the village church of Oxgodby where he is to spend the summer uncovering a huge medieval wall-painting. Immersed in the peace of the countryside and the unchanging rhythms of village life, Birkin experiences a sense of renewal. Now an old man, he looks back on that idyllic summer of 1920.

Lucky Jim   Kingsley Amis

Jim Dixon has accidentally fallen into a job at one of Britain's new redbrick universities. A moderately successful future beckons, as long as he can survive a madrigal-singing weekend at Professor Welch's, deliver a lecture on 'Merrie England' and resist Christine, the hopelessly desirable girlfriend of Welch's awful son Bertrand. 'A flawless comic novel . . . It has always made me laugh out loud' Helen Dunmore, *The Times*

Under Milk Wood   Dylan Thomas

As the inhabitants of Llareggub lie sleeping, their dreams and fantasies deliciously unfold. Waking up, their dreams turn to bustling activity as a new day begins. In this classic modern pastoral, the 'dismays and rainbows' of the imagined seaside town become, within the cycle of one day, 'a greenleaved sermon on the innocence of men'.

READ MORE IN PENGUIN

Published or forthcoming:

Swann's Way Marcel Proust

This first book of Proust's supreme masterpiece, *A la recherche du temps perdu*, recalls the early youth of Charles Swann in the small, provincial backwater of Combray through the eyes of the adult narrator. The story then moves forward to Swann's life as a man of fashion in the glittering world of *belle-époque* Paris. A scathing, often comic dissection of French society, *Swann's Way* is also a story of past moments tantalizingly lost and, finally, triumphantly rediscovered.

Metamorphosis and Other Stories Franz Kafka

A companion volume to *The Great Wall of China and Other Short Works*, these translations bring together the small proportion of Kafka's works that he thought worthy of publication. This volume contains his most famous story, 'Metamorphosis'. All the stories reveal the breadth of Kafka's literary vision and the extraordinary imaginative depth of his thought.

Cancer Ward Aleksandr Solzhenitsyn

One of the great allegorical masterpieces of world literature, *Cancer Ward* is both a deeply compassionate study of people facing terminal illness and a brilliant dissection of the 'cancerous' Soviet police state. Withdrawn from publication in Russia in 1964, it became a work that awoke the conscience of the world. 'Without doubt the greatest Russian novelist of this century' *Sunday Times*

Peter Camenzind Hermann Hesse

In a moment of 'emotion recollected in tranquility' Peter Camenzind recounts the days of his youth: his childhood in a remote mountain village, his abiding love of nature, and the discovery of literature which inspires him to leave the village and become a writer. 'One of the most penetrating accounts of a young man trying to discover the nature of his creative talent' *The Times Literary Supplement*